Stitches and Scars

a novel by
Elizabeth A. Vincent

OMNIFIC PUBLISHING
DALLAS

Omnific Publishing
P.O. Box 793871, Dallas, TX 75379
www.omnificpublishing.com

First Omnific ebook edition, May 2010
First Omnific trade paperback edition, May 2010

Library of Congress Cataloguing-in-Publication Data

Vincent, Elizabeth A.
    Stitches and Scars / Elizabeth A. Vincent – 1st ed.
    ISBN 978-1-936305-17-9
    1. Young Women—Fiction. 2. New Hope—Fiction. 3. Friends—Fiction.
    4. Doctor—Fiction. I. Title

10 9 8 7 6 5 4 3 2 1

Book Cover Design by Amy Brokaw
Book Interior Design by Barbara Hallworth

Printed in the United States of America

For my "Sophie," Michelle,
who has been there since the beginning,
when all of this was just an idea.

Chapter 1
Epiphany

Sophie, you have got to be kidding me!" Kate yelled over the dressing room door.

"Just come out and let me see it," her friend pleaded.

"No freakin' way am I coming out there. It barely covers my butt!" Kate turned around to look at herself in the mirror. The red dress she had just squeezed herself into left very little to the imagination. It fell just below her butt, and her chest was at serious risk of falling out.

"Wait, is that the red one?"

"Yeah, the red one that's so small it's now cutting off my circulation. What is this, a size two?" Kate pulled at the bodice of the dress, attempting to get her blood flowing again.

"Sorry, that one is mine; here it is in a six. Oh, and try this one too." She threw the same red dress over the door, followed by a hot pink one. "Oh, and these too," she said as she tossed over at least five more dresses in all different colors.

"Soph, what it is with all the colors? I'm trying *not* to stand out," Kate said, tossing the pile of colorful fabrics on the chair.

"Well, it's the trend right now. Just bear with me. You want this night to be something you remember, and there is nothing wrong with standing out. Plus, who knows—you might just meet someone."

"Fine, but can you at least give me a few black ones—something a little less…loud?" Kate knew she would be giving in and buying something other than black, but it didn't mean she was willing to give up without a fight.

"I'm already two steps ahead of you, babe. Here."

Another batch of dresses was flung over the door, all of them black. Kate was beginning to regret ever agreeing to this little shopping trip, but Sophie always had a way of getting what she wanted. Plus, she was right. Kate did want to remember this night.

It was the first time her art would be displayed in a legitimate, well-known gallery, and she was beyond excited. She definitely wanted to look nice and make a good impression. And after looking through her closet, she realized that in order to do that she'd need to find a new outfit. Originally, she *was* planning on coming alone and getting a simple black dress. But then again, she did have Sophie as a best friend whose profession was buying clothing. She had an eye for what would look good and a passion for making people look their best.

"Do you have one on yet?" Sophie asked, showing the patience of a five-year-old.

"Almost." Kate reached around and pulled up the zipper.

"Not bad," her fashionista friend said, eyeing her over as she opened the door. "We can do better though. Try on the navy one next."

Kate turned around and looked at the pile of dresses. "Umm, which navy one?"

"It's right there, near the bottom." She pointed her delicate finger at the corner piece of fabric sticking out from under the rainbow pile of silk and satin.

After a little maneuvering, Kate stepped into the navy dress and was fumbling with the zipper when Sophie cleared her throat from the other side of the dressing room door. "So, have you heard anything from Scott lately?"

Kate immediately froze when she heard his name. There was hesitance in Sophie's voice and Kate knew that she hated bringing him up just as much as she did. But as her best friend, she was concerned.

"No, not since the last time." Kate quickly got dressed, and stepped out without looking in the mirror in an attempt to distract Sophie's current thought process.

A huge smile spread across her face and she clapped her hands. "Oh, Kate, it's perfect! I knew that would be the one. See, I told you we would find something. Now all we have to do is find some shoes." She quickly spun around and headed off for the shoe department, audibly debating whether to go with a sling back heel or a peep toe.

Kate smiled as she realized how good she had become at distracting her friend. Of course, shopping was a huge help. She knew she wouldn't stand a chance at the game of distraction if they were just sitting at home. Either way, she had succeeded for now.

Still smiling, she turned to face the mirror. Her brown hair was in disarray and hung loosely over her chocolate eyes. With a flip of her head, she swept it aside, fiddling with possible hairstyles. With her hair out of the way, she finally got a good look at herself and realized Sophie was right, the dress was perfect. Not too flashy or loud. The length was respectable and the back showed off just enough skin. She felt sexy but still conservative.

Scott would love me in this. As soon as the thought came to mind, she quickly pushed it aside and reminded herself that this was not going to be enjoyed by him, or by any other male for that matter. Tonight she was flying solo.

Before she had time to wallow in the fact that she had no one, Sophie came barreling around the corner holding a stack of shoeboxes.

"I couldn't decide what color or what type, so I grabbed a few of each. Let's start with the metallic ones; they'd be fun."

"Fun? Right. They would be fun," Kate said sarcastically.

"Come on, we're supposed to be having fun, and shoes *are* fun. What about these?" She held up a metallic pewter peep toe. "These will be like a party on your feet!"

Kate laughed at her use of words. Sophie always knew how to make everything interesting, and she was right—the shoes were fabulous.

"You're right, those will definitely be a party on my feet. I'll have to tell them to behave themselves if they get out of hand tonight." With a laugh, Kate grabbed the shoes and slipped them on.

"So, what do you think?" her friend asked, biting her nail.

"You already know I love them. Would I ever question something you picked out?"

"Yes, in fact, you have questioned me on, I believe . . . six different occasions." Besides having great fashion sense, Sophie had an amazing memory; nothing ever slipped past her.

"Hey, six times isn't bad. You're lucky, that's all." Kate teased back.

"True. I guess after twelve years of friendship, six is a small number." Sophie smiled to herself, obviously pleased with this fact. "Okay, let's finish up and head over to the food court. We're meeting Elle for some lunch in ten minutes."

Kate went back into the dressing room to change, taking one last look in the mirror. *Tonight is going to be great, I can just feel it,* she thought. Quickly changing back into her jeans and tee, she grabbed her purse and walked over to the sales counter where Sophie was explaining the fine art of accessory shopping to the sales lady. Kate watched her friend talk adamantly with her hands, her white-blond bob swinging past her shoulders with every motion.

"The right shoes can make or break an outfit, and don't even get me started on the importance of the right jewelry. Some people are just lost in the world of fashion, and it is our responsibility to show them the right way." The sales lady was listening earnestly, leaning forward on her elbows.

"Here, I'm all set." Kate put her dress and shoes up on the counter, breaking up the conversation. She felt bad interrupting, but knew that if she didn't, Sophie could and would continue on for hours. Plus, Elle was waiting, and she hated waiting.

A few minutes later, they were walking through the mall toward the food court.

Kate watched the people as they walked by, wondering where they were heading and who they were meeting. Her mind started to wander back to Scott when Sophie cleared her throat and broke her train of thought. She should know by now that whenever a conversation started this way, it was going to be an interesting one.

"So, I noticed how you kind of danced around the whole Scott question earlier."

"Oh, yeah?" Kate tried to sound surprised, but Sophie was always too perceptive.

"You know I can tell when something is on your mind, and I know when you're keeping something from me. So, just drop the act and spill it." She looked up at Kate, her blue eyes wide and wearing a sad face that she knew her friend couldn't resist.

"Fine." She knew she wouldn't win, so why try? "He sent me a text the other night."

"What!" Sophie stopped walking and put her hands on her hips. "He texted you and you didn't tell me! What did it say?"

"Geez, Soph, keep it down." This was why Kate hadn't told her. She knew that she'd throw a fit. "It wasn't that big a deal," Kate responded. But she was lying; it definitely was a big deal.

"Then what did it say?" Sophie was still standing with her hands on her hips, feet planted firmly on the ground. Kate reached in her bag and pulled out her cell phone.

"Here, you can read it. But at least start walking so we don't…cause a scene."

Walking over, Sophie took the phone and started punching the keys. Kate held her breath in preparation for what she knew would be coming.

"He misses you? *He misses you!* Are you kidding me?" She stopped once again and was now screaming at the phone. "He can't say that! What type of twisted text is that?"

Kate felt her face go red as she dropped her voice. "Could you please not yell?"

Sophie froze and looked around, finally noticing the passing people who were staring. "Sorry," she whispered. "But you know I can't help it. And where does he get off saying that? You guys broke up. He can't say he doesn't want to be with you and then say he misses you. That's…that's just…" she stammered, trying to find the right word and finally settled with, "wrong."

"I know it's weird, but I mean…we were best friends. You can't just lose your best friend and not expect to miss them." Kate was justifying his actions, like she always did, and she knew it would bother Sophie. So it caught her off guard when she didn't receive an immediate response.

Instead Sophie just stood there, silently thinking. Eventually she spoke up. "Katherine Elizabeth Thomas, I know he was your best friend. '*Was*' being the key word here. But the moment he broke your heart, he gave up the right to call you that anymore. If he thinks he can just keep dragging you along like this by contacting you whenever he has a moment of weakness, he is seriously mistaken. I will not let him hurt you any more than he already has."

Kate looked in the eyes of her concerned friend and couldn't argue. She knew she was right. Just as much as Kate still wanted to talk to and be friends with Scott, she knew she couldn't. Every time he made contact with her, it always turned out the same way. He said he missed her, she said she missed him. And after a few days of being "just friends," he would say that they were getting too close.

This had happened a few times over the last six months, and each time Kate was left broken and crying. One time in particular was exceptionally hard, but she blocked that out, didn't let herself even think about it. Sophie and Elle were there, like always, to pick up the pieces and help her get her strength back. Kate knew she owed them her sanity and quite possibly even more.

"Soph, I know how you feel and you know how I feel. This time I am not budging. It's been three days since I got his text and I still haven't responded, and I'm not going to. In fact, here." She held out her hand, took her phone back and erased his message. "There. Now I won't even be able to look at it any more."

"That's my girl," Sophie said with a smile. She skipped over and linked her arm with Kate's. "Now, let's go have some lunch."

When they made it to the food court, it wasn't hard to spot where Elle was sitting. On most days, people were either lined up around her or sitting close by, blatantly staring. Today they were mostly staring, but there were a few brave boys that had approached her. Her exotic beauty was something everyone noticed. Standing at five foot ten with dark brown hair that almost looked black and flawless tan skin, Elle was a force to be reckoned with, and that wasn't just because of her looks. The two best friends casually walked over and took their seats on either side of the ever-stunning Elle. Upon noticing them arrive, the boys quickly said goodbye and left the three girls alone.

"Giving out your number to minors again, Elle?" Sophie teased.

"Oh, come on, they were at least eighteen. Besides, they were just being nice and wanted an autograph." Elle returned her attention to the boys and gave them a playful wink.

"You're such a tease. I swear, I will never get used to the effect you seem to have on guys."

Kate had known Elle for just as long as Sophie had. Elle and her older brother, Logan, moved to Virginia during high school, after their parents' divorce. Although Kate and Sophie were already tightly knit, it didn't take much for Elle to meld into their pairing. All three were different from each other, yet similar enough to bring exactly what the other needed into the friendship. They were a perfectly balanced, fiercely loyal trio, and nothing ever could or would come between them.

Their friendship lasted through high school heartbreaks and the even bigger ones that followed in college. They remained close, even when they went their separate ways for a few years. Elle went off to L.A. to pursue modeling full-time,

Sophie went to Paris to study fashion, and Kate went to London and studied art. They never went more than two days without talking on the phone, and they made sure their trips home were scheduled to be at the same time. It had only been in the last two years, after the gang moved to the Philadelphia area, that they finally lived close together again.

"So, what's on the agenda for tonight?" Elle questioned while sipping her sweet tea.

"Well, I'm getting to the gallery early, probably around seven. You guys can come whenever you want." Kate tried sounding casual about the whole thing, but her insides were a mess. She knew that she'd be a ball of nerves until they showed up and stood by her side.

They, being the best friends they were, noticed her nervousness and responded just as she assumed they would. "We'll be there around seven thirty," they said in unison.

With a sigh of relief, Kate felt herself relax slightly. "Thanks," she said, hearing her voice waver. "I'm just so nervous, I think it will help having you guys there."

"It's going to be great, you'll see." Elle reached over and squeezed Kate's hand. "Besides, who knows? Maybe some rich old millionaire will buy all your work and sweep you off your feet."

"Why does he have to be old?" Sophie piped in.

"Okay, so not old, but definitely rich *and* good looking." Elle raised her perfect brow in challenge.

"That's better," Sophie nodded. "Maybe a hot, young doctor, or lawyer, or investment banker or something." Kate could see the wheels turning as Sophie dreamed about her friend's unlikely fairytale future.

"All right, you two, let's just focus on getting me through the exhibit, and then we'll take it from there." Kate was already nervous enough, and the thought of either of her friends trying to set her up with someone tonight made it even worse.

"Fine, but after tonight, we get to take you out for some hunting," Elle purred while a wicked smile stretched across her face.

"Ohh, someplace fun, like Rain. They always have good guys there." Sophie's eyes were wide, and Kate could feel her excitement.

"Soph, you already have a good guy. No, let me rephrase that. Logan is a great guy. You already have a great guy." That sounded better.

"I'm not talking about me, silly. I'm talking about *you*." She was still dancing in her seat, smiling at Kate.

"Let's just take it one night at a time, all right?" As soon as the words left Kate's mouth, Sophie's face fell in disappointment. "Okay, okay," she said quickly. "We'll take it one night at a time, starting with tonight, and then tomorrow night, we'll go to Rain." She tried to sound excited but was sure there was no disguising her voice.

"It will be fun, you'll see. Right, Elle?" Their blond friend looked over at her partner in crime for some encouragement.

"It will be a blast, like always. It has been a little while since I've gone hunting, though. I may need to sharpen my weapons." She gave a little shoulder shimmy and leaned forward, showing some cleavage.

"You are such a man-eater." Kate laughed.

Elle winked. "And you love me for it."

The three girls spent the rest of their meal talking about plans for the next few weeks. They were interrupted when Sophie's phone started buzzing. She answered with a huge grin on her delicate face.

Kate and Elle both knew that look. There was only one person who could cause a smile like that, and that was Logan. Standing at just over six feet, Logan was just as attractive as his sister. They shared the same dark hair and eyes, and his smile could melt any girl's heart. He and Sophie had been dating since high school. Except for the time they'd spent apart while she was in Paris, they were inseparable. Everyone knew they were perfect for each other and it was only a matter of time until they got married.

Sophie snapped her phone shut. "Sorry, guys," she apologized. "I should probably get going. I'll be over at five thirty to help get you ready?" She looked at Kate expectantly.

"When have I ever gotten ready for a big event without your help?"

"I know, I was just checking. I'll see you later then." She leaned down and gave her two friends a quick kiss, before grabbing her bags and heading off.

"What would we do without that nut keeping us in order?" Elle laughed.

"I don't have the slightest." Kate shook her head and stood to throw her trash away, Elle following behind her.

Together they walked to the parking garage.

"I'll see you at home. I'm going to stop off at the store and grab some stuff. Do you need anything?" Elle asked, rummaging through her purse for her keys.

"Some nerves of steel, if they're selling it." Kate looked back at her with worried eyes.

"You'll do great; you won't need any. You'll see." She leaned forward and gave her a quick hug.

"Thanks," Kate said, hanging her head. "I'll see you at home."

They said their goodbyes, and as Kate walked to her car, her mind easily wandered back to Scott. She hated that she still thought about him so much, especially at exciting times like this. She knew that it would take some time to get over him, but it was taking longer than she expected. But he had been her best friend, and she missed him. She missed laughing with him. She missed their long conversations, and comfortable silences. She just missed … him.

It was with that thought that a light flicked on and everything suddenly became clear. For the first time in a long time, Kate realized that she only missed him as her *friend* and nothing more. She would always love him, but not in the romantic way that she had. While she missed their conversations and time spent together, she didn't ache for him. She didn't miss his kisses or his touch. She didn't even miss the comfort she used to feel when wrapped in his arms.

She found herself smiling as she came to this realization. This epiphany had brought with it a new feeling of determination.

I'm moving on with my life and I'm going to take some chances.

She wasn't exactly sure how she was going to do that, but something told her that tonight was going to be her start.

Chapter 2
First Glances

Walking into the gallery was probably the longest and most nerve-wracking walk of Kate's life. Butterflies were wreaking havoc on her insides, and if it wasn't for the deep breathing she'd done in the car on the way over, she was certain she'd be sick.

With shaky hands, she pulled open the large glass door of the gallery and stepped inside, searching quickly for the bathroom. She had to make sure all of Sophie's hard work hadn't just been blown away in the wind. Thankfully, it wasn't that bad. Just a little finger-run-through and it was perfect. She stepped back to take one final look.

Kate smiled because she liked what she saw. For the first time in a while, she felt … sexy. The dress was great and surprisingly comfortable. Sophie had made sure to keep the hair simple and left it down in waves. Though at the time Kate had been hesitant on the smoky eye make-up, looking at herself now, she was glad that she let her friend work her magic.

Well, it's now or never. She took a deep breath and exhaled. Feeling herself relax a little, she headed into the gallery.

It was pretty crowded, more than she had expected it to be. Glancing at her watch, she realized there was still about twenty minutes until Elle, Sophie, and Logan showed up. Seizing the opportunity, she decided to walk around and look at the other work on display.

About halfway through, she came upon one of her own pictures. Her heart thumped loudly in her chest, and she felt a wave of accomplishment rush over her. Standing back a few feet, she took a minute to admire her work as it hung before her. She still couldn't believe it was hers.

Staring at the bold palette of colors, her mind drifted back to the day she'd taken it. It was not the happiest day of her life, but it ended up leading to great things. She and Scott had just ended their relationship, and this time she knew it was different. It was final.

After their fight, she'd needed to get away and have some time alone, time to think. She'd climbed in her car and drove out of the city, leaving the hustle and bustle behind her. Without paying attention to any of the passing exits, she eventually pulled off and parked the car when she came upon what looked like a state park. Grabbing her camera, she'd started walking, not sure of where she was going but sure that she'd know once she got there.

Ultimately, she ended up sitting under an amazing tree. It was unlike anything she'd ever seen before. The black bark twisted and wrapped around the trunk in waves, making it appear as if it was actually moving. The branches reached towards the sky, like fingers stretching for the stars. She sat under its protective canopy for an immeasurable amount of time and wondered how old it must have been. How many people had sat in its shade just like she was at that very moment? She had lost track of time, hadn't even noticed until the sun began to set. Light streamed through the branches of the tree and cast an orange-red glow over everything. It was as if someone put a tinted lens in front of her eyes—rose colored glasses that made everything look even more beautiful. Everything around her was aglow. It was at that magical moment that she knew things would be okay. Somehow they would all work out. She had pulled out her camera and hoped that the picture would capture the moment forever. Hoped that the lens would do the beautiful tree justice.

Later, when she got back in her car to head home, she took a moment to look around at her surroundings. Not sure of exactly where she was, she had driven to the closest town. As soon as she saw the sign, she knew it was where she was meant to be. *New Hope.* She was never a person who looked for signs, but there was no denying this one. Just the name alone gave her a sense of beginning, of starting over. She knew it was exactly what she needed, and after driving through the charming, artsy town, she knew she'd found it: her new hope, her new home.

"It's beautiful, isn't it?"

A deep voice from behind Kate broke her train of thought. She jumped and quickly whipped around to see who it was. Her body turned faster than her legs and she began to lose her balance. Unable to stop herself, she stumbled forward and face planted into the stranger's chest. His feet shuffled for a second, but he quickly regained his balance as he helped her gain hers.

"Sorry, I didn't mean to scare you."

Before Kate even looked up, she was apologizing. "No, I'm sorry. I was just lost in a memory and I—" Her words caught in her throat the instant she finally looked up and met a beautiful pair of smoky blue eyes. It took her a second to realize that she'd stopped talking, and her jumbled mind quickly grasped for words.

"I mean, I'm … I'm really sorry; I wasn't paying attention." She looked down, trying to hide the obvious embarrassment that she felt.

"No, I'm the one who should apologize. I shouldn't be sneaking up on beautiful ladies like that." A smirk spread across his face, and Kate could feel the heat rise to her cheeks.

She kept her head down as she tried to think of something to say. He seemed to sense her embarrassment and came to the conclusion that she felt uneasy.

"Sorry, I'll just let you enjoy the art."

He started to turn away, and as he did, Kate's body reacted instinctively. She reached out and grabbed his hand, feeling a tingling prick at her fingers when her skin touched his. With wide eyes, she stared at her own hand realizing what she'd done.

"Um, sorry, I didn't mean to just grab you like that. I don't normally do that … I just … um, what I mean is, you can stay here if you want. You don't have to leave." Kate stumbled with her words, trying not to sound like an idiot.

He liked what he heard and smiled at her again. Unable to look away, Kate studied him, took in every detail. The lines of his jaw were strong and angular, a harsh contrast to the friendly lines around his eyes. His brown hair was left natural and unstyled, no gel holding it in place. It was so different from Scott's perfect hair. And his eyes were the most interesting shade of steel blue that she'd ever seen. Kate realized she was staring, yet she couldn't look away.

Eventually he broke their gaze and turned to Kate's picture.

"It's beautiful, isn't it?" he repeated and took a step closer to get a better look.

"I've always loved trees." Kate shrugged. "There's just something about them. They seem so strong and powerful." She heard the words that were coming out of her mouth and suddenly felt a little stupid. *Who talks about trees like that?*

She chanced a quick glance in his direction; instead of looking at her like she was crazy, he smiled.

"Where was this taken?" he wondered aloud.

"I don't really remember, to be honest. I just came upon it one day while I was walking. I keep saying I'm going to try and find it again, but I still haven't tried."

His eyes grew wide upon hearing her words. "You took this?"

Kate wasn't sure if he sounded shocked in a good way or a bad way. "Yes, why do you look so stunned?"

"I'm not, I'm just … surprised." He shrugged.

Surprised? What, a girl like me can't possibly take a good picture? Who does this guy think he is? She could feel herself getting angry.

"What do you mean 'surprised'? You don't even know me, how does that surprise you?" Her voice grew louder. She was aware that she was acting ridiculous and jumping to conclusions, but she couldn't help herself.

Before she could say another word, he held his hands up, palms facing out, as if surrendering. His eyes looked playful and his sexy smile got even bigger.

Great, now he's smiling at me. Here I am trying to sound tough and he just smiles. Not that I mind, but still. She placed her hands on her hips, feeling a little like Sophie, and waited for his response. Very slowly, he started speaking as if he was carefully choosing his words so he wouldn't upset her further.

"I'm sorry if I upset you. By no means was I surprised in a bad way. On the contrary, I am actually very impressed. It's not every day that I get to meet the talent behind the work. Not only are you beautiful, but you take a beautiful picture as well."

Kate stood completely frozen with her jaw hanging open in shock. She wasn't sure what she was expecting him to say, but it definitely was not that. She tried to speak but nothing came out. All she could do was stand there and look into the eyes of the stranger.

She was fairly certain there were other people in the room, but she couldn't be sure. In that one moment, time ceased to exist. The air between them grew thick, and she felt the heat rushing through her body, from the tips of her toes all the way to her hairline. Never in her life had she experienced something like this, and from the look on his face, neither had he. When her head started to spin, she realized she wasn't breathing. Trying not to gasp, she sucked in some air and attempted to concentrate, but her mind was blank. Just as she opened her mouth to say something, his phone rang. With apologetic eyes, he stepped away to take the call and blended into the crowd.

When his back was turned, Kate dropped her head in her hands and tried to make sense of what had just taken place. Less than a minute later, she heard someone yell her name.

"Kate!" Sophie spotted her and started weaving her way through the crowd. As soon as she was close enough, she wrapped her arms around Kate's neck. "Oh, I'm so excited for you. Everything looks great; the place seems crowded. Aren't you excited?" She leaned back and looked at her friend and immediately sensed something was off. "What's wrong?"

Realizing that she must look a little dazed, Kate attempted to relax a bit and act normal. "Nothing's wrong, I'm just a little nervous." Her eyes dashed around the room, looking for the man she was just speaking with.

"Looking for someone?" Sophie asked.

"Um, yeah," Kate mumbled, completely distracted. She continued searching for him and felt her heart sink when he was nowhere in sight. It was a minute before she realized Sophie was staring at her. She obviously wanted an explanation for Kate's odd behavior, but Kate couldn't give one. How could she explain something that she didn't even understand?

"Where are Logan and Elle?" she quickly asked, looking to change the subject.

"Logan's parking the car, and Elle went to find the bathroom." Sophie continued to study her face but didn't say a word, for which Kate was thankful.

"Let's go find her and get some drinks. I'm thirsty." Kate grabbed Sophie's hand and headed off to the bar. She wasn't sure if this distraction would work, but she could try.

☙

The rest of the night flew by, and Kate continued to look for the mystery man. Unfortunately, she never saw him again, and it put her in a sulky mood. She tried to act happy but wasn't sure if her friends were buying it.

Elle had her arm linked with Kate's as they headed to their cars. "What's with you tonight?" Elle asked.

"What do you mean?" Kate tried to sound surprised by her question.

"We just had an amazing night, and I feel like you're not even here."

Kate dropped her eyes to the pavement. "I just have a lot on my mind, that's all."

"Does it have anything to do with the text Scott sent you?" Elle asked. The mention of Scott's name always made Kate pause, usually because it stung a little. But this time, she paused because he was actually *not* the person Kate was thinking about.

"Sophie told you, huh? Not that it really matters anyway. I'm not calling him. I actually had an epiphany earlier today, and I've decided that I'm over him." Kate rolled her shoulders back with pride.

"Good for you. So does that mean you're going hunting with me tomorrow night?" Elle asked, unable to hide the smile that was now on her face.

"Would I ever let you hunt alone, Elle?" She too couldn't help but laugh at their ridiculous term for picking up men. They made it up in high school and never stopped using it. After all, it fit. For one, there are a lot of beasts out there. Second, you can get hurt while trying to catch one. And third, when you finally got the kill or the "right one" it was always worth it.

"Good. Because I have a feeling it's going to be a great season." Elle smirked as she got into her car. Pulling away, she gave a wave and was out of sight in no time.

For the second time that day, Kate found herself walking to her car all alone and thinking about a guy. But this time, it wasn't Scott. She kept replaying the moment she shared with the mystery man over and over in her mind. The way he smiled, and the way he looked at her. There was something different; she knew it, and she *felt* it. She didn't know what it was or who he was, but someday, somehow, she hoped to find out.

Chapter 3
Hunting

Kate. Kate, wake up." Kate could hear Elle's voice getting louder in her ear as she began to come to. Before falling asleep last night, her last thoughts were of the man with stormy gray-blue eyes, and thankfully those thoughts led to a wonderful dream.

Not wanting it to end, she pulled the covers up over her head and attempted to ignore her roommate. "Go away! I'm not done dreaming," Kate managed to moan.

"Oh, dreaming again, are we? Who is it about his time?" Elle teased. "Come on, I want details. Was it that guy from the dry cleaners again or was it the waiter from 90 Main?" She started bouncing on Kate's bed and pulling the pillow out from under her.

"All right, all right, I'm up. Geez, you're starting to act like Sophie." Kate sat up, running her fingers through her messy hair.

"What can I say? She has a way of rubbing off on me. Plus, wouldn't you rather I get you up now instead of waiting for her to get here? You know she hates being late."

"What are you talking about?" Kate asked, confused.

"We're going out for breakfast, don't you remember?" Elle walked over to her roommate's desk and started flipping through the photographs that were spread out. "I swear, last night you were not with it. It was like you were on some other planet."

"Sorry about that. I don't know what was with me."

Secretly, Kate knew why she had acted a little off, but she didn't want to admit it. She was still a little shocked over the whole thing and couldn't understand how a stranger had been able to affect her so much.

"It was probably just nerves," Elle added. "Although you had no reason to be nervous. We all knew you would be a hit, and you were!"

"I'm still in shock over it. I mean, I thought if I was lucky, I'd sell something. I just wasn't planning on being *that* lucky." Kate smiled as she remembered the four pieces she'd sold.

"Does that mean breakfast is on you?" Elle turned around, raising her eyebrows.

"Of course it is. Isn't it customary by now? I got the money this time, so I'm paying."

It was an unspoken rule in their friendship that, whenever one of them got a big paycheck, that person would be the one footing the bill for the celebration breakfast. In the past, it had usually been Elle. Not only was she the first one with a full-time job, but as a model, she landed a lot of work. Eventually, Sophie got her dream job as a clothing buyer for a huge department store and made a better living for herself than she expected. Although, they could have paid her in shoes and handbags and she wouldn't have complained. This time, Kate had the success, and she was more than happy to take her turn.

"Okay, so hurry and get ready. Sophie will be here in an hour. And don't forget to wear comfortable shoes." Elle walked out of the room smiling.

"Wait, what did you say?" Kate asked when her friend's words finally registered. She thought she knew what she had said, but needed to make sure. "Did you say 'wear comfortable shoes'?" she confirmed.

Elle never told Kate to wear comfortable shoes. Mainly because she thought women should only wear heels. And since Kate was fairly certain they weren't going to the gym this morning, this left only one option.

"Elle, are you planning on doing some shopping today?"

"Actually, *we* are doing some shopping." Elle turned on her heel and headed off to her bedroom.

"But I had plans today!" Kate yelled while running after her.

"Come on, it will be fun. We want to get something new for tonight. You want to look great, right?"

Kate thought over her day's schedule and realized that most of the items on her list could be put off until tomorrow.

Elle could sense her friend's wavering decision and quickly took advantage of her weakness. "We can call it quits whenever you're done. You just tell us you've had enough, and we won't complain."

"Fine, but you better promise me. When I say I'm done, we leave. No ifs, ands, or buts, got it?" She tried to sound firm, but couldn't stop the laugh that was bubbling under the surface.

"Whatever you say, Ms. Thomas," Elle said with a giggle. Unable to retain her composure, Kate gave in, laughing right along with her.

After a few minutes of laughter, Kate straightened up and tried sounding more serious.

"Okay, so I sounded like my mom. But I meant what I said. And *you* have to tell Sophie your promise. You know I can't say no to her."

"All right, I'll call her now. That way she's prepared when she gets here." Elle walked into her room, looking for her cell phone, and Kate headed back to the bathroom to get ready for their shopping excursion.

Two pairs of shoes, six new outfits, and five hours later, Kate plopped down on her bed, exhausted.

"Now I know why you wear those awful shoes shopping," Elle said as she crawled into Kate's room.

"See, you don't think they're so bad now, do you?"

"I still don't think you should wear them when you're not working out, but I do *understand* why you do. I shouldn't have worn my new Ferragamos. They weren't broken in enough." Elle rolled onto her back and held up her feet, examining the damage.

"They are now."

"Yeah, and I have the blisters to show for it." She pointed her foot in Kate's direction.

"What are you going to wear tonight? Do you want to borrow my sneakers?" Kate teased.

"Tonight won't be a problem. Ever heard of Band-Aids? Plus, if I wanted to wear sneakers, I would wear mine. I do own a pair, you know. After all, you can't work out in heels. The people at the gym won't let you; believe me, I've tried."

"Why am I not surprised that you actually tried that?"

"Tried what?" Sophie walked into the room and flopped down on the bed beside Kate.

"Wearing heels to work out," Kate replied.

"Oh, they won't let you do that at the gym. Although the exotic dancing class they offer lets you." She had a little smirk on her face that they knew all too well.

"Sophie Jackson!" Kate feigned shock.

"What? It was a great class. And a better work out than I thought. Of course, the real workout came later with Logan." Sophie had an innocent look on her face, but they could see the twinkle of delight in her eyes.

"Too much information. That's my brother, you know." Elle scrunched her face up as if she tasted something bitter.

"Sorry, I can't help it. You're my friend and sometimes you're gonna hear things you don't want to." Kate could tell Sophie was enjoying the torture and sat back to watch.

"I know, I know. But can you please try to be a little discreet?" Elle begged.

"Fine, I'll *try*." She smiled, easily dropping the subject. "What time do you want to head into the city? I was thinking we should grab something to eat here first, or we could just eat there. How about eight o'clock?"

Kate glanced at her watch. Mentally calculating her time, she decided that eight o'clock would give her enough time to take a nap and relax a little. "Eight sounds great. I need some rest after today," she said, crawling over to her pillow and letting out an exhausted sigh.

"Just make sure you're up by five. I'll come over and we can get ready together."

Sophie slid off the bed and strolled out of the room.

Kate rolled over to the edge of her bed and looked down at Elle. "Are you going to sleep on my floor?"

"Maybe. It depends on whether I can make it to my room or not." With shaky arms, Elle slowly got to her hands and knees and then crawled out of the room.

⁂

"Hurry up, Kate! I don't want to miss our reservations!" Sophie banged on the door impatiently.

"I know. I'm coming!" Kate swiped on her lip gloss and took one final look at herself in the mirror.

Tonight is definitely a hunting night, she thought to herself. Feeling a slight boost in confidence, she grabbed her clutch and headed out.

"Now, *that* is an outfit," Elle said while eyeing Kate as she walked into the room.

"Thanks. You look great too." Then again, Elle always looked great. Her tall tan frame and perfect body put other girls to shame. She had legs that went on for miles and the sort of exotic features that people paid money for.

"The boys at Rain are not going to know what hit them," Sophie chimed in with a smile.

Kate looked over at Sophie. She stood only a few inches shorter than Elle but was just as graceful and beautiful. Her blunt cut bangs framed her large doe eyes and her pin straight white-blond bob accentuated the sleek lines of her face. With a wardrobe any fashion aficionado would love, Sophie always looked as if she walked off the cover of *Vogue.*

Stepping forward, Elle wrapped her long arms around her two best friends. "Are you guys ready to go hunting?" she asked in a sultry voice.

"Ready." They nodded.

"Let's go find you girls some prey," Sophie said in her sing-song voice. She bounded out the door and both Kate and Elle followed behind, fast on her heels.

☙

They made it to Rain around ten o'clock. The night was still young and the club was just starting to get crowded. Once they made their way around the dance floor, they found an empty table and ordered a round of drinks.

"Well, so far, I'm not seeing anything. I want some big game, not a small easy catch." Elle slumped down in her seat, looking depressed.

Kate and Sophie laughed at the hunting terminology she used, but realized that she was pretty much right. When it came to Elle, very few men were actually her "type."

"Oh, come on, we just got here. You never know what will happen," Sophie said confidently. "Let's dance."

Elle rolled her eyes but complied. "I'll give it until midnight."

An hour later, the dance floor was packed. Kate was surrounded by sweaty bodies and the heat was suffocating. Looking for an out, she motioned to her two friends that she was taking a break and made her way off the dance floor.

As she walked through the crowd of bodies pressed together, swaying to the fast rhythm of the music, she felt the weight of someone's stare. Hesitantly, she looked to the side and caught the face of a man following her with his eyes. A chill ran up her spine, and she felt the hairs on her arms stand up. She quickly turned her attention to the direction of the bar and told herself to stop being paranoid. After all, she was at a club; people were everywhere.

Finally at the bar, she waited patiently for the bartender to work his way toward her. She took a moment to observe the people surrounding her. One of the things she always loved about Philly was the mix of cultures that flooded the city. It was a melting pot and everyone came from different walks of life. She couldn't imagine living in a place that didn't have a mesh of cultures. She loved it. Still lost in thought and playing with a cardboard coaster, she felt someone stand close behind her.

"Hello there, pretty lady," came a slurred, scratchy voice.

Realizing that someone was talking to her, she spun around in her chair and came face to face with the man who she'd seen just a moment before, watching her. Her stomach dropped and she swallowed thickly, trying to ignore the unease she felt. *Surely I'm just overreacting*, she thought though she didn't believe it.

"Why did you leave? I was having fun watchin' you." He slumped down in the seat next to her and put his hand on her shoulder.

Kate shrugged and tried to turn her shoulders away, but he was already turning her chair towards him.

"Come on, stay and talk a little. I bet we would hit it off. And if we do, we can always go back to my place." He leaned in and Kate could smell the stale cigarettes on his clothes and the bitter stench of his breath. His yellow eyes were sunk deep into his worn face as he stared down at her.

Something about the way he talked and looked at Kate made her skin crawl. Her instincts told her to get away from him. Knowing the best way to deal with creeps like this was to be blunt and straightforward, she took a deep breath and mustered up the courage to say what she was thinking.

"I know some girls might enjoy it when men like you hit on them. But trust me when I say that you have zero chance of scoring here, believe me. Move on." She swung around in her chair, feeling braver than ever and started to walk away. Before she got more than two feet, a rough, calloused hand grabbed her wrist and yanked back, twisting her arm behind her.

"Now, what's a nice girl like you doing talking like that? Maybe I should teach you a little lesson. Teach you how you should be talking to men." His breath blew in her face, and her stomach churned.

"Is everything okay, honey?" Kate heard the voice from behind her and immediately knew it sounded familiar. Her heart skipped a beat when she realized who it was.

The man who was holding Kate in his grasp dropped her wrist and stepped back. Finally free, she turned around and saw a pair of familiar gray-blue eyes. The mystery man from the gallery stepped closer and extended his hand. Without a moment's hesitation, Kate reached for him and let him pull her to his side.

"I take it you'll be leaving for the evening?" The gray-eyed man glared at the drunk. "Or would you prefer me to escort you out?" His voice was firm, and there was an underlying current of anger that made Kate shiver in all the best ways.

"No, I was just on my way out." The drunken man looked down at Kate and winked before he turned to leave.

She must have been holding her breath through the whole ordeal, because as soon as he left, Kate let out a huge sigh. Feeling her body relax, she turned and looked up into the same gray eyes she had dreamed about last night. She felt her legs go weak.

"Why don't we sit for a second," the man whispered into her ear as he led her over to a chair.

Kate felt completely stupid for reacting the way she was and tried to gather her senses.

Get a grip, she told herself. "I'm fine, really. That guy was a creep, though. Thanks for stepping in." Kate looked down at her wrist, noticing its red surface. He must have grabbed it harder than she thought.

"Here, let me take a look at that." The gray-eyed man reached forward gently and took her wrist in his hand.

As soon as his hand touched hers, she felt her heart jump to life and start racing. Hoping that he didn't notice her reaction, she dropped her eyes to the floor.

"What, do you have some first aid training or something?" she asked, while trying to hide her face.

"Something like that," he said with a smirk as he turned her wrist over in his hand.

Kate looked up and watched his face as he studied her wrist, his sexy smirk still in place. He was even more beautiful than she'd remembered. Her dream had not done him justice.

"It looks like you'll just have some bruising," he said after a few minutes and gently placed her hand back in her lap. "You may want to put some ice on it when you get home, though." Their eyes locked, and Kate could feel the palms of her hands getting sweaty. "Well," he continued, "this is the second time we've met, and I still don't know your name."

"That's because I didn't give it," Kate teased.

"Ah, so *that's* how you're going to play," he said with a laugh.

"Play? Why, I don't believe I know what you're talking about." Kate batted her lashes exaggeratedly and didn't hold back her smile.

"I'll go first. My name is Ethan. It's nice to meet you." He extended his hand and waited for her move. He had a moment of doubt where he wondered if she'd turn him down, and let out a silent sigh of relief when she placed her hand in his.

"Kate. And it's nice to meet you too." They shook hands and both took their time releasing their grasp, not wanting to lose the connection they felt. They sat in silence, staring at each other for what Kate felt was hours but was pretty positive was only a few seconds. She felt the same tangible energy from yesterday swirl around them and her head started swimming. The room around them began to spin, and Kate knew she had to breathe or it was likely she'd pass out. Slowly pulling her eyes away from his, she looked down at the table, willing herself to take a breath.

"Do you come here often?" Ethan asked.

"Sometimes, but only when we want to go hunting," Kate blurted out. Her eyes grew big upon realizing what she'd just said. "Umm, I mean, yeah, sometimes when my friend's boyfriend goes hunting." She stumbled with her words and failed miserably.

Ethan held back his laugh. "Hunting?" he repeated curiously.

Kate quickly tried to change the subject. "So, did you have a good time at the gallery last night?"

"Yes, but I would have liked to have stayed longer. Sometimes my work pulls me away and—"

The distinctive ring of Ethan's phone cut him off mid-thought. With a resigned sigh, he pulled his phone out of his pocket. He immediately recognized the number from the hospital and knew that he didn't have a choice but to answer. "Speaking of work," he said, holding up his cell. "I'm going to have to take this." He looked apologetically at Kate as if waiting for permission.

"Oh. No, go right ahead. I should probably get back to my friends anyway. I'll see you around." Kate smiled shyly and started walking back to the dance floor before Ethan could stop her.

The further Kate walked away from him, the louder the voice of protest in her mind became. *What are you doing?* The voice yelled. *Turn around and ask him for his number or something!*

She knew that if she was going to make a move, she'd have to act fast. Holding onto what little courage she had, Kate closed her eyes, took a deep breath, and turned around to face him. But when she opened her eyes and mouth to say something, he wasn't there. Glancing around desperately, she searched the bar thinking that maybe she'd just missed him. He was nowhere in sight.

Chapter 4
Magic

Kate searched the dance floor looking for Ethan, but it was pointless; he was nowhere to be seen. Disappointment settled in her stomach, and she went to find Sophie and Elle.

"Did you think we left you or something?" Elle yelled into Kate's ear. "You looked frantic."

"Yeah, are you okay?" Sophie stopped dancing and looked into Kate's eyes, trying to read the expression on her face.

"I'm great. Aside from the creepy guy that tried picking me up, refused to take 'no' for an answer, and about ripped my hand off, I'm fine."

Kate attempted to sound aloof about the whole situation, but she still felt anxious. And it wasn't because of the creepy guy. It was because of the gorgeous guy who'd saved her from him. It was the second time she'd met him and the second time she felt an indescribable pull towards him. He was a complete stranger, and yet all Kate wanted to do was be alone with him. She'd never felt an instant connection to someone before—attraction yes, but this was different. She couldn't quite explain it, but whatever it was, it was intense. And to make it all worse, she didn't even know if she'd ever see him again.

Ethan. Her heart fluttered as she repeated his name over in her mind.

"Where is he?" Elle's yelling broke Kate's train of thought.

"I don't know. I tried looking for him, but I think he left," Kate said sadly.

"You went looking for him! Katherine Thomas, don't you ever go looking for a creep like that by yourself. What if he did something to you?" Now Sophie was yelling, and Kate couldn't understand what she was talking about.

"You know the rules. Always come find us."

Kate looked back and forth between her friends, and it was a moment before she realized who they were talking about.

"Ohhh, you're talking about the creepy guy," she said.

"Wait, what are *you* talking about? Who else would we be referring to?" The look on Sophie's face showed she was just as confused as Elle.

Kate didn't know how to explain what she was talking about without sounding crazy, but she also knew she had to say something. *Here goes nothing,* she thought. "I was thinking about the guy that kind of…saved me from the creepy guy." It sounded weird saying 'saved,' but she couldn't think of any other way to phrase it.

"Saved you?" Elle tilted her head to the side, and then looked over at Sophie to see if she wasn't the only confused one.

"All right, so *saved* is the wrong word. The creepy guy started getting a little rough, and Ethan came over and pretended he was with me. He basically told the guy to stay away from me and leave, or he would kick his ass." Kate smiled to herself, remembering how it felt to even pretend she was with Ethan.

"I think we need to sit. You have some explaining to do." Sophie grabbed Kate's hand and led her off the dance floor with Elle following behind.

"Spill it, Thomas," she shouted as soon as they sat down.

"Yeah, because we're both familiar with that goo-goo eyed look of yours."

"Elle, I'm not goo-goo eyed," Kate snapped, trying to deny the obvious.

"All right, you're not goo-goo eyed, but there is something going on. And who is Ethan?"

Kate took a deep breath and exhaled. She didn't know what to say. On one hand, she could play it off as nothing and tell them that he was just some guy she'd met. On the other hand, she could tell them exactly how she was feeling and how utterly confused she was about the whole thing.

She figured honesty was the best policy, especially when it came to Sophie and Elle. They would find out at some point anyway, so she knew she might as well get it over with. Taking another deep breath, she began her story.

"Last night when I was waiting for you at the gallery, I bumped into this guy. Well, not really bumped, I kind of…fell into him." Kate smiled at the thought and then continued where she left off. She told them how he'd been surprised when he found out she was the photographer, and she laughed when she described the way she practically yelled at him for making assumptions.

"I wanted to know why he was so shocked. It's not like he *knew* me or anything. And the crazy part is that he just stood there smiling at me, which of course flustered me even more. He did apologize eventually, and he said he was impressed with my work. He said it was beautiful, and he said ..."

Kate's voice trailed off as she remembered the words he'd said to her. She was so lost in her own little memory that she barely heard the whimpering coming from her two best friends.

"Well, what did he say?" Sophie asked, leaning forward in anticipation.

"He told me he that he thought ... *I* was beautiful." Kate's smile was so wide she thought her cheeks would split.

"Then what happened? What did you say?"

"Kate, please tell me you took him into the coat closet," Elle murmured.

"Elle, no! I didn't take him into the coat closet. I'm not as brave as you. And even if I wanted to, his phone rang, interrupting us. And then you guys got there."

Sophie sat back in her chair with a smirk. "*That's* who you were looking for all night."

"So you aren't *denying* that you wanted to take him into the coat closet?" Elle was still leaning forward, engulfed in her own thoughts of a closet romp.

"Yes, Soph, that is who I was looking for. And no, Elle, I honestly wasn't thinking about jumping in the coat closet."

"Not that good looking?" Elle said, scrunching up her nose.

"No, believe me when I say this—he was so good looking I could barely stand it. I just wanted to reach out and touch him, if only just to prove that he was real. It was so strange too; we only spoke for a moment, and then we just stood there for I don't even know how long. All we could do was stare at each other. And I could feel this energy between us. I've heard of physical chemistry before and I thought I knew what that was, but this was different—completely different."

Kate knew she sounded stupid trying to explain the unexplainable. But that was just it; she didn't know how to else explain it. She didn't even know what *it* was.

"I know you guys probably think I'm little nuts." Kate laughed nervously.

Sophie placed her hand on Kate's and smiled at her. "I don't think you're nuts. I know exactly what you're talking about."

"You do?"

"Yep, I felt that way the first time I saw Logan."

"You did?" Kate racked her brain trying to think back to when the two of them had first found each other.

Elle let out a loud laugh. "You're not talking about that whole 'magic' thing again, are you, Soph?"

"That's exactly what I'm talking about." She hit Elle on the arm, then looked back at Kate. "I just called it something different. I called it magic and you called it a weird, energy, physical pull, attraction thingy." She was still laughing at her friend's description when she leaned over and put her head on Kate's shoulder.

"So, when are you guys going out?" Elle asked.

"That's the problem, we aren't."

"What?" Elle yelled. "You just sat here ranting about this Ethan guy, sounding just like Sophie if I may add, and you aren't even going to go *out* with him?"

Clearly annoyed with Elle's comment, Sophie opened her mouth to say something, but snapped it shut before turning her attention back to Kate. "Elle has a point. You just spoke about Ethan with more excitement and passion than you've talked about any guy before, Scott included. You can't just let him slip by."

"You think I want him to slip by? I would love to go out with him. The problem is that I don't know anything about him; I don't even *know* him. I just learned his name tonight. I wanted to ask him for his number or something, but he got called away again." Kate exhaled and slumped back into her chair feeling defeated.

Sophie, sensing her friend's sadness, sat up and tried to lighten the mood. "Well, then, we'll just come here every Saturday night until you find him again."

"That's right," Elle added. "See, I knew hunting tonight would turn out great for one of us."

"I haven't caught him yet," Kate reminded them.

"Don't worry, Kate," Sophie said. "You'll catch him. You just have to think positively."

Elle wrapped her arm around Kate's waist and gave her a slight squeeze, showing that she too agreed with their optimistic friend.

"Okay, so now that we all agree on you and Ethan, let's hear more about this creepy guy. What exactly did he do to you?" Sophie's eyes narrowed in anger.

Kate spent the next few minutes explaining exactly what happened, making sure to give every little detail.

Sophie's face was full of worry. "I can't believe nobody else saw him. Did he hurt you?"

"My wrist is a little sore, but it's no big deal. I've had worse," Kate joked.

"You don't think he's still here, do you?" Elle was sitting up in her chair, eyeing the surrounding men.

"I don't think so. If I were him, I would have listened to Ethan." Kate remembered the look on Ethan's face when he held her to his chest. The rage in his eyes was plain to see, and she wondered briefly if he reacted that protectively to all defenseless girls. She wasn't sure, but for the moment, she allowed herself to believe that it was just her.

"Well, if that creep comes back, I would love to show him what I think of him." Sophie once again had that glint of hatred in her eyes.

"Agreed," nodded Elle.

Elle was one of the toughest girls Kate or Sophie knew. Most men underestimated her and that worked to her advantage. All they saw was a pretty face and hot body. Usually, they didn't get very far before her sharp tongue informed them of who they were dealing with. The fashion world always made statements about her "diva" attitude, but her friends knew her better than that. Kate and Sophie knew that the real Elle was kind, funny, and loving. She was the most loyal friend that anyone could ask for. She'd just done a perfect job of creating a tough exterior to keep her protected from the mean and sometimes hurtful industry she was in.

"I doubt I'll see that creep again," Kate commented. "And if he shows up, I'll be more prepared. We didn't take self-defense classes for nothing."

"Yeah, but in the heat of the moment, some of those moves are harder than you think," Elle reminded them.

If anyone knew the truth of that statement, it was Elle. On more than one occasion, she'd had to defend herself against some "overly-friendly fans" as she liked to call them. All it took was one scary encounter and the three friends found themselves in self-defense classes to make sure nothing like that happened again.

"All right." Sophie sat back in her seat. "I'll forget all about the creep I want to beat down if you tell us more about Ethan."

"Sophie is right, you know," Elle agreed. "We've heard all about his chivalry, but I haven't heard enough about the rest of him."

"What do you want to hear? I didn't get a great look at his body, but what I saw was nice, very nice." Kate smiled.

"What else? What about his face? What color are his eyes?" Sophie leaned forward excitedly, waiting for the exact description she knew Kate would give her.

And so she did. Kate went on to describe Ethan's blue-gray eyes and how they had pierced through her. Simply talking about him made her heart speed up, and she could feel the blood pulsing quickly through her veins. She couldn't stop thinking about him and didn't want to.

The three friends sat at their table for the rest of the evening, and they continued to ask Kate random questions.

She tried to pay attention enough to answer, but she couldn't help but think about what Sophie had said earlier. The more Kate thought about what had happened between Ethan and her, the more she agreed. The way Sophie described it was perfect. It was … magic.

Chapter 5
Impasse

Ethan walked out of Rain feeling more confused than when he'd entered. He couldn't believe she was there. After he'd left the gallery last night, he wondered if he would ever see her again, and now she was in the building that he'd just walked *out* of. He debated about whether he should just go back inside, but knew he couldn't. He had to get to the hospital.

It took all of his strength to keep his legs moving away from *her*. He laughed at his luck. Twice he'd bumped into the most amazing girl he'd ever met, and twice he'd been called away from her.

Over the past twenty-four hours, Ethan had replayed their meeting over in his mind numerous times. He could still see her standing there in the gallery. She immediately caught his eye with her fair skin against the darkness of her deep blue dress, and the way her hair framed her face and brushed her bare back. And then, after speaking with her and looking into her deep brown eyes, Ethan knew he didn't want to leave her side.

Their conversation, though short, left him wanting to know everything about her. And there was something else—something he'd had never felt before. He didn't know how to describe it, but it was powerful. Up until tonight, he thought that maybe he'd been imagining the whole thing.

But then he saw her tonight, and she was just as beautiful as he'd imagined. She was talking to another man and Ethan knew he should wait until she was finished. Then he watched as the man angrily grabbed her and pulled her close.

Ethan wasn't prepared for the feelings that stirred inside of him, and before he knew it, he was walking towards them.

Not sure how she would react, he looked at her tentatively, waiting for a sign that she was comfortable with his actions. To his relief, she'd followed along and went to his side. He took it upon himself to tell the asshole he could get lost, and then he spent the next few minutes talking with the photographer he never expected to see again. Just like the previous night, he felt an indescribable pull toward her and just like before, it left him feeling more confused than ever.

The sound of Ethan's phone beeping broke his train of thought. He didn't have to look to see who the text was from. Trent, his best friend, had just gotten a new phone and was obsessed with the new keypad feature.

Hey bro. Sorry I'm running late. On my way.

Crap, I forgot to call Trent, Ethan thought, quickly dialing his number in the hope that he would catch him before he got to the club. The phone rang at least five times before he picked up. Ethan could easily picture his friend cursing his new gadget, trying to figure out how to work it. When he finally did answer, all he could hear was yelling.

"Ah, damn! Hold on, Ethan. I just dropped the phone." There was fumbling and cursing on the other end, and Ethan laughed under his breath. "Sorry. I'm still trying to figure this thing out. It doesn't help that the phone is so damn small I can barely push the buttons. They should really make them a little larger."

"Trent, in the cell phone world, smaller is considered better."

"Yeah, yeah," he mumbled. "How come you're calling me? I thought we were meeting at Rain?"

"That's why I'm calling." Ethan braced himself for his friend's reaction. "I just got a call from work."

"Come on, man! I thought you were clear for tonight. It's been way too long and we need to get out and meet some girls."

"Trent—"

"I know what you're going to say. You *technically* already have a girlfriend. But you know as well as I do that it's going nowhere. Plus, aren't you dropping her tomorrow?"

"Tactful, Trent, very tactful. You could be a little nicer about it."

"What? She's no good, Ethan, and you know it."

Ethan thought about what Trent had said and knew he was right. He and Cindy had been dating for almost three months, and he'd recently realized it was going nowhere. She was too controlling and obsessive when it came to their relationship. If Cindy had it her way, they would be moving in together, picking out rings, and setting a wedding date. Three things which were far from Ethan's mind, especially with her.

"All right," Ethan admitted. "You're right about the 'not going anywhere' comment. And yes, I am planning on talking with her tomorrow."

"Then what's the hold up?"

"There isn't one, really. I just don't want to dive into another relationship right away. Can't I be friends with someone and then see what happens?"

"Dude, you sound like I'm telling you to go get a wife. I'm just trying to get you laid." Trent laughed.

"I think I can take care of myself in that department. And I haven't needed your help since high school, if I remember correctly."

"Wait a minute, I totally hooked you up with that girl sophomore year at college. What was her name … Susan, Susan King.'

"Clark. Her last name was Clark. And I would hardly consider introducing me to her hooking me up. Plus, I would have asked her out on my own."

"True, but you did meet her at my party. Therefore I still had a hand in it," Trent bragged.

"I can't argue with you there. Now, are we done talking about my relationships? I'm almost to the hospital."

"Yeah, I'm done, for now," he teased. "Are you on for tomorrow night?"

"Um, tomorrow is Sunday, right?" Ethan mentally flipped through his calendar. "Yeah, I only work the morning shift. I'll be done by late afternoon. But I have to talk to Cindy tomorrow night or it's going to drag on for another week."

Trent couldn't hide the amusement in his voice. "She's still avoiding you, huh?"

"I swear she knows it's coming. Every time I try to get together with her to talk, she comes up with some excuse and then another week goes by and we're still together."

"You want me to call her?"

Ethan knew that Trent was probably teasing, but he also knew him well enough to know that he *would* do something like that. "No, I can take care of it. And I'm not doing it over the phone."

"Why not? It's easier that way. You avoid the whole 'it's not you, it's me thing.' And you don't have to deal with the tears. Trust me on this one. Tears are no good."

Ethan laughed at his friend's view of relationships. As a player for the NFL, Trent got his fair share of girls. All of them attractive and all of them dumb as doorknobs. He never dated anyone longer than a month, and it didn't bother him. As far as he was concerned, he was going to be a bachelor for life. Ethan, however, knew him well enough to know different. He just hadn't found a girl strong enough to match him.

"I don't think doing this over the phone would be the best thing. I know Cindy well enough to know that if I told her over the phone, she wouldn't believe it. She would show up the next day like nothing had ever happened and play dumb." Hearing the words come out of his mouth made Ethan realize just how bad the situation had gotten.

"Man, she is nuts. The sooner you end it, the better. All right, so you go out with her after work. Dump her crazy ass, and then we can meet up afterwards. Sound good?"

Ethan rolled his eyes. "Sounds good. I'll call you later and let you know what time."

He hung up the phone still laughing at Trent's tactless use of words. He was never one for buffering his true feelings. He was right about Cindy being nuts, though. Breaking up with her wasn't going to be an easy thing and Ethan knew it. But it had to be done, especially after meeting Kate.

Kate. Just the thought of her name made his blood pulse faster. Ethan knew the moment he saw her that he wanted to ask her out, but he also knew he couldn't. It wasn't the right thing to do. He needed to have all ties broken with Cindy before he acted on anything. It wouldn't be fair to either of them, and Cindy, although overbearing and obsessive, deserved better.

His only fear was that he'd lost his chance. That he'd never see Kate again. He had never been one to believe in fate, but there was no denying that fate was indeed involved. It was what brought them together again tonight. Now all he could do was wait and see if fate would intervene again.

❧

It was late and the halls of the hospital were empty when Ethan arrived. *Why did Henry call me if it was so slow? And where is he anyway?* he wondered. Just as he reached for his phone, Henry walked around the corner.

"There you are, Ethan. I was beginning to wonder if you were still coming." As Henry walked closer, Ethan got a better look at his face. He knew that Henry had been working a double shift, but his eyes were alert and focused, something that only came with years of experience.

"Sorry, I got held up on the phone. Your son was giving me advice on women again." Ethan laughed.

"Please tell me you didn't take any of it. Out of the two of you, *he* is the one in need of relationship advice."

"Oh, believe me, *I* know that. He's just looking out for me."

"Always the protective brother." Henry wrapped his arm around Ethan's shoulder. "I'm really glad you two have each other. It's always made Lori and me glad knowing that, even though we couldn't give Trent a sibling, he never really missed out on having one." He gave Ethan's shoulder a quick squeeze before stepping back and handing over his charts. "You told me to inform you if Mr. Bennett took a turn for the worse. I could have explained this to you over the phone, but I knew you would want to be here anyway."

"Of course. How is he?" Ethan's current mood shifted from happy to concerned at the thought of his patient, his friend. He took the chart from Henry and looked over his notes.

"We aren't expecting him to make it that much longer. We're keeping him comfortable, though. He keeps asking for you. The tough old man seems determined not to rest until he sees you."

"He can be that way sometimes," Ethan said, shaking his head disapprovingly. "I better get going. I'm sure he's tired." He turned away from Henry and headed over to the elevator.

"Ethan." Henry's voice stopped him in his tracks. "Let me know if you need to talk. I know it can be hard, losing someone you've grown attached to."

"Thanks." Ethan felt the emotions churning inside him as he stepped onto the elevator and pushed the button for the third floor.

Mr. Bennett was one of the first patients Ethan saw four years ago when he first moved to Philadelphia. He was doing his ER rotation, and Mr. Bennett came in complaining of a persistent cough and difficulty breathing. After numerous tests, he was diagnosed with lung cancer. Ethan referred him to an oncologist, and he began his treatment.

His wife of forty years never left his side, and Ethan clearly remembered thinking that she was the strongest woman he'd ever met. She often said to him, "You do whatever it takes to be with the one you love." Ethan had never experienced that kind of love before, but he was sure she was right. She stood by her husband's side while he went through chemotherapy and had numerous surgeries to remove the tumors.

During the man's recovery, Ethan paid him visits, often sitting for hours. Mr. Bennett had been a music teacher, which was one of Ethan's many interests. He'd often bring in recordings of his favorite pieces or an album from a new band he'd recently discovered. They'd discuss the universal world of music and the ways it had changed over time. After a few months, his oncologist said that he was in remission and he could go home to be with his family.

About six months ago, his wife, Dorothy, passed away, and Mr. Bennett ended up back in the hospital. This time the cancer was back and it had already spread to his lymph nodes and liver. With his wife not beside him, it seemed as though he'd given up. Ethan remembered feeling so angry and upset that he wasn't fighting. Two weeks ago, he went to visit him and told him how he felt.

"You're giving up," Ethan told him. "Do you really think Dorothy would have wanted that?"

Mr. Bennett looked at him and smiled. "I'm not giving up, kid. Do you realize that the sooner I'm out of this body, the sooner I'll be with her? This has been the worst six months of my life, and I'm ready to be with her again. Part of me went missing when she left, and I know I can't feel whole again unless I have her near me."

That short conversation had been the thing to make Ethan realize what he wanted. He wanted to love a woman like that. He wanted to ache when she wasn't near him. He wanted to feel like he was only whole when he was with her. He didn't feel that way about Cindy and that wasn't fair to her or to himself.

The elevator doors opened with a ping, and Ethan's mind returned to the present. He began the long walk down the sterile hall until he reached Mr.

Bennett's room. Knowing that he wouldn't want sympathy or a sad face, Ethan mustered up the best smile he could and walked though his door.

"Hey, there, kid." Mr. Bennett opened one eye and peered at Ethan.

"Hi, Mr. Bennett. I would ask how you're doing today, but I'm sure you would say what you always do."

"Yep, I'm still dying." He let out a muffled chuckle. Since Mr. Bennett had made up his mind to not fight any more, he'd had an almost morbid sense of humor. The nurses were always so disturbed by it, but Ethan knew him well enough to understand his way of thinking. "I'll be seeing Dorothy by tomorrow night. I can feel it." He smiled.

"Umm hmm," Ethan said while looking over his chart.

He never knew what to say when he talked that way. He wasn't sure what he believed about life and death. But he did know that if there *was* something out there, a life after this one, then he would want it to be with the ones he loved. So why not believe it?

"Are you feeling comfortable?" Ethan asked, trying to change the subject.

"I better be. They've got enough drugs pumping through me." He lifted his hand, pointing out the tubes and bags that were attached to him.

"They're just doing their job. They want you to be comfortable," Ethan assured him.

"I know, I know. It makes it harder for me to think this way; my head's all foggy."

"Well, that's because you need some sleep. I'll come back and check on you tomorrow morning." Ethan flipped his chart closed and turned for the door.

"Dr. Montgomery?"

"Mr. Bennett, I've told you before. Please call me Ethan."

"And I've told you to call me John," he retorted.

"Okay then, John. What do you need?" Ethan waited for a minute so he could gather his thoughts.

When John finally spoke, his words came out softly and Ethan had to step closer to hear him correctly.

"I just wanted to thank you for being a friend. Not everyone understands my decision and you've always seemed to get it. I know you say you'll see me tomorrow, but I think someone else may have other plans." He looked to the ceiling before reaching over and placing his hand on Ethan's.

It was clear what he was saying, but Ethan didn't know how to respond. He was silent while he searched for the right words to say.

"Tell Dorothy I said hello." Ethan squeezed his hand a final time and walked towards the door, pausing before he left. "I'll be seeing you," he said as he took one last look at the face of his friend.

Chapter 6
Code Blue

Kate woke the next morning blinded by the sun streaming through her window. Her mind was so preoccupied last night that she'd forgotten to pull the blinds before going to bed. Now she lay there staring out the window, thankful that she'd forgotten.

A smile took her lips as she watched the clouds dance across the blue-gray sky. The very same blue-gray that was sure to become her favorite color. She closed her eyes and tried to picture Ethan's face and the eyes that matched the sky outside her window. The same eyes that penetrated straight through her. The very ones that made her imagine he knew what she was thinking without saying a word.

His strong jaw line and perfect straight nose were etched in her memory. And the way his mouth turned up at the corners still made her weak in the knees.

Kate enjoyed the next half hour or so just thinking about Ethan. She finally decided to face the day when the smell of freshly brewed coffee awakened her senses. She could hear Elle rummaging around the kitchen and laughed when she wondered if she was actually attempting to cook something.

When Kate walked into the kitchen, she found Elle fiddling with the electric skillet.

"Need a hand with that?" She tried hiding her amusement, but she didn't think Elle bought it.

"I can do it. What? Do you think I can't cook or something?"

Kate walked over and took the cord from Elle's hand, inserted the correct end into the skillet and plugged it in. "First off, I've known you for way too long to *think* you can't cook. I *know* you can't cook."

Elle flashed an evil look and squared off her shoulders. "Okay, so cooking is not my strong suit. But I can make a mean margarita and you know it."

"Now, you've got me there. Your skill with making drinks far exceeds mine." Kate smiled, happily admitting defeat.

"All right, since we both agree that I can't cook, what are *you* making us for breakfast?"

"What would you like?" Kate asked, already knowing the response.

"I was thinking your 'fly-away buttermilk pancakes' sounded pretty good." A wide childlike grin spread across her face.

"Would you like berry sauce with that?" Again, Kate asked even though she knew the answer.

"Yes, thank you." She nodded. "Can I call Sophie?"

"Do you even need to ask? I'm sure she's on her way here already." Before either of them made a move, they heard someone at the door. The quick, impatient knocking was all too familiar.

"Coming, Soph!" Elle turned to get the door, and Kate set about preparing their breakfast. She was grabbing the fruit out of the refrigerator when Sophie skipped into the kitchen.

"Are we having your famous pancakes and berry sauce?"

"Of course. Would I make anything less for my two best friends?"

"You know you could make anything and we'd eat it."

"I'll take that as a compliment."

Sophie reached around Kate's waist and gave her a quick hug. "You should, because that's exactly what it was."

"Thanks." Kate smiled.

The three friends talked about their plans for the day while Kate continued getting breakfast ready. Something about being in the kitchen was relaxing for her. She always thought that if she hadn't studied photography, she would have gone to culinary arts school. Now she got her cooking fix by preparing meals for her friends. They were always more than happy to taste her latest creations, and she enjoyed having someone to cook for.

"What are your plans for today?" Elle asked as she checked the pancakes.

Kate handed her a spatula. "I'm not quite sure yet. I have to drop some photos off for a client in the city, then I'm thinking about taking a run in Fairmount Park. It's been a while since I've run the trails there. After that, I'm free. Why?"

"We want go see that new movie about the girl with all the dresses. Are you in?"

"You know me. I'm a sucker for romantic comedies. What time does it start?" Kate glanced over at Sophie who was sitting at the counter looking through the newspaper.

"They have shows at two-ten, four-twenty, seven-twenty, and nine-thirty. Let's do an earlier time so we can go out for dinner after."

"Sounds good to me," Elle said as she flipped over the last of the pancakes.

"Me too," Kate agreed as she handed Elle a plate and poured the berry sauce into a bowl.

℃

By the time they finished eating breakfast, they'd all decided to separate for the rest of the morning and get their errands done.

Elle and Sophie left, and Kate headed into her room to get ready for her jog. She wasn't always a runner; in fact, she was the complete opposite. The thought of just running for no apparent reason didn't really appeal to her. But after her second breakup with Scott, she decided she needed a way to release all of her pent up energy. After just a few days of going through the motions, she found herself actually enjoying the rush of energy it gave her. Running alone and feeling the silence that surrounded her really gave her the time to clear her head and simply think. Now, whenever she had something weighing on her mind, she *had* to go for a run—it was a necessity.

Kate made the familiar drive into the city and dropped off the photos from a client's wedding she'd done a month ago. The traffic this time of day was awful, and by the time she made it to Fairmount Park, she was anxious for a run.

Pulling on a hat and gloves, she set out on a familiar trail that she used to run when she lived there. In the past, whenever she started her run, her mind automatically went to thoughts of Scott. However, today she couldn't get her mind off of Ethan.

She wondered if she'd ever be able to find him again. Most likely he lived in the city and that left her chances slim to none. Her best bet was just as Sophie and Elle had suggested: go to Rain every weekend and pray that he shows up. *But what if he doesn't go to Rain often? And what if I do meet him again and he's not interested?* she thought.

Her stomach twisted at the idea, and she forced herself to push the fear from her mind. Surely he felt the same connection that she'd felt. And if he didn't... well, she couldn't think of it. Picking up her pace, she pushed herself a little harder, hoping to dispel the unease that was creeping in.

She kept up her fast tempo for another mile and felt her legs begin to grow heavy. The stretch and pull of her tendons was invigorating, and she welcomed the slow burn as she continued at a steady rhythm. Climbing a small hill, she drove herself upward, her breath coming out in gusts of white in the cold air. On her way down the slope, she felt the loose gravel crunch beneath her feet as she slipped over the unsteady surface. Before her mind could register what was happening, she was falling. She attempted to steady herself, but felt the familiar sharp pain in her ankle as it twisted beneath her. Her leg gave out and her body went down. The momentum from her fall left her tumbling down the incline, rolling over branches and rocks until finally coming to a stop.

At the bottom of the hill, she lay panting, trying to catch her breath and assess the damage to her body. She already knew from the throbbing in her ankle that she'd twisted it. Taking a calming breath, she tried to sit up, but when she did, she felt a searing pain in her side. Glancing down, she noticed that her shirt was dirty, ripped, and stained with blood. She wasn't sure how deep of a cut she had, but from the way it felt, it was bad enough. She contemplated making a trip to the hospital and having Dr. Williams take a look.

When she and Elle had moved to Philadelphia, she made a few trips to the hospital to visit Dr. Williams, but it was never for her own health. It was always for Elle. The first time was because she had a nasty fall and broke her ankle. All the subsequent times were for either sprained wrists or shoulder pulls—injuries that Kate wasn't sure were 100 percent real. But she always kept her mouth shut and played the supportive friend. After all, she'd had her fair share of crushes over the years.

Dr. Williams was one of them. He was always so nice to Kate, and there was something about him that reminded her of her dad. And it wasn't just his good looks, that's for sure. For someone who looked like a model who'd walked off the pages of Lands' End, he was extremely humble. In fact, he seemed to have no idea that all the nurses—and pretty much all of his patients—were left speechless by his presence.

After coming to the decision that going to the hospital was probably her best bet, Kate slowly stood. It took her a moment to regain her balance and took even longer to make it to her car. Thankfully, it was her left ankle and not her right, which meant she could still drive. She'd hate to have to call Sophie or Elle and have them make the trip into the city for nothing.

By the time Kate made it to the hospital and to the check-in desk, she was feeling a little woozy. The throbbing ache on both her stomach and ankle was growing worse. She waited at the desk behind another woman and felt her face break into a cold sweat. Trying to relax, she took a few calming breaths, but the next thing she knew, everything went black.

Kate opened her eyes to a familiar white tile ceiling. It took her a second to understand how she'd ended up in the hospital, but then it all came back to her. Out of the corner of her eye, she caught a glimpse of someone and turned to see who it was. A tall red-haired nurse heard her stirring and quickly spun around to face her patient.

"Hello." She sounded happy that Kate was awake, and this made her wonder how long she'd been unconscious.

"How long was I out?" Kate asked, while looking around the room for a clock.

"Oh, only a few minutes. Just long enough to skip to the front of the line." The young nurse talked to Kate and handed her a clipboard of papers. "I need you to fill these out before you leave. Take your time. I'll let the doctor know you're awake and ready." She gave Kate another kind smile that scrunched up her freckled nose and walked out of the room, pulling the curtain closed behind her.

Kate sat up on the gurney she'd found herself on, stared down at the paperwork in front of her, and began filling it out. For the most part the questions reminded her of the forms she filled out at her doctor's office, just a little more detailed.

While listing the dates of her last physical, she heard the door open. She continued filling out the paperwork when she noticed the curtain being pulled aside and someone walk in. Quickly glancing up from her papers, she saw the doctor walk over to the counter. He had his face down and was looking over what Kate could only assume was her chart. He didn't speak and hadn't acknowledged her presence, so she returned her focus to the clipboard.

It was a moment before he finally spoke, but when he did, she froze. Her heart fluttered, and she quickly lifted her head to confirm who it was. His back was still turned to Kate, but she knew it was him. His velvety voice was something she couldn't just imagine. It was Ethan.

"Miss Thomas. What brings you into the emergency room today?" Just as he finished speaking, he turned around.

Kate hadn't taken her eyes off of him, and she dared not blink on the off chance that she was, in fact, dreaming. When Ethan's eyes finally met hers, he too froze. They were both silent for a moment.

A beautiful smile spread across his face as he stepped toward her. "Well, isn't this interesting." He laughed.

"Uh-huh" was all Kate could say. She felt the color rise to her cheeks and the embarrassment set in. *Why is this happening to me? Of all places I see him again, it's the hospital!* she groaned to herself. *Not to mention the fact that I'm totally sweaty, gross, and bloody.*

Ethan sensed her embarrassment and let out a little laugh. "If I didn't know any better, I'd think you were following me," he teased, helping her relax a little.

"Come on, give me a little credit. If I were following you, you would never know it," Kate said with a smile.

His eyes grew wide, but he didn't look away and his smile didn't fade. "Now that we're clear on your stalking capabilities, what can I do for you today?"

Kiss me, take me home, and never leave my side. Do I need to continue? Kate wished she had the guts to say exactly what she was thinking, but at the moment she was not that brave. Instead, she settled for something a little less crazy. "Well, I fell while I was out running."

"You're a runner?"

Kate couldn't tell if he was asking her as a doctor or if he was taking a personal interest. Either way, she wasn't going to miss the chance to get to talk with him.

"I try to run every day. It helps me clear my head. Plus, the view down by the water is beautiful, and I haven't had a chance to run there in a while."

"Really? I'll have to check it out sometime." He was still smiling at her, and she took that as a good thing.

"So anyway," she looked down at her lap and fiddled with the hem of her shirt, "I was running and I lost my balance. I can usually stop myself before I get too hurt, but this time," she paused, "the hill won." Kate looked up at him and smiled when she noticed he looked slightly amused. "My left ankle is twisted and I'm fairly certain I have a mean cut somewhere on my stomach. I'm not sure how bad it is—couldn't really get a good look. But it feels bad." She scrunched her nose in discomfort.

"And you figured it would be better to let a professional handle it." It was a statement not a question.

"Right. It has been a few months since I've seen Dr. Williams, and I didn't want him to think I was ignoring him."

As soon as the words were out of Kate's mouth, she was aware of how they must have sounded. "Oh! I mean, I…I…" She scrambled to come up with a better explanation. "Dr. Williams has treated my friend a few times. So I've gotten to know him. He's really nice…reminds me a lot of my dad."

Ethan watched as she floundered through her explanation. Not bothering to repress his grin, he tucked Kate's chart under his arm and leaned back against the counter. There was something about her that amused him. She was always doing or saying something he wasn't expecting. He found it intriguing. "Dr. Williams is a great doctor. He's actually taught me a lot. But he isn't working today, so you're kind of stuck with me, if that's all right."

"Fine with me," Kate said, holding back the desire to tell him it was *more* than fine. "As long as you know what you're doing." She looked at him skeptically.

"I think I'll be able to handle it," he said with a smirk. "Let's start with your cut. I want to get any bleeding under control. I'll just step out while you put this on." He walked toward her and handed her a paper gown, then turned and left the room.

Kate took the moment alone to gather her thoughts and take a calming, deep breath. *It's okay, it's no big deal. He's a doctor—he sees this stuff all the time. Plus, I'll be in my sports bra.* She continued to give herself a pep talk and tugged the bottom of her filthy shirt over her head. Just as she slipped her arms into the paper gown, the door opened.

"All right, let's take a look." Ethan pulled on a pair of gloves and sat down on a rolling chair, pulling up beside Kate. Without lowering her eyes, Kate pulled the front of the gown back and held her breath.

"It does look pretty deep," Ethan said, leaning in. "You really did a number on yourself."

Kate nodded still not looking down. "I'll take your word for it." She tried to relax and stay calm, but having him this close made it hard. Her heart was pounding so fast she knew he could hear it.

"Just relax and take some deep breaths. That always helps." Kate's eyes were closed but she could hear the smile in his voice. She let out a long sigh and tried to ignore the fact that his hands were touching her bare skin.

"It looks like you will need a few stitches, but it's not too deep." Ethan stood from his chair and began gathering everything he'd need. Kate watched him out of the corner of her eye. His white lab coat stretched taut across his broad shoulders and she couldn't help but fantasize about how they would look bare. Her thoughts were interrupted when he turned around.

"Okay, are you ready to get started?" he asked.

"Ready as I'll ever be," Kate mumbled, trying to clear her mind.

"I'll be careful, don't worry. You probably won't even end up with a scar." His smile was reassuring.

Kate lay back on the gurney and stared at the ceiling. Ethan moved so gently that Kate barely noticed he was even touching her. Doctor and patient remained in comfortable silence for a few minutes before either of them spoke.

"So, are you from the area?" Kate asked, figuring it was a pretty safe question to start with.

"No. I've lived in a few places over the years, but Philly has been my home for the past four. I was born in Boston, but my family moved to San Francisco when I was a baby. Went to medical school at Hopkins, and after I finished, I needed to find a place to complete my residency. My best friend Trent and his family had moved here and said it was a great area, so I took his word for it."

"Don't you miss your family?"

"I do miss my parents, but they visit a lot and recently bought a home not too far from here. Also, I try to make it home a few times a year. I'm the only child, and Trent is the closest thing I have to a brother. I see him every day, so that makes it pretty easy. What about you? Are you from the area?"

"I grew up in Arlington, Virginia."

"And what brought you here?"

"One of my best friends got a job here, and my other best friend and I decided to tag along. We wanted a change in scenery. It's great because we're all within driving distance of our families. I'm actually living in New Hope now and I love it there."

"So, do you live with them, then?" It was a simple question, but Kate felt the weight behind it.

"Elle and I live together. Her line of work is pretty flexible, and she's only a short train ride from New York City. Sophie keeps a room at our place, but practically lives with her boyfriend. But she does take pity on us *single* girls by going out with us every once in a while. They were the ones I was with last night at Rain."

Ethan stopped stitching and looked up at Kate with a smile. "You mean the ones you were hunting with?"

Kate blinked. "What are you talking about?" she asked innocently.

"Oh, I think you know exactly what I'm talking about. You three must be killers. I do feel bad for your prey, though."

She was so shocked that she couldn't speak and when she finally could, she didn't know what to say. "It's not like that," she stammered, trying to explain.

"There is no need to explain," he said with a laugh. "I think it's pretty funny." He shrugged and kept his eyes down while finishing the sutures. He placed the last piece of tape over the protective gauze and helped her to sit up again. He backed his chair up slightly as Kate swung her legs over the side of the gurney, facing him. Then he looked directly into Kate's eyes. They were dark and full of life.

"Can I ask you something?" he asked her.

"Yes," she responded in an almost-whisper. She hadn't a clue what he was about to ask, but in that moment she knew that she would answer him honestly.

"What exactly do you do with your prey once you've caught him?" He was still looking into her eyes, and they both felt the intensity between them thicken. His hands were still pressed against her skin as he leaned forward slightly, waiting for her response. He knew he should stop himself, but no matter how hard he tried, he couldn't. It was like one magnet being pulled to the other.

Kate's heart started beating faster and her breaths came in short pants. She couldn't speak. They both knew that if either one of them leaned in another few inches, their lips would touch. Kate shivered at the thought of being that close to him, being able to taste him and breathe him in. His eyes were locked with hers, and she could see the sparks of excitement.

The room around them faded away, and Kate knew at that moment he was feeling the same pull that she was. Ethan leaned forward and paused for only a second, as if waiting for permission. Her eyes began to close as she leaned towards him in acceptance. Kate could feel his breath on her mouth as their lips almost touched. The sound of the door opening startled them both, causing them to jerk away from each other. Ethan quickly pushed back in his chair and grabbed Kate's file, flipping it open. With a defeated sigh, Kate turned and lifted her legs back onto the gurney, feeling the blood slowly rush back into her body and relieving the ache in her ankle. The red-headed nurse who had been in the room earlier stepped in and looked from doctor to patient and back again.

"How is everything going? Do you need me for anything? I was just heading out for lunch and thought I would check."

"No, I think we're doing fine." Ethan kept his head down and continued to read over her chart. The nurse turned around and was heading for the door when Ethan spoke up. "Lisa?"

"Yeah?" The nurse turned back to face him.

"Could you grab an ice pack for Miss Thomas, please? I'm sure her ankle could use it."

"Sure," she said with a bat of her lashes. "I'll be right back."

As soon as they were alone again, Ethan turned back to face Kate and stared blankly. She could sense that he wasn't sure what to say, and neither was she. A few minutes ago, they were only a few inches from each other. The energy between them had been undeniable, and she knew he felt it, just as he knew she had. They had been so close to kissing, and yet now they sat as distant from each other as they could in the small room and were at a loss for words.

Kate wondered if perhaps he was regretting what almost happened, and that thought brought with it a wave of rejection. It wasn't until he started to smile that she felt some relief. He opened his mouth to speak, but stopped when Lisa walked back into the room.

"Here you go." She placed the ice pack on Kate's ankle gently. "Do you need anything else?" she asked Ethan, who was already shaking his head. "I'm heading out then." As she turned to leave the room for the last time, Kate looked over at Ethan, wondering what he was going to do next.

In one fluid movement, he stood and started to walk towards her, but paused when Lisa walked back through the door again. Kate let out an annoyed sigh. Ethan heard her frustration and felt the same way. He gave Kate a quick wink before turning his attention to Lisa.

She was only in the room for a second and yet it took an entire minute for what Lisa said to register in Kate's mind. And even then, she couldn't be sure if she had heard her correctly. She looked at Ethan and the expression on his face said everything.

Her stomach dropped and her eyes closed as she silently repeated Lisa's words.

"I almost forgot to tell you. Your girlfriend called about an hour ago. She said she's sorry she won't be able to meet you for dinner tonight. But she'll call you later."

Chapter 7
Broken

The instant Kate heard the words come out of Lisa's mouth, her heart sank. Did she just say *girlfriend?* she wondered. *I am such an idiot.* She hadn't looked at Ethan since his face had confirmed that what she'd heard was true. Kate mentally scolded herself for being so stupid and for actually assuming that he was single and interested. *He's just like all the other jerks I've met. How could I be so dumb?*

"Kate?" His voice was reluctant.

"What?" She knew he wanted her to look at him, but she refused.

"Could I please explain what just happened? I want to—"

"No," she cut him off.

Kate didn't want to hear anything he had to say, and the more she thought about it, the angrier she got. Part of her didn't know if she was angrier at herself or him. She knew it was ridiculous to be angry at him. It wasn't as if the two of them were dating; they had just met. She felt stupid and humiliated for thinking that perhaps he'd felt the connection she had. Apparently he didn't. Then again, he had almost kissed her.

"Kate, please. I…" He paused and took a step closer to her.

Kate exhaled and tried to gather the courage she knew it would take to look him in the eyes and say what she wanted to. She pushed the ice pack off her foot in frustration.

"Look Doctor..." she fumbled, trying to remember his last name, then realized she had never learned it. "Dr. Whoever-you-are. Thank you for stitching me up. I think my ankle is fine, and I'd like to get going now, if that's okay." She tried to remain calm and hold back her anger.

His eyes looked pained, and for a second, Kate regretted her rudeness, but then remembered it wasn't she who had the girlfriend. Her brief moment of weakness was shoved aside, and she let the frustration and anger return.

Swinging her legs off the gurney, she stood. Her quick motion left her a little light-headed and she staggered slightly, trying to regain her balance. Ethan stood quickly to steady her with his arms, and a chill surged down Kate's spine at his close proximity. Clenching her fists, she had to fight the urge to run her hands over his body. Her nose was filled with the scent of him and it clouded her thoughts. Realizing that she was still upset and knowing that if she stayed there another minute she would end up doing something she would regret, she stepped away from him. He was still silent. Kate didn't chance looking up into his eyes again as she turned to leave.

At the door, she paused. "Thank you," she whispered, and then walked out.

❧

Kate didn't remember the thirty-five minute drive home. She didn't even remember walking up the stairs of her townhouse. Her mind was so jumbled she couldn't think straight. Every time she began on one train of thought, her mind jumped to another.

As Kate put her keys in the lock, she realized that her friends were probably on the other side of the door. She looked down at herself. She had left the hospital so quickly she'd forgotten to grab her shirt. Her shorts were filthy, and she was pretty sure her hair was a mess. If someone saw her and didn't know what had happened, she was positive they would think she was attacked by a bear or something. Quickly redoing her hair, she tucked the loose strands behind her ear and then tried to rub off any dirt that was still on her skin.

At the moment, Kate didn't feel like explaining her appearance to her friends, and she was sure they would want all the details. All she wanted to do was be alone for a few minutes. She had to think through everything that had happened in the last two days and try to make some sense of it.

"Hello?" Kate called out, announcing her arrival home. There was no response and she sensed the townhouse was empty, but she walked down the hall to Elle's room just to make sure. A feeling of relief washed over her when she saw her roommate wasn't there. At least now she'd have time to clean up and get hold of herself.

With tired legs, Kate trudged to her room and grabbed some clean clothes. On her way to the bathroom, she caught a glimpse of herself in the mirror. She didn't look quite as bad as she felt. Her muscles ached in protest as she leaned down to turn on the water. Kate knew in a few hours they would feel even worse, so she grabbed some ibuprofen from the medicine cabinet.

After letting the tub fill with hot water, Kate stepped in. Luckily, she'd had stitches before and knew how to care for them. It would be at least another day until she could get them wet, so sponge bathing would have to do until then.

She sat down in the low water and let the bottom half of her body relax while making sure to leave her upper torso above the water line. Sitting back, she breathed in the steam. The longer she sat, the quieter her mind became. While her thoughts still centered around Ethan, she had finally reached two conclusions. The first was that he was indeed interested in her—she wasn't imagining that. He did almost kiss her, and she wasn't imagining the spark or immediate connection they felt. But the second thing she was certain of trumped the first: Ethan had a girlfriend. He was unavailable and she would have to accept that.

Every thought Kate continued to have was followed by the fact that canceled out everything else, that Ethan had a girlfriend.

"Kate, are you in there?" Elle's voice cut through Kate's thoughts.

"Yeah, I'll be out in a sec." Kate didn't know how long she'd been soaking, but her fingers were starting to prune. She stood up, carefully babying her sore ankle, and grabbed a towel. She dried off, got dressed, and opened the door to find Elle sitting on her bed, looking through the fashion edition of *People*.

"Hey, where have you been? I came home and you weren't here," Kate asked.

Elle looked up and noticed Kate's slight limp. "What happened? Did you sprain your ankle?"

"Something like that. I fell while I was running. It's really not that bad. But the stitches hurt a little."

"Stitches? Where?"

As Kate lifted her shirt to show the injury, Sophie slipped into the room unnoticed.

"What happened?" Her loud voice made the other two girls jump.

"Geez, Soph, don't sneak up like that." Elle took a breath and turned her attention back to her magazine.

Ignoring her friend, Sophie walked over to Kate and looked at her bandage. "You really need to be more careful."

Kate was used to both her friends worrying by now and knew it was only because they cared so much. "It's not that bad. I even drove myself to the hospital."

As soon as the word hospital fell from her lips, Elle's head snapped up and a smile spread across her face. "Was he there? He was, wasn't he? Why didn't you call me to take you? You know I like going when he's working. Was he wearing the blue scrubs? Or was it the green ones? Oh, I love the green ones, the way they hug his—"

"Elle!" Kate cut her off. "Dr. Williams is married. Besides, he wasn't working today. Someone else stitched me up." She tried to keep her voice from wavering but Sophie, being the perceptive friend that she was, noticed.

Elle, however, hadn't noticed anything and continued talking. "I know he's married. But that doesn't mean I can't look at him. Plus, a little harmless flirting never hurt anyone. Oh, Henry," she sighed dramatically before flopping backward onto the bed.

"He's not a candy bar," Kate laughed. She kept her eyes trained on Elle, but could feel the weight of Sophie watching her.

Her observant friend cocked her head to the side, trying to figure out what was off. "Who stitched you up?" she finally asked.

"Umm." Kate paused. She was planning on telling them everything that happened, but hadn't planned on how. "It's actually kind of funny," she said, while trying to sound casual. Elle had now noticed the tremor in her friend's voice and sat up. Both girls watched her closely. "It was Ethan."

Sophie's eyes went wide but Elle's face scrunched in confusion. "What was Ethan?" she asked.

Sophie knew exactly what Kate meant. "The doctor, the doctor was Ethan," she clarified.

Elle's jaw dropped. "Are you kidding me? He's a doctor?" she shouted.

"What happened? What did he say? Did you exchange numbers? When are you going out with him?" Sophie bombarded Kate with questions and bounced on the tips of her toes. They were getting way ahead of themselves.

"Calm down. I'll explain everything. Just let me speak." Kate took a breath. "Yes, Ethan was the doctor who stitched me up. He was really nice. No, he was *great* actually." She felt her heart skip just speaking about him. "We talked and I got to know a little bit about him. I told him about you guys and how long we've been best friends. It was mostly just harmless chit-chat until we talked about ... going hunting."

"What? You told him that we call it hunting?" Both of their mouths hung open in shock.

"Not really. See the other night at the club, I kind of let it slip. I thought he hadn't caught on, but apparently I was wrong."

Sophie was now leaning forward in anticipation. "So, what did he say?"

Feeling a rush of emotion, Kate closed her eyes and started talking. "He asked what we did with the guys that we caught." The two friends were silent, so Kate kept her eyes shut and continued. "Then he leaned forward, and waited for me to give him the okay."

"He kissed you!" they both interrupted.

"No, but he almost did. The nurse walked in just as he was about to." The disappointment was clear on Kate's face and in her voice.

Sophie gasped. "What happened when she left?"

"She only left for a second to get me an icepack. And we just stared at each other."

"She did leave eventually, though, right? Then you jumped him?" Elle asked.

"Of course she did, Elle," Sophie replied. "Although she probably didn't pounce on him like you would have. Oh, I'm so excited! When are you guys going out? I want to meet him. Make sure he picks you up here. I'll even have Logan come over, that way he can give the guy's approval. I knew you would find him again and now we'll be able to—"

"He has a girlfriend," Kate said, cutting off her friend's rant.

It took Sophie a second to process what Kate had said. And when it did, she looked livid. "What?" she snapped.

"He has a girlfriend," Kate repeated slower this time.

"How do you know that?" Elle asked skeptically.

"Because when the nurse came back in the room, she told him that his girlfriend had called and said she wouldn't be able to make it for dinner."

"Jerk," Elle yelled.

"Bastard." Sophie joined her.

"No good piece of crap."

"Cheater!"

Kate looked back and forth at her friends as they verbally abused Ethan. As much as she wanted to join them, she couldn't. Deep down she felt he was none of those things. She'd only talked to him a few times, but the feelings she had around him were only good ones. She was just disappointed she would never find out who he really was. She wouldn't get the chance to know him on a different level.

"Okay, okay, you can stop. Thanks for being so nice. But really, guys, I can't be all that mad. It's not like anything actually happened. We didn't even know each other."

"Kate, you know as well as we do that he was flirting with you. And what you said about him almost kissing you today…"

"Believe me, Soph, I've had time to think about everything that happened. And I *am* a little upset; but more than anything, I'm bummed and annoyed at myself for getting so worked up over some guy I didn't even know. Remind me not to do that again."

Kate's friends could sense her desire to stop the topic of conversation and immediately gave her a hug. Elle was the first one to break the silence.

"How about a change of plans? Instead of going out for dinner and a movie, how about bringing the food and movie here?"

"Are you sure? You both really wanted to see that movie." Kate didn't want to throw a wrench in their plans, but the thought of being comfortable at home sounded really good.

"We can see it another day. Besides, I think it would be a great night to do facials. What do you think, Soph?"

"I'm in. Plus, I'm in serious need of a microdermabrasion treatment, and I can't get in with Salina until next week." She walked over to the mirror that hung on the wall and ran her fingers over her face.

"I'm in too," Kate agreed. "I need it after the day I've had."

Sophie rubbed her hands together. "All the more reason to do some pampering." She spun around and stopped when she reached the door. "It's a good thing you didn't break your ankle today. A beautiful pedicure really deserves to be displayed on a non-cast foot." She gave one last smile and disappeared down the hall.

Elle and Kate glanced at each other, shaking their heads and fighting off laughter.

"She does have a point," Elle said between laughs. "It's a good thing you didn't break anything today. That would have really sucked." Kate continued laughing and nodded. "All right, I'll go find us some take-out menus."

As Kate watched Elle leave the room, she thought about what both of her friends had said. Today could have gone a lot worse than it had. She hadn't broken anything, and there would be no permanent damage to her body. In a few weeks, she'd only have a scar to show for her fall. But somewhere deep inside her, Kate knew that statement was false. Something did feel broken, and the scar that would remain would not just be a physical one.

Chapter 8
Mr. Collins

Ethan watched as Kate walked out of the exam room. He couldn't believe what had just happened. Part of him wanted to run after her and explain everything. He wanted her to know that he was breaking things off with Cindy. He wanted to tell Kate that the few times he had spent with her had been amazing. That the pull he felt towards her was indescribable. That seeing her smile made his heart race, and that even though the whole thing freaked him out, he didn't care. All of these things he wanted to tell her and he just couldn't. Instead, he stood there, frozen in place, watching her leave.

What is happening to me? I'm acting like love struck teenager, Ethan thought, running his hands over his face in frustration. He couldn't understand the effect this girl he hardly knew was having on him. He was torn. His mind was telling him two entirely different things. One part of him thought he was crazy for feeling the way he did and to just forget about her. The other part of him was so excited that he'd finally found her—the one person he was sure he'd never find. The only thing both sides of his brain agreed upon was the fact that he needed to end things with Cindy.

Ethan looked down at his watch. He had two more hours until his shift was over, and he had to get in touch with Cindy before then. Since she'd canceled their dinner plans yet again, he knew he'd have to get creative. It took him a moment to decide what to do, but once he did, he knew it was his best shot.

Ethan dug out his phone and placed a call to Cindy's roommate. He left a message with her explaining that he got Cindy's message, and to let her know that he'd be going out with Trent and he'd call her later. He felt bad for lying, but he knew this was the only way.

He hung up the phone, hoping the message would be relayed. Now all he could do was wait. He knew Cindy well enough to know that she was obsessive about her Sunday night TV shows. And if she thought Ethan had plans, she would definitely stay home and stick to her normal routine. Now all he had to do was show up and hope that she would be there.

It was a little past eight by the time Ethan made it to Cindy's place. He pulled up in front of her house and noticed her living room lights were on. Feeling relief that she was home, he put his car in park and cut the engine. With one deep exhale, he climbed out and made the walk to her front door.

He paused for a moment on the front porch and tried to gather his thoughts. Rolling his shoulders, he attempted to somehow physically erase the nerves that were brewing before he began knocking loudly. He could hear the TV blaring from inside and wasn't sure if she'd heard him. The second time, he was positive she had.

"I'm coming! I'm not deaf! I heard you the first time. Whoever you are, you better have a damn good excuse for bothering me. Don't you think eight o'clock on a Sunday night is a little late to be knocking on doors? Whatever you're selling I'm not—" Cindy swung the door open, her words cutting off immediately. Her blond hair was pulled back in a bun, and she was dressed in pajamas. Her light blue eyes went from enraged to serene as soon as she saw it was Ethan.

"Ethan, I'm so sorry. I didn't know it was you." Her voice was extra sweet, a complete one-eighty from the vicious tone she'd yelled in.

"I'm glad I wasn't trying to sell something," he said sarcastically. He wished he could say that he was surprised by her behavior, but he wasn't. He'd seen this other side before, but only a few times.

"I thought you were going out with Trent tonight. Did you miss me so much you had to come see me?" She walked towards Ethan and wrapped her arms around his shoulders, planting kisses along his neck.

"Actually, I came here to talk to you about something." He leaned back from her and looked her in the eyes. Sensing his seriousness, Cindy untangled her arms and stepped back. "Can we sit for a minute?"

Taking the lead, Ethan walked into the room and sat down on her couch. Once she was beside him, he froze. He knew what he wanted to say, but was suddenly finding it very difficult. After a moment, he decided that best way to handle it was to just spit it out.

"This isn't working," he finally said.

"What's not working, honey bun?"

Ethan looked at her. "This." He motioned his hand in a circle between the two of them. "This isn't working." He was fairly sure that his statement and gesture was the universal language used by all people during a breakup. Surely she would know what he was talking about without having to explain it to her. He was wrong.

"Oh, Ethan, I'm so glad you feel that way too! We are definitely ready to move on."

He ran his hand through his hair, relieved at how well this was going. "I'm glad you understand."

"Understand? That's an understatement—I'm thrilled! When should we start looking at places?"

"Looking at places?" he asked, confused.

"Yeah. If we're gonna move in together, we need a place, don't we? My house is too small and it needs too much work. And I like my roommate and Trent, but I don't think either of us is interested in having a third roommate."

Ethan sat, slack jawed. *How in the world did she interpret that wrong?* His so-called universal body language didn't work as well as he'd thought. "Uhh, that's not exactly what I meant." He waited, hoping that she would suddenly understand. When she didn't, he continued. "I'm not interested in dating you anymore."

Cindy's back went straight, and she cocked her head to the side. "What?" she asked.

"I'm not interested in moving any further in our relationship."

Her eyebrows pulled together as if she didn't understand him. "So, what are you saying?"

"I'm saying that I think we shouldn't date anymore." Ethan waited for her response.

She smiled coyly. "Ethan, I know what you're trying to do and it's not going to work."

"What are you talking about?"

"I'm talking about this little game of cat and mouse you're playing." Her eyelids fluttered.

"What game of cat and mouse?"

"You know, the one where you try to make me think you're not interested anymore just so I'll cry and beg you to stay. Well, I'm not going to play it. You know as well as I do that we're perfect for each other. So let's just drop this whole thing and go upstairs. I promise you we can still make up." She got up from the sofa and walked behind it, leaning forward and running her fingers down Ethan's chest in an attempt to distract him.

As Ethan processed the words that came out of her mouth, he almost started laughing. Here he was trying to break up with her, and she thought he was trying to move their relationship to the next level.

"Look, Cindy, I know you think I'm playing a game with you, but I'm not." He took her hands in his. "I came over here tonight to end things. I don't think we should be involved in a relationship anymore. I'm sorry things didn't work out, and I truly hope you find someone who makes you happy." Ethan squeezed her hands gently and stood to leave.

As he reached for the doorknob, he caught sight of quick movement out of the corner of his eye. He spun around just in time to see Cindy throw a blue vase filled with flowers in his direction. As he ducked down, the vase shattered against the wall behind him, splattering his shirt with water. *I take it the real Cindy has made her appearance,* he thought to himself as he quickly opened the door and hurried to his car. As he reached the driver side door, he swore he heard her yelling something that sounded like, "Call you tomorrow." Ethan rolled his eyes in disbelief and climbed into his car.

He was still reeling when he pulled away from Cindy's house. He never thought he'd have to convince her that he was serious. She wouldn't accept it. She was insistent that he was playing some twisted game, but Ethan was not the kind of guy to do that. He was always fair and gentlemanly. And given the proper opportunity, he always spoke truthfully about his feelings.

Ethan's cell phone rang, interrupting his thoughts. He half expected it to be Cindy asking what time he'd be over tomorrow. Thankfully, it wasn't her.

"Hey, Trent. What's up?"

"Are you done yet, or are you still there? Is that psycho holding you hostage?" he asked, trying to stifle a laugh.

Ethan couldn't help but laugh himself. "No, I just left."

"How did she take it?"

"Just like you thought she would. She was in denial. I'm beginning to realize how Elizabeth Bennett felt when Mr. Collins wouldn't take the hint she truly wasn't interested." He knew it was odd to compare his situation to that of a fictional character, but that was the closest thing he could think of.

"Elizabeth who?"

"Elizabeth Bennett. From *Pride and Prejudice*." He knew Trent wasn't much of a reader, but he knew he'd read it in high school; they all had to.

"Pride and what?"

"It's a Jane Austen novel. We read it in high school, remember?"

"No. I don't remember that sort of stuff. Plus, it sounds like it was a chick book, and you know damn well I don't read chick lit." Ethan knew he was right. Trent had rarely read the assigned books in high school, and if it happened to be a 'chick book,' he definitely hadn't read it.

"Let's just forget about me comparing anything to a book, okay?"

"Whatever you say, 'chick lit reader.'" He let out a loud laugh.

"It was an assignment, Trent," he said in defense. "You know how I was in high school. I did every assignment."

"Yeah, but it sounds to me like you really enjoyed it enough to be talking about it, what, twelve years later?" Trent continued, not letting up in the least.

"It's a classic. And I have a good memory, that's all. Drop it." He paused, half expecting his friend to continue. Thankfully, he didn't.

Trent quickly changed the subject. "Are we still on for Rain tonight?"

"Yeah, I'm heading there now. Are you already there?" Ethan questioned as he glanced at the clock on the dash. Ending things with Cindy hadn't taken as long as it felt.

"I'm leaving now, so I'll catch you there. And you better bring your 'A' game tonight, bro. I'm planning on us both leaving with a girl."

"Whatever you say, man. I'll see you in a few." Ethan hung up his phone and pressed his foot to the pedal. Trent's comment about leaving with a girl tonight reminded him of the one girl he truly wanted to see: Kate. Just thinking about her made him smile. He raced downtown hoping that maybe tonight he would get lucky and see her again.

Ethan's first night out as an official single guy was not as eventful as he had hoped. He couldn't concentrate on anyone Trent introduced him to. He kept searching for Kate. He wanted desperately to see her smile, to hold her hand. He wanted to tell her that he didn't have a girlfriend and that he wanted nothing more than to spend time with her, get to know her better.

After two hours of Ethan's blatant disregard for any female, his friend had enough. They both left the club just as alone as when they had arrived. Ethan could sense Trent's displeasure and knew he wanted to say something. As soon as they were home, he did just that.

"What was with you tonight? I was introducing you to girls that would clearly hook up with you, and you weren't giving them the time of day." He looked like someone told him his dog died.

"I'm sorry. I was just … distracted, that's all." Ethan hadn't decided if he should tell him about Kate. There wasn't that much to tell anyway. Plus, if he told him the truth about the way he was feeling, he was sure Trent would think he was crazy. After all, who falls for a girl he barely even knows?

"Don't tell me you're thinking about that psycho."

"No. I've just had a lot on my mind, that's all. Work has been hard." He knew his work excuse would be sufficient to end any further discussion on his attitude. Trent had enough experience with his dad being a doctor to know that some days it can really wear on you.

"Work, huh? That sucks. I still don't know how you and Dad do it."

"Someone has to, right?" Ethan tried to lighten the mood and felt a slight sting for not telling him the real reason for his distractions earlier.

"Do you think you'll be up for going out next weekend?" Trent's mood was no longer somber, and his eyes looked excited.

"Yeah, I'll check my schedule." That seemed to be enough to appease Trent. He grabbed a beer out of the fridge, sat down on the couch, and flipped on EPSN, or the 'channel of the gods' as he liked to call it.

Not being in the mood to sit and watch replays of tonight's games, Ethan headed into his bedroom. He was still feeling the disappointment of not running into Kate tonight as he lay in bed thinking about the last time he'd seen her. It couldn't have been more than twelve hours ago, and yet it felt like an eternity. He missed her. He didn't even know her and he missed her. His last thoughts were of Kate sitting on that gurney in the exam room and how beautiful she was.

It was the most realistic dream he'd ever had. Kate was sitting in his exam room, just like she had been before. Her deep brown eyes bored into his as he moved closer. The pull between them was just as strong as the first time they'd met, and he couldn't stop his fingers as they traced over her collarbone and down her back.

He watched as goose bumps rose on her naked flesh where his fingers had just been. Without stopping, he continued moving his hands along her back, tracing small circles until he felt her body relax. Ethan looked at her face only to see that her eyes were closed and her full lips were parted as she released a quiet sigh.

Slowly leaning forward, he paused just as his lips brushed hers. She whispered his name so softly that he felt it more than heard it.

"Ethan," she said again, although this time her tone sounded different. She repeated it again and each time her voice grew louder.

"Ethan, wake up, man. Your alarm's been going off for fifteen minutes. I'm not doing this again tomorrow."

Ethan rolled over and looked up at Trent's annoyed face. "Sorry. I guess I didn't hear it."

"For the fourth day in a row? You have got to get a new alarm clock," Trent said while leaving the room.

Ethan sat up rubbing his eyes, looked over at his clock, and realized he would be late for work if he didn't hurry. With a groan, he uncomfortably climbed out of bed and headed into his bathroom to take another cold shower. Normally, he'd enjoy a nice hot one to get ready for the day, but the past four mornings, cold showers had definitely been necessary. *When is this going to end?* he thought with a sigh. The past four days had been torture. He was dreaming about Kate every night and thinking about her all day. One unanswered question continued to float around in his head: When would he see her again?

His answer came later that afternoon when he was on his way home from work and decided to stop off at the grocery store.

"Where is the bread aisle?" he asked himself quietly. He had been in this grocery store only once before, and even then he remembered getting turned around.

After asking an employee, he eventually found what he needed and headed over to the produce section. He looked down at the piles of fruit and wondered where to begin. Even after all the years he'd lived on his own, he'd never figured out the best way to pick certain fruit. He was always getting confused. Were you supposed to smell it, see how heavy it was, or press on it and check if it was ripe? Not wanting to deal with the challenge, he settled on apples since they were probably the least difficult.

As he turned to rip off one of the plastic bags, someone caught his eye. He knew it was her as soon as he saw her silhouette. Kate. She was standing in front of some vegetables, deciding which ones to choose. He watched her from a distance as she bit her bottom lip, contemplating her decision. Something about her intense expression and concentration made him laugh.

Before he had a chance to realize what he was doing, his feet were moving toward her. It was like an unseen force pulling him closer. He wanted to reach out and touch her, but knew that he couldn't. Not only did he not know her well enough, but the all-too-vivid dreams he had been having were just that—dreams.

"I don't know about you, but I never know the best way to pick out produce. It's always been a mystery to me." Ethan kept his voice casual, but he saw her stiffen when she heard him speak. He turned his head to look at her and watched as her brown eyes slowly met his.

Chapter 9
Innuendos

Kate stood outside of a client's apartment and looked over her grocery list again to make sure she had everything she needed before heading to the grocery store. Tonight she was testing out a new Italian recipe. Logan, Sophie, and Elle had all agreed to be the guinea pigs, and she was excited to use her new gnocchi paddle. Flipping open her phone, she called home.

"Hey, it's me."

"Hi. Get everything dropped off okay?" Elle asked.

"Yep. And they referred me to one of their friends. If everything works out, I'll have another wedding in August."

"Look at you! Big time photographer booking up her schedule."

Kate laughed. "I do what I can," she teased. "So anyway, I called because I'm going to run to the store on my way out of the city. Do you need anything?"

"No, I think I'm good. Besides, I've got my eye on a new Louis Vuitton bag. Who needs food when you can have a great bag?"

Kate laughed simply because she wasn't shocked in the least by her friend's priorities. She could remember more than one occasion when both Elle and Sophie lived off coffee and ramen for weeks so they could splurge on great clothes or accessories.

"Okay, I'm leaving then. I'll be home in a while."

As Kate made her way to the grocery store, she found herself looking at every car she pulled up next to. Usually she kept her eyes on the road, but things had changed over the past four days. She tried to tell herself that she was just being more observant of her surroundings, but she knew what the real reason was. She was hoping that by some miracle she would spot Ethan. She hadn't been able to get him out of her mind and was beginning to think she was going crazy.

Yesterday she'd pulled up to a light and caught a glimpse of someone who reminded her of him. She knew it probably wasn't, considering she wasn't even in the city, but she was grasping at straws, just hoping that maybe he'd be in her town. She sat at the light long after it had turned green before the guy finally looked over at her. When she saw it wasn't him, she immediately sped off, cursing herself for getting carried away with her wishes.

Last night as she lay in bed, she thought of ways that she could 'accidentally' bump into him at the hospital. After realizing all of them were ridiculous, not to mention pointless, because he already had a girlfriend, she finally gave up and fell asleep, only to dream of him again. Dreams that had started out pretty tame were getting more intense. She found herself waking up every morning feeling more and more sexually frustrated, which made her a little snappy. This morning's dream had been the best so far, which of course brought with it a new wave of desire to see him again.

She pulled into the grocery store parking lot, feeling slightly disappointed at another failed sighting, although she wasn't sure what she expected. There were far too many people living in the city. Chances were she wouldn't see him again, and if she did, it wouldn't be while driving.

Kate grabbed her list and bag and headed into the store. She went about her normal routine and started in the produce section. Bag in hand, she looked over the bell peppers and racked her brain trying to remember what color her recipe had called for.

"I don't know about you, but I never know the best way to pick out produce. It's always been a mystery to me."

Kate froze, hand outstretched. She knew that voice and the person that went with it. For a second she wondered if perhaps she'd imagined it—a side effect from dreaming about him so much lately. Then again, her dreams had not done the voice she had just heard justice; it was even better than she remembered.

She slowly turned toward him, hoping that her imagination wasn't good enough to create an illusion. She looked up into his stunning blue eyes and couldn't stop the smile that spread across her face. She stared at him, standing there, looking positively delicious in his scrubs before she realized what she was doing.

He asked you a question, dummy. Now answer! her brain shouted at her. She tried to pull her eyes away from him so she could think coherently, but was unsuccessful.

"Umm … yeah, I know what you mean. Produce can be tricky," she stammered, still locked in his gaze.

Ethan smiled. "I would go with the red ones. They always seem to be the sweetest."

"What?" she asked in a daze, blinking.

Her blank stare made Ethan laugh. She was so lost in her thoughts that she seemed to not understand a word he'd said.

"I said you should go with the red bell peppers. They're usually the sweetest," he repeated, this time breaking eye contact with Kate long enough for her to regain her senses.

Upon realizing that she was blatantly staring, she dropped her eyes and felt a wave of embarrassment rush over her. Grabbing a plastic bag, she busied herself with the peppers in front of her and proceeded to shove them into the bag.

"So, what are you making?" he asked, hoping to start a conversation.

"The bell peppers are just for a salad. I'm actually making gnocchi for the main dish," she said, while continuing to add peppers to her bag.

His eyes lit up. "Really?" Gnocchi was one of Ethan's favorite dishes. For a split second, a vision flashed in his mind. Kate stood beside him in the kitchen as they worked together. It only lasted a second, but it was perfect.

"Yeah, it's one of my favorites, although you can't really go wrong with Italian food. It's Logan's favorite too, so I'm hoping it turns out okay."

The excitement Ethan felt just a moment before faded as her words registered in his mind. He hadn't thought that perhaps she had a boyfriend and was unavailable. "Oh … well, I hope it turns out," he said with a smile.

"Thanks. After all, what are friends for, right?" Kate clarified. "His girlfriend—my best friend Sophie—can't cook to save her life. Every so often, I offer to make them all a home cooked meal, and it saves her the task of attempting to make his favorite dishes."

"Well, in that case, I really hope it turns out great. Sounds like Sophie should be thankful to have a friend who's willing to cook her boyfriend meals."

Kate blushed at his compliment and shook her head. "No, she's an amazing best friend. She's done so much for me that I should probably be cooking for her every night."

"I know what it's like to have a friend like that." He nodded.

"Trent, right?"

Ethan's eyes widened. "I'm surprised you remembered his name."

"I *have* been known to pay attention when someone's talking, you know," she teased, feeling a flutter in her heart.

"No, that's not what I mean. It's just nice. To hold someone's attention enough that they remember something small like that."

Ethan's eyes grew soft as he looked at her. She felt as if there was something more he wanted to say but didn't. Silence hung in the air, and she felt the tingle of energy pulse to life between them. Her heart raced and her hands itched to reach out and touch him. Something told her that if she didn't keep talking, the chances of her body taking control and doing something rash in the middle of the grocery store was quite possible.

"So, what are you cooking tonight?" Kate asked, swallowing thickly.

"Me? Nothing. I'm not buying anything big, just the usual bread and fruit." He looked down at his basket, noting the few things he had. "I don't cook that much anyway. Not that I don't enjoy it; I just don't see the point when there's only two of you."

As soon as Ethan mentioned cooking for two, her breath caught and all the facts came rushing back. It left a bitter taste in her mouth, and before she had time to sensor her words, they poured out freely.

"What, is your girlfriend not much of a cook? Do you guys usually go out for dinner, then?" His eyes widened at Kate's reaction, but then he smiled and looked amused, which of course made her even more annoyed. Again, her words spewed out uncensored like word vomit. "Why are you smiling at me like that?"

"I like watching you get flustered. You look beautiful."

Kate tried to form a coherent sentence but came up with nothing. Ethan wasn't sure if her lack of words was a good thing or a bad thing, but since she wasn't yelling, he figured it couldn't be that bad.

"Do you want me to answer your questions?" he asked. She still couldn't form words, so she simply nodded.

"When I said that I didn't cook because there were only two of us, the person I was referring to was Trent, my roommate. And no, my *ex*-girlfriend did not cook."

Kate felt her heart skip and her chest tighten in the best possible way. She tried to play it casual, and bit down on the inside of her cheeks to keep from smiling.

"And, well," he continued, "I guess I already explained to you why I was smiling."

Just thinking about his compliment made Kate even more flustered. She tucked her hair behind her ear and dropped her head. It was a moment before she calmed down and looked back at him. When she did, she couldn't withhold her smile. Finally, the guy she'd been thinking about for the past week was standing in front of her, suddenly available.

As soon as the thought came to her mind, a little voice in her head said she was jumping the gun. After all, she wasn't entirely sure he was interested. All she could do was remain calm and see how things played out. Gathering all of her courage, she told herself to relax.

Calm down, act cool. Just think like Elle, she encouraged herself. *What would Elle do?*

Kate held back a devious smile as a plan formed in her head.

"There are some *tricks* to picking out produce you know. I can show you a few if you want." Kate gave him a look that she hoped he would interpret as flirty. Apparently it worked, because his beautiful smile returned along with a new glint in his eye.

"I'm all yours," he said with a slow drawl.

In a rush, all the air blew from Kate's lungs, and she felt her heart slam against her chest. She forced herself to concentrate on breathing so she wouldn't pass out. Her knees were already feeling weak, and if he had any idea what the small comment he made did to her body, she wouldn't stand a chance at the little game she was about to play.

She took a step closer to him and placed one of her palms flat on his chest. "Well, in that case, Doctor, where do you want me … to start?" Kate let her eyes slowly roam down his body before returning to his glorious face.

Ethan's throat closed up. Just having her look at him the way she was drove him wild. He swallowed deeply, trying to calm himself. Something in the way she was acting made him think they were about to play a little game, and he was up for anything she was ready to dish out.

"You can start wherever you'd like," he said with a lift of his brows.

Thankful that he was going to play along, Kate reached out and grabbed a bell pepper. "Well, most vegetables are the same. You want to make sure they are *smooth* and *firm*." Kate took his hand in hers, placing it on the bell pepper she was still holding. "Here, you feel how smooth it is? Now give it a slight squeeze."

Ethan froze. "Holy crap," he muttered under his breath. His mind instantly filled with images of Kate. The controlled part of his brain was telling him to snap out of it and gain some focus, but it was proving harder than he thought. Taking a calming breath, Ethan attempted to clear his head and keep his feet planted firmly in place as she reached around him. Kate's dark hair swept in front of his face, filling his senses with her sweet perfume.

"Now, with cucumbers, it's pretty much the same." She held out her hand. "You're just looking for one thing. You want them to be nice and hard." She took her eyes away from the cucumber and looked up at him.

With her close proximity, Kate could literally feel the heat radiate from him. She closed her eyes and breathed him in. The familiar flicker of warmth grew in her stomach, spreading heat through her body. Her mouth watered as she imagined how good he would taste on her tongue. *Oh man, I want to kiss him*. She almost whimpered at the thought.

Ethan shifted his feet, and it took Kate a second to realize that she wasn't the only one who felt that way. As much as she wanted to continue with her demonstrations, she felt a little bad for putting him in that predicament, especially in public.

Kate took one last inhale and stepped away from him slowly, trying to keep her eyes from drifting. But, like always, they had a mind of their own. Her eyes went wide and she felt her face burn. Quickly turning away, she attempted to hide her face, but knew it was pointless. One look at Ethan, and she knew she'd been caught. Surprisingly, the expression on his face was not one of embarrassment. In fact, he looked as though he was enjoying himself. His eyes were alight and matched his mischievous grin.

"I think you've just made me a *big* fan of the produce aisle." He gave her a quick wink and continued to smile.

"I'm glad I could help," Kate said, holding back a giggle. "After all, vegetables are good for your body."

The two of them continued to stare at each other in silence, both of them feeling the spark between them crackle to life.

"Shall we move on to fruit?" Ethan held out his hand and just like that, Kate knew she'd let him take her anywhere. She watched as their fingers intertwined with each other's, and she quieted the screaming voice of excitement that rang in her head.

"So what are your 'tips' for picking out fruit? Are they better than your vegetable pointers? Because if they are, I'll have to prepare myself." He shifted slightly.

"What? Was that hard for you? You don't think you can take too much more *information*?" she teased, hoping that he would catch her double meaning.

"Oh, I can handle more *information*. But it would require us leaving the grocery store, and you haven't finished your shopping." Ethan's eyes held hers and Kate knew without a doubt he was being serious. The thought of leaving with Ethan made her knees go weak.

"All right, then, I'll take it easy on you." She gave him a quick wink and let go of his hand. Kate knew if she was going to carry on a coherent conversation with Ethan, she would need all of her energy focused on the words coming out of her mouth and not on the desire she felt to grab him and leave. "What fruit should we start with?" She looked around at the selection before her and waited for him to choose.

"I like all fruit, but I really only feel safe picking out the basics."

"Okay, so you've got the apples, bananas, and oranges covered. Am I right?"

He nodded. "Right."

Kate laughed. Never in her life would she have pictured herself in this situation, teaching a guy the finer points of produce shopping. And not just a good looking guy, but someone who could make her body feel the way it did.

"What is so funny?" he asked, looking around for the source of her laughter.

Kate twisted the hem of her shirt between her fingers. "It's nothing really. I just never thought I would do something like this."

"Something like what, exactly?" he asked, amused.

"Show you, a doctor, how to pick out produce." She went from laughing to shy in a matter of seconds and dropped her eyes to the floor.

Ethan stepped forward and tucked her hair behind her ear. His voice lowered and he looked her in the eyes. "You may not know this, Miss Thomas, but they didn't teach us *everything* in medical school. I'm glad that you're willing to fill in the blanks. You're a great teacher."

"Thanks for the compliment." Kate smiled.

"You are very welcome."

"So…" She paused. "What are some of your favorites?" She walked over to the nearby bin and picked up a cantaloupe. Holding it in her hands, she turned around to face him. "How about cantaloupe?"

"Cantaloupe I like, but it *is* a melon and I find melons to be the most puzzling."

Kate's lips twitched and she fought off the laughter threatening to escape. She knew he was talking about fruit, but her mind was still wandering in the sexual danger zone.

"Sorry, that probably sounded like I have no idea what to do with uh… with umm… melons," he stammered, running his fingers through his hair and shoving them in his pockets nervously.

Kate watched the beautiful man get flustered and was shocked at how sexy she found him at that moment. His nervous fidgeting, the way his body swayed from one foot to the next, the slight pink color of his cheeks, the way he licked and bit on his bottom lip. He seemed so vulnerable. And as much as she would have loved to watch him squirm a little longer, she couldn't.

"I know what you mean about melons being tricky." She gave him a little wink, signaling she wasn't going to give him a hard time. "With watermelons, you go by weight. Pick one that feels heavy for its size. And with cantaloupes you go by smell." She held the melon up to her nose, closed her eyes and breathed in.

Ethan had to stifle back a moan. The woman in front of him was the perfect example of a real life angel and yet everything about her drove him crazy. It took all of his strength not to pull her towards him and ask if he could handle her *melons* right there in the middle of the produce section.

"Mmm, it smells perfect," she purred, the sound of her voice driving him even crazier. "Here, smell." She held out the melon and waited for his move. Ethan looked at her cautiously before stepping forward and mimicking her motion.

"It does smell good. First shot and you picked a great one." He smiled down at her. "Do you want to take this one?"

"No, why don't you have it. I'll grab another one." She reached down into the bin, and when she stood back up, he was gone. *Great, another disappearing act. This guy has got that down to a science,* she thought as she looked around. It took all of two seconds for her to spot him at another section of the produce department, and when their eyes met, he signaled for her to come to him.

"I thought you pulled one of your disappearing acts again," she said, nudging him with her elbow, once by his side.

"I'm sorry. I thought you saw me walk over here. And I am sorry about the other times too. Sometimes I get called away with work."

"You don't have to apologize for that. I completely understand. Why did you come over here anyway?"

"Well, after showing me all of your little tips, I'm sure you think I'm a complete idiot." Kate opened her mouth to correct him, but he held up his hand, motioning for her to stop. "I wanted to show you that I do know how to pick out some things, especially my favorites." He held up a package of strawberries and flipped open the lid, removing a bright red berry.

"The trick to picking out a good strawberry is much like the cantaloupe. You go by smell." He brought the strawberry up to his nose and breathed in its scent, then held it out. He watched Kate's eyes carefully, never looking away as she leaned in. "Smells delicious, right?" She nodded. "And for most people that would suffice. But for me, I like to make sure they taste as good as they smell." He pulled the strawberry back to his mouth and took a bite. Kate's eyes went wide as her mind filled with images of kissing that delicious mouth.

Without realizing that she'd stopped breathing, she began to feel light headed. Inhaling quickly, she made herself concentrate on the simple act of pulling air into her lungs.

"Want a bite? It's really good and *juicy*." Ethan smirked at her and held out the strawberry. The look on his face let Kate know that that he was more than aware of the effect he was having on her.

She cocked an eyebrow. *Fine, Ethan, you want to play again, let's play,* she thought with a devious smirk.

Slowly taking a step closer to him, she pressed herself against his chest and looked up into his eyes, which were focused solely on her. Giving her lips a quick lick, she opened her mouth and waited for his move. In one fluid motion, he lifted the strawberry and held it a few inches away. Knowing that if she wanted the full effect she couldn't rush it, she leaned in and let her tongue slowly reach for the berry. She licked at the juice from where he'd just taken a bite, and when she did, she heard him swallow loudly.

Repeating the step a second time, she then used her tongue to pull the berry into her mouth. Kate closed her eyes as she bit down, letting some of the juice drip onto her lips. The sound of his breath came rapidly and the quick rise and fall of his chest pressed against hers.

Ignoring the desire she had to climb up his body, she focused on chewing slowly, accentuating every movement. When she was done, she opened her eyes and stepped back. She didn't have to look into his eyes or see his face to know what he was thinking. The tension in his jaw said it all. Feeling quite satisfied with her demonstration, she very casually licked her lips.

"You're right; those are really good, very…*juicy*. I think I'll get some myself." She reached down and grabbed a package of her own, all the while holding back a giggle of satisfaction. Knowing that she couldn't end on a better note, she decided it was a perfect place to end their conversation. "Well, Ethan. I think I better get going. I need to get dinner started, and my friends are not the most patient people." She turned away from him and silently pleaded that he'd stop her.

"Wait." He reached out and grabbed her hand. "I'd like to call you sometime, if that's okay."

Kate's heart thrilled at his words, and it was all she could do not to blurt out her number. But then Elle's voice entered her head and reminded her to make him work for it. "You're a doctor, right? And you work at the hospital?" He looked a little confused by her questions since he knew she already had the answers, but he nodded anyway. "Good, then that means you're a smart guy. If you want to see me again, I'm sure you'll figure out how." Kate gave him one last wink and turned around pushing her cart slowly, making sure to give him a nice view as she swayed away.

Ethan couldn't take his eyes off of her as she walked away from him. When she stopped and turned around, he smiled, taking in every last detail of her beautiful face.

As soon as she was out of his sight, he let out a sigh. He was exhausted. Never in his life had he had such a sexually frustrating, emotionally draining, thrilling, enjoyable experience. Laughing quietly to himself, he replayed everything from the past few minutes and turned his cart around. He only got a few feet when he noticed a pile of peaches. Rolling his eyes, he said a silent prayer of thanks that peaches were not part of Kate's demonstration. Something told him that if she had grabbed a peach during their little game, he would have literally lost all control. His pulse quickened at the simple thought, and he let out another exhausted sigh while picking one up. *Produce will never be the same again,* he thought, before opening his mouth and taking a big bite.

☙

Kate's drive home was a blur. She was in complete and utter euphoria as she replayed everything that happened. The way he looked at her like she was the only one there, the way his eyes glistened with excitement, the way he smelled, the way he smiled at her, everything. She didn't have to look at her reflection to know that she had a huge smile on her face.

She was still floating as she walked up the steps of her townhouse and opened her front door. Once inside, she could hear the laughter of Sophie and Logan coming from the kitchen. With her groceries in tow, she made her way through the door. Just as she thought, Logan was standing in the kitchen with Sophie clinging to his back, her arms wrapped tightly around his neck.

Kate froze, right there in the middle of the doorway, and waited until both of her friends were focused on her. Then she dropped her bags on the floor and flung her arms and head up into the air victoriously.

"He's *single*!!"

Chapter 10
Rumble

Elle sat on her bed, flipping through another fashion magazine. Lately, she hadn't been able to get her fashion fill. She knew from past experience that meant one of two things. Either she was in need of another serious shopping excursion, or she needed a job.

Considering the fact that she had just gone shopping last week with her girls, she knew that meant only one thing. She needed to get another job lined up. Sophie kept telling her to be patient, but Elle was worried. It had been a little while since she'd landed anything really big and she was beginning to feel scared. With a sigh, she reached for another magazine when her cell rang. After assuring Kate that she didn't need anything from the store, she hung up, satisfied to hear the smile in her friend's voice. The past four days had been interesting. After Kate came home from the hospital with the news that her Dr. Hottie had a girlfriend, she seemed a little off. Both Sophie and Elle knew that she was ready to move on after her break up with Scott, and they were hoping that this mystery guy Ethan was going to be the one to help with that. It was disappointing to all of them to learn he was taken.

Kate had made it pretty clear to the two of them that she was just going to forget about him and write the whole situation off as one big misunderstanding. Of course, both Sophie and Elle knew that there was no way he was fading away any time soon. They had never seen her so affected by someone before, at least not since Scott. And even then, it was different.

Their relationship had seemed to be based on convenience. They had become such good friends and had grown to love one another. It just seemed fitting that it should have taken the next step. That was probably why it ended so badly. How do you end a relationship and lose your best friend in the process? They both missed each other's friendship so much that they were confused as to what that meant. Did they miss each other as lovers and partners? Or did they simply miss the platonic friendship they had? Where did they draw the line?

Elle had to admit she was glad when the whole fiasco was finally over. It was one of the hardest times in Kate's life, and it killed Sophie and her to see their best friend in such heartache.

Now the only thing Elle had to do was set Kate up on a date, get her back into the dating scene again. After all, Elle could spot a sexually frustrated person a mile away, and Kate was definitely in that category. She needed to find someone and the sooner the better.

Elle was flipping through her mental Rolodex of guys that she could hook Kate up with when the phone rang. Pleased to see it was her manager, she answered her phone with a smile.

"Hello, Graham."

"Hello, beautiful. How is my gorgeous Elle doing on this fine day?" His thick British accent always made Elle feel like she'd stepped into a movie.

"Well, that all depends on what news you have for me."

"News? Can't I just call my sweet girlfriend to chat?" he asked.

"Graham, why are you teasing me?"

"Darling, you know I don't tease. I just like being playful." He was stalling and even Elle could tell.

"I know what you're doing, Graham. I can tell when you're hiding something from me. Please, you know how I can't handle surprises."

"All right, fine, but I'm only giving in so quickly because I love you and because I can hear the stress in your voice. You know what stress does to your skin. It does nothing but cause breakouts and give you wrinkles."

"So...?" She waited for him to start talking.

"Well, last week, I had lunch with my old friend Samuel. We went to that fabulous little bistro I told you about, the one with the great beet salad. So anyway, it turns out he's now working with Alexandre Beaumont, the French designer, and he's on the search for a model to open next month's show here in New York. Naturally, I shift our discussion to business because you know I can't miss out on an opportunity like this."

"Uh-huh," Elle said.

"So, you'll never believe who shows up right when it's getting good and interrupts our conversation."

"Who?" she asked, truly puzzled.

"Sheridan Wyatt."

Elle froze. "What was she doing there? I thought she was in China."

"Well, apparently, she decided to come back to the States and try things here again."

She let out a sigh of annoyance. "So, why was she at lunch?"

"That's the best part. She showed up saying that it was just an amazing 'coincidence.' I know how she works, sweetheart. She'll stop at nothing to get all the inside information she can get her hands on."

"Sneaky bitch." Elle felt her insides get hot thinking about the one girl who had made her career more difficult than it needed to be.

"Don't I know it? Anyway, we had just started talking names when she practically pulled up a chair and started saying how she would love the opportunity to work with them again."

"Ugh," she groaned. "What did he say?" Elle held her breath while waiting for his response.

"He told her that they would be in touch with her agency if they were interested."

Elle relaxed slightly, but then remembered that it didn't mean a thing. She'd gone head to head against Sheridan before and had lost out. Of course, Graham had blamed it on marketing at the time, saying that the wide demographic was looking for a different 'look.' But they both really knew the truth. Sheridan slept her way through the modeling world. Her specialty was landing photographers. All it took was one and she was in.

The funny thing was, if anyone asked Elle, she would be the first to admit that having a great body can get you things in life. But sleeping with someone to move up in a job was where she drew the line.

"When do they make their decision?" she asked.

"They already have, that's why I'm calling." Elle didn't have to ask. Graham didn't sound the least bit excited, and if there was one thing he wasn't good at it was masking his feelings. As soon as Elle realized that she not only missed another great opportunity, but that he was calling to inform her that she'd lost out, she got angry.

"You called me acting like you might have good news, and then just drop a big ol' bomb on me? Seriously, Graham, I am this close to looking for another manager!" She wasn't serious, but was definitely mad enough to try sounding like she was.

"Oh, shut it, Elle. Do you honestly think I would let an opportunity like this slip by?"

Now she was confused. "What are you talking about?"

"I'm talking about how I charmed the pants off of Samuel and told them that no one would be better for the job than my smart-ass Elle. Of course, I may have said something about you having the perkiest set of breasts this side of the Equator."

"Are you serious? You really did that? And you really think my breasts are that great?"

"Yes, yes, and yes. And after sending him prints of your previous work, he agreed. They want you up here on Saturday for a fitting."

"Are you serious?" she asked happily. "Thank you so much. This couldn't have come at a better time."

"You are more than welcome, darling." He paused. "Now for the good news…" he trailed off.

Her brows furrowed. "Good news? I thought that was the good news?"

"On a normal basis, yes, it would be. But today is different. I just got a phone call from my friend at *Sports Illustrated*."

As soon as the words left his mouth, Elle froze. She'd done a shoot with them a few months before, for their yearly swimsuit issue. She knew that it had the potential to be big—big because there was a chance to end up on the cover. But since she hadn't heard back from them, she figured she'd lost out on the chance.

"Have they made this year's choice?" she whispered, almost afraid to ask.

"Not yet," he said slowly. "But, he did tell me that you are one of their top two choices."

Elle's jaw hung open in shock. "You're kidding, right?"

"I'm afraid not."

"I…I…I can't believe it," she stuttered. It took a moment until she could form words and once she could, she was overflowing with thanks. "You are seriously amazing, and if you were straight, I would be begging to go out with you. And you know I don't beg for anything, especially when it comes to men."

"My dear Elle, you sure know how to boost a man's ego," he teased. "I'll have my office send you the info about this weekend, arrival time, etc. Now, go out and celebrate. I'll call you tomorrow. Oh, and Elle, you realize what this means, right?"

Elle nodded. "It means that I could—"

"Land the coveted cover of the *Sports Illustrated* swimsuit issue," Graham finished with a tone of awe.

If Elle had a hard time finding words before, there was definitely no finding words now. Landing the cover of *Sports Illustrated* was something she'd dreamed about forever. It would change her career.

Hanging up the phone, Elle let out a squeal that even Sophie would be proud of and grabbed her purse. She intended to do just as Graham suggested and celebrate. And if there was one way to celebrate, it was eating chocolate covered Oreos from the Goodie Bag on South Main Street and drinking margaritas.

Racing down the road with the windows partially down, Elle let the cold wind whip around her. With the music blaring, she was lost in her own world when she heard a loud bang. Her car swerved to the right, and Elle immediately knew she'd blown a tire. *Crap, crap, crap. Changing a tire in heels is the last thing I feel like doing right now,* she thought with a roll of her eyes.

Her dread was not because she didn't know how to change a tire. Her dad's business in the automotive industry made him a car aficionado, and he made sure to teach his little girl the basics, like changing a tire.

Elle pulled over to the shoulder, making sure she was far enough away from any other passing cars, and popped the trunk. Thankful that she wouldn't have to wait for AAA, she grabbed her spare, wheeled it around to the front of the car, and went back for the tools.

Just as she bent down to jack the car up, she noticed a vehicle pull over. Actually, she heard it before she saw it. Music was blaring at a deafening level. Elle's eyes flashed upward long enough to see that it was a huge black SUV, not a small car like she'd assumed. Neon lights surrounded a license plate that read RUMBLE. *Typical jock. You've got to be kidding me,* Elle thought with a laugh.

The music abruptly ended as the driver turned off the SUV and stepped out. She watched as a tall man walked towards her. His fitted shirt clung to his chest, accentuating his muscles, and the sun glistened off of his light blond hair. He walked toward her, and there was no way Elle could stop her eyes from roaming. Something about him looked familiar, yet she couldn't place his face. Pushing those thoughts away, she peeled her eyes away long enough to gather her thoughts and started to unscrew the lug nuts.

"You look like you could use some help." His attempt to make his voice sound sexy made Elle laugh.

"I'm fine, thanks."

"Yes. You. Are." He spoke slowly, and she could feel the weight of his eyes watching her.

Elle looked up at his face and was greeted by a wide smile and bright green eyes. For a second, she felt her heart flutter, but ignored it when she remembered what he had said.

"Thank you for that astute observation. Now if you'll excuse me." She turned back to the tire and finished with the last nut, all the while knowing he was still watching her.

"So, you know how to change a tire?" She looked back to him with wide eyes as if acknowledging the obvious. "But you're … you're … beautiful," he stammered.

"Does exhaustive research show that beautiful women can't possibly know how to change a tire?" She forcefully heaved the tire off the wheel hub and began rolling it around to her trunk.

He followed behind her and continued talking. "Umm … no, that's not what I meant, it's just—"

"Why in the hell can't a beautiful girl know how to change a tire?" she spat, cutting him off. "See, this is what's wrong with men. They make stupid assumptions." Elle walked back around to the front, lifted the spare, and shoved it in place.

"Look, I'm sorry if I offended you. I was just taken off guard. It's not every day I meet a hot girl who knows how to change a tire. It's impressive."

She peered up at him with squinted eyes, trying to read him. Was he just being a smart ass or was he honestly serious? He continued looking at her and his smile grew even bigger, showing off a set of perfect white teeth. Her heart thumped loudly in her chest, and she immediately reprimanded herself for gawking. Forcing her eyes away from him, she told herself he was just another guy, nothing special.

"Impressive? Would it also surprise you that I'm a girl who can actually drive a stick?" It was a simple statement, but it was clear by the look on his face that he took it out of context. She let out an exhausted sigh. "Typical man. I make a simple non-sexual statement and you assume it means I want to have sex with you."

"Hey! I didn't say anything about having sex with you. You really are a spit fire, aren't ya?"

"What?" She stared at him blankly.

"You heard me. Look, I pulled over here because I thought maybe you needed some help. Now are you going to let me help or not?"

She was shocked. Never in her life had a guy actually talked back like that before. Yell profanities? Cry? Grab their balls and run? Yes, but never stand up and say what they actually felt.

"Fine, you can help." She gave in. His sexy smile returned, and he rolled his shoulders back in pride before reaching for the wrench. "What do you think you're doing?" she asked.

"You said I could help."

"Help, yes. Take over? No."

"Aww man, what do you want me to do then?" He hung his head much like a little boy being punished by his mother. Elle's insides grew warm, and she felt herself giving in.

"Here, you can hold these." She shoved the lug nuts into his huge hands. He opened his mouth to say something, but quickly snapped it shut with one glare from Elle. She didn't say another word as she went about her work.

Just as assumed, it didn't take her long. When she was finished, she looked down at her filthy hands and realized she still had to go to the store. With a mischievous grin, she looked over at the stranger who was still beside her. "You still want to help?"

"I thought I was helping," he said in a mocking tone while cocking his head to the side.

"Smart ass. I mean, you want to do something really useful?" She took a step closer to him.

"Sure. What did you have in mind?" He lifted his eyebrows suggestively.

"Take off your shirt," she said.

The jock's face lit up like a kid on Christmas morning. He let out a hearty laugh. "Whatever you say."

He reached his hands over his shoulders, grabbed onto the back of his shirt and pulled it forward over his head. Elle could tell even before he had his shirt off that he had a good body, but she wasn't expecting what she saw. And she couldn't stop the gasp that escaped her mouth.

She stood wide-eyed, starting at the gorgeous creature before her. In her line of work, she'd seen her fair share of half-naked men, but never in her life had she been turned on like she was at the moment. His chest was perfect: ripped abs and chiseled pecs all under gloriously tan skin. She felt her jaw go slack and heat spread through her entire body. Quickly snapping her mouth shut, she swallowed and turned her attention back to her grease covered hands.

"Well … what do you want me to do?" he said, shrugging his shoulders.

Let me lick you. Or better yet, take me right here on the side of the road, she thought before shaking her head, attempting to clear her mind.

"Give it to me." Elle held out her hand, making sure to keep her distance. She didn't trust herself to get too close to the slice of heaven standing before her. Mostly because her body tended to have a mind of its own and right now it liked what it saw.

The stranger looked down at Elle's hands, covered in grease and all he did was laugh. Clearly he'd figured out her plans. His light green eyes lit up and he tossed her his shirt, hitting her in the face.

With a roll of her eyes, Elle went to work getting every last bit of grease from her hands. She kept her eyes down and pretended to ignore the man that was still standing in front of her. To say he annoyed her was an understatement. His cocky attitude and smart ass comments got under her skin. Yet there was something in his smile that melted her heart.

"Here." She took a step forward and pressed his shirt against his chest. Before she could pull away, his large hand covered hers, pushing her palm flat against his pecs. "Thanks for all your help," she said, sliding her hand out from under his and dragging it down his bare stomach.

Oh my … please help me now, she moaned silently to herself.

"No problem. I'd be more than willing to *help* you out anytime you need it," he said with a laugh, sending vibrations up the length of her arm.

"Yeah, I bet you would." Elle spun on her heel and walked over to the driver's side. Climbing into her seat, she could feel his eyes on her, watching her every move.

"So that's it?" He looked down and shuffled his feet side to side, kicking some loose pebbles around.

He didn't have to explain his question. Elle knew exactly what he was referring to. He expected her to be the typical girl. The girl that would bat her lashes, give him her phone number, and practically beg for a call. But Elle McLean was not that type of girl. If he wanted her number, then he was going to have to ask, although something about him told her that he was not the kind of guy who did that. Girls swooned after him, not the other way around.

"Yep, that's it. Unless, of course, you need help changing a flat tire," she said innocently.

"No, I'm good. But if I ever need any help, I know the right girl to call."

"I never gave you my number," she said, while closing the door. His mouth hung slack and he blinked slowly. "Thanks again for your help," Elle said. "Your shirt really came in handy." She gave him her most mischievous smile and slowly drove away.

❦

Trent watched as the hottest girl he'd ever seen drove away, leaving him standing on the side of the road like some love sick adolescent.

Hot damn, what a girl, he thought. He'd had his fair share of beautiful women, but she was gorgeous. Not only that, she was a gorgeous smart ass who knew how to change a tire. And her apparent disinterest drove him crazy. He was used to girls falling all over him, practically begging to get in his pants, and she didn't even bat a lash. He wondered briefly if something was wrong with her. It took him all of two seconds to realize that there was absolutely nothing wrong with her. In fact, she was the complete opposite. She was everything right. But if she was so right, why didn't he ask for her number?

Trent knew the answer to his question as soon as he thought it. He never asked for chicks' numbers. That's how it had always been and how it would always be. He shrugged it off as her loss and climbed back in his SUV.

A half hour later, he walked into his condo, slamming the door behind him. The entire car ride home had done nothing but give him time to think about the tire chick and make him aggravated that things hadn't turned out the way he planned. He was making his way into the kitchen for a beer when he noticed Ethan putting away some groceries.

"Bad afternoon at your parents, T?"

"Yeah, you could say that," he said while walking over to the counter to sit down. There was a moment of silence between the two friends, and Ethan eyed the grease smudged shirt.

"Something wrong with the SUV?"

"No." Trent crossed his arms.

"Look, I'm not going to talk to you if you start moping. Just tell me what happened."

Trent didn't want to sound like a complete idiot, but he knew in this situation it would most likely be inevitable. "I was on my way home from my parents' when I saw a girl on the side of the road with a flat tire. I pulled over to offer my help."

"And by 'offering your help,' do you mean you offered to get into her pants?"

"No, I was being nice. I just asked if she needed any help, I swear." He held up his hands defensively. Ethan looked doubtful, but didn't say anything. He waited for his friend to continue. "Anyway, I offered and she said she didn't need help. She already knew how to change a tire."

"Lots of girls know how to change tires," Ethan said with a shrug.

"Not girls like *her*. Man, you should have seen her. She was wearing these high heels and this skirt. And her legs? Man, they were amazing. She was gorgeous, and you know I've seen a lot of good looking girls. She was the hottest I've *ever* seen."

Ethan watched his friend in amusement. "So, when are you going out with her?"

"I'm not," Trent said dejectedly.

"She turned you down?" Ethan laughed. "Trent, that has gotta be the first time that's ever happened. Well, except for Kathy Harris but that was in ninth grade. What did you do to her?"

Trent suddenly felt very defensive. His ego had already taken a beating and he couldn't bear much more. "Hey, first off, Kathy Harris only said no because she was infatuated with you. And I didn't *do* anything to this girl. You should have heard her, E. She had a mouth on her. I swear I've never been talked to like that before. I have to admit it was kind of a turn on, but that's beside the point. We aren't going out because she didn't give me her number."

Ethan closed his eyes and took a calming breath. "Please tell me you didn't ask her out because she didn't play into your stupid little game."

"It's not a game, man. You know how I am."

"If you mean that I know you're a complete ass, then yes, I know how you are. You finally meet a girl who wouldn't put up with your crap, and you let her walk away because she didn't give you her number?"

Trent listened as his friend lectured him. Normally, he would fight back, but today he didn't. He knew Ethan was right. "Okay, so it was stupid of me. But it's too late now. Maybe I'll get lucky and see her again someday."

Ethan stopped talking and shook his head as he went back to putting his groceries away. After the third bag of fruit, Trent looked at him with narrowed eyes.

"What's with all the produce? Are you making some big dinner or something?" Ethan paused for a second, but didn't say a word. "Ethan? I said, what's with all the produce?"

"Nothing, I just felt like getting some more fruit and stuff." He shrugged his shoulders casually, but there was no hiding the slight tint of pink that colored his cheeks.

If Trent knew Ethan—which he did—there was only one thing that made him blush and that was girls. "All right, who is she?" he asked, drumming his fingers on the granite countertop.

"She who?"

"Dude, Ethan, I know you. You met someone, I can tell. So who is she?" His friend shrugged again, attempting to play it cool. "You know I won't give up until you tell me. I can get really annoying if I need to. Do I need to remind you about summer camp of ninth grade?"

Trent thought back to that summer the two friends spent at Camp Trexler. After they got home from a summer of fun, Ethan wasn't acting like himself. He refused to tell his friend what was going on. Eventually Trent got him to admit it involved a girl and wouldn't let it go. He'd followed him around for days singing, whining, and repeating anything he said until Ethan finally broke down. He eventually admitted to making out with one of the senior camp leaders, something that Trent still gave him major kudos for to this day.

"Fine. Yes, I met someone," Ethan said.

"I knew it! Was it today?"

"No, it was actually a week ago." Trent listened closely as Ethan told him all about the mystery girl he met—Kate was her name. He told him about what happened at the hospital, how he almost kissed her, and how Lisa dropped the bomb about Cindy.

"I never liked that Lisa girl. There is something about her. It's like she's always plotting something." Ethan nodded. "So did you see her today, then?" Trent watched Ethan unload the last bag of groceries and waited for his response.

"Yeah, on my way home from work, I stopped off at the grocery store, and I bumped into her." He closed the fridge with a click and leaned back on the stainless steel surface.

"And . . . ?" Trent asked with wide eyes.

Ethan stood up and started to walk out of the room before stopping in the doorway.

"All I'm gonna say is that I'm officially a *big* fan of the produce section. I sure as hell won't ever look at it the same way again." His face lit up with a wide smile, and he turned on his heel to leave.

Trent sat in shock. He couldn't believe Ethan was leaving him hanging. How could he drop a bomb like that and not explain? He quickly hopped down off his chair.

"Wait!" he yelled. "Did you jump her? You did, didn't you? You got down and dirty with her right there in the middle of the produce section. Come on, tell me! You were playing with her melons, weren't you? Oh, man, you are so the luckiest S.O.B. I've ever met!" Trent followed after his friend, begging for the details of his illicit grocery store rendezvous.

Chapter 11
Reservations

Kate looked back and forth between her two friends and wondered if they'd know who she was referring to.

"Who's single?" Logan asked with puzzled eyes.

Sophie didn't have to ask. There was only one person who Kate wanted to be single, and that was Doctor Ethan.

"What?" she yelled, hopping off Logan's back. "How did you find out? Did you just see him? What did he say? What did you say? Are you guys going out, then?" She was so excited that one question ran into the other.

"I just saw him at the grocery store," Kate said with a smile.

"And?"

"We talked for a while. And I helped him pick out produce." She tried to hide her blushing face as she grabbed her bags, headed over to the kitchen, and started putting things away.

Sophie gave Logan the 'girls talk' look, and he disappeared into the living room to watch some TV.

"Why are you blushing like that?" Sophie asked, knowing there was something going on.

"Blushing like what?"

"Oh, don't try and play coy with me, missy," she said while waving her finger in Kate's face. "I can tell there is something going on behind that smile of yours. Now spill it!"

Kate fiddled with the corner of her shirt, trying to decide where to start. Just as she opened her mouth to speak, the door opened and Elle walked in.

"What's up, bitches? Who's up for some amazing chocolate covered Oreos and margaritas?" She walked into the kitchen, bags in hand, and a huge smile on her face. Both Kate and Sophie stared in wonderment. They were used to Elle's more than colorful ways of greeting them, but this was different. There was something else going on.

"What happened to you?" Sophie asked.

"What? I can't be happy without you guys thinking something's going on?" Again, the two girls looked at each other with wide eyes.

"Umm…" Kate mumbled. "It's just that you seem really, really happy." She looked at Sophie with pleading eyes, begging for help.

"Kate's right. You only get this happy when you've had a great lay. And since I'm pretty sure you've only been gone an hour or so, I'm guessing that's not it." Sophie pulled her brows together and shrugged. "I suppose it could be possible. You are pretty ballsy," she pointed out.

"All right, Soph, you can stop jumping to conclusions. That's not why I'm happy," she said with a roll of her eyes. "Then again, I *did* meet someone."

"You did?" Kate asked, while leaning forward in interest.

Elle's eyes glazed over, her mind stuck on something else while she spoke. "Yeah, I got a flat tire and some hot jock pulled over and tried to help. You know, since I have the words 'helpless big-breasted bimbo' stamped across my forehead."

"So, you let him help you?" Sophie asked surprised. "That's a first."

"Yeah, Elle, he must have been really hot for you to allow that to happen." Kate watched her friend closely for any reaction. She had a feeling there was more to her story.

"Oh, believe me, he was hot. And there was something about him that looked familiar. Then again, I'm pretty positive I'd remember a hot asshole like him." She shook her head, dismissing her previous thoughts. "Anyway, yes, he was hot and cocky and adorable and annoying." She prattled off a few other attributes and told them the entire story. Both Kate and Sophie stared with their jaws hanging open.

"So… are you going out with him, then?" Kate asked hesitantly.

"Did you not just hear what I said? You guys, he was a complete… I don't know, he was just so…" She rubbed her hands across her forehead in frustration.

"Hot," Sophie said, finishing her sentence.

Elle dropped her shoulders and let out a little sigh of defeat. "Yeah, he was hot. It still doesn't change the fact that he was an ass." She sat down at the table, propping her head up with her hand.

Kate sat down next to her. "What's the problem, then? Why didn't you give him your number?"

"Because!" she yelled. "He is one of *those* guys!" Elle blinked at her friends like they should know what she was talking about.

"Oh no! Not one of *those* guys," Sophie teased.

"You know what I mean. Look, can we just stop talking about this? Besides, he's not the reason I'm so happy." She waived her hand around dismissively.

Sophie's eyebrows pulled together. "He's not?"

"Why are you so chipper, then?" Kate asked.

Elle casually stood up, walked over to the counter and started pulling out the Jose Cuervo and limes, obviously taking her time in an attempt to drive her two friends crazy.

"Oh, you know, maybe it has something to do with the fact that I got a call from Graham earlier," she said with an indifferent tone.

"And?" Sophie asked, bouncing on the tips of her toes.

"And he gave me some great news."

Both girls waited anxiously while Elle reached into a bag and pulled out a chocolate covered Oreo. "I've been booked to open a show for Alexandre Beaumont next month," she said casually while taking a bite.

"You have?" Kate hit her friend's shoulder in excitement, causing flecks of cookie to crumble to the floor.

"That's great news." Sophie added. "I told you to be patient."

Elle nodded and took another bite. "That's not all he told me. There's more," she said with a full mouth.

"More?" both girls said in unison.

She swallowed. "He told me some other pretty amazing news." The smile on her face grew wider and her friends knew it was big.

"So?"

"I'm one of their top two choices." She blurted quickly, not able to contain it any longer.

Sophie and Kate looked at each other. "Whose choice? What?" Kate asked.

"Spill it!" Sophie yelled, unable to take it anymore.

"I'm one of the top two choices for the cover of the swimsuit issue of *Sports Illustrated*!"

"Shut up, shut up, shut up! Are you serious?!" Sophie's high pitched squeal rang in the air.

"Dead serious," Elle said, still in awe. "You guys, I'm just so excited. I mean, being in the spread was a big deal, but being on the cover? If I land that … it'll be surreal."

Kate stepped forward and wrapped her arms around her two friends. "I think this means we need to go out and celebrate," she suggested.

"How about I make reservations at Union Trust Steakhouse?"

Kate's eyes lit up. "I've wanted to try that place out. It's been getting great reviews and the interior is supposed to be amazing. You know, it used to be a bank," she said excitedly.

"I know, silly," Sophie said proudly. "After all, this celebration is for you too, you know."

"What?" Elle asked, eyeing them both.

"Kate hasn't had a chance to tell you *her* big news yet," Sophie said with a smirk. "Go ahead, tell her."

"He's single," Kate said with a smirk.

Just like Sophie, Elle knew exactly who she was talking about. "He is? How did you find out?"

"I bumped into him at the grocery store, in the produce section." She paused for a minute and smiled. "We talked for a little while." Kate dropped her eyes to the ground shyly.

"Wait a minute." Elle crossed her arms. "What's going on? What happened between you two?"

"Right? I sensed something too!" Sophie added. "She was just about to crack when you walked in."

"Actually, Elle, I think you would be really proud of me," Kate said with a wide grin.

"Why? What did you do? Did you jump him? You did, didn't you? Right in the middle of the produce section. Man, what I wouldn't give to see *that* go down." Elle's eyes glazed over as she became lost in her own world.

"No, I didn't jump him. I just gave him some pointers on picking out produce." She shrugged indifferently.

"What kind of pointers?" Sophie asked, taking a seat beside Elle.

"You know, the usual. You want to make sure you pick out the cucumbers that are nice and *thick* and *hard*," she said in a casual tone. "Make sure you feel how *smooth* and *firm* the bell peppers are, that sort of thing. I thought for sure he'd lose it at one point, but he actually stepped up his game and fed me a strawberry right in the middle of the store."

Both Sophie and Elle stared with wide eyes and slack jaws. They were speechless.

Logan, who, up until this point, had been in the living room, was the only one to speak. "Damn. That guy didn't stand a chance. I bet he's home right now taking the coldest shower of his life." He shook his head, feeling sorry for the complete stranger who had been tortured by Kate's sexual innuendos. "Humph, the produce section," he laughed to himself as he walked back into the living room.

"Kate," Elle said calmly. "If I wasn't so shocked right now, I would be kissing the ground that you walk on. You make me so proud."

"Thanks, I try," her proud friend said with a triumphant smile.

The group of friends spent the next hour preparing dinner and discussing Kate's encounter with a now single Ethan. Both friends agreed that Kate's choice not to give him her number was a risky move, but worth it.

Later that night, Sophie called to make reservations for the following evening. "It's all set," she said, flipping her phone shut. "We have reservations at seven, so make sure you're there by quarter till. I don't want to lose our table."

"We'll be there, don't worry," Kate said as they walked into the living room. Elle was sitting on the couch, yelling at the TV, while Logan sat in the recliner, shaking his head back and forth.

"What kind of a play was that?" she yelled. "Stupid idiot, you've got to be kidding me."

Sophie laughed as she climbed into her boyfriend's lap. "Your sister is nuts when it comes to sports," she whispered in his ear.

"Believe me, I know. Her sports rage can be scary." He laughed and pulled Sophie into his chest. "What do you say we get out of here? Head home where I can draw you a nice warm bath and then crawl into our warm bed ..." His voice trailed off.

"Why, Mr. McLean, are you trying to seduce me?" Sophie said with a bat of her lashes.

He looked down at her, his brown eyes alight. "Maybe I am. Are you okay with that?" He smirked.

She gave him a quick wink. "Baby, I'm more than okay with that."

Without a second word, Logan stood up and tossed her over his shoulder. He turned to the other two girls in the room. "Bye, Kate. Bye, sis. We'll see you guys later," he said as he walked through the doorway.

"Bye, girls! We'll see you tomorrow night. Don't forget be on time!" Sophie yelled, straining her head so she could catch one last glimpse of her friends.

The two girls looked up just in time to see the door slam shut. "Those two are perfect for each other. If I didn't love them both, it would make me sick," Elle said, turning her attention back to the TV.

Kate agreed with a nod and pretended to focus on the game when really her mind was preoccupied with thoughts of a certain doctor and whether or not he'd find her phone number.

❧

After giving Trent a few details about his shopping experience so he would leave him alone, Ethan was finally able to take a cold shower. He tried to keep his mind clear of thoughts of Kate, but it was impossible. She was all he could think about.

His body was exhausted and all he wanted to do was crash, but he couldn't. Just the thought of having Kate's phone number and address within his reach kept his adrenaline pumping. He quickly got dressed and headed back to the hospital.

Ethan made his way past the nurses' station without anyone noticing. Although he knew it wasn't a big deal to be seen, he also knew that looking up a patient's information for personal use was not acceptable. But he did have honest intentions of doing a follow up call. Just to make sure Kate's stitches were healing properly. Or at least that was what he was telling himself.

He headed for the locker room first. Four days ago, when Kate walked out of the exam room, she'd left behind her shirt. He wasn't sure if he'd ever see her again, but had kept it just in case. Now he was beginning to see how keeping it could really work to his advantage. It would give him an excuse to stop by her home this weekend.

Just as he opened his locker to grab the shirt, someone caught his eye.

"Hello, Dr. Montgomery." Ethan jumped slightly when he saw Lisa. It was as if she appeared out of nowhere.

"Hey, Lisa. Didn't hear you come in."

"Well, that's just because I'm so light on my feet," she giggled.

It was clear that she was flirting and that was not something Ethan felt like doing at the moment. "Um, yeah. I guess that could be it," he mumbled.

"So," she paused. "Cindy came in today."

"Oh, really? That's great." He tried to act as if nothing had happened between the two of them on the off chance that Cindy hadn't mentioned the breakup.

"She told us about you two breaking up." Lisa frowned.

"Yeah, well. It just wasn't working out. She is a nice woman, though, and I truly hope she finds someone." He started to walk away in the hope that Lisa would sense his desire to end their conversation.

"Does that mean you're on the market, then?" She scurried along beside him.

After his experience with Cindy, Ethan wasn't at all interested in dating anyone that was involved with the hospital. Mixing his personal life with his work life was not a good move. He knew that now. And while Lisa was always a nice enough girl, he just didn't feel anything there. She, on the other hand, had been hitting on him since his first day. After the first few weeks of shameless flirting on her part, she had asked him out. He'd talked his way out of the date back then and, luckily for him, she started dating someone seriously shortly after.

"On the market?" he repeated her question. "I guess you could say that, but I'm not really ready to date right now. And when I do, I'm going to keep my personal life separate from work, if you know what I mean."

"Oh." Her face fell. "Well, are you going to the dinner tomorrow night?"

"Dinner?"

"Yeah, remember, a bunch of us are getting together for dinner to discuss the new hospital policies."

As she spoke, Ethan suddenly remembered what she was talking about. The dinner was planned a few months ago, and it had simply slipped his mind.

By now, the two of them were standing at the medical records desk, and Ethan was starting to feel a little anxious. He hadn't actually decided whether he would be going to the dinner or not, but right now he was willing to do whatever it took to have Lisa leave him alone.

"Oh, that's right. The dinner at Union Trust. We were meeting at five o'clock, right?"

"Actually, we changed the time. We're meeting at seven o'clock instead," she said with a smile.

"OK, then. Seven o'clock it is."

"So you'll be there?" Lisa asked, twirling a lock of hair around her finger.

"Yeah, it would probably look bad if I didn't show."

"Right, well, it looks like you're in a hurry, so I'll let you go. I'll let everyone know that we'll be there."

Ethan watched Lisa walk way and felt a wave of relief wash over him. He looked back to the records desk and felt the palms of his hands start to sweat. Realizing that he was only a few feet away from the information he ached to find out, he quickly slipped into the medical records room and began his search.

Chapter 12
Nicknames

"Elle, you have to hurry up! You know that Sophie will freak out if we're late." Kate stood in the kitchen, looking at the clock, cursing every second that ticked by.

Elle had been running around all day getting prepared for her weekend away and had returned home only fifteen minutes ago. When Kate had told her they had to leave, she had just stepped out of the shower, hair soaking wet and nowhere near being ready. Now they were sure to be late, and she knew they wouldn't hear the end of it from Sophie.

With a sigh, Kate walked down the hall to her friend's room and knocked on the door.

"Come in!" came a muffled yell.

Kate poked her head in and saw Elle pulling a shirt over her head.

She started speaking before Kate even opened her mouth. "I know we're going to be late and I know Soph will kill us."

"How much longer do you think you need?" Kate asked with a smile.

"More than she'll be willing to give." She let out an exhausted sigh. "Look, why don't you go ahead and tell her I'm on my way. That way, she won't be mad at both of us. That's the last thing we need," she said as she rolled her eyes.

They were both well aware of the wrath Sophie could cause, and it wasn't something they liked to experience.

"All right, I'll go, but I'm warning you, I can only soften her up so much. And you know the longer she has to wait, the more upset she'll be."

"I know, I know. I'll be ten minutes behind you, maybe less. I promise." She quickly ran off to the bathroom, brushing her fingers through her damp hair.

&

The drive into the city was second nature for Kate. It was as if her car knew the way. She loved watching the towers peeking up in the distance or the skyline etched out against a wall of orange sunset. Even the old warehouses held their beauty.

Most days, her mind was preoccupied with clients and upcoming jobs, but today it was focused on an excuse to tell Sophie. She decided, like always, that honesty worked best. She would simply explain that Elle was out getting ready for this weekend's fitting and that she lost track of time. Hopefully, it would be enough to appease their impatient friend. After all, this dinner was in celebration of Elle's new job. And of course, the fact that Ethan was now single.

Just thinking about him brought a smile to her face. She spent most of last night lying in bed, thinking over the day's events. She still couldn't believe she was as brave as she had been. Never in her life would she have pictured herself doing something like that. There was just something about him that brought out a side of her that she'd never seen before. It was refreshing and exciting. There was only one problem. As much as she enjoyed all the new feelings that he stirred up within her, she couldn't help but feel scared at the same time.

She wasn't sure if she was ready to fall for someone again, to take that step and open herself up. She was just finally starting to heal from Scott, and she assumed the first guy she'd meet after him would be the re-bound guy. Someone who would take her out and help get her back in the dating world. She never expected to meet someone like Ethan and feel such an immediate connection. There was something special about him, and she recognized it the first time they'd met. It was like her body and soul recognized his. She knew it sounded strange, but that was the only way she could describe it and make sense of it. Either way, she knew it wouldn't matter how she felt unless he called her. *He'll call. Don't worry, he'll call,* she assured herself.

Kate pulled up to the restaurant and climbed out of her car, giving the keys to the valet. She took a moment to admire the beautiful marble exterior of the restaurant. Taking a quick glance around, she couldn't spot Sophie or Logan anywhere. Hoping that maybe she'd beaten them there, she pulled her coat tight around her and headed into the restaurant.

Ethan spent most of his morning working out and strategically planning how he was going to contact Kate. Finding her phone number and address turned out to be easier than he thought it would. As it turned out, plenty of doctors made follow-up calls to check on their patients. But no matter how many times he told himself what he did was okay, he still saw the words 'HIPAA violation' flash in his mind.

After hours of contemplating his next move, he finally came up with two strategies. The first was to call her and ask her out. The other was to stop by her house and drop off her shirt, which he was hoping would also result in a date. The more he thought about it, the more the second option appealed to him and that was simply because he wanted to see her. He didn't want to wait another few days to see her face. He wanted to see her smile and feel his heart race the way it did when he was near her.

Since his work schedule kept him busy all day and he had the employee dinner that evening, he planned on stopping by tomorrow. *Tomorrow, tomorrow, tomorrow,* he kept repeating to himself in order to bring him even the slightest bit of comfort.

His day flew by quickly, and before he knew it, he was fighting traffic on his way to the restaurant. Not wanting to be late and owe everyone a round of drinks, he quickly parked his car and ran into the restaurant.

The hostess greeted him with a smile. "Hello, how can I help you this evening?"

"I'm meeting a group here. It may be under Henry Williams, or Hospital of the University of Pennsylvania, I'm not sure."

The girl looked over her list with furrowed brows. "I don't see any reservations by that name. Could it be under any other?"

Ethan thought quickly, running through other possible names. Before he had a chance to say anything, someone spoke up from behind him.

"It's under Lisa, Lisa Connelly."

He felt her hand slip around his waist and he paused. *Please for the love of all that is holy do not let this be what I think it is,* he thought with a groan. He put his hand on top of hers and lifted it off his waist.

"Lisa. What's going on? I thought we were meeting everyone here for dinner."

She looked at him with a smile and shrugged. "Well, we *were,* but after I found out about you and Cindy breaking up, I couldn't resist."

"Resist?" he asked puzzled.

"Come on, Ethan. I know your rules about dating people you work with. I knew I'd never get you to ask *me,* so I kind of found a way around it."

He couldn't believe what he was hearing. He thought his excuse was good enough, but Lisa was determined to find a way around it.

"Lisa, as much as I'm flattered that you planned this whole thing out, I don't think—"

"I knew you'd be happy," she squealed, cutting him off and throwing her arms around his neck. "I knew that working together was the only thing keeping you away from me."

Ethan closed his eyes in exhaustion. He couldn't understand why when he spoke to girls they always took every word out of context. First Cindy and now Lisa.

Just as he placed his hands over hers in an attempt to remove them from him, the restaurant door opened. The street light from outside framed the silhouette of someone standing in the doorway. It took four seconds for Ethan to recognize who it was and when he did, he froze.

Kate's eyes immediately caught his, and the puzzled look on her face quickly changed to one of hurt as she dropped her head. Her purse slipped from her shoulders and Ethan's mind went blank. He pulled Lisa's arms from around his neck and took a step in Kate's direction.

The closer he stepped, the more Kate's hurt turned to anger. She couldn't believe she'd been stupid enough to believe that Ethan had told the truth about his breakup. And even if he had told the truth, he obviously wasn't interested in her if he was going out on dates with other girls.

Ethan was only a few feet away, when the door opened once again and in walked his past. The woman who just arrived bent down to get Kate's purse, and when she stood back up, she noticed Ethan. Her eyes went wide with recognition.

"Bones?"

"Squish?" he asked with a disbelieving tone. Ethan couldn't believe his eyes. Standing before him was Elle McLean, his childhood friend.

Kate looked in confusion from Elle to Ethan, not quite believing what she heard.

"Oh, shut up, Bones, you know I hate that nickname," Elle spat.

"Yeah, well, I believe I told you on more than one occasion that my name was Ethan and not Bones," he said while giving her a knowing look.

A sudden rush of panic hit Kate. If Elle knew Ethan, then it meant only one thing. They dated. As if confirming her biggest nightmare, the two of them hugged. Sparks of jealousy burned inside of her, but she kept her mouth shut. After all, Ethan wasn't hers to claim.

"What are you doing here? I thought you were still in San Francisco."

"I was there until medical school. Then I moved east. I had a connection with some family friends that moved here to Philly and it was too good for me to pass up. What about you? I thought you guys moved to Detroit?"

"We did initially, but then my parents separated. We moved with my dad to Virginia right before high school and made the move up here a few years ago. It's close to New York City, so it's perfect for work."

"That's right, you're modeling. Didn't you do something for Coors Light a while back?"

"Yeah, I was the 'Tap the Rockies' girl for a little while." She waved her hand around.

"What are you up to now?" Ethan asked, honestly interested.

"I actually just landed a great job. And I did a spread for the swimsuit issue of *Sports Illustrated* a few months ago. I'm hoping I get the cover," she said with a huge smile.

"You did? Squish, that's awesome. Congratulations. My roommate would flip out if he found out that I actually knew a model in that issue."

"Really? I'll have to meet him sometime and make his day," she said with a sly wink.

"He would definitely enjoy that." Ethan laughed. "So how is Logan doing these days? Is he still in Detroit?"

"No, we wouldn't separate from each other like that. He's my lifeline. There was no way I was moving without him."

By now, Kate was completely floored. She couldn't believe that the guy she'd been obsessing over for the past week was an old friend of Elle's. The only thing she feared was that, at one point, they were more than friends. Kate considered herself a fairly confident woman, but being compared to someone like Elle was sure to make even the prettiest of women doubt their appearance.

There was a break in conversation, and Elle finally noticed her friend standing silently beside her.

"Ethan, I want you to meet my best friend, Kate Thomas."

Kate looked at Ethan, and even though her heart started to pound loudly, she still felt a little angry. He'd lied to her.

He stretched out his hand. "It's a pleasure to meet you, Kate," he said with a smile.

"I wish I could say the same," she said under her breath.

Elle tensed and turned to look at her friend, attempting to read her harsh expression. Then without saying a word, she relaxed and looked at Ethan, who was still watching Kate with intense eyes.

"Sorry, Ethan. Kate's has been a little snappy lately. You'll have to forgive her." She raised her perfectly formed eyebrow.

"I haven't been snappy, Elle," she retorted.

"Yes, you have been ever since you met that 'Dr. Hottie' of yours a week ago," she argued back, under her breath.

Kate glared, but Elle didn't notice. "She's been a bit of a witch lately," she said to Ethan. "It's the effects of being sexually frustrated beyond a normal capacity." She nodded matter-of-factly.

Kate's eyes went wide and her cheeks flushed red. "Elle," she said in a whisper through clenched teeth. Her friend still hadn't noticed her apparent mortification and continued talking.

"See, this doctor she met a week ago has made her crazy. She even did this whole 'produce porn' thing—which, to be honest, made me quite proud. But that's not the point. The point is that this guy she met has her panties in a twist. And she's taking it out on everyone around her. And she keeps having these dreams where she—"

Kate reached out and clamped her hand over her friend's mouth. Heat radiated from every inch of her body. She was mortified. But she didn't care how embarrassed she was. She was determined to stop Elle from speaking another word.

Just as she was about to push her outside, the door opened again and in walked Sophie and Logan, linked arm in arm. Kate was immediately thankful for the distraction and felt herself relax for the first time since she'd walked in the restaurant.

"Man, Ethan, it's been what … sixteen, no, eighteen years?" Logan hugged his friend and had a smile that stretched ear to ear. "You haven't changed too much, except you're not skin and bones anymore."

"Neither have you. And I see you still can't get rid of this sister of yours," Ethan joked back.

The group continued talking, all except for Kate who stood in silence not wanting to risk looking up at Ethan. She felt like she was having one of those crazy dreams where you're standing naked in front of everyone and there were no clothes in sight. It took her a few minutes and a couple deep breaths to gain back even a little of her composure.

Tentatively lifting her head, she peered over at Ethan who was engrossed in the conversation. As soon as he noticed her motion, he turned from Logan and looked directly at her. She inhaled and held her breath as he leaned toward her, placing his hand on her forearm.

"I dream about you all the time," he whispered while squeezing her arm slightly.

And just like that, Kate's anger clicked down a notch. Having him at such a close proximity made her knees weak. Somehow, in the past twenty-four hours she'd forgotten just how strong an effect he seemed to have on her physically. Taking a deep breath, she let herself enjoy the moment.

She was so lost in her own hot, sexy Ethan fantasy world that she hadn't noticed the girl whom Ethan was with earlier was now standing beside her. Elle, however, was not oblivious to the girl or to what just transpired between Kate and her childhood friend.

"Well, Ethan. Who is your lady friend?" she inquired.

Kate turned and, for the first time, actually looked at his date. She recognized her immediately. It was the nurse from the hospital who had interrupted their almost-kiss.

"Oh, I'm sorry. I forgot to introduce you. This is Lisa Connelly. We *work* together at the hospital," Ethan said, staring intently into Kate's eyes.

Lisa shook everyone's hand and paused briefly when she reached Kate. Her eyes lit up in recognition, but didn't say a word. "It's really nice to meet all of you. I haven't had a chance to meet very many of Ethan's friends outside of work," she said with a sugary sweet smile.

Sophie perked up. "Well, in that case, why don't we all sit together? I've heard so much about you, Ethan, and I'm sure Lisa would like to hear all about Elle and Logan." Kate shot an evil glare at Sophie, but it went unnoticed.

"That sounds great! I'd love to get to know Ethan's friends better." Lisa smiled. "I'll go ask the hostess if she can arrange that." She was gone before a word could be said, and Kate felt her earlier nausea return. The last thing she felt like doing was sitting through an entire dinner with Ethan and his date. She dropped her eyes and turned away, looking for an out. Just when she thought it couldn't get any worse, she came face to face with her own past.

"Katie?" His voice echoed in her ears and she froze. Kate would recognize his deep voice anywhere. It was the one voice that brought her so much happiness and, at the same time, sorrow worse than she'd ever known. She knew it was Scott. The one person she never wanted to see again, yet yearned to see at the same time.

Looking up into the familiar dark eyes that brought with them a million memories, Kate's heart responded immediately of its own accord. It was as if it could remember the way he could make her feel. He looked wonderful, as always—the epitome of tall, dark, and handsome. His hair was perfect, just as it had always been, and the black tailored suit he wore accentuated the body of perfection that lay beneath it.

Kate stood, locked in his gaze, until she noticed someone next to him. She didn't want see the person who had taken her place, and she didn't want to care that he was with someone. But she did look and she did care. The woman was tall and blond and stunning. And the slinky gold dress she wore must have cost as much as Kate's entire wardrobe.

"This is Samantha, my girlfriend," Scott said while turning to look at his date.

An imaginary blade drove through Kate's chest as his words registered in her mind. *His girlfriend. He has a girlfriend,* she repeated, and each time, it stung a little worse. She'd expected him to move on, but never thought she'd see it with her own eyes. Plus, as much as she hated to admit it, part of her wanted to be the first one to move on, not him. If she thought she was having a dream before, then this was definitely a nightmare. The room around her started to spin, and Kate knew she was close to passing out. Too many emotions were swirling inside, and her mind was screaming for a way to escape.

At the exact moment her legs went weak, she felt a warm arm wrap around her waist. She knew in an instant who the arm belonged to, and as much as she wanted to remove it, she couldn't. Something in his touch calmed her and gave her the strength to lift her head.

"Hi, I'm Ethan. It's nice to meet you." He extended his free hand and shook the new girlfriend's hand and then turned to look at Scott.

Ethan knew he might be overstepping his boundaries, considering he didn't have any claim on Kate, but he knew he had to do something. The look on her face was enough to tell him that she wasn't okay. Her dark, beautiful eyes that were once full of emotion were suddenly hollow and glazed over. At that moment, Ethan made a promise to himself that he would do whatever it took to make sure he never saw that look on her face again.

Considering he'd addressed Kate as 'Katie,' which was clearly a nickname, Ethan assumed that he was someone from her past. And based on the reaction she'd had, it didn't take much to assume that he had played an important role.

"I'm Scott, Scott Christiansen," Kate's acquaintance said before introducing his girlfriend a second time.

Ethan noticed the way Kate's body stiffened upon hearing the word 'girlfriend' and wondered how this Scott character didn't notice the effect he was having on her. His instincts took over and Ethan immediately wanted to take Kate away. He wanted to make her forget all about the man in the suit.

Much to Kate's relief, Sophie stepped forward. "Scott," she said with a nod of her head. Turning her attention back to Kate, she leaned in. "Our table's ready." Sophie looked at her friend with concerned eyes, silently asking if she was okay.

Kate gave a slight nod and looked up at Ethan. "Are you ready?" she asked.

He nodded and pulled her closer to his side. "It was nice meeting you," Ethan said to Scott and his girlfriend, and led Kate away.

"Bye, Katie. It was great seeing you again." At the sound of Scott's voice, Kate paused.

"You too, Scott." She gave him a half smile and then continued walking.

By the time they made it to their table, Kate had shrugged out of Ethan's arms and took a seat directly across from him and Lisa. There was an awkward silence that hung in the air. It seemed that everyone was aware of the effect Scott had just had on Kate, except of course Lisa, who was clueless to everything. The silence only lasted a few minutes before a very cheerful Sophie chimed in.

"Okay, so explain the nicknames," she said with a lighthearted laugh.

Ethan looked at his two childhood friends and smiled. "Well, when I was little, I was a little skinnier than I am now." He shrugged.

Elle let out a loud laugh. "Kind of skinny? Ethan, you were skin and bones."

Everyone at the table joined in Elle's laughter, including Kate. Ethan watched her out of the corner of his eye. *She really is beautiful,* he thought. Her dark hair and eyes in contrast to her pale, creamy skin. The curve of her neck as it sloped down to meet her shoulders. He was so lost in thoughts of Kate that he hadn't noticed Lisa nudged him.

"Ethan, Earth to Ethan," she said with a hint of annoyance.

He shook his head, clearing his mind. "I'm sorry, what were you saying?"

"Sophie asked how you came up with Elle's nickname."

"Oh, right. Sorry." He peered over at Elle who looked quite irritated by the posed question.

"Do you want me to tell them, Squish, or do you want to do it?" he asked with a smirk.

She let out a huff and grabbed her uniquely folded napkin, smoothing it over her lap. Ethan took her silence as a positive and went on to explain. "Well, Elle didn't always look the way she looks now. She was a little…" He hesitated trying to find the right words to use so she wouldn't be insulted.

Elle's back went ramrod straight, sitting up in her chair. "Fat," she yelled. "Okay? I was fat! I was a squishy, awkward, too tall, chubby, soft child. Not all of us were always so skinny," she continued to yell while looking at Kate and Sophie accusingly.

Both friends looked at each other with wide eyes of disbelief. Sophie then turned her attention to Logan and gave him the same disbelieving look.

He put his hands up, palms facing out, and shook his head. "Not my place to tell you."

"I didn't expect for you to tell me she was fat when she was little," Sophie snapped. "I just thought that I would have seen pictures or something," she said with a shrug.

"Yeah, Elle," Kate added "We've known you since high school and we've seen tons of pictures. I don't remember you looking fat in any of them."

"That's only because I made sure you never saw them. Any pictures from the age of five to twelve have been secretly stashed."

"Yeah, and don't ever try finding them either," Logan said with a laugh. "This one time, Mom somehow stumbled across one and tried to show it to Elle's boyfriend. I'll never forget the look on your face," he said, eyeing Elle. "Man, if looks could kill."

"Whatever, 'Stretch,' you hid your pictures too." Elle lashed out.

"I only hid them because I was a nerd. Besides, I can't help it that I was too skinny."

Elle rolled her eyes. "We're brother and sister, Logan. We came from the same gene pool and *you* ended up with the 'skinny as a kid' gene."

Logan leaned across the table and reached for his sister's hand. She begrudgingly looked at him.

"Well, we both know who got the beautiful gene." Elle's demeanor changed instantly. She softened as soon as he made his comment.

That one simple act showed Ethan that nothing had changed over the years. Logan was still the big brother; he knew Elle better than anyone, and the bond the two of them shared was indescribable.

The waiter finally greeted the table, successfully bringing all conversation to a halt. He had only made it halfway around the table for drink orders when Kate heard her cell phone beep signaling a text. Digging through her bag, she retrieved her phone and paused when she saw the number. She recognized it at once, but wondered why he'd be texting her, especially right now.

> *katie it was really hard seeing you tonight.*
> *you look great. i miss you. please call me.*
> *always - scott*

Kate stared at her phone. *What is he talking about? It was hard for him?* she wondered. He was the one with the new girlfriend. Her eyes began to sting, and she blinked back the tears that were threatening to take over. Needing a minute to clear her head, she excused herself from the table. She refused to shed another tear over Scott Christiansen, especially in the middle of a restaurant. As she made her way to the front of the restaurant, she completely bypassed the restrooms and went directly outside.

The cold January air blew around her face, stinging her cheeks and awakening her senses. She hadn't brought her jacket with her and the humid wind ripped through her clothes, chilling her to the bone. Wrapping her arms around herself, she tried to both keep warm and bring some comfort to the pain that was aching in her chest.

There were only a few cars parked along the side of the building, and thankfully she found a spot behind a van that would work as a perfect barrier from the wind. Kate leaned up against the brick wall with a thud and buried her face on her hands. Her mind was swarming with so many thoughts that she couldn't think straight. Here she was going out with her friends, celebrating a newly single and available Ethan, when what happens? She runs into him on a date. Then to make matters worse, she runs into Scott.

Her emotions were already running wild and seeing him seemed to push her over the edge. She wasn't expecting to have the reaction she did. But seeing Scott with someone else brought on feelings of jealousy. She knew she had no reason to feel jealous, but she couldn't help it. She had a history with Scott, and that didn't go away with the ending of their relationship.

Then there were the feelings she was having for Ethan, someone she hardly knew yet felt an immediate intense connection with. She remembered his words from earlier about dreaming of her and felt her body flush warm at the thought.

"Kate?" She heard his deep voice and her thoughts came to a halt.

Looking up slowly from her hands, she saw Ethan standing directly in front of her. Just the sight of him took her breath away. The wind was blowing his charcoal gray pants and white button-down shirt across his body. His shirt clung to the contours of his chest, and for the first time, Kate saw just how amazing his body was. His dark hair was moving whichever way the wind took it, and Kate wondered briefly if he tried to look sexy or if it just came naturally. Realizing that she was blatantly staring, she dropped her eyes.

"Kate, are you okay? I noticed you seemed upset after checking your phone. Is everything fine?" he asked, his voice laced with concern.

Fine? Kate thought. *No, everything is not fine.* Her confusion and frustration peaked, and she scrambled to her feet.

"No, Ethan. Everything is *not* fine." As angry as she was, she couldn't look into his eyes. She knew from previous experience that if she did, she would melt into them and not be able to think coherently.

"Do you want to talk about it?" he asked.

"Talk about it? I don't even know where I would start. I'm just so confused."

"Confused?"

Maybe it was the sound of his voice that broke her. Maybe it was the fact that she couldn't bear to hear the pleading tone of his voice. Whatever the reason, she gave up and started ranting.

"The guy that was in there was Scott Christiansen. He was my best-friend-turned-boyfriend for longer than I can remember.

"The last six months of our relationship were hell. We broke up and got back together at least three times, and each time, I told myself it wouldn't happen again. But I gave in; I gave in because he said he missed me. And I didn't for one second think about the way it would affect me when he changed his mind again. I was always there, waiting on the back burner for him.

"The last time it ended was a few months ago. We haven't had any contact since then, other than the random cryptic texts he sends me. This was the first time I've seen him, and he ends up having a girlfriend."

She took a long breath and exhaled while shaking her head.

"To be honest, I'm surprised I felt any jealousy whatsoever. I mean, I don't have those kinds of feelings anymore. I'm not in love with him. There was just something about seeing him with someone else. Knowing that he's moved on and I'm still here. I'm waiting for a person who isn't even available. It's pathetic really."

This time when Kate paused, she looked up at him. Her brown eyes met his blue, and she allowed herself to be entranced. They held each other's gaze for an immeasurable amount of time until they both felt the energy swirling between them, mixing with the wind as it circled about.

Kate reminded herself to relax so she could keep some sort of focus and remain coherent enough to speak. "You were here with her, and it … surprised me, to say the least. I couldn't breathe." She ran her fingers over her face. "I guess that doesn't say much, considering I often find myself not being able to breathe when I'm around you. I blame the eyes," she admitted shyly. "It's just that … I felt like there was something between us and to be honest, I can't even believe I am saying these things to you. There's just something that happens to me when I'm near you. I find myself being able to say and do things that I would never normally do. Like at the hospital and at the grocery store and—"

As she spoke, Ethan stepped forward. She paused and looked up at his face. His eyes were burning with an emotion that she'd seen before but couldn't place. Her brows furrowed and she opened her mouth to speak when he took another step closer, closing the distance between them instantly.

He swiftly wrapped his arm around her waist and pulled her close to him. She could feel his quick breath as it brushed across her face, warm and inviting. He stood a few inches taller than her so she had to raise her chin to look in his eyes. He walked forward quickly— lifting her off the ground slightly so she wouldn't trip in his haste—forcing her back until she came in contact with the brick wall. As soon as they hit, he leaned down and pressed his lips to hers.

Kate's once-racing mind came to a screeching halt. All of her questions and doubts faded away. Ethan was kissing her, something she had wanted since the first time she saw him. Her only thoughts were of him.

He continued to kiss her eagerly, never letting her lips take control. She pulled away just enough to catch her breath and grab hold of his bottom lip, sucking on it gently. Ethan moaned quietly into her mouth and waited with patience for her to let his tongue touch hers. They gently slid over each other, exploring the sensations of one another's mouths and reveling in the moment.

The smooth texture of his tongue and delicious taste of him made Kate's knees weak. Her body relaxed and Ethan supported her weight by pulling her in closer. She locked her arms around his neck and pulled herself up, wrapping her legs around his waist. She knew it was brave of her, but there was no stopping the desire she had to be close to him. To just feel him pressed firmly against her. Once every line of their bodies was touching, Kate dropped her head back and sucked in a breath of air, enjoying the sensation of his body against hers and his mouth on her skin.

Ethan kissed along her neck, biting and nipping his way up to her jaw. Her skin felt just as soft as he thought it would, and he couldn't get enough of it. He trailed his hands up and over her waist, pushing the pads of his fingers into her back and wishing more than anything that he could feel the smooth skin that lay hidden beneath the thin blue material. He gently grazed his lips along her jaw line until he reached her ear, tenderly kissing the hollow space beneath her lobe.

"Kate," he whispered. "I've never done this before," he confessed. "I've never even felt this way, for that matter."

"Me either. Never this intense and never this sudden." She looked down at his face and saw his eyes full of wonderment.

"There's just something about you," he continued. "I can't help but follow my heart. And I left that with you a week ago."

Kate didn't know what to say. What do you say to something like that anyway? Instead of searching for words, she decided a kiss would be the best response, especially at the moment while they were still so close to each other.

This time they slowed down. It was softer and slower. They let their tongues swirl with each other's, learning the way in which they each moved. At moments, they would separate only to look into each other's eyes and place soft kisses everywhere. Ethan kissed her eyes, her forehead, her cheeks, her jaw, and her lips—every line and curve that he'd been dreaming about for the past week.

Every place he touched left Kate's skin on fire. Her body was now alive, and the heat that was coursing through her veins was radiating off of her, causing a light sheen of sweat to gather at the nape of her neck. As she kissed Ethan's forehead, she could taste the slight saltiness of his sweat. The knowledge that she wasn't the only one sweating made her giggle.

"What's so funny?" he asked with a puzzled expression.

"It's nothing really. I just find it funny how we're both sweating like it's ninety degrees outside when it's probably closer to forty."

He dropped his head forward as he laughed, his hair falling onto his forehead. Kate brushed it back and ran her fingers through his hair before placing her palm flat against his cheek. "You really are beautiful, you know that?" she whispered.

He gave her a perfect smile and leaned in, placing a light peck on her lips. "You, Kate Thomas, are the beautiful one." He stepped away from the wall and spun around, while still holding on to her.

As much as she loved hearing the words, she couldn't hide her embarrassment. She laid her head on his shoulder in an attempt to hide her face.

"Hey, don't look away from me. I've been waiting all week—forever—to see you." His fingers traced along her jaw and lifted her chin up so he could see her. "As much as I would love to stay out here all night with you, I have a feeling that people are going to come looking for us if we don't go back," he said with a sigh.

"Knowing Soph, she'll call the police if we aren't back when our meals arrive."

"She really does seem like a handful," he laughed.

Kate rolled her eyes. "You have no idea."

"I'm guessing she's got to be pretty great since Logan is with her."

"The best," she agreed.

With that, Kate began to untangle herself from his hold. She unwrapped her legs from around his waist, and he gently lowered her to ground. The two stood, arms still around each other not wanting to separate. Eventually they pulled apart, but Ethan was sure to keep her hand in his, as they made their way back into the restaurant.

Now that they were standing away from each other, Kate could feel the effects of the cold wind. A shiver shook through her body, causing a rush of goose bumps to cover her skin. Ethan noticed and pulled her close, rubbing her arms in an attempt to warm her.

"Thanks," she said. "I didn't think about grabbing my coat. Aren't you freezing?" she looked up at him.

"No, I'm pretty warm actually. It must have something to do with being around you."

"Sorry," she smiled, not at all apologetic.

"Don't be," he chuckled. "Being in your presence does things to me," he shrugged. "And since I'm not leaving your side, I better learn how to deal with it."

Upon hearing his words, Kate's heart began to race. *Where did he learn to say things like that?* she thought.

As they walked back into the restaurant, Kate started to worry about what their excuse would be. Surely Sophie and Elle would be able to tell something had happened between them. They were, after all, her best friends and were more than familiar with her 'hot and bothered just made out' face.

"You know I'm not really dating Lisa, right? She kind of tricked me into this whole thing," Ethan said, interrupting Kate's train of thought.

"Really?" Relief laced her voice. "She tricked you?"

"Yeah. It's a long story. I'll explain it all later." He pulled the door open and stepped into the warmth of the restaurant. The two stayed side by side, and when they reached the table, Ethan regretfully released her hand.

Kate sat down, took a deep breath and looked up at her two friends, who were now looking at her with knowing eyes.

"Have a fun time in the *bathroom*, Kate?" Sophie asked with a smile.

Elle joined her. "I don't know, Sophie. I think I saw her *jump* into that *coat closet*."

Kate smiled back at her two friends and felt her face get warm. Thankfully, they didn't say anything else. She'd had enough humiliation for one night.

☙

The rest the evening continued, and Ethan and Kate stole quick glances at one another from across the table. At one point during the dinner, Logan gave a brief run down of their past with Ethan. She was sure it was mainly for Lisa's benefit, but Kate listened nonetheless. After all, anything that had to do with Ethan interested her.

Logan cleared his voice and slipped into teacher mode. "We grew up with Ethan in San Francisco. Our parents knew each other from charity events and other volunteer organizations. At first, we didn't know what to think about the quiet boy, but after he gave Elle her nickname and stopped letting her boss him around, we realized he fit in perfectly. We pretty much spent all our time together until the fifth grade when my dad got transferred to Detroit. After our parents split, we moved to Virginia, and well, you guys know the rest."

"To be honest, I never thought we would see you again, Bones," Elle said as she nudged him with her elbow.

"Yeah, well, here I was thinking I'd get lucky and never have to put up with your crap again," Ethan teased back.

"You're just going to have to learn how to deal because now that we found you, I have a feeling we aren't going to let you go. Isn't that right, Kate?" Elle asked, while turning to her friend.

Kate's throat tightened and she glared at her friend. For the second time in one evening, Elle had embarrassed her beyond belief. She was beginning to think that paybacks were in order. Just as she opened her mouth to retaliate, Sophie stepped in. It didn't take the most observant person to notice the frustration on Kate's face.

"I think it's time we get going. Elle has to catch an early train, and I'm sure you all have busy schedules." Sophie grabbed her purse and stood.

Following her lead, everyone else gathered their things and headed for the door. Kate glanced over at Ethan and wondered if he would say something to her. She was still unsure about everything that had happened earlier. Yes, they'd shared an amazing kiss, but what did that mean?

Before she had time to make a plan of attack, they were outside and everyone was walking to their cars. They all wished Elle good luck one last time. As Elle got in her car, she told Kate she'd see her at home. Kate waved goodbye to her friend and turned around only to find that both Sophie and Logan were nowhere in sight. She stood awkwardly looking at a smiling Lisa and Ethan.

"Umm … so yeah, I guess I'll see you later then," she said, looking into Ethan's blue-gray eyes that sparkled even in the dark, catching what little light there was surrounding them. Kate held her breath at the sight of him. She studied his features frantically, not knowing when she would actually see them again. Closing her eyes tight, she took a breath. "I'll see you," she said one last time, before turning around and scurrying off to her car, all the while berating herself for leaving so quickly.

It wasn't until she reached her car that she considered turning back around. She paused for a moment and gave herself a pep talk before deciding to just go back. But before she moved an inch, a hand slipped around her waist. Ethan spun her around and pushed her against her car, wrapping his hand around the base of her neck, his fingers tickling her hair. He pulled her face to his and covered her lips with his, sending her heart into overdrive. The desperation of his kiss eventually softened and he slowly pulled back, looking down at her seriously.

"I'm not letting you walk away this time."

"But I—"

He placed his finger to her mouth. "I mean, I'm not letting you walk away without a kiss and a promise that I will see you again soon." Ethan smiled down at her, enjoying the flush of color on her cheeks and flash of emotion he saw in her eyes.

"All right then, I promise." Kate smirked. "I take it you found my number?"

"I'm pretty sure I broke every HIPAA prohibition possible, but I got it." He lifted his eyebrows playfully.

"Good, then I'll be waiting for your call." Kate leaned forward pressing her body firmly against his as she kissed him one last time, committing his taste to memory. Then carefully opening her door, she climbed in.

"I'll call you later," he said, and then he closed her door.

They looked at each other through the glass of the car window for another moment before Kate pulled away. She had just barely made it out of the parking lot and onto the street when she heard her phone signaling that she'd received a text.

Immediately assuming it was Scott, she groaned. She didn't feel like dealing with him at the moment. Wanting to end the night on a positive note, she grabbed her phone and was just about to shut it off when she changed her mind. Flipping her phone open, she clicked on the inbox.

Is it later yet?

Chapter 13
Penny Walk

Kate held her phone in hand and stared at those four little words. *Is it later yet? Is he serious?* she thought, her heart racing. The blaring sound of a horn made her realize that she'd come to a complete stop in the middle of the road. Cringing in embarrassment, she quickly tossed her phone on the seat beside her. Maneuvering her car to the side of the road, she slipped it into park and took a calming breath before grabbing her phone again.

She re-read the message probably twenty times, analyzing every possible meaning. Dropping her head back on the headrest, she focused on the gray fabric ceiling of the car and thought about how best to respond. After a minute of planning, she flipped her phone open and pushed reply.

Yes it's later. Where r u? ~ K

She pushed the send button and squealed internally as she awaited a response. It didn't take long.

In the restaurant parking lot. Where r u?- E

Reading his message quickly, she smiled, imagining him sitting in his car doing the same thing she was.

Where do u want me? ~ K

Fairmount Park. do u have a penny?- E

A penny? Kate wondered. *What does he want with a penny?* She shook her head when she realized it didn't matter what he wanted. She would go anyway.

Got one, c u in 15 ~ K

She quickly tossed her phone down and slammed on the gas, fighting her way through the city streets. Her adrenaline pumped through her veins, and she turned up the volume on her radio, hoping the music would help calm her.

It took her less time than she thought it would. Arriving at the park, she felt embarrassed for rushing, but as soon as she pulled in, she noticed Ethan leaning against the outside of his car, his legs crossed at the ankle and his arms wrapped lazily across himself. Realizing he must have sped even faster than she had, she smiled and her embarrassment faded.

Kate put the car in park and killed the engine. The song she had been listening to stopped abruptly and left a ringing sensation in her ears. Ethan was at her door and opened it before she had a chance to reach for the handle.

He greeted her with a huge smile. "*Love You Madly?*" he asked.

"What?" she gaped, her mind a jumbled mess.

"The song, '*Love You Madly*.' It's a good one."

Kate scrambled for a response, laughing at herself for being so thrown off by his comment. She nodded. "Yeah, that's right."

"I like the one about the girl in a long jacket and a short skirt."

"So, you're saying you like that sort of thing?" Kate said with raised brows. "I'll have to keep that in mind." She winked.

Without a moment's hesitation, he took a step forward, and wrapped his arms around her waist. He leaned down and Kate was certain he was going to kiss her. But instead, at the last second, he turned his head to the side and nuzzled into her neck. Ethan inhaled slowly, enjoying the natural scent of her skin and watched as goose bumps covered her flesh. He kissed the base of her neck and worked his way higher.

"You could wear anything, Kate, and I'd still devour you." Kate's knees went weak and her head filled with thoughts of Ethan. She swallowed slowly and heard him chuckle softly in her ear. "Do you have that penny I asked for?" He leaned back and looked down at her.

"Uh-huh," she mumbled, still not able to form coherent sentences.

"Good. Let me go grab my flashlight."

As he turned away, Kate watched him with curious eyes.

"What are we doing, anyway? I mean, what could we possibly be doing with a penny and a flashlight?"

Ethan quickly returned from his car, flashlight in hand, and laughed at the tone of her voice, full of doubt and confusion. "You'll see," he said with his arm outstretched. She looked down at his open hand and gently placed her small hand in his. The satisfaction he felt at that one moment was enough to make his chest tight. He smiled to himself happily as they began walking, hand in hand. When they reached a tee in the path, Ethan held out his other hand. Kate still had no idea what he was doing, but she placed the penny in his open palm nonetheless.

She watched in silence as he flipped the penny in the air and switched on the flashlight. A few feet away, facing heads up, was the coin.

"Heads means we go right, tails means we go left," Ethan said, bending down to retrieve the coin.

"What?" she asked still confused.

He shrugged his shoulders and gave Kate an innocent smirk. "It's called a penny walk."

"A penny walk?"

"Yes. Every time we come to a crossing, we flip the coin. Whichever way it lands is the direction we go. Heads we go right and tails we go left. You simply walk and talk. The one rule is that you have to follow whatever the penny tells you. You almost never end up back where you started, so basically it means you can end up walking forever, which in turn means you can end up talking forever."

"So you *want* to get lost?"

"No." He reached out and placed his hand on Kate's face, gently rubbing her cheek with his thumb. "I want to talk to you and not have to think about it ever ending."

She almost laughed and looked into his eyes, expecting to see humor, but instead saw the most sincere, honest face she'd ever seen. He was being serious. Kate allowed herself to breathe and to actually consider that what he'd just said to her was true. "All right." She paused. "Let's go." She grabbed hold of his hand and waited for his move. At this point, they hadn't talked very much and Kate wasn't sure how to start their conversation.

She was slightly nervous at the thought of opening up to someone. Kate tended to be a private person, and other than Soph, Elle, Logan, and her family, there weren't many people who knew the real her. *Other than Scott, of course,* she thought, then quickly pushed it aside. She wanted tonight to be only about her and Ethan, and right now, he wanted to get to know the real her. She smiled as she realized that just maybe he wanted to know her as much as she wanted to know him.

"What are you smiling about?" Ethan asked, when he noticed her smile.

"Nothing," she lied.

Ethan stopped walking. "I forgot to mention one other rule of the penny walk."

"Oh really? And would that be?"

"You're not allowed to lie."

Kate rolled her eyes and knew she'd been caught. His comment reminded Kate of something from earlier that evening.

"Speaking of telling the truth, how did you know I was upset at the restaurant?"

"I could just … tell," he said hesitantly.

Kate raised a brow. "Now, *that* didn't sound very truthful."

"You are trying to change the subject. I asked you first," he stated.

"Fine." She gave in with a sigh. "I was smiling earlier because I was excited that you actually wanted to get to know me, just as much as I want to get to know you." She closed her eyes, dropping her head in an attempt to hide her embarrassment.

"Kate," he said, his voice deep and rich. "Please look at me." She opened her eyes and met his. "You don't know how happy it makes me to hear you say that." He paused for a moment, holding her gaze. "And the only reason I knew something was wrong tonight was because I couldn't keep my eyes off of you. And there was something in your eyes. I don't know, I could just tell." He shrugged his shoulders. "Plus," he continued, "if anyone else had been that observant, I'm sure they would have noticed." He made the statement sound so obvious, like it was no big deal. But to Kate it was.

"Thank you for noticing," she said with a smile. "It was an interesting night, to say the least, and it could have gone a lot worse than it did."

"I should be the one thanking you. If you hadn't gotten up to leave, I never would have followed you," he said with a wink.

Kate smiled at the memory and took a step closer to Ethan as they began walking again. He was the first one to ask questions. He wanted to know everything. He already knew that she grew up in Virginia, but he wanted to hear all the details of her childhood. He asked if she'd had any make-believe friends, what her favorite cartoons were, what music she enjoyed, when she'd decided to be a photographer, what teachers inspired her.

He asked about her parents, what they were like, and if being an only child was the same as it was for him. He wanted to hear all about her friendship with Sophie, Elle, and Logan. He bombarded her with question after question, some as simple as favorite foods, some more intimate like religious views and political stances.

It wasn't until he asked about her first crushes and past boyfriends that she grew nervous.

"I didn't ... umm ... I didn't really have a lot of boyfriends," she mumbled.

"Kate, I thought we were being honest with each other," he said teasingly.

"I am being honest."

He chuckled quietly. "Somehow I find it very difficult to believe that *you*," he looked at her with eyebrows lifted, "didn't have many boyfriends."

"Look, there was one guy I dated in high school. His name was Mark and he broke my heart. And then there was Scott and well ..." She trailed off attempting to find the words to describe what he'd done to her. "Break her heart" didn't seem fitting. It was more like he broke her spirit. She felt her eyes well up with tears with the mere thought of him. She couldn't understand why he still had such a hold on her. It was as if no matter how badly she wanted to move on, he always found a way back in.

Ethan noticed the same sad look in Kate's eyes that he had earlier at the restaurant—the same hollow look that he'd told himself he never wanted to see again. Quickly turning to face her, he placed his hands on her shoulders. "I'm sorry I made you think of him." His voice was so quiet and kind, it made Kate's heart melt.

"It's not your fault. I just get so mad at myself sometimes for letting him affect me."

"He really did a number on you, didn't he?"

"I guess so." She shrugged.

"Is it weird of me to hate him for that?" he asked.

Kate looked at him with squinted eyes, not fully understanding him. He saw her confusion and continued to explain.

"I mean, I don't know you that well, something which I hope changes very soon," he said, smiling. "But I can't help but hate this guy for hurting you so much." He placed his hand on her cheek. "I would never hurt you, Kate.

I know you don't have any reason to trust me, you barely know me, but I'm more than willing to show you. There's something here, between us. I know it. So I'll take whatever you can give. However you want me in your life right now, I'll be it."

Kate had a sudden onset of guilt. Up until this point, she hadn't realized how much her past relationship with Scott could hold her back. Everything ending between them was the hardest thing in her life, but she'd thought once she found someone else she would be able to move on, to forget all about him. But it hadn't happened that way. Would it get better? How would she know if the wound Scott left behind was fully healed, and how could she ask Ethan to wait around until she figured it out?

"That's not fair," she whispered.

"Why don't you let me decide what's fair?"

"I can't do that. I'm the one who has issues, not you. And to be honest, I don't think I could handle it happening to me again." She confessed, dropping her head, a wave of sadness overwhelming her. Just the thought of having her heart broken again was more than Kate could handle.

Ethan knew what she was doing. He knew that she was talking herself out of giving them a chance because she was afraid. He racked his brain trying to think of what he could say or do to make her realize he wasn't going anywhere.

"Do you want me here?" he asked, plain and simple.

"Yes," she hesitated. "But that doesn't mean you should want to be here or that I'm not scared of getting hurt again."

He smiled. "All I need to know is that you want me here. I've already told you I won't hurt you. I won't leave you with another scar." He started to laugh. "After all, didn't I tell you at the hospital that I'm a skilled doctor? I don't leave scars," he said with a wink, clearly trying to lighten the mood.

Kate laughed and remembered their conversation at the hospital. She couldn't believe that only one week had passed and now here she was with him. The whole situation was starting to get a little overwhelming, so she was more than happy to accept the change in subject.

"Why, yes, Doctor, I believe you did tell me I wouldn't scar," Kate said in a flirty tone that even Elle would be proud of.

"And did you?" he asked with raised eyebrows.

"That's something I'll have to let you check out for yourself." She winked and bit on her lips in an attempt to hide her smile.

His eyes widened. "I think that's something I could arrange. I am, after all, a very *thorough* doctor."

"Well, then, I'll have to make sure you give me a very *thorough* examination."

With those words, Kate was finished thinking. All she wanted was to be lost in Ethan. She leaned in slowly, molding her body to his. As soon as he recognized what she wanted, he lowered his head and brushed his lips across her mouth, leaving her lips tingling. Kate's heartbeat accelerated and heat ran quickly through her, igniting every inch of her body, making her even more aware of his touch.

Ethan moved one of his hands from her waist to her back. He stroked her soft skin slowly, working the hem of her shirt up slightly. The cold night air flowed up her back, spreading goose bumps over her skin, and his warm hand felt like fire against the cold sliver of exposed flesh. She arched her back and pulled away slightly, creating a gap of space between them.

He looked down at her, hunger in his eyes. "Kate," he said in an eager tone.

She didn't respond with words. Instead she leaned in, tracing her tongue on his lip until he parted his mouth, granting her exactly what she wanted. He slid his tongue over hers, gently following her movements. Their kiss turned more passionate, and Kate allowed her hands to roam over him, following an invisible path up his stomach to his chest. She traced the curves and dips of his body, feeling his taut muscles shift, responding to her touch.

As she slid her hands down his arms, her head was filled with thoughts of only Ethan. They broke apart, and Kate turned her head into his neck. She breathed him in, trying to describe the scent. Something about him reminded her of warm vanilla. She kissed her way down his neck to the exposed hollow of his collarbone and back up to his ear.

"I could kiss you forever," she whispered, before tracing his earlobe with her tongue and kissing the soft skin that hid underneath. She heard herself speaking and was shocked at how brave she was being. It wasn't like her to be so bold, yet there was just something about him. Her body responded in a way that she'd never experienced before. Not even with Scott. Kate knew that if she was indeed going to take things slow with Ethan, she was going to have to get some self-control. There was no doubt that she wanted him; she wanted him more than anything and part of her knew that he felt the same way. She just needed some time.

It was getting late, and both Ethan and Kate knew that if they didn't leave soon, they'd end up doing something that they would both regret. And enjoy. Kate reached up on her toes and gave him another long kiss, before pulling away and getting lost in his eyes.

"I have had a wonderful night, but I should probably get going."

She heard him exhale softly. "Yeah, I guess we'd better, huh?"

The disappointment in his voice was clear and it made her heart skip. Reaching down, she took his hand in hers and felt the comfort from earlier. Together, they walked in silence back to their cars. Kate felt the same panic she'd felt earlier when walking out of the restaurant. *When will I see him again?* she wondered. The question hung on the tip of her tongue until finally she pushed the words out in a slur.

"Can I see you tomorrow night?" she asked, squeezing her eyes shut.

Ethan laughed. "You ask that like I'm not going to want to see you."

"I was just … you know … worried that maybe you—"

"Kate," he said, cutting her off. "I thought I already told you I wasn't going anywhere. I have a feeling there won't ever be a time when I won't want to be with you."

She swallowed slowly to calm her nerves. "Okay, so you're not going anywhere," she repeated, trying to convince herself. "Does that mean I can see you tomorrow?" she asked again.

"Actually, I'm working a night shift tomorrow."

"Oh." She blinked quickly, trying to hide her disappointment.

"But can I call you tomorrow?"

She nodded and gave him what she was sure was a goofy smile. But she couldn't help it; she simply couldn't hold it back.

Kate turned to get into her car, but Ethan grabbed her hand to stop her. He twisted her around so she was facing him and placed his hand on her cheek. Leaning in, he gently pressed his lips to hers causing her mind to grow fuzzy. Before she wanted it to be over, it was. He pulled away and looked down at her.

"Sleep well, Kate. Have pleasant dreams."

"You too," she whispered.

"Oh, I don't think that's going to be a problem," he said with a smirk.

Kate laughed as his statement brought back memories of what he'd said earlier at the restaurant. *I dream about you all the time,* he had said.

Quickly reaching up on her toes, Kate gave him one last peck before getting into her car. "I'll be waiting for your call," she said as she slammed the door shut.

Ethan stood outside her car smiling for a moment, then climbed into his own. He wasn't sure how many hours they'd spent together, but he was certain he could have spent even longer with her. For him, tomorrow couldn't come fast enough.

They both pulled away from the park, heading in opposite directions and both thinking about each other.

❧

By the time Kate made it home, it was one o'clock in the morning. She couldn't believe she and Ethan had spent almost four hours talking. *Four of the best hours of my life,* she thought with a sigh.

Relieved that all the lights were off when she arrived home, she silently crept up the stairs. Kate didn't feel like answering all of the questions she knew Elle would have for her. And she didn't even want to think about the plethora of questions Sophie would bombard her with. There was no doubt in her mind that her other best friend would be at her door first thing in the morning to get all the details.

She made her way into her bedroom, kicking off her flats and slipping out of her black pants and blouse. Tossing them in a heap on the floor, she then headed into her bathroom where she stood in front of the mirror looking at her reflection. The face reflected back at her was one she almost didn't recognize. Her ear-to-ear grin was alive and full of energy. Even the color of her eyes seemed lighter and more vibrant. She took a deep breath and exhaled, reveling in the exhilaration that came with the prospect of new love.

Kate finished her nightly routine and lazily slid into a tank top before crawling into bed. Pulling the covers up around her neck, she let her mind replay the evening. Closing her eyes, she tried to remember the exact details of his face when he smiled at her. She unconsciously touched her fingers to her lips, thinking of the way his felt pressed up against them. His kisses were the last thing she thought of as she drifted off to sleep, her fingers still held to her mouth.

❧

"Kate. Kate, wake up."

Perfect dreams of Ethan were interrupted as Kate came to. She could hear Elle whispering in her ear before the gentle nudging began.

"Come on, Kate. I know you're awake," Elle begged.

"You better have a good reason for waking me up," Kate said, her voice still raspy from sleep.

"I do." Her friend's tone was shocked as if surprised she'd suggest otherwise.

"A reason that does not involve Ethan," Kate clarified while pulling the covers over her head.

"Katherine Thomas!" Elle yelled as she grabbed the blanket off her sleeping friend. "You know I'm getting on the train in the next hour and I have to know what happened. Soph will be here by lunchtime and she'll get all the details. I refuse to be left out just because I'll be out of the state," she finished with a huff.

"Fine, what do you want to know?" Kate sat up sluggishly and took her blanket back, pulling it up over her bare legs.

"Did you kiss?" Elle asked in an almost whisper.

Kate paused. "Yes."

"You did! I can't believe it. I mean, I can—I'm just surprised. I still can't believe that he was *the* Ethan you've been talking about this entire time." She shook her head.

At Elle's words, Kate realized that she hadn't actually told her friend that the Ethan she'd been talking about was the same Ethan that was her childhood friend. "Wait a minute. How did you figure that out, anyway?" she asked curiously.

Elle looked at her like she was crazy. "Give me some credit. It wasn't that hard to figure out. The way you two were looking at each other. Not to mention the sexual tension that I think everyone in the restaurant felt. And then you two disappeared and when you came back you had the I-just-made-out-and-it-was-hot look all over your face. Then I knew it was definitely him."

Kate laughed. Her friends knew something had happened just like she thought they would.

"So, are you going out with him tonight?" Elle asked with a smile. "Because you know, I *am* going to be out of town and the townhouse will be empty..." She trailed off suggestively.

"No, he has to work the night shift. But he said he'd call me. Plus, I know what you're suggesting and *that* is not going to happen anytime soon."

"Why not? You like him, don't you?"

"You know I do. It's just that … I don't know. I'm nervous about getting hurt again."

"That little jerk," Elle burst out with a shake of her head.

Kate was taken aback. "What are you talking about?"

"I'm talking about that ex-boyfriend of yours. I swear, Kate, if he were here …" Her eyes were full of anger as she thought about the things she would like to do to Scott.

"I know. Believe me, I know. To be honest, I'm just shocked and upset and scared about the whole situation." Elle looked at her friend, waiting for further explanation. "I'm shocked that I have these feelings for Ethan—feelings that are stronger than I could imagine especially after such a short time. I'm upset with myself because I can't seem to get over the way Scott hurt me. It's like the fear of getting hurt is paralyzing me. I'm just afraid it will happen all over again, and I know I won't be able to handle that. I'm scared to fall in love again. And I'm even more scared because I think I'm already falling. How is that possible? I barely know him!" she wailed, feeling exasperated.

"Kate." Elle leaned forward and placed her hand on her flustered friend's knee. "You're never going to move on if you don't try. You've *got* to open yourself up. That's all part of falling in love. Now, I'm not saying you have to dive right in, even though you feel you already have. But I *am* saying you're going to have to put your trust in Ethan. And as for not knowing him very long? Well, I know him. Granted it was a long time ago, but he was great then and he seems great now. Plus, if it's there," she paused, "it's there. Remember what Sophie said about magic." She rolled her eyes and let out a small huff. "I can't believe that I just said that. She is so rubbing off on me."

"I won't tell Sophie, don't worry." Kate promised with a laugh.

"All right." She smiled. "I need to get going. The last thing I want is to miss my train. I'll call you later to find out how your *phone call* went," she said with a wink as if "phone call" meant something else.

Kate rolled her eyes. "Yeah, okay, now go and show the world what you're made of."

Her gorgeous friend stood and struck a pose before grabbing her chest. "God didn't bless me with this hot body for nothing."

"That's right." Kate nodded. "Now do us proud."

The two friends gave one another a hug, and as Elle was walking out of the room, she paused. "Don't forget what I said, Kate. It's magic. So just…let it happen." She gave one last smile and left.

As soon as Kate heard the door close, she rolled over, burying her face in her pillow. She was still exhausted from her late night and figured she could afford to sleep in a little longer. Especially since Sophie would most likely be making an appearance today. No sooner had she finished her thought than she heard someone at the door.

With a groan, she pulled back her covers and trudged to the door. "Sophie! Why did we let you keep your key if you're always forgetting it? I was trying to get back to—" Kate flung the door open and froze mid-sentence.

There, standing before her, was Ethan. He was wearing blue scrub bottoms and a thin, worn, long sleeve tee shirt, holding the biggest basket of fruit she'd ever seen.

Chapter 14
Fruit Smoothies

Ethan. What are you doing here?" Kate asked.

She was wearing nothing but a light blue tank top and dark gray underwear. As much as he tried, Ethan couldn't stop his eyes from roaming over her body, taking in every curve and inch of bare skin. He was aware that she'd asked him a question, but at the moment, words seemed to fail him. "I'm sorry," he said, finally mustering an apology.

"No!" she practically shouted. "Don't be sorry. I'm glad you're here. I just wasn't expecting you." She blushed slightly.

Relief rushed over him when he realized that she was, in fact, happy to see him. It was something he'd feared since early this morning, after making the rash decision to drive up and see her. Of course, he'd tried sleeping, but it was of no use. Thoughts of her kept him awake and eventually, he gave in to his desires.

"Sorry I surprised you like this. I must have awoken you."

At his words, Kate's eyes went wide. She quickly looked down at herself and realized that she was barely dressed. Her face turned bright red as she attempted to fix the tangled pile of hair on her head. "Oh, umm," she paused, her eyes looking everywhere but at him. "No, you didn't wake me. Elle did," she said quietly.

"Is Elle here then?" Ethan tried to act curious even though he was hoping that she wasn't home. He wanted to be alone with Kate.

"No, she just left to catch her train."

"That's right; she's doing a fitting this weekend," he remembered out loud.

"So, do you want to come in?" She looked at him and smiled.

"Yes, that would be great." Ethan walked into her townhouse, still grasping the large basket filled with fruit. "I thought that, since we wouldn't get a chance to see each other tonight, I'd stop by and make you breakfast. Well, smoothies, really."

She closed the door behind them and leaned up against it for a minute, looking at him with a strange expression.

"What?" he asked, not sure what she was thinking.

"It's nothing. I just like the way you look holding all that fruit. It brings back some great memories." She smirked.

"That is a *great* memory. I don't know if I told you or not, but I will never be able to look at produce the same way again." He laughed and shook his head back and forth. "I took the coldest shower of my life when I got home.

Her eyes went wide. "You did?"

He almost wished he could feel embarrassed about his comment, but he didn't. He gave a quiet sigh before he decided to be completely honest. "Yes, a very cold shower and even that didn't help. You have to know the effect you have on me by now, especially after last night."

Ethan looked into her eyes and watched her fiddle with the fabric of her shirt. She dropped her head shyly and started to twist her foot around, nervously drawing imaginary patterns on the hard wood. She was beautiful, even when she was nervous.

He could tell that she wasn't going to be the first one to speak. In the few conversations he'd had with her, Ethan had learned that when she dropped her head, it meant she was trying to gather her thoughts and find the right words to say. He hated to see her struggle. "Do you have somewhere I can put this?" He held up the full basket.

"Sure," she said with relief.

She turned the corner and led him down the hall to what he assumed was the kitchen. Again, Ethan couldn't help but let his eyes wander down her body, taking in her bare legs and the way her hips shifted from side to side. Quickly looking away so he wouldn't get caught, he turned his attention to the kitchen.

It was bigger than he expected. Dark counters wrapped around two sides of the room in an L formation. Honey colored cabinets lined the walls reaching higher in some places than in others, drawing attention to the height of the ceiling. In the center of the kitchen stood a granite-topped island with bar stools lining one side.

"Your kitchen's great."

"Thanks, it's the main reason we chose this place. I love cooking, so it works out great for me."

"That's right, you can make gnocchi," he said, remembering yet again something from their encounter at the grocery store.

Kate's eyebrows pulled together as she thought of how he knew that. Then she remembered. "Ahh, the grocery store," she realized out loud.

"The grocery store." He nodded.

With a smile, Ethan walked over to the island and started removing some of the fruit. He wasn't sure what her favorite was, so he grabbed all he could find.

"I'm not sure if we have enough fruit here for two shakes," she teased sarcastically.

"What makes you think I'm making two?"

She looked at him with raised eyebrows. "Oh, so you're not hungry?"

"I'm a guy, Kate. I'm always hungry."

"How could I miss that?" She smiled and playfully winked. "So, what kind are we making?" Her eyes danced over the fruit on the table.

"What's your favorite?"

"In a shake, I like peaches, bananas, strawberries, and maybe some blueberries. But I will eat some cantaloupe and cherries separately, if that's okay?"

"You can have whatever you want." Ethan began to sort through the basket and pulled out the fruits that she'd mentioned.

"What about you? What do you like in your shakes?

He thought for a moment before speaking. "You already know I'm a big strawberry fan, and peaches are probably a tie for first, so those two are a definite. The combination you suggested sounds great."

"Well, then, let's get started." She smiled up at him and held his gaze for a little longer than necessary. Ethan was once again struck by her beauty, and his hand twitched with the desire to touch her. Slowly reaching his hand forward, he lightly grazed her cheekbone, feeling the silkiness of her skin slip beneath his fingertips.

Kate closed her eyes and turned into his palm, before placing her hand over his. "I'm really glad you're here," she whispered.

"Me too, more than you probably know."

They shared a moment of silence before Kate returned her attention to the fruit. She quickly went to work opening a drawer and rummaging around. In no time at all, she found what she was looking for and placed the small paring knife on the counter. Grabbing a colander out of the cabinet below, she walked over to the sink.

Ethan watched her move around the kitchen, gathering the items she needed. She really seemed in her element. Something about it brought a feeling of happiness to him that he hadn't expected. He wasn't sure why, but soon decided it was because she was happy and comfortable around him.

"Will you bring that fruit over here?" she asked, looking briefly over her shoulder.

Without a moment's hesitation, he grabbed the fruit and flew to her side. She began ripping open the bags, placing the fruit in the colander and washing them off. When she opened the package of strawberries he automatically stood a little straighter.

"Are you all right?" She looked over at him.

"Yeah, I'm fine," he lied. *Although, it seems I can't retain any sort of composure when you're near me with fruit,* he added silently.

Kate shrugged off his odd response and went back to washing fruit. Then, as if someone turned on a bulb, it hit her and she knew why he'd reacted as he had. She smiled to herself, biting back a laugh. Slowly turning to face him, she held out a strawberry. "Want a bite?" she purred.

It was clear by her tone that the playful Kate was back and Ethan swallowed. "Sure," he managed to say, while holding out his hand.

She eyed his hand and shook her head. "No hands, please," she said, taking a step closer and placing the strawberry to his lips.

He swallowed again—louder this time—and leaned in to take a bite. Her breath caught as he bit down, taking the berry into his mouth. Quickly finishing, he reached down into the sink and retrieved one of his own. "Your turn," he said, while holding another strawberry to her mouth.

Holding back a giggle, she leaned in and slowly parted her lips, waiting for Ethan's move. He lifted the berry to her mouth and she bit down hard, making juice drip onto her bottom lip. Kate lifted her hand in an attempt to wipe it off, but was stopped when Ethan grabbed hold of her wrist.

He shook his head. "No hands, please." He smiled, then leaned down until his face was level with hers. Softly sliding his tongue out, he licked the red juice that had gathered at the corner of her mouth, then kissed her properly.

"Wait," she said, pulling back quickly.

Ethan froze, thinking that perhaps he'd done something wrong. "Are you okay? Did I do something? Am I moving too fast for you?"

"No, no, that's not it. I need a minute. I just woke up, so hang on a second." She placed her finger to Ethan's lips. "Don't move," she commanded as she quickly ran out of the room.

Kate hurried to her bathroom and grabbed her toothbrush, smothering it with enough toothpaste for three people. With her toothbrush still in her mouth, she ran into her bedroom and searched desperately for something to put on. Only finding an old pair of shorts, she settled on the gray cut offs and pulled them on with one hand as she continued to brush vigorously. When she was satisfied that she'd removed any trace of morning breath, she rinsed out her mouth and splashed her face with the cool water, washing away any nighttime grime.

After one look in the mirror and a swipe of her lip-gloss, she knew it wasn't going to get any better with the time she had. With a satisfied shrug, she practically ran back to the kitchen, wondering if perhaps Ethan being there was all a wonderful dream. Much to her satisfaction it wasn't a dream, and Ethan was standing exactly where she'd left him, strawberry still in hand, waiting patiently. His blue eyes locked with hers when she entered the room.

Her heart was pounding so loudly she wouldn't have been surprised if he could hear it from where he was standing. She tried taking some quick breaths, but they didn't seem to calm her at all. Instead, she kept reciting the words Elle had said earlier. *It's magic, just let it happen. It's magic, just let it happen,* she repeated.

With a slight boost in confidence, she walked toward him, holding his gaze. "So, where were we?" she asked, standing directly in front of him.

"I believe you were here." He grabbed her waist and pulled her closer to him. "And I was here," he said as he brought his lips to her mouth. Their lips formed together perfectly, recognizing each other at once. Kate could smell him all around her and that alone sent electricity through her body. When they finally separated, they were both gasping for air, panting like they'd just finished running a marathon.

Ethan kept his arms around her waist and rested his chin on the top of her head. There was something about simply holding her that made him feel content.

Kate laid her cheek against his chest. She could hear the quick beating of his heart and could feel the rise and fall of his chest with every breath. "Ethan," she sighed.

"Yes," he whispered, dropping his lips to her ear.

"I think we better make those smoothies now," she said out loud for the mere purpose of trying to convince herself.

"Are you sure that's what you want to do?" he asked, as he lowered his head slightly, dragging his nose across her jaw line.

Kate's head began to get hazy. She shook her head, and told herself to get some control. Taking a deep breath, she pulled back abruptly. "I think I need some ice." Quickly walking over to the refrigerator, she pulled open the freezer door. She stood there for a second, letting the cold air awaken her senses and wipe away any foggy confusion that still lingered.

It was clear to Kate that her body and mind were having a battle with each other. Her mind was telling her to go slow, to take her time and figure out if she could really trust Ethan and make sure he wouldn't hurt her like she'd been hurt in the past. Her body was telling her something else entirely. And she knew she couldn't trust it, especially when she was around him. It was as if his simple presence made her throw all caution to the wind.

She continued to go back and forth between her two halves until she realized that she hadn't listened to her heart. *What does my heart tell me?* she asked herself. Closing her eyes, she took another deep breath and allowed herself to *feel*.

It didn't take long for her to come to a conclusion. Her heart was a mix between the two sides. Her heart wanted him; she wanted him. Yes, it might be hard, and yes, she was still confused, scared, and worried. But it didn't matter. It didn't matter that she'd been wounded before. She wanted to be loved again, even if it meant taking a risk. *It's magic, just let it happen,* she thought.

Quickly turning around, she faced Ethan who was sitting on the granite island. He was leaning forward resting his hands on his knees, his head hanging down. Kate suddenly realized that he probably took her sudden mood change as a rejection and immediately felt awful.

"Ethan?"

"I'm sorry, Kate," he said without lifting his head. "I really didn't mean to upset you. It's just that when I'm around you I forget that I've only known you for a week." He let out a sigh. "I keep forgetting that you need to take it slow. I'm letting the desire and feelings that I have for you take over, and I'm sorry. I just wish I could make you see that I won't hurt you. I won't make you feel like you can't—"

"Ethan," she cut him off before he could finish. "Look at me, please."

He lifted his head slowly, his hair hanging across his forehead, his blue eyes gray with emotion. He took her breath away.

"Kiss me," she whispered, barely audible to her own ears. But somehow he heard her.

"Kate, I'm fine with taking things slow, both physically and emotionally."

Hearing him say that only drove her further. She knew she still had some things to work on and she wasn't saying that she wanted to marry him tomorrow, but she did know that she wanted him—her heart wanted him. And that was enough.

"Kiss me," she said again, louder this time.

Ethan watched her with cautious eyes as he slid off the counter and walked over to her, hesitating when he was a few feet away. He didn't want to do something she wasn't ready for and, most importantly, something that she didn't want to do. He looked deep into her brown eyes, trying to read her emotions, to make sure.

Kate felt bare, exposed, like he could see right through her. She wasn't sure what he saw, but it must have been reassuring because he closed the rest of the distance in one swift movement and kissed her.

He pushed her up against the refrigerator with the freezer door still opened. The cold air poured out over her shoulders, adding to the chills he already caused. He quickly moved from her mouth to her neck, kissing and tasting her skin. Kate let her head fall back—practically inside the freezer—as his kisses traced her collarbone. Gripping his hair in her fingers, she sighed.

Upon hearing her reaction, Ethan looked up. He gave her his perfect smile before returning his attention to her lips. She gladly welcomed the feel of his tongue, something that she knew she'd never tire of. They kissed and nipped playfully, not able to get enough, until the sound of the freezer pumping on suddenly broke their connection.

"Maybe we should close the door," Kate panted.

Ethan got an idea and a mischievous grin spread across his face. "Not yet. Didn't you say you needed some ice?" he asked, raising one eyebrow.

"For the smoothies," Kate said.

"Then allow me." With that, he reached over her shoulder and dug into the freezer behind her. Before she had time to turn around, he brought an ice cube to her mouth. His eyes focused on her lips as he slowly began tracing them with the ice cube.

She parted her mouth and allowed her tongue to reach out for the ice, wetting it slightly, as he slid it against her warm lips. Ethan's body shifted as he leaned in and gently kissed her, removing the excess water with his tongue.

Kate had never felt this way before—so alive and powerful, yet so weak at the same time. The ice was so cold that, after a few minutes, her body shivered and she involuntarily curled her shoulders in.

She heard him chuckle softly. "Is something wrong?"

"No, it's just cold," she sighed, barely able to speak the words.

"Here." In one swift motion, Ethan had his hands wrapped around Kate's waist. He slammed the freezer door shut and lifted her onto the counter next to the sink. "Is that better?"

Kate nodded and sat back against the cabinets, relieved to finally be sitting. Now at least she wouldn't have to worry about her legs giving out. Ethan stood in front of her, and she parted her legs slightly, allowing him to move closer.

"How about some fruit?" he asked.

She only nodded. She couldn't speak. Her mind was a mess, and the vision of Ethan standing in front of her, breathing heavily, was driving her insane. Before he had a chance to grab anything, Kate shot her hand out and grabbed some cherries.

Cherries were not something she'd gotten to use at the grocery store and she was more than ready to tease. Holding a perfect pairing of cherries out in front of her, she smiled as she brought them to her mouth, reaching out with her tongue. She slid it around each one slowly before taking them both into her mouth. The skin was smooth on her tongue, and she held them there for a moment before releasing them.

Ethan's back went ramrod straight and his breathing was loud. Kate kept her head down slightly, looking up at him from under her lashes. His eyes seemed darker, grayer, as he watched her. The energy between them worked as a magnetic force, drawing him in until he was just inches from her face. Kate lifted one of the cherries and placed it in his mouth then leaned in and grabbed the other one between her teeth. Pulling back slightly, they split the stem, separating the two.

A smirk took Ethan's lips as he chewed and searched the nearby colander for his next selection. Reaching down into the sink, he grabbed a peach and stood up, still smiling. He brought the peach to Kate's face and marveled at the similar color while he gently grazed it across her cheek. The smooth surface felt like velvet on her skin and when the sweet aroma hit her nose, she felt her mouth begin to water. By the time it reached her lips, Kate was ready for a bite. She opened her mouth and stuck out her chin in preparation but was disappointed when he abruptly pulled it away.

Instead, he lifted the peach to his mouth and bit down. The juice from the fruit dripped on his chin and without waiting a second, Kate leaned forward to lick it away. She intertwined her fingers in the hair at the nape of his neck and pulled him close to her. Tasting the sweet flavor of the juice on her tongue was delicious, and it made her head spin. Slowly slipping one free hand up and over his shoulder, she traced down the back of his arm and finally to the hand that held the peach.

She grasped it in her hands and broke their kiss so she could take a bite. Ethan stood back, and Kate took the biggest bite she could. His eyes grew large as he watched her mouth. Then, he was on her so fast she didn't get a chance to respond. He tasted her lips and kissed her just as she had done a moment before. Kate's body relaxed, and her hand lazily dropped the peach to the floor.

Ethan stood up and pulled her off the counter in one swift motion. He wrapped his arms around her and nuzzled his face into her neck, breathing loudly in her ear. Kate ran her hands up and down his back, feeling the curve of his body and the warmth of his shirt as it clung to him.

Their breathing was erratic, coming in heavy gasps. Letting her body relax, Kate laid her head on his shoulder and sighed. He held her wrapped in his arms until their breathing settled. It was a few moments before Kate lifted her head and looked into Ethan's beautiful eyes, which seemed to glow.

She couldn't keep the smile from her face.

"I like seeing you smile," Ethan admitted. "It makes me happy."

"Me too." She nodded and placed her head back on his shoulder. After a shared moment of silence, Kate's stomach growled loudly. She let out a little laugh. "I guess it's time to eat."

"What? The strawberry, cherry, and one bite of peach weren't enough for you?" he asked teasingly.

"Yeah, not quite. I may be a girl, but I like to eat."

"All right," he said as he lowered her to the ground. "Let's make some breakfast. But before I help, could I use your bathroom?"

"Sure, it's down the hall on the left. I'll get started on our shakes."

He gave Kate a quick wink that made her heart flutter, and he walked out of the kitchen. As soon as he was out of sight, she bent over and rested her head on the counter. Her mind was screaming and her heart felt like it was going to jump out of her chest. All she could do was smile. The sound of the front door opening brought her out of her daze.

"Katherine Elizabeth Thomas! You get out here right this minute and tell me what happened last night!" the voice shrieked.

Sophie's voice trailed down the hallway and Kate stood up, suddenly frantic. She had been so lost in her own world with Ethan that she had forgotten all about the possibility of Sophie stopping by. She didn't have time to stew over her thoughts before Sophie came through the doorway.

"So?" she asked, propping her large black sunglasses onto the top of her head.

"What?" Kate teased, knowing full well what her friend was talking about.

"That was him, wasn't it? That was the Ethan from the gallery, the club, the hospital, and the grocery store. That was the same Ethan at the dinner last night, wasn't it?" She rose to the tips of her toes in anticipation.

"What makes you think that?" Kate played dumb.

"I just do. Plus, the way he was looking at you was not the normal way a guy looks at someone he's just met. Then, after you both came back to the table and you looked like you do after a hot make out session, I knew there was something going on. I put two and two together. You don't have to be a rocket scientist to figure it out. I would say I'm shocked, but I'm not. You know what I said about it being magic."

Kate listened to her friend's rant and couldn't help but laugh. She was just as observant as Elle was.

"It's not funny." Sophie placed her hands firmly on her hips.

"I'm sorry. I'm not laughing at you. I was just thinking about something." She shook her head. "Hey, did Logan come with you? I didn't hear him."

Sophie peered over her shoulder and waived her hand around. "He's here, but he's probably in the other room watching TV. Besides, I want to hear all about the kiss, and I don't think he wants to be around to hear all the delicious details."

Kate laughed again and turned around to focus on making the fruit smoothies.

"You aren't really going to do this to me, are you?" Sophie groaned.

"I don't know what you want to hear." She shrugged. "Ethan followed me outside after I got the text from Scott and—"

"What text from Scott?"

Sighing, Kate turned to the sink and continued washing fruit as she explained. "He sent me a text that basically said it was hard for him to see me with someone and that he missed me and wanted me to call him."

Sophie's jaw was hanging open. "That little piece of sh—"

"Soph," she cut her off. "Can we not talk about him right now? Besides, I thought you wanted to hear about Ethan."

"Okay, I'll let it slide for now because you already know how I feel about the situation. Sorry, back to your story." She held up her hand, gesturing for her to continue.

Grabbing two glasses out of the cupboard, Kate placed them on the table and started into her story. "Basically, he saw me get flustered or whatever, and he decided to follow me outside and see if I was okay. I, of course, started ranting like I do when I get nervous and angry. And well…" Kate paused and looked over at Sophie, surprised that she hadn't interrupted her yet.

Instead her blond friend was standing still, a look of wonderment on her face. Her eyes dashed around the kitchen as she took in the surroundings. They shot over to the large basket of fruit, the half-eaten peach that was still on the floor, and the two glasses that sat on the table. When she looked back at Kate, her eyes were wide as she finally noticed her friend's appearance. Kate rolled her lips in, attempting to keep the smile from her face, and dropped her eyes.

"Kate, is there something you want to tell me?" Sophie asked in a tone that said she already knew the answer.

Kate didn't get a chance to speak before she heard the most beautiful sound in the world. It was the one voice that made her heart flutter, her knees weak, sent chills up her spine, and made her flush, all at the same time.

"Hello again, Sophie. It's nice to see you this morning." Ethan walked past a very stunned Sophie who was now staring with her mouth open wide. He slipped his arm around Kate's waist and smiled down at her before looking back up. "Want a fruit smoothie?"

Chapter 15
Information

Kate looked up at Ethan in awe. Clearly, he was not at all bothered by Sophie's presence. She wasn't sure what she expected, but she thought he might be a little embarrassed for being caught in her house in the early morning. Kate turned to face her friend who was still frozen in place with wide eyes. At least she had closed her mouth.

"What do you like in your fruit smoothie?" Ethan asked again, still completely at ease.

"Umm…" Sophie mumbled. Kate laughed. Seeing Sophie shocked was rare, but seeing Sophie *speechless* was achieving the impossible. "Do you mind if I steal my friend for a second?" she finally asked. "I promise I'll bring her right back." Before either Ethan or Kate could respond, Sophie was dragging her friend out of the room.

"Ouch. Has anyone ever told you that you're freakishly strong?" Kate complained. She wasn't released until they reached the bedroom and she was shoved to the bed.

"All right, Thomas, spill it." Sophie stood with hands on hips, determined to get an answer.

"Soph, I know what you thinking. And nothing like that happened." Kate laughed when she heard herself. It sounded more like a conversation between a mother and daughter than that of two best friends. "I would think that if something did happen, you would be happy for me," she feigned being hurt.

Sophie dropped her hands immediately, walked over and sat down next to her friend. "Of course, I would be happy for you, are you kidding? I think I'm just a little shocked, that's all. I mean I saw you looking…" she waved her hand around, "…like you just rolled out of bed, and then Ethan walked in."

Kate's heartbeat picked up instinctively at just the mention of his name, and she felt herself smile.

"You really like him, don't you?" Sophie continued. Kate nodded, but what little doubt and fear she had was apparent on her face. "You're scared?" Sophie asked, being the observant friend that she was. Kate nodded again and bit down on her lip in worry.

"He's not Scott." Sophie placed her hand on Kate's knee. "Logan kept me up late last night, telling me story after story about him and Ethan. I'd heard him mention him before, but never like this. He was a great friend to him, and he sounds like an amazing guy." She paused. "He is *not* Scott."

It was the second time she had told Kate that he wasn't like Scott, and every time she said it, Kate felt her stomach churn. "I know he's not Scott. And I trust him when he says he won't hurt me—which is crazy because we're just starting to get to know each other. There's just something about him and the way I *feel* when I'm around him. Is it weird to say that I feel safe?" She looked at her friend who was positively beaming.

"No, it's not weird at all. I think it's normal to feel that way about the person you're meant to be with."

Meant to be with? Kate let the words float around her head before pushing them back, filing them away for later. There would be plenty of time for her to stew over her feelings. Right now there was only one thing she wanted and he was in the other room.

Ethan wasn't sure how long Kate would be under interrogation, so he figured he might as well make himself useful and make the smoothies. Just as he began to cut up some of the fruit, he heard the TV switch on in the other room. Up until that point he wasn't aware that anyone else was in the house. He hadn't been given an official tour of the townhouse yet but was fairly certain he could find his way around. Following the sound of the TV into the other room, he found Logan spread out on the couch.

"Hey, Logan, I didn't know you were here."

Logan sat up quickly and smiled as he took in Ethan's appearance. "I should be saying the same thing to you. What are you doing here so early?" he asked with raised eyebrows.

Ethan shook his head. "It's not what you think."

"*Sure.* That's what they all say," he teased.

Little sparks of jealousy ignited at the simple thought of someone else vying for Kate's attention, of someone else being in her home. Ethan knew it was ridiculous because she'd dated before, but he couldn't stop his emotions.

"Whoa, that's not what I meant," Logan said quickly upon seeing the look on Ethan's face. "Kate isn't the type of girl to just have guys sleep over. Come to think of it, I don't even think there's been anyone since Scott."

Ethan's nerves settled slightly, but not entirely. It seemed that the mere mention of Scott made his blood boil. He wanted to know about him, wanted to know all the details that Kate hadn't told him. He knew that he shouldn't ask, but he couldn't help himself.

"Logan, can I ask you something?"

He looked at Ethan for a second before answering. "You want to know about Scott, don't you?"

"I know I don't have a right to know everything. But I just can't help it, I want her to..." he trailed off, not saying anything else as he walked over and took a seat on the love seat.

"You really like her, don't you?"

Ethan turned to face him. "I do like her—a lot. And from what she's said, she likes me too. She's just scared of getting hurt again. Apparently this Scott guy did quite a number on her, breaking her heart numerous times." He could feel himself getting angry just thinking about it.

Logan sighed. "He broke her heart, all right," he said, shaking his head. "It took all my strength not to beat his ass after what he did to her. The only thing that kept me from doing it was Kate. She said he didn't deserve to be hurt. Can you believe that? *She* told me that *he* didn't deserve to be hurt."

This statement didn't surprise Ethan at all. In the time he'd had to get to know Kate, he was quickly learning that she was anything but ordinary. She was nothing like the other girls he'd known, and for that, he was thankful. "So what happened?" he asked still curious.

Logan looked at his old friend for a moment. "You know I'm only telling you this because you're my friend. And even though it's been years since we've talked, I have a feeling you haven't changed. You're still a good guy; I can tell."

Ethan nodded and Logan continued. "Kate and Scott were friends for years before they actually started dating. They met back in Virginia. We all thought it would be a little weird for them, that it would take some time to adjust from being just friends to being together in a relationship, but it didn't. In fact, it was the exact opposite. It was like they were finally where they should be. They were serious for about a year before things started getting strange. Scott started pulling away, making comments that sounded like they were coming from a good friend, not someone you were in love with. At first, Kate wasn't even aware. Sophie tried telling her that something was up and that she thought Scott and Kate should talk, but Kate insisted things were fine.

"About two weeks later, Scott broke up with her for the *first* time. He told her that they were getting too serious and that he wasn't sure they should be together any more. Kate was crushed. It was even worse because she had no clue he was feeling that way. Lots of times you know the relationship's over before you actually say it, but Kate was clueless.

"About a month later, Scott called her and asked her to meet him for coffee. She was hesitant and we all told her she shouldn't go, but she felt like she needed some closure.

"I don't know exactly what was said during that 'meeting' over coffee; all I know is that Kate came home wrapped in Scott's arms, smiling like nothing had ever happened.

"Things seemed to pick right back up where they left off and everything was going great, until two months later, when Kate came home in tears. It took Sophie and Elle almost an hour to get her to calm down enough to tell them what was wrong. As it turned out, Scott told her he was having doubts again. He kept saying something about it being 'too easy.' He said that there was no way love could be that simple and that it was too easy to fall in love with his best friend. He told her he wanted to still be friends and that he hoped it wouldn't affect the relationship they had. At first, Kate thought that she would try to be his friend and nothing more. But the longer she was around him, the harder it became. Eventually she told him that she couldn't do it any more. She either had to be in his life completely or not at all.

"He wasn't happy about it. In fact, he was calling and texting her all the time. She never returned his calls, so one day he showed up here. I still say that if Soph had been here he would have ended up in the hospital." He laughed

"So what happened when he showed up?" Ethan leaned forward in anticipation.

"Now *that* conversation, Soph and Elle know nothing about."

"Why?"

"Because Kate never told them." He shrugged.

"Why didn't she tell them?

"Because they already hated Scott for hurting her the first two times. Anyway, he showed up at her door and told her that he would marry her if—"

"*If*?" Ethan interrupted. "*Would* marry her? What is that supposed to mean?"

"He said that he wanted another chance, and that if she changed for the better and things kept moving forward, then he would marry her."

Ethan felt sick. "What? That's not a proposal. And why would he want her to change!" His anger grew the more he thought about it.

Logan held his hands up. "Look, man, believe me, I know. I couldn't believe it either. But Kate being Kate threw her whole self into it. She knew they were perfect for each other. She knew that this time it would be different because in the end, she was going to marry him.

"She took him back and it lasted for about three months. That time when she came home, she didn't even cry. She couldn't—it was like she was dead. Sophie and Elle thought it was just because he broke her heart again. The reality was that *she* was broken; her spirit was broken. We all hated him. And after she told me what he had said, what he had promised her? I wanted to kill him. It took all my strength not to beat him down. But Kate begged me. She begged me not to hurt him and she begged me never to tell Elle and Sophie the whole story. So I didn't. I knew it would only make things worse anyway. You don't want the wrath of Soph or my sister on you. Believe me." He rolled his eyes in an attempt to lighten the mood.

"It's been a few years since I've felt the wrath that is Elle McLean, but I'm pretty sure it hasn't changed much. If anything, I'm sure it's only grown worse," he agreed.

"You have no idea." Logan laughed.

The two guys sat in silence for a moment, and then Logan leaned forward resting his hands on his knees and looked Ethan in the eyes. "You know you're my friend, Ethan, but I'm going to tell you this right now. If you hurt her in any way, I'll kick your ass."

Ethan looked back at him just as seriously. "If I hurt her, I'll let you."

Logan's stern face melted into a smile, and he lay back down on the couch, grabbing the remote control. "Hey, I have a question for you." He lifted his head off the pillow and looked at his friend. "What are you doing here, anyway? Isn't it a little early to be stopping by?"

Ethan dropped his eyes and ran his fingers through his hair. "Uh, I just stopped by to make some breakfast for Kate," he mumbled, trying to sound casual.

"Hmm." Logan's eyebrows furrowed, not sure what to make of his friend's statement. He lay his head back down and flipped through the channels before pausing. "What are you making?"

Ethan's throat clenched tight and he coughed. "Umm, breakfast drinks."

"You mean like ... fruit smoothies?"

Ethan could hear the smile in Logan's voice, but couldn't risk looking at his face. "Yeah," he confirmed simply.

"I'd be a fan of fruit too, if I were you."

The two finally looked at each other and fell into laughter.

"You have no idea, man," Ethan laughed out. "Produce has *never* looked so good."

The two friends sat on the couch laughing for a few minutes until the TV caught their attention. Silently, Ethan sat back and let the moment soak in. Besides Trent, he didn't have many close friends, and after dinner last night with the group, he couldn't help but feel like this was where he was supposed to be.

Another minute passed and Sophie walked into the room. She curled up on Logan's chest and nuzzled into his neck. They looked so happy together, and he automatically thought of Kate and wondered where she was. Ethan stood and had just taken a step toward the kitchen when a slender but firm hand grasped his arm. He turned to see Sophie looking up at him, her wide eyes serious.

"She likes you, so don't mess it up. You hurt her and I'll hurt you." She smiled at him sweetly, looking like an angel—an angel that could cause the very fires of Hell to rise and destroy him.

"I won't," Ethan promised.

"Good." Her smile widened as she spun around and bounded back onto Logan.

Ethan walked into the kitchen, making a mental note to never cross Sophie. As soon as he was through the doorway, he saw Kate resting her head on the granite counter. Silently making his way to her, he slipped his arm around her waist and leaned down, placing his lips to her ear.

"I was waiting for you," he whispered. "Why didn't you come in and sit with us?"

"I figured I would just get to work and finish these smoothies." She shifted and he could tell that she wasn't being completely honest.

"Kate," he sighed, turning her around to face him. Placing his hand on her chin, he lifted her beautiful face to his.

It didn't take long for her to give in, especially when he was looking at her the way he was. "I walked in and didn't know where I should sit. I just figured that I'd come in here so I wouldn't have to worry about where I should be."

Ethan's stomach twisted when he realized that she actually doubted where she belonged. To him the answer was simple. "Where you should be, is anywhere I am." He smiled down at her. "Now let's make some smoothies." He slid his hand down her arm and grabbed hold of her hand, intertwining their fingers as he led her to the sink.

Four smoothies later, Ethan looked over the still half-full basket of produce and laughed. "I think I may have gotten a little carried away with the fruit."

"You can get carried away with fruit any time you want, as long as I'm around." Kate smirked.

Ethan's eyebrows lifted. "I'll keep that in mind," he said before leaning in to kiss her.

With a quiet sigh, Kate pulled away. Her eyes were closed and her full, perfect lips were pulled up slightly at the corners. She inhaled deeply and opened her eyes, focusing on Ethan's face. "Let's get these out to Soph and Logan before I let you get carried away again."

She grabbed two of the four glasses and turned away. Ethan enjoyed the view and watched her hips sway side to side. Kate came to a stop in the doorway and peered over her shoulder. "Are you coming?"

With a quick nod, Ethan grabbed the other two glasses and followed after her. Sophie and Logan were still in the same position they were in a few minutes ago, and this time, Kate didn't hesitate about where to sit. She took a seat on the loveseat and patted the open space beside her. Ethan gladly accepted and wrapped his free arm around her shoulder.

The group sat in silence, watching football highlights from recent games. The playoffs were coming around, and the Eagles had secured home field advantage, Ethan knew this couldn't have made Trent any happier. He was just angry that he wasn't able to play since tearing his ACL during the middle of the season.

"What do you think the Eagles' chances are of taking it all the way?" Logan asked, still engrossed in the screen.

"You want my opinion or Trent's?" Ethan asked with a laugh.

"Trent?"

"Didn't I mention him the other night at dinner?"

"You said you moved out here because you had a friend in the area, but you never told me about him. His name's Trent, what does he do?"

"He plays football, actually. Although right now, he's watching from the sidelines. He got injured earlier this season."

At Ethan's words, Logan looked away from the TV. "Really, you mean he plays pro? For who, the Eagles?" He was now sitting up at full attention. "Are you talking about Trent *Williams*?"

"Yep," Ethan said with a pop. "And yes, he can get me good tickets." He answered the question before Logan could even ask.

"Are you serious? You can get us tickets?"

Ethan nodded, and just as Logan started pumping his fist in the air, Sophie hopped off the couch and plopped down at Ethan's feet. Apparently she wasn't the only one excited about the prospect of getting tickets.

"Is he single?"

Her question threw Ethan off guard. "What?"

"I said, is he single?"

"Yes," he answered slowly, still not understanding her question.

"Then we need to hook him up with Elle."

Ethan didn't get a chance to respond before Logan cut in. "No, no, no." Sophie turned to face him with a pout. "Don't look at me like that. You know as well as I do that Elle doesn't date athletes, or 'jocks' as she calls them," he said while meeting her pleading gaze.

"Come on, Logan. Who knows, maybe this guy will be different." She shifted back over to Logan and knelt down on the floor so she was eye level with him. She gave him her best puppy dog face, and Logan could feel his defenses falling.

"No," he mumbled miserably.

"Yeah, I'm not sure that's such a good idea. I mean, I know Elle is a spitfire and could probably handle anything you throw at her, but I don't think she's Trent's type." Ethan stumbled for an excuse, trying anything he could to help out his friend. He looked to Kate with pleading eyes and she only smirked. She knew exactly what Sophie was doing and exactly what the outcome would be.

"Besides," Ethan continued. "Trent can be a little rough around the edges sometimes. He needs someone like … like …" He was grasping at straws, trying to find the perfect definition for the girl that would be ideal for Trent, when it hit him. "He needs someone like the tire chick," he blurted out.

Sophie's button nose scrunched in confusion. "Tire chick? Ethan, I don't know what you're talking about, but that makes no sense."

"And it wouldn't. At least to you guys. See, about a week ago …" He turned to Kate. "Come to think of it, it was the day that I ran into you at the grocery store. Anyway, apparently Trent pulled over to help this girl who had a flat tire. It turned out to be a big mistake on his part because she already knew what she was doing. She must have run him through the wringer too." He laughed remembering his friend's worn expression.

"I tell you what," Ethan continued. "I have never seen him so whipped by a girl in all my life. She put him in his place and didn't swoon over him in the least. He's not used to that happening; girls usually fall all over him. I told him he should have asked for her number, but he, for some reason, has this rule when it comes to women. He thinks that—" Ethan paused mid-sentence as he noticed the look on both girls' faces. Their jaws hung open and their eyes were bulging. "What?" he asked curiously.

Both Sophie and Kate turned to one another and squealed. They both knew exactly who Ethan was talking about and couldn't believe it. The two girls started shouting out random words like, *it's him … the tire … hot … shirt … half-naked,* and *grease,* which only left Logan and Ethan more confused.

"Wait a minute. Who are you guys talking about?"

Sophie stopped her bouncing long enough to look at Ethan. "It's Elle," she said.

"What's Elle?" Logan asked.

Taking a deep breath, Sophie attempted to calm herself before speaking slowly, accentuating each word. "The girl that Trent met on the side of the road with a flat tire was Elle."

"What?" both guys said in unison.

"I said, the girl that Trent met on the side of the road, the one who knew how to change a tire, the one who used his shirt to wipe the grease off her hands, the one who wouldn't give him her number, *that*, my dear boys, was Elle."

Both Logan and Ethan sat in stunned silence. When they finally spoke, it was with a tone of awe. "How can that be possible? It's all so … I don't know." Ethan shook his head.

"Wow. Talk about coincidence. Things like that don't just happen," Logan added.

Sophie took a step forward and looked down at Ethan. "It happens all the time. When things are meant to be, they have a way of working out." She smiled at him, then peered over at Kate.

The two looked at each other, and Ethan placed his hand on top of Kate's, squeezing it gently, letting her know that he agreed with what Sophie said.

"So. Now that you know that Elle was the girl Trent was talking about, are you still against setting them up?" Sophie placed her hands on her hips.

"I guess not," Ethan shrugged.

"Good. That's what I thought."

Kate sat up excitedly. "Why don't we all go out when Elle gets back in town? I know she doesn't like getting set up on blind dates, but I have a feeling she won't mind once we tell her who it's with."

"Don't you dare!" Sophie yelled.

Kate stared at her in shock. "What? Why not?"

"Come on, we can't just tell her that it's *him*," she said with a scrunched-up face. "We need to make it a little fun."

"Soph," Kate warned. "What are you planning in that little head of yours?"

"I'm not exactly sure yet." She bit down on her bottom lip, concentrating.

"Man, Elle is going to flip when she finds out he plays for the Eagles," Logan said with a laugh as he turned his attention back to the TV.

"*She's* going to flip? What about Trent? You guys don't know him. He is going to have an aneurysm when he finds out he's going on a date with a girl from the *Sports Illustrated* swimsuit issue."

"You can't tell him!" Sophie squeaked. "And you can't tell Elle, Logan. Neither can you." She pointed at Kate. "The three of you have to swear not to say anything until I figure this whole thing out."

"All right."

"Fine with me."

"Okay."

None of them wanted to stand in the way of Sophie, who had already grabbed a pen and paper and started writing things down.

The group sat for a while watching TV and enjoying their smoothies. Every time Ethan lifted his glass, he would steal glances at Kate. He was entranced by the soft lines of her profile as she focused on the game and the way her lips grazed the edge of her cup.

After catching him twice, Kate finally spoke up. "Would you like a tour?" she asked innocently. A smile played on the corners of her mouth.

With a nod, Ethan stood and pulled her to his side, wrapping an arm around her waist.

"It's not huge, but it's enough for us," she said, as they walked up a set of stairs.

Ethan paused when he noticed the pictures that lined the walls. "Did you take these?" he asked in amazement. He'd seen her work before at the gallery, but that was only a few pieces.

"Uh-huh," she confirmed with a nod.

"They're amazing." Ethan walked by each one slowly, admiring every detail. There was no specific theme to any of them. Some were landscape shots, others architectural. There were even a few of Sophie and Elle. "What do you prefer to shoot?" he asked, still absorbed by her work.

"I don't have a preference really. I like to do a little of everything. I can't choose. I mean, the world is such a magnificent place."

"Yes, it is." He reached over and placed his hand on her cheek, feeling the heat of her warm skin.

She closed her eyes and smiled against his hand. "Come on, I want to show you something," she said as she pulled his hand from her face and led him further down the hall.

She paused just outside of a door. "My room," she said, looking anxious.

He smiled encouragingly. She sighed and pushed open her door. He walked into her room and tried to absorb everything at once. The walls were the color of the ocean, a gray-blue that stood out in contrast to the crisp white curtains that framed the large window next to her bed. Dark hardwood floors peeked out from beneath the edges of shell-colored area rugs.

Ethan walked past the over-filled bookcases, dragging his fingers along the worn bindings, reading the few titles that he could still make out. Next to her dresser stood a mahogany desk, covered with papers and photographs. Eager to see more of her work, he made his way over to them, but paused when the wall above it caught his eye. The entire wall was adorned with pictures. Not one frame was the same and not one picture was reminiscent of the other.

"Kate," he said quietly. "These are…" He trailed off, not knowing what words to use to do them justice.

"Do you like them?" she asked shyly.

"Are you kidding? They're amazing. You're so talented."

She dropped her eyes timidly, and Ethan was overcome by the woman standing before him. Taking a step forward, he wrapped an arm around her waist and pulled her to him. "Beautiful," he whispered, looking into her soft brown eyes and silently asking for permission to kiss her.

When she nodded, he leaned in slowly and brushed his lips against hers before deepening the kiss. She wrapped her arms around his neck. Parting her lips, she breathed into his mouth with a quiet sigh.

As they clung to each other, Ethan lifted her up and sat her on top of the desk. Papers crinkled beneath her as she leaned back, knocking over various containers of office supplies. He hovered over her as they continued to kiss, completely lost in each other. The shrill ring of Ethan's phone interrupted them.

"Sorry," he groaned, pulling out his cell. "Hello?" The agitation was clear in his voice and he made a conscious effort to control his irritation.

Kate bit on her lip to keep from laughing. It was clear that he wasn't happy with being bothered and that thought made her happy. She listened to his conversation and felt her heart drop when he agreed to go in to work. Apparently, a Dr. Hunter had a family emergency and needed him to cover for her.

"Yeah, well, you'll just owe me big time," Ethan said with a laugh, before hanging up and looking at Kate. "I'm sorry. I can't stay longer." He hoped she could hear his honesty. There was nowhere else he'd rather be than right there with her.

"It's okay. I understand," she said with a half smile.

Ethan leaned forward and gave her another kiss, running his fingers through her thick hair. Twisting a piece around his finger, he felt something metal. He untangled his hands and removed the foreign object—a shiny silver paper clip.

"Guess that's what happens when you make out on a desk, huh?" Kate giggled and grabbed the clip from his fingers.

Helping her down from the desk, the two silently made their way back downstairs and to the front door. "Can I take you out tomorrow night?" he asked, worried that she might say no.

"I'd love that." She smiled.

"Great. I'll pick you up at six-thirty?"

"Sounds great. I'll see you then." She leaned in and kissed his lips softly.

Each of them committed the other's touch to memory, knowing that it would be what got them through the night.

"Bye," Ethan said one last time and turned away, forcing his feet to walk away from her.

Chapter 16
Counting Down

Kate lay in bed the next morning, letting the sunlight burst through her window, warming her body through the blankets. Thoughts of Ethan had preoccupied her mind all night. She continued to replay the way his rich voice sounded when he said her name, the way his carefree laugh made her heart skip, and the simple pleasure she felt from just being next to him.

She knew she must have dreamt of him during the night and was disappointed that she couldn't recall every detail. Finally giving up, she took a deep breath, reaching her arms up over her head and stretching her muscles after being still all night. She rolled over and looked at the clock. *Eleven hours. Eleven hours and I get to see him again,* she thought. Excitement bubbled in her stomach and gave her a jolt of energy. She flipped the covers back and got up, ready to start her day. Hopefully if she kept herself busy, six-thirty would be there before she knew it.

Walking over to her desk, she switched on her laptop, smiling as she remembered what had taken place there last night. She instinctively placed her fingers to her lips. *Eleven hours, eleven hours,* she repeated over and over as she clicked on the inbox of her email. Scrolling through her unread messages, she noticed an all-too-familiar name. Her heart stuttered and she held her breath. Scott Christiansen. Her first instinct was to delete it, but she found herself wavering. What felt like an eternity later, she clicked it open to read.

*Katie - I'm sorry about the text the other night. It was just
weird seeing you there with someone else. I really do miss
you. Can we meet up sometime for coffee?
Always,
Scott*

Not blinking, she stared at the message until the black font began to bleed together into illegible squiggles. The unforgettable ache returned to her chest, pressing down on her. She dropped her head and took a calming breath in hopes of relieving some of the pressure. *Why does he do this? Why does he always come back?* she wondered, already knowing the answer. The history between them was too great. They would always be tied to one another.

Frustration built inside of her, layering brick by brick on top of the hurt. She clenched her jaw tight, and suddenly her bedroom was too small. The walls closed in around her and she felt trapped. Needing oxygen, she grabbed her favorite sweatshirt and keys and ran out of her house.

As soon as she made it outside, the cold air seemed to help clear her head, but only slightly. She bypassed her car and started on foot. Making her way down the street, she took a left on Main and picked up her pace. She walked quickly at first, matching the pace at which her mind was racing. Eventually, she slowed and forced all thoughts of Scott and his email from her mind. Glancing down at her watch, she noted the time. *Ten hours, ten hours,* she repeated in an attempt to turn her thoughts to Ethan.

With another calming breath, she pushed open the door of her favorite coffee shop. The delicious smells of freshly ground coffee and buttery pastries filled her senses, making her mouth water. As Kate stood in line, her eyes focused on the tile floor beneath her, but her mind was somewhere else entirely.

"Miss? I said, can I help you?" The young girl's loud voice from behind the counter woke her out of her daze and she looked up.

"Sorry, uh, yeah, I'll have a—"

"Hazelnut latte, and I'll have a double espresso." A deep voice spoke up from behind her. Kate's entire body stiffened as she slowly turned around. Standing in front of her for the second time in two days was Scott. He met her eyes with a casual smile. "Glad to see you're still drinking the same thing." He took a step forward to pay. Kate, upon realizing what he was about to do, shot her arm out, effectively cutting him off.

"I can pay for it myself." She kept her voice firm.

"I know you can. But why don't you let me get it this time?"

This time? Does he think there's going to be another time? she thought, her eyes widening.

"As friends, Kate. Let me buy this for you because you're my friend," he clarified.

He smiled again and she felt her frustration subside. He always seemed to have that effect on her. No matter how upset she was at him or how angry he made her, all it took was one smile and she always gave in.

"Fine," she said with a huff. She waited impatiently for her drink, and once it was ready, she grabbed it off the counter and turned to leave.

"Hey, where are you going so fast?" He maneuvered himself in front of her. "Don't you want to sit for a minute?" His dark eyes were focused on hers. "After all, it's not every day I'm in New Hope."

Her immediate thoughts were to say no and walk away, but the longer she looked at him, the more she found herself giving in.

"Just as friends," he reassured again with a smile.

"Okay, but just for a few minutes. I have things to do today." She tried to look serious, but Scott only seemed amused. He let out a loud laugh as he sat down at the closest table. She huffed loudly in response and flopped down in the chair next to him.

"I sent you an email yesterday," he said casually.

"Yeah, I got it," she spat.

"Oh-ho, being a little snappy, are we?" he asked, holding back a laugh.

"Yes, I am. And I think I have every right to be a little snappy."

"And why is that?"

"Because, Scott, you can't do that. You can't text me while you're on a date, saying that you miss me. And you shouldn't be sending me emails saying that it was weird for *you* to see *me* with someone else. You were there with your girlfriend, Scott, your *girlfriend*."

He held his hands up, surrendering. "Hang on. Technically, I wasn't on the date when I sent you that text. I had already dropped her off." Kate rolled her eyes and opened her mouth to retort when he continued. "And it *was* a little weird seeing you there with someone else." He looked down at his cup and paused. "Who was that guy, anyway? Is he your boyfriend?"

She thrilled at hearing the term boyfriend in regard to Ethan but wasn't about to have a conversation about it with Scott. "What are you doing here, Scott?" she asked instead.

"I was north of here, dropping something off for a client and thought I'd check out the town. Now," he sat forward on his arms. "Is he your boyfriend?" he asked again.

"I'm not talking to you about this." She sipped her drink.

"Why not?"

"Because you're not in my life anymore, and I don't need to tell you everything." She knew it sounded harsh, but she also knew it was the only way he'd drop the topic.

"Fair enough," he said with a nod. "I noticed that Sophie and Logan are still together. That's great. Are they going to get hitched any time soon?"

Her stomach twisted into knots before it dropped, heavy like an anvil. The four of them used to talk about getting married, living next door to each other, and watching their kids play. The memory brought back a wave of pain that Kate wasn't prepared for.

"I've gotta go, Scott," she whispered as she grabbed her coffee and stood up quickly.

Scott stood up just as fast and wrapped his arm around her waist, keeping her there. Kate hesitated. His hands felt different from the last set that had held her. They felt familiar, yet frightening at the same time. Scott pulled her close to his chest and dropped his head.

It had been a long time since she'd been that close to him, feeling his warm arms encircle her. For a moment, she felt like she was back where she belonged. Her body remembered his touch and the way it felt to have him close.

"I've missed this, getting to hold you," he said, his voice deep.

Hearing the words come out of his mouth made Kate's stomach churn. Obviously her body was quickly remembering the other feelings he could cause. Like the pain, the aching throbbing pain that his words could inflict. Kate took advantage of the moment and pushed away from him. She kept her head down and didn't say a word.

"Kate." He paused. "Katie, I'm sorry. I didn't mean to … look, I just want to try and be friends with you again. I miss you."

She held her hand up, signaling for him to stop. "Just … not right now, okay? I'll talk to you later."

Before Scott had a chance to say anything else, Kate pushed through the door and hurried out onto the street. She tossed what was left of her latte in the trash and started to run. By the time she made it to her townhouse, she was out of breath. She slammed the door behind her and flung herself down onto her couch, burying her face in a pillow. Using what air she had left in her lungs, she screamed, hoping that all the emotions she felt would be expelled along with it.

She couldn't believe he'd actually said he wanted to be friends with her. It was impossible, wasn't it? She tried to wrap her brain around the idea, tried to look at it from every possible angle. She wasn't sure how long she sat on her couch thinking, but by the time she was finished, she'd decided that she didn't have to make a decision yet. It wasn't as if Scott asked if they could be friends again tomorrow. He simply said he *wanted* to be friends again. Therefore, she didn't need to tell Scott anything right now. She would simply continue on the path she was on and see where it led. And right now, her path led to Ethan.

Her body seemed to relax at the mere thought of Ethan. After the morning she had, all she wanted was to be with him—to lose herself in him and forget all about what happened with Scott. She glanced down at her watch again. *Eight hours and forty-five minutes, eight hours and forty-five minutes,* she thought with a smile. Her daydream of Ethan was interrupted when her cell rang.

"Hey, Soph," she answered, then leaned back on the couch.

"Are you home right now?" her friend asked frantically.

"Yeah. Why, what's going on?"

"I'll tell you when I get there."

Sophie hung up the phone before Kate could ask another question, and instantly there came a knock at the door.

"It's me, open up," Sophie yelled.

Kate stood up quickly and hurried to the door. "I'm coming!" she called out. Yanking the door open, she barely had time to step out of the way before Sophie barreled into the room. Her white-blond hair was pulled up in a messy knot and her eyes were wild.

"Do you know where Elle keeps her address book?" she yelled, scurrying down the hall.

"Umm, I'm not sure. Why? What do you need?" Kate followed after her.

"I need numbers! Specifically Graham's, but if I can't find his, anyone that knows him will do."

Kate walked into Elle's room to find her frantic friend digging through drawers. "Why do you need his number?"

Sophie wheeled around and looked at her like she'd suddenly sprouted two heads.

"Because I need to make plans."

Kate knew exactly what plan she was referring to and could only laugh as she thought about what her friend must be arranging. "Soph, do you think you could be getting a little carried away with all of this?"

"No," she said too quickly, before diving back into the drawers.

If there was one thing Kate had learned over the years, it was never to question Sophie—especially when she had a plan. She was never one to be deterred from a goal.

"Found it!" she squealed, waving her arms around.

"So, are you going to tell me what your plan is? Do I even want to know?"

"Yes, you want to know. And I'll tell you when it gets closer. Elle is too good at reading you. She'll know if something is up." Her eyes twinkled in mischief.

Kate laughed. "Sounds fine with me. It's safer if I don't know; wouldn't want something to slip out by accident."

"Good," she said with a smile. "So what's the plan for tonight? Has he told you where you're going?"

"No. But honestly I don't care where he takes me. All I care is that we'll be together." Kate shrugged.

"Yes, it matters. How are you supposed to choose an acceptable outfit if you don't know where you're going?" Sophie asked, as if her statement was common knowledge.

"I'm sure I can find something that will work for whatever he has planned."

"I don't think so, missy," Sophie said, waving her pointer finger. "Get your butt on that phone right now and call him."

"I'm *not* calling him. He's at work."

"At least try. If he's busy, you can leave a message, and he can call you back."

"No," Kate said, folding her arms.

Sophie stepped closer and challenged Kate. "Yes."

As much as Kate wanted to stand firm, she could feel her defenses falling. Her friend's persuasive ways were only part of it. In reality, she was aching to hear Ethan's voice.

"When is he picking you up?" the blonde asked, watching Kate closely, no doubt seeing the defeat in her eyes.

"In roughly eight in a half hours, give or take five minutes." Kate glanced down at her watch to confirm.

"Anxious, are we?" Sophie smiled.

"Maybe."

Kate turned around and started to walk out of the room, hoping that perhaps her friend would forget about the phone call.

"Go ahead and try to distract me, Kate!" she yelled after her. "I'm not leaving until you call him and I get to help you pick out an outfit."

Kate walked into her bedroom laughing. Planning to let her friend stew over things for a while, she settled in to do some work. Spending the next few hours at her desk, she finished editing pictures from a wedding she had recently shot. The entire time, she stole glances at her clock, feeling the butterflies get more intense as the time ticked slowly by. By the time five o'clock rolled around, she was so nervous she couldn't work any more. While shutting down her computer, she decided to relax and watch some TV before her date.

But before she had a chance to stand, Sophie barged into her room. "Okay, I've waited long enough. It's time to call." She picked up the phone and tossed it to her friend.

Kate went back and forth, debating whether she wanted him to answer. On the one hand, she wanted to hear his voice, and on the other, she didn't want to bother him. It only rang twice.

"Kate? Is everything okay?"

"No, no, everything's fine," she assured him.

He sighed. "Good. I thought for a minute you were canceling on me."

Sophie, annoyed that her friend wasn't getting to the point, gave her a not-so-friendly nudge.

"Ouch, Soph," Kate said, rubbing her arm.

Now Ethan was laughing. "What's she doing now?"

Kate eyed Sophie evilly. "She wants me to find out what you have planned for tonight."

He paused for a moment before speaking. "I'm not sure it would be appropriate to tell her." His voice was deep and sensual.

"Yes, well, I don't think we need to tell her *everything*," she flirted back. "But seriously, she won't leave me alone until I know something. She has a problem when it comes to fashion."

"You can tell her that I'll be taking you somewhere casual but nice. You'll be fine in pants."

"Pants, I can do. Let's see if she allows it." Kate laughed. "Okay, so I'll let you get back to saving lives. I'll see you soon?"

"Soon. I can't wait. I've been counting down the hours all day," he said.

Her heart skipped. "Me too," she admitted.

"I'm so glad to hear you say that. I'll be there in an hour and a half and not a minute later."

Kate ended her call with a big smile on her face. She looked to her friend on the bed beside her and was met with a smile that matched her own. "Work your magic," she said simply.

Sophie jumped off the bed and ran into the bathroom. "Let's get to work!"

With a calming exhale, Kate took once last glance at her watch. *One hour and twenty-eight minutes, one hour and twenty-eight minutes,* she recited as she followed after her friend.

℘

The last half hour of work dragged on, and Ethan continually checked his watch, counting down the minutes until he would see Kate. He had been so excited when she'd called that it only made him want to see her more. He planned on showering quickly at work, cutting out any extra time it would take for him to go home first.

As he made his way out of the hospital, he stopped off at the gift shop to pick up some flowers. Sure they were a little cliché, but he was a classic romantic at heart, and Kate deserved only the best. He was just about to head to his car when he heard the voice of the one person he'd been avoiding all day.

"Hello, Dr. Montgomery."

The thought crossed his mind to ignore her and continue walking, but it was obvious that he'd heard her. He turned around and was greeted by the ever-floozy Lisa.

"Where are you off to? Do you have a hot date or something?" she asked in a nasal voice.

Apparently, Ethan telling her that he wasn't interested in repeating their impromptu surprise date the other night still hadn't settled well with her. "As a matter of fact, yes, I do," he stated.

Her face puckered slightly as if tasting something bitter. "Well, isn't that nice. You have a great time, then, *Doctor*."

"Oh, I will." He smiled back pleasantly.

He climbed into his car and sped out of the parking lot, glancing down at his dashboard to check the time. *Forty-five minutes, forty-five minutes.*

Ethan raced up I-95 and sped through the winding roads toward New Hope. By the time he pulled onto Canal Street, he felt winded and anxious, which was ridiculous since he'd been driving, but he did all the same. Hurrying out of his car, he made his way up to her door. Taking one deep breath, he knocked.

Only a moment later, the door swung open and he was met with the most beautiful vision. Kate stood in front of him dressed in all black. Her chestnut hair fell down around her shoulders, with a few strands sweeping in front of her wide expressive eyes. She smiled at him shyly, and he grinned back, feeling completely at ease now that he was with her again.

"Hi," he managed to say.

"Hey." Kate's eyes trailed down his body. Even under his black coat, she could see how nice he looked.

"These are for you." Ethan held out a bouquet of bright gerbera daisies. Her face lit up and he knew that no matter how cliché his decision to get them for her was, it was the right one.

"Thank you. That's so nice of you." She smiled.

Ethan stepped forward with the flowers held out and leaned in, placing a soft kiss on her cheek. "There. That's a much better hello," he whispered, against her cheek. "Why don't you go put those in some water before I do something else and cause us to lose our reservations."

She giggled quietly and spun around. As she took a step away from Ethan, he finally got a view of the shirt she was wearing. The back of the sweater scooped down low and left her entire back open. Her skin looked so soft and fair in contrast to the dark sweater that all he wanted to do was touch her. He wasn't aware that he'd moaned out loud until Kate looked back at him.

"Are you okay?" she asked.

His mouth hung open as he searched for words. "I'm more than okay," he finally stammered. "That shirt is amazing on you."

Kate looked down and fiddled with the hem of the shirt. "Thanks."

"No, thank *you*," he said, not able to hide the rough tone his voice had just taken.

She smiled again and shook her head as she walked in the direction of the kitchen. With her out of sight, Ethan allowed himself a minute to regain his composure. If he was going to make it through this night without throwing her down on the table at the restaurant, he would need to get some control.

"So," he said when she walked back into the hall. "I thought that maybe we'd eat at a restaurant here in town. And since it's not too cold out, I thought it would be nice to walk there. I haven't had a chance to see much of the main street yet."

"That sounds like a perfect idea." Reaching out her hand, she intertwined her fingers with his, and pulled the door closed behind her.

They walked in comfortable silence until they hit Main Street. That's when Kate started pointing out the shops that were her favorites. Ethan noticed the way her eyes lit up when she spoke about the town she'd grown to love. The galleries, the little boutiques, the diverse culture that surrounded her were what drew her in. She grew excited about the littlest details, and he couldn't help but smile as he watched her.

"Oh, and Gerenser's has got the most amazing ice cream. Their strawberry is my favorite." She gave him a playful wink and went on to explain the next shop they passed.

It didn't take long before they reached the bridge that crossed a section of the canal. They both slowed to a stop. "Have you seen a show at the playhouse?" Ethan asked, looking across the water.

"No, not yet. I plan on it though."

"Maybe that's something we should plan together," Ethan suggested, wrapping his arm around her.

"I'd like that." Kate nodded as she pressed herself into his side. The two stood, wrapped up in each other, listening to the sounds of the water rushing below them. In the back of her mind, Kate knew this moment was one that she'd remember forever. The feelings she was experiencing, the happiness of being with him, of simply being in his company, were something she would never forget. It would forever be engrained—a perfect memory.

Eventually it was time to head to the restaurant. Side by side they walked, and Ethan veered them to the right, down Ferry Street. There, nestled along the water, was the yellow house with white trim that was Martine's River House Restaurant.

Her eyes lit up. "I've wanted to try this place."

"Well, it's a good thing we're eating here then." Ethan smiled and pulled the brown wooden door open.

They were greeted immediately and led through the restaurant to their table. Kate lifted her eyes to the dark beams that ran the span of the ceiling. Green plants and white lights announced the entrance to the glassed-in porch where tables were set in white floor-length cloths with accents of blue. They sat down at a table by the window, which offered a beautiful view of the Delaware River.

"So, is tonight my turn?" Kate asked, once their drink orders were placed and they were left alone.

"Your turn?"

"To ask you every question imaginable." She laughed.

"Go right ahead." Ethan motioned for her to begin.

Her brows rose as she thought. "Favorite color?"

"Blue."

"Favorite food?"

He withheld a laugh and tried to answer with a straight face. "Peaches and strawberries."

Immediately, Kate dropped her head back and laughed freely. "I should have known that one," she said, shaking her head from side to side. "Okay, what about childhood make-believe friends? I told you all about my imaginary unicorn, which by the way, you'd better never tell anyone about. What about you, did you have any?"

"George."

"Who?" she asked with a smirk.

"George," Ethan repeated in a matter of fact tone. "George was my make-believe friend that helped me fight crime. I didn't have a brother so I had to be imaginative."

Kate burst out laughing. Ethan soon joined her, and it took a minute before they could speak easily.

"Favorite movie?" she asked, after composing herself and taking a sip of water.

"'Quiet...what's that smell?'" Ethan quoted.

She swallowed. "What?"

"It's from *Batches*. I guess you haven't seen it. One of my favorite lines is when Mike Myers asks him how he got home and he says—"

Kate cut him off before he could get another word in and recited the line from the movie perfectly, even attempting a British accent. When she was finished, she realized how loud she must have been and clamped her hand over her mouth. "Sorry," she said in a hushed voice, trying to suppress a giggle.

"Are you kidding?" he laughed. "That was great."

"Yeah, well, it's one of my favorites too."

They continued quoting lines back and forth until their waiter took their order. It wasn't long before their meals arrived, and once they did, the conversation slowed, but only slightly. Kate continued to ask questions between bites, and Ethan continued to answer, adding bits of random information here and there. He couldn't remember the last time he was so engulfed in a conversation or so consumed by a person in all his life. It was thrilling, to say the least.

On numerous occasions, he found himself staring at her mouth, watching the way it moved as she talked or the way she licked her lips between bites. Not wanting her to notice, he attempted to focus on something else, but that didn't work either. Her expressive eyes were just as intoxicating and had a way of pulling him in. He hadn't realized how entranced he was until Kate stopped talking and cocked her head to the side.

"What?" she asked, breaking him out of his trance.

He blinked. "I'm sorry. I just got a little distracted."

"Distracted?"

It wasn't until Ethan really looked at her that he realized she was completely unaware of what had transpired. She was clueless as to how beautiful she was to him, and that only made him want her more.

"You're beautiful, and I don't think you understand how entirely drawn to you I am."

Her already large eyes grew wide at his response and her lips spread into the smile that Ethan was beginning to think he wouldn't be able to live a day without seeing.

"Do you want to get out of here? We can get our dessert to go."

Her words caught Ethan off guard, but he wasn't about to turn her down. He couldn't imagine a more comfortable setting than sitting on a couch with

Kate and eating dessert. Signaling for the waiter, they placed their order for the chocolate mousse and paid the bill.

The comfortable conversation they'd had during dinner continued the entire walk home. When they turned onto Kate's street, she was in the midst of telling a story about her first camping experience with her two best friends.

"You should have seen their faces when I told them there were no bathrooms. I thought for sure they were going to kill me," she said with a laugh.

Her eyes sparkled as she talked about her friends. Her adoration for them was evident. And after seeing the way they acted around her, Ethan knew their feelings were mutual.

"I don't know Sophie very well," he started, "but from what I can gather, she's a lot like Elle. From what I've seen, Elle's pretty much the same as she was when we were kids, and I can guarantee you, she would never have gone to a place with no running water."

They were in the hallway just outside the kitchen when Kate turned around. "I always forget that you know Elle and Logan. It's so nice not having to worry about them approving of who I date. Their opinion is important to me and you're important to me..." Her voice trailed off, nervous that she'd said too much. "Do you want some water or something?" she asked quickly trying to change the subject.

"Sure."

She took a deep breath and walked into the kitchen, flicking on the under-counter lights, casting a soft glow around the kitchen. Ethan followed behind her and watched the small curve of her back as she grabbed two bottles of water out of the refrigerator. Her skin looked so soft and smooth that he wanted nothing more than to touch it. Turning around slowly, she looked into his eyes, and Ethan wondered briefly if she could see how much he wanted her.

Taking a step toward her, he took the two bottles from her hands and placed them on the counter. Finally getting what he wanted, he reached around her and placed his hands on her bare back, sliding his fingers across her silky skin.

He leaned in. "You're important to me too, you know," he whispered in her ear.

Kate closed her eyes and let the words he spoke register in her mind. She relaxed under his touch and inhaled calmly. Turning her head to the side, she grazed her lips across his jaw until she met his lips. She kissed them twice, softly, before moving back to his jaw and down his neck, leaving a trail of kisses behind her.

"Let's go in the other room and have our dessert," she breathed into his ear before turning away and grabbing their water bottles.

Her words went straight through Ethan's body. He felt like a teenager around her and was finding it hard to know how to act. He was lost in her, everything about her.

With a quiet groan, he picked up the take-out bag and followed in the direction Kate had gone. She was already in the living room, seated on the couch with her feet curled up under her. He paused in the doorway, admiring her beauty. The dim light from the side lamp reflected off her skin, making her glow. When she noticed his watchful eyes, she patted the seat beside her. He followed her silent order and sat down, fighting off his urges to make out with her like an adolescent schoolboy. Looking for a distraction, he decided dessert would be the safest bet. He grabbed the Styrofoam box and opened it up. The rich aroma of chocolate wafted through the air.

"Umm, that looks and smells delicious." The pitch of her voice rose and her eyes were wide.

"What is it with women and chocolate?" Ethan asked with a laugh.

"Oh, come on, who doesn't like chocolate?" She grabbed the container from his hands and held it up, showing the contents. "You can't tell me this doesn't look delicious."

Completely ignoring the chocolate filled container, Ethan looked directly into Kate's eyes. "Yes, it does. It looks delicious." He leaned forward slightly, hoping that she would understand his advances.

Without taking her eyes from his, she placed the container on the coffee table and shifted closer. "I guess that part of dessert can wait," she said in a low voice.

Thank you, Ethan thought and immediately grabbed hold of her waist, pulling her toward him. They both clung to each other, not able to get enough. He pulled away from her lips only long enough for her to catch her breath and turned his attention to her neck. Sliding his nose along her jaw line, he breathed in her scent, all woman and delicious. He stopped just short of her earlobe and gently traced it with his tongue. Kate released a breathy sigh that sent chills down his spine.

"You have no idea what you do to me," he said roughly.

She hummed in response and dropped her head back to one side, exposing her bare neck. He kissed along the path of a blue vein that ran the line of her throat and felt the pulse under his tongue as he tasted her skin. His hands were itching to move, desperate to touch the curves of her body, and when Kate arched her back toward him, silently urging him onward, he did just that. Swallowing thickly, he followed her lead and allowed his hands to roam her waist, her smooth back, her firm stomach. She was perfect.

Kate kept her eyes closed and was lost in the sensation of his mouth on her lips and her neck. Everywhere he touched felt on fire and it was almost overwhelming.

Sensual kisses slowed until they were tender and loving. Ethan memorized every inch of skin he felt and every freckle he saw. He traced the lines of her face and the curve of her lips before covering them with his once more. When they finally parted, both of them appeared to be in a daze. Light flickered in Kate's heavily lidded eyes, and the pink of her cheeks looked like a permanent blush. She curled up beside him and nuzzled into his neck.

"Do you want that dessert now?" she asked, her voice slightly raspy, like raw silk.

"That sounds great." He nodded, maneuvering their bodies into a more comfortable position. "There, now I'm ready for some chocolate."

"I thought you'd never say that." She laughed, quickly reaching for the mousse. Scooping a large bite onto her fork, she popped it in her mouth and immediately moaned in satisfaction.

"Good dessert?" he asked.

"What, this?" She motioned to the mousse. "Oh, this is all right," she said in an indifferent tone.

Ethan was shocked. "All right? You *do* know that's one of the chef's specialties right?"

"Like I said, it's all right." She shrugged. "I simply think the first dessert I had was better." She smiled and gave him a playful wink.

Ethan returned her smile and didn't argue. After all, he didn't have to taste the mousse to know she was right.

Chapter 17
Desperate Times

Ethan woke the next morning to the shrill sound of his cell phone cutting through his sleepy haze. Blindly feeling around on his nightstand, he looked at the screen with squinting eyes, not recognizing the number.

"Hello?" he asked, confusion lacing his voice.

"Hey, Ethan. It's Sophie."

"Oh, hey, how's it going?"

"I'm fine. But I'll be *great* if you can help me out with something."

Making a mental note that Sophie wasn't much for small talk, he propped himself up on his pillows and wiped the sleep from his eyes. "Okay, shoot."

"I need you to talk to Trent and see if he can get us football tickets for two weeks from tonight."

"I don't think that will be a problem. He'll probably have us sit in one of the boxes with the other players' families."

"Really? That's even better."

Ethan could almost hear the gears shifting while she absorbed the new information. "Does this have something to do with your master plan?" he asked knowingly.

"Yes. And if you don't do your part, it won't work, so I need you to swear to me that you will." Her voice rose to a desperate level.

"I swear. I'll talk to Trent, and we'll be there with bells on," he assured her.

"Good." Sophie felt her anxiety click down a notch. "Now, there is one more *little* thing I need you to do," she said casually.

"And what's that?"

"I need you to keep the new *Sports Illustrated* issue away from Trent." Her words rushed out, toppling over one another, but she was fairly certain he'd heard her. There was silence on the other end.

Sophie didn't know Trent at all, but from what Ethan had told her about him, she knew that he was a huge *Sports Illustrated* fan and the swimsuit issue was probably his favorite. It was *every* man's favorite issue.

"Ethan, are you going to say something?" The silence continued. "Ethan?"

"Sophie, I don't think you realize how hard that's going to be. There are few things in life that Trent counts down for. The Super Bowl, Thanksgiving, the Annual Philadelphia Car Show, Christmas, and the swimsuit issue of *Sports Illustrated*."

"Come on," she begged. "If there is one person I know can do it, it's you. I need you to do this or nothing else will work." She was met with silence once again and found herself holding her breath.

"Fine." He sighed. "I'll try. But I can't promise anything."

"Thank you, thank you, thank you!" she squealed. "Now, the issue is released the same day as the game, so make sure to check the mailbox. He can't see it before the game. Do whatever it takes. Desperate times call for desperate measures, Ethan."

He laughed at her choice of words. "Whatever you say, Sophie."

The two said their goodbyes, and Ethan laughed once more to himself. He'd never before met someone with Sophie's enthusiasm and excitement for life. She was quickly becoming one of his new favorite people.

Rolling over in bed, he took a moment to relax and enjoy the picture that hung on his wall. His thoughts immediately turned to Kate. At the time he'd purchased it, he had no idea that he would meet its maker again. He knew she was special the first moment he saw her and never in his life had he experienced something like that. Just thinking back to that moment and the energy he had felt made his body feel alive.

He remembered exactly how she looked. How her dark eyes grew angry when she thought he doubted her talent. Watching her get flustered when he told her that he thought she was beautiful. At the time, he knew he'd probably never see her again and he needed to have something to remind him of her. That's when he'd decided that he needed the picture, *her* picture. The very one that they'd met in front of.

He stood in front of it now, admiring the colors that danced off of it. The orange-red hue that grew darker as it met the gray sky. The way the tree stood alone, strong and dark against the colorful backdrop. It was beautiful, just like the person who took it.

Ethan hadn't told her about his purchase. He was hoping that someday soon he'd be able to show her. He smiled as he thought of her and grabbed his phone. It was still early, but he was willing to take his chances. It went straight to voicemail, and even though he was disappointed he couldn't speak with her, he was glad to have heard her voice. After leaving her a brief message, he grabbed his shoes and headed out to the living room.

Trent was sitting on the couch half-naked, eating a bowl of cereal and watching ESPN. He noticed Ethan walk in and flashed him a knowing grin.

"How was your night?" he asked with implication while swallowing another mouthful.

"Great," Ethan replied simply. "How was yours?"

"Oh, come on. You finally score a hot date with the produce chick, and you're not gonna dish?"

"Her name is Kate. And no, I'm not dishing on anything."

"Fine," he said, returning to his Cocoa Pebbles.

Looking for a way to change the subject, Ethan turned his attention to the TV. The announcer was discussing the upcoming playoff games, and he figured it was perfect timing to act on Sophie's wishes. "Hey, do you think you could get a bunch of us in for the game?" he asked casually.

Trent faced him with raised eyebrows. "Maybe."

Ethan knew exactly what he was getting at. Trent wasn't going to give in unless he did. "Fine. We went out to dinner, had a great discussion, went back to her place, and hooked up."

Ethan was never the kiss-and-tell type, but Sophie's phrase 'desperate times call for desperate measures' kept running through his mind.

Trent's smile grew even wider and he pumped his fists in the air, splattering milk from the end of his spoon. "Now that's what I'm talking about. It's about time."

"What are you talking about? It hasn't been that long," Ethan defended himself.

Trent's celebration stopped short and he looked at his friend. "Okay, so maybe it hasn't been that long if you count Cindy. But seriously, do you really want to count her? The psycho harpy needs to be erased from your memory." He waved his hand around as if swatting a fly. "How's that going by the way? You see her at work yet?"

Just the mention of Cindy made Ethan's skin crawl. "Thanks for bringing that up," he said sarcastically. "I think she'll be in later today."

One of the many down sides of Cindy being a medical sales rep was that it was inevitable that Ethan would run into her. No matter how hard he tried, it was bound to happen.

"Good luck with that," Trent snickered while turning to the TV. "Oh," he paused. "Just so you know, the countdown has begun. We are down to fourteen days."

"What?"

Trent looked at his friend like he was an idiot. "Come on, Ethan, you know I don't count down days unless it's something good."

Suddenly it hit him. "*Sports Illustrated*," he said out loud with a nod.

"No, Ethan. It's not *just Sports Illustrated*. It's the swimsuit issue of *Sports Illustrated*—the issue that every guy waits months to get. And I, for one, am dying to see who they got for the cover this year. They're keeping it under wraps."

"I'm sure whoever they get will be spectacular." Ethan walked into the kitchen when he remembered that Trent still hadn't answered his initial question. "So can you get us into the game, or what?"

"Are you forgetting who you're talking to? I can get you into the box; don't you worry."

He shook his head laughing and grabbed a cereal bowl. At that moment, Trent walked in and Ethan noticed for the first time that his friend was wearing his scrubs. "Trent, do you think you could not wear my work clothes to sleep in?"

"What? They're comfortable. Besides it's not like you don't have, like, twenty pairs."

"Yeah, well, make sure you wash them before returning them."

"Who says I'm giving them back?" he asked with a grin.

Ethan rolled his eyes and laughed. "Fine, keep them."

"Thanks, bro." He grabbed the box of Cocoa Pebbles and poured another bowl. "Hey, you never told me how many people are coming to the game."

"Uh…" He stalled, not knowing if he should tell him about Elle, but figured it couldn't hurt. After all, Trent had never learned her name. "There will be six of us, including you. And we're all going out after the game."

"Six? Who's all going?"

"Me and Kate, my old friend Logan—you remember me telling you about him, right? Anyway, he'll be there with his girlfriend, Sophie, and … his sister, Elle," he mumbled through her name.

Apparently, his attempt failed. Trent choked on his cereal as he looked at him with wide eyes. It took him a minute before he could start talking. "Are you talking about chubby Elle? The girl you knew when you were little? What did you call her again? Softy, mushy?"

"Squish. We used to call her Squish. And Trent, she doesn't look like that now. She's really … nice."

"Nice? Ethan, you *do* know that 'nice' is like the code word for 'fat,' right?"

"Don't worry," he said with a laugh. "I'm sure you'll be able to handle her."

"Whatever, man. I'll go, but you're going to owe me big time," Trent said, walking back into the living room.

Once his friend was out of earshot, Ethan laughed to himself. "No, Trent, I'm pretty sure you'll owe *me* big time."

℮

The first half of Ethan's work day went by quickly, but it was daunting. Try as he might, he couldn't shake his sour attitude. Of course, everything changed as soon as Kate returned his call. Simply hearing her voice seemed to make all the difference. They made plans to meet up later that night after he finished with work, and Ethan hung up feeling an immediate change in his mood.

"Well, it looks like someone is having a good day," Henry said upon seeing Ethan's smile. "Does this have something to do with a certain lady by the name of Kate?"

"Trent told you, I assume?"

"Of course," he said with a nod. "She's a sweet girl. And I'm glad to see you happy."

"Wait, what?" he asked, turning to face him. "How do you know Kate?"

"I've treated her friend a few times, and Kate's always been the one to bring her in."

"Oh," Ethan realized aloud as he thought back to the conversation he'd had with her more than a week ago.

"You'll have to bring her over to the house sometime for dinner. I know Lori would love to meet her. You know how she feels about meeting the girls you date."

"I know," Ethan said with a laugh. Lori was like a second mother to him, and she was always concerned about his well-being. Nothing brought her more joy than knowing that he and Trent were happy. "I'll talk to Kate and get back to you."

"I'll let Lori know. She'll be thrilled. Especially since that son of ours hasn't dated anyone seriously in over a year," he said, rolling his eyes.

"He'll find someone soon enough. He just hasn't met his match. Actually, he has," he said to himself out loud, "he just doesn't know who she is yet." Henry looked at him with furrowed brows, confused by his cryptic statement. "Don't worry. You'll find out soon enough," he assured.

"Whatever you say, Ethan." He shook his head. "I have to go finish my rounds. I'll see you later."

"All right, see ya."

Still laughing to himself, Ethan made his way over to the nurse's station, but froze when he heard a familiar laugh. He swallowed slowly and continued on his route. Surprisingly, Cindy was not alone. Slouched down beside her was Lisa. *Great, now I have to deal with both of them,* he thought with a groan. "Ladies," he said, tipping his head in acknowledgment.

"It's so good to see you again, Ethan," Cindy sneered. "It's funny that you should walk up right now. We were just discussing you," she said in an overly sweet voice.

"Really? Interesting, since I never discuss you."

Cindy's fake façade fell for an instant before her smile returned. "Oh, I'm sure that isn't true. Surely you must have mentioned me to your new girlfriend?" Ethan's back stiffened, but he didn't respond. Apparently Lisa had done her job in filing everyone in on the hospital gossip. "And if not her, then I'm sure you've mentioned me to your parents. By the way, how are they doing? It's been ages since I've talked to Sabrina. I was thinking about giving her a call and arranging a friendly tennis match the next time she's in town."

"They're doing fine, actually," he stalled. "And calling them won't be necessary. I'll make sure to give them your regards." He handed Lisa one of the charts in his hands. "When you're finished spreading the latest *news,* I'd like for you to check on Mr. Harris in room two-fifteen. He's still waiting on his meds."

Lisa's eyes were wide as she studied his face, surprised by his attitude. "Okay, sure," she said warily.

Ethan quickly turned on his heel and walked away. His mind couldn't even wrap around the idea of Cindy calling his mother right now. But he wasn't about to put it past her.

Unfortunately, Cindy had met his parents on one of their visits, and his mother seemed to take a liking to her. Whether it was just because she wanted him to finally settle down, he wasn't sure. But whatever the reason, she got it in her head that the two were going to get married. 'A perfect match' she'd called them. Cindy's parents were well-known in the community and very well off. *As if that's a perfect reason to stay together*, he scoffed to himself. How she couldn't see through Cindy's act was still a mystery to him.

The pressure to call his parents and inform them of his break-up was building. He knew it had to be done—especially since he wanted them to know about Kate. He wanted them to see how happy she made him and how perfect they were for each other.

With a smile on his face, Ethan walked down the hallway and allowed himself to imagine his life in twenty years with Kate by his side.

Chapter 18
Revelations

Two weeks. I can't believe it's been two weeks. Two of the most amazing weeks of my life, Kate thought as she stared blankly at the computer screen in front of her. For the past fourteen days, she and Ethan had seen each other almost every day. They would sit and talk for hours either on the phone or cuddled up on her couch. His voice had become the first thing she heard in the morning and the last voice she heard at night. Their relationship was growing into something that she knew was special, and she was certain he felt the same way.

Everything in her life was just as it should be, and surprisingly, her relationship with Scott was included in that. Taking some time to settle down after the last run in she'd had with him, Kate thought about what he'd said. He wanted to be friends again. At the time, she wasn't sure it was possible, but her opinion soon changed. It started with a few friendly emails where he'd tell her the random happenings of his day. At first she didn't respond to them, but the more he wrote, the more comfortable she felt. After all, they had been friends first before anything had happened between them. It was easy to have a casual friendship.

He'd even mention his girlfriend, Samantha, and Kate would, in turn, tell him about what she and Ethan had planned for the evening. His mentioning his girlfriend didn't bother her like she thought it might. In fact, it only proved that they could indeed be friends and nothing more.

The only time her heart ached was when he'd mention their old friends. Cutting off contact with Scott had its price, and it came in the form of his friends—the same friends she'd grown to love over the years. But now things were different. If she and Scott were finally able to be friends—just friends—then that meant she'd have that connection again.

Her thoughts were interrupted when she heard the banging of kitchen cabinets. She knew that only meant one thing: Elle was awake and she was trying to cook. Kate quickly closed her email, not wanting to risk Elle walking in and seeing it. She felt bad about hiding her friendship with Scott from her roommate and Sophie, but knew that it would only make things complicated.

"Where in the hell is the coffee?" Elle yelled out as Kate walked into the kitchen.

Elle continued to ramble to herself as she slammed cabinet after cabinet shut. Lately her nerves had been running thin, which was surprising considering the turn her life had taken in the past two weeks. Ever since finding out she was a top choice for the cover of *Sports Illustrated*, she'd been waiting with bated breath to find out if she'd gotten it. And just over a week ago, while she was in New York for business, they told her that she was this year's choice. Along with the cover came a lot of promotional work that would keep her schedule busy for the next month. The most important, and for *her* the most exciting, was taking place the same day the magazine was released. As the year's cover model, it was arranged that she flip a coin at the start of the Eagles game. For Elle, the news was almost as exciting as landing the cover. She'd been on cloud nine ever since. But now that the day was actually here, she was a ball of nerves.

"Do you need help?" Kate asked quietly in an attempt to not anger the beast.

"Yes. And why the hell can't I find anything in this stupid kitchen?" she spat back. As soon as the words were out of her mouth, she spun around and met her friend's eyes with a repentant face. "I'm sorry," she sighed. "I'm just so nervous about this whole reveal that they have set up. I mean, why couldn't they just release the information like they normally do? I can't seem to function."

"Elle, you're never nervous," Kate reminded her. "You're going to be great. Plus, we'll all be there."

"Speaking of that, when are you going to tell me more about this guy you're setting me up with?"

"There's really nothing to tell." She shrugged. "His name is Trent, and he's Ethan's best friend."

Elle knew her friend was hiding something; she could feel it. "Yeah, you keep acting secretive." She pointed her finger at Kate. "But I'm warning you, if this guy ends up being some crazy psycho, I will get revenge on your sweet ass."

"Who has a sweet ass?" Sophie chirped as she poked her head into the kitchen, causing both Elle and Kate to jump.

"Hey! What are you doing here?"

"I just stopped by to see how you were doing. I figured we could hang out for a bit before the game." Sophie smiled.

Elle swept her hair up into a clip. "I'm a little nervous, slightly more so now that you mentioned the game." She eyed Sophie. "But it's nothing that can't be flushed out with a little kickboxing."

"Ah, nothing like taking out all the built up tension on a punching bag," the blond friend agreed.

"Or a horny gym rat," Kate added.

"I couldn't agree more." That being said, Elle grabbed her keys and a newly poured cup of coffee, then headed to the door. "I'll catch you guys later."

Both friends yelled their goodbyes, and once alone, looked at each other with mischievous grins.

"Do you think she has any clue who Trent is?" Sophie asked.

"Are you kidding? She's so nervous about flipping the coin, she can't focus on anything else."

"Perfect." Sophie smiled. "Now it's all up to Ethan. Let's hope he can keep his friend distracted."

"Have some faith, Soph. Ethan can do anything." Kate laughed. "This is going to be good."

"No," Sophie corrected. "This is going to be *great.*"

❧

"Trent. Hey, Trent! Get up." Ethan tossed a pillow at his friend's head and hoped that did the trick.

"Ethan," he warned. "You better not be waking me up unless you have a big cup of coffee and the *Sports Illustrated.*"

"Uh, no. Sorry, I don't. But I can go make us some coffee, if that will help."

Trent lifted his head and saw his friend dressed in his hiking gear. "Why are you dressed like you're going for a hike?" he asked him.

"I'm dressed like this because *we* are going hiking."

"No, I'm not going," Trent moaned.

"Come on, it'll be fun."

"No, no, no." He shook his head. "Today is 'SISSI' day. I'm not going anywhere."

"SISSI day?" Ethan asked curiously.

His friend rolled his eyes and let out a frustrated sigh. "*Sports Illustrated* swimsuit issue."

"Oh, come on, Trent. You'll have plenty of time to pick up a magazine. We'll just go for a little while."

A staring contest was begun between the two friends, and when Ethan didn't let up, Trent groaned. "Fine, let me just grab my stuff."

With a satisfied smile, Ethan left his friend to get ready and prepared himself for the apologizing that he'd be doing in the not too distant future.

⌒

"For the last time, Trent, I'm sorry that we got lost."

"There is no *we*; *you* got us lost." Trent rolled his eyes. His normally carefree attitude had drastically changed after the fifth hour of walking. Their short little hike ended up taking all day because Ethan apparently 'forgot' how to get back to the car. Now they were pressed for time.

"We could always call the girls and tell them that we'll meet them later," Ethan suggested. Trent didn't respond. Ethan knew better than anyone that his friend never missed kickoff. He even recalled a time when Trent compared it to skipping the stockings at Christmas and going straight to the tree. To him, everything had a specific order to be followed, and it didn't work any other way. He was always there, on the sidelines, when the game started, whether he was suited up to play or not.

"Just pull over at the 7-Eleven so I can get the magazine."

At Trent's words, Ethan stiffened. "How about we go home first, and then we can—"

"No." His friend cut him off.

With a defeated sigh, Ethan pulled over at the closest 7-Eleven and wondered how bad it would be when Sophie found out he didn't hold up his side of the plan.

Trent walked into the convenience store and made his way over to the magazine rack. Skimming the covers, he saw every magazine except the one he was looking for.

"Can I help you find something?" the store clerk asked with a knowing smile.

"Ah, I'm just looking for—"

"The *Sports Illustrated*?" the man finished.

"Yeah, how'd you guess?"

"Every guy that's come in this morning has purchased one. I sold the last one an hour ago. I've never seen them go so fast. It is quite a cover."

He raised his eyebrows. Silently cursing Ethan for making him late, Trent spun on his heel and was just about to walk out when the man spoke up again. "You're not an Eagles fan, are you?"

With a chuckle, Trent looked back at him. "You could say I'm one of their *biggest* fans. Why?"

"Apparently she's going to be there tonight, at the game."

"What? Who?" he asked in confusion.

"The girl from the cover. Didn't you see the paper this morning?" the clerk picked up a paper and tossed it to Trent.

Flipping open to the sports page, he noticed the article on the bottom right corner. "*Sports Illustrated model expected to flip.*" His eyes quickly scanned over the article. It explained that the model who had graced the cover of this month's issue was flipping the coin at the start of the game.

Trent's once gloomy mood changed instantly. He tossed some money on the counter and walked outside with the newspaper in hand and a smile on his face.

Ethan noticed his friend's expression. "That great of a cover, huh?"

"Don't know. They were out."

"And you're okay with this?"

"I am now." He reached over and punched Ethan's shoulder before tossing the article on his lap.

Ethan's eyes narrowed as he skimmed over the paper and read the information he already knew. He was just thankful that there wasn't a picture. The last thing he wanted was to be the reason Sophie's plan didn't work. "Well, let's go."

With an excited nod, Trent turned up the volume on the radio and sat back. His plans for the evening were quickly looking up.

"They said they'd let us know where to meet them," Ethan said for the second time. He watched as his friend shifted from one foot to the other.

Ever since they'd arrived at the stadium, Trent had a one-track mind. All he cared about was getting on the field so he could get a closer look at the model everyone was talking about. Since they'd arrived, Ethan had almost corrected his friend twice that 'the model' he continued to refer to had a name. He was surprised at how hard keeping a simple detail from his friend actually was. Thankfully, his cell phone rang and he didn't have to think about it much longer.

After a short conversation with Kate, he snapped his phone shut and looked to his eager friend. "They want us to meet them in the hallway out in front of the tunnel."

"Sounds good to me." Trent quickly took off without a second thought, and Ethan followed close behind him.

They made their way through the stadium, and once closer to the tunnel, Trent finally slowed down. There were more people standing around than usual, and he hoped it had something to do with the mystery model. But before he could get a good look, Ethan led them over to a small group that stood off to the side and began making introductions.

"It's nice to meet you," Trent said after meeting Kate. "This guy won't shut up about you. You know, I've wanted to thank you. Ever since he's met you, we've had a serious influx of produce in the house. I don't think I've ever felt so healthy."

Kate burst into laughter. "What can I say? I'm good with produce." She shrugged.

Trent laughed with her, then turned his attention to the group of people standing close by. "Wonder if they're all here because of the swimsuit chick. I hear she's hot." He shook his head. "They've been keeping her identity under wraps. Usually they aren't so secretive."

Logan listened closely and was just about to comment when his phone rang. Turning away for a moment, he only spoke a few words before ending his call. "That was my sister," he said to Trent. "She's just a little nervous."

Trent furrowed his brow, and then it hit him. "That's right—Squish," he said aloud. "She's your sister."

"Yep," Logan confirmed.

Nodding his head, Trent looked a little closer at the guy standing in front of him. He wasn't bad looking for a dude, and he hoped that maybe Logan and his sister had that in common. Just thinking about suffering through a blind date made his head hurt. His only solace was the fact that he'd be watching a game from the sidelines. After a good game, he could endure anything. Even a date that he didn't want to be on.

"There she is. Hey, Elle, over here!" Sophie's musical voice rang through Trent's ears, pulling him from his thoughts.

Closing his eyes briefly, he prepared himself and slowly turned around. He scanned the area, looking for anyone who might resemble Logan, but didn't get far before he was distracted. He caught a glimpse of the most perfect set of legs in red heels walking toward him. Fearing that if he allowed himself to continue to the rest of her body, he'd be a goner, he kept his eyes focused on the legs.

Eventually his eyes won out and he gave in, slowly lifting his head. Elle's hips swayed side to side like a metronome keeping the rhythm of her strut, and the red dress she wore clung tightly to the curves of her body. He felt a lump forming in his throat, and he hadn't even looked at her face yet. He inhaled deeply and closed his eyes, willing her to be gone when they opened. There was no way she could be as good as his imagination could make her up to be.

After a few calming breaths, he felt his body begin to relax. Then he heard her voice. A voice that he was fairly certain he'd recognize anywhere. The same rich, commanding voice that he assumed he'd never hear again.

"Well, if it isn't Mr. Rumble himself," Elle purred, crossing her arms.

Trent rocked on his heels and opened his eyes, finally focusing on the face that he now knew belonged to that amazing body. "Hey, tire chick. What are you doing here? You come to hang in the parking lot on the off chance someone might get a flat?"

She smiled back cunningly. "Well, you know, I sat around all day wondering where I'd find clueless people. Then it hit me. Dumb jocks will be at the football game. And since most of them don't know their dick from a wrench, I figured my expertise could be useful."

Trent was so mesmerized by her lips that he barely caught everything she said. But his ears perked up what she started talking dirty. "If you want to keep talking dirty, I'm sure we could find a better place to carry on with this conversation."

She pursed her lips together, annoyed, but her eyes held a glint. "As tempting as that sounds, I think I'll pass. Now if you'll excuse me, I have a date that's waiting." Elle turned away, tossing her dark hair over her shoulder and took a step toward her best friends who were watching her with wide eyes. "What?" she questioned.

Behind her back, Trent looked at Ethan and pointed, silently mouthing the word 'Squish.' Ethan nodded and grinned ear to ear. In the two seconds it took Trent to realize that the tire chick was in fact Elle, his blind date, his confidence doubled. He walked over to her casually and froze directly behind her.

"Where is this Trent guy anyway? I thought you guys said he'd be here," Elle ranted.

Leaning forward slowly, Trent placed his lips against her ear. "I'm right here, darling," he whispered.

Elle's back stiffened and her breath caught. She was still for only a moment before whipping around to face him. Miscalculating the distance between them, she ended up a lot closer to him than intended. "Sorry," she mumbled as her brown eyes flickered up to his green.

In that brief second, Trent saw the vulnerability that lay within her. The strong, gorgeous, confident, sexy woman had weaknesses and he knew he wouldn't stop until he found all of them.

Ethan took advantage of the odd moment of silence and stepped forward, holding out his hand in introduction. "Elle, this is my best friend, Trent Williams."

As soon as she heard his full name, a light went off. "Trent Williams? As in Trent Asher Williams?" She eyed him suspiciously, but couldn't hide the shock on her face. She knew that he looked familiar when she first saw him, but had never put it together.

"In the flesh." He smiled, realizing that she finally recognized him. She slowly looked him up and down, and although Trent felt like a piece of meat, he couldn't deny that he liked it.

Elle let out a quiet sigh, and Trent knew he had her, hook, line, and sinker. "Can't say I'm too impressed, you look bigger on TV," she said with a shrug. And just like that Trent's upper hand was nonexistent.

Sophie, sensing the tension building between them, stepped in. "Well, why don't we get this show started," she said, rubbing her hands together.

"Sounds like a great idea," Logan agreed, wrapping his arm around her waist, smiling.

At that exact moment, one of the men who'd been standing with the larger group stepped forward and stood directly in front of Elle and Trent. He had a few magazines in his hand. "We want to get a few copies of these signed for a raffle drawing, if that's all right."

Trent, knowing that this was a perfect moment to show off for Elle, straightened his back and puffed out his chest confidently. "Sure, I'd love to, anything for the fans." He reached forward and was just about to take the magazines when they were pulled away. Puzzled, he looked at the man who was staring directly at Elle.

"I'm talking to Miss McLean." He directed his attention to Elle. "We've got a table set up if you'd like a place to sit, and I've been informed that they'll be ready for you on the field as soon as you finish."

"What the—?" Trent's mouth hung open and he turned to Elle.

"Sounds great." She smiled.

Trent was taken aback. *What about being on the field?* he thought. Trying to understand what he'd just heard, he quickly looked to Ethan.

With a simple nod, Ethan looked down at the stack of magazines Elle held in her hands. Following the direction of his friend's eyes, Trent froze when he saw the cover that he'd been waiting months to see. The model was beautiful. Her legs, her hair, her smooth skin, her flat stomach, the voluptuous curve of her hips, her dark eyes, and full lips were almost too much for him to take in. She was perfect, the epitome of an exotic beauty surrounded by white sand and green palms, and she was standing less than five feet from him.

Within the five seconds it took him to absorb every detail of the picture, he'd had at least fifteen different fantasies, all of them revolving around the woman that stood in front of him. The same woman who, not too long ago, had cut him off at the knees and in one fell swoop, swept him off of his feet.

Elle looked up from signing the magazines and glanced at Trent, desperate to see his reaction to the cover. Try as she might, she couldn't help but be attracted to him. Yes, he was the jock she met on the side of the road that she swore she'd never go after, but there was just something about him that drew her in.

Then to find out that he was *the* Trent Asher Williams—the same T.A.W. who had over fifteen touchdown receptions as a tight end last season—was almost too much to take in. She silently scolded herself for not recognizing him earlier and allowed her eyes to dash over to him again briefly. As it turned out, a brief glance was all it took and Elle's imagination ran wild.

She took a calming breath and told herself to get some control and focus on the simple task of writing her name. "There you go," she said, handing the magazines over.

"Great," the man said. "Now if you'll just follow me."

Elle faced Trent. "I'll catch your act after the game," she said coolly before turning around.

She didn't get far before she felt a large warm hand wrap around her waist. "Actually, I think I'll catch *your* act down on the field," he said, raising his eyebrows.

"Excuse me?"

"One of the many perks of being a player, a football player, that is. I get to sit on the field for the game. Mind if I join you?" He smiled widely, and Elle was left momentarily stunned.

"You can do whatever you want." She shrugged. "I'm not going to stop you."

"Really?" He moved his eyes up and down her body. "*Whatever* I want?"

"Oh, shut it." Elle shook her head, feigning disgust.

"Whatever you say, babe." He laughed boisterously.

"Don't call me babe," she snapped one last time, before turning away and following after the stadium representatives.

As they made their way down the hall and through the tunnel, Elle couldn't help but strain her ears in an attempt to hear Trent's voice. Every once in a while, she would hear him chuckle or laugh about something that one of the security guards said in passing. Her every focus was on him, and she was completely oblivious to where they were going. She simply followed the man in front of her, who hadn't stopped asking her questions.

As they got closer, she could hear the sound of the crowd getting louder. It had a constant hum like a giant bees' nest, and she was going to walk right into the center of it. The butterflies that had once been lying dormant were now fluttering around frantically inside her stomach.

"Sounds pretty amazing, huh?" Trent's deep voice rang from behind her.

"Amazing," she agreed.

"If you can behave yourself, 'Miss. Sassy,' I might just—"

"Miss Sassy? Look, you—"

Trent lifted his finger and placed it to her lips. "Let me stop you from saying something you'll regret." Her jaw closed shut with an audible snap, but she continued to glare. "As I was saying, if you behave yourself, I may be able to give you a behind the scenes tour."

Her eyes lit up and she knew there was no hiding the blatant excitement on her face. "Do you think you could introduce me to Andy Reid?"

"Maybe…" He trailed off, looking at her with confused eyes. "Why?"

"Because since he was hired back in '99, you guys have won five division titles and have captured five trips to the NFC Championship Game. And starting in 2001, you guys won the NFC Eastern Division four consecutive years in a row. Did you know that's the longest streak in franchise history? Plus, he's currently one of only two coaches in the league who effectively has the power of general manager. The only other is Bill Belichick."

Trent stood slack jawed and staring. "How did you … I mean what … do you …?" He fumbled with his words, and before he had a chance to gain some composure, the announcer's voice was piped over the loud speakers.

"Tonight, we have someone special doing our coin toss. This year's *Sports Illustrated* swimsuit issue cover model, Miss Elle McLean."

The stadium erupted with noise, and Elle's stomach dropped. She turned to look at Trent who was finally starting to look collected.

"You'll do great," he assured her. "I'll be waiting." His smile returned, and Elle felt her heart skip.

Smiling back, she gave him a quick wink before quickly strutting out onto the field. The thunderous applause mixed with the hoots and hollers seemed to literally vibrate off her skin. It rang in her ears and sent a feeling of exhilaration through her veins.

The walk to centerfield took longer than she'd imagined, and she found herself lost in thought. And she wasn't lost in the thrill of the moment, or in the excitement of actually being on a pro football field, or even in the anticipation of tossing the coin. She was lost in thoughts of Trent. The guy who she'd met on the side of the road not so long ago, who had been in her thoughts every day since. The same guy who was standing on the side of the field, waiting for her and who she'd have the rest of the evening to get to know—if she wanted to. That decision was all up to her.

Before she was aware of it, she was in the center of the field and the coin was placed in her hand. She looked down at its shiny surface and carefully turned it over, focusing on the two sides. *Why not let fate decide?* she thought. If it landed on heads, she would give in and get to know Trent. She'd give him the benefit of the doubt. If it landed on tails, she'd push him away like all the others.

Elle took a deep breath and closed her eyes before flipping the polished coin in the air. Her heart felt like it stopped beating for that short second, and she held her breath with anticipation. All the noise, the loud clapping, the yelling was blocked out, and all she could hear was the air pulling in and out of her lungs. The coin landed on the ground with a thump, and she slowly opened her eyes. Leaning forward slightly, she focused down on the silver reflective surface that gleamed up at her. A smile tugged at her lips.

Chapter 19
Heads Up

Elle continued to smile as she focused on the face of the coin. For a split second, she doubted her choice, wondering who in their right mind left a decision like that up to fate. Either way, she *had* left it up to fate, and fate decided heads.

A hard pounding on her back woke her from her reverie. "Good job, sweetheart. Now, let's get you off the field."

She lifted her eyes to the ref and had a split second where she'd forgotten where she was. But then the words the ref just spoke rang in her ears.

"My name is Elle," she corrected with a hit of annoyance. One of the bulky players on her right chuckled, but she didn't look away.

"No disrespect intended," the ref said, holding up his hands.

Just as she opened her mouth to comment, two men were at her side to escort her off the field. The crowd around her erupted, and she felt a wave of sound hit her. The blissful sound of a Jimi Hendrix song was piped around the stadium, and Elle matched its rhythmic beat to her strut. As soon as she was close enough to spot Trent, her eyes met his and she smirked. He was leaning back against the wall, legs crossed at the ankles and his arms folded over his chest. His blond hair hung over his forehead, barely reaching his eyes and his shirt pulled snug across his shoulders, accentuating the muscles that lay beneath. She unconsciously licked her lips as she continued to watch him.

Trent's eyes were trained on Elle. He couldn't look away from her even if he wanted too. There was something about her that drew him in like a moth to a flame. When she reached him, she stopped and matched his crossed arm position.

"Damn, I'd like to play ball with you. I wouldn't mind that tackle," he said with raised eyebrows.

"Really, Trent, is everything sexual for you? Is that the only thing your brain can process?"

"Not entirely," he said, giving her his wide smile that was quickly becoming the kryptonite to her hard-ass exterior.

"You're such a pig," she said quickly, before turning around and hiding the smirk that was threatening to give her away. Starting to walk, Elle turned around and peered over her shoulder. "Are you coming or what?" she asked. "You'll never get anywhere if you stay there, but suit yourself." Her heels clicked on the hard floor as she walked away, and his footfalls soon started after her. "Besides, I'm sure I've got some hot executives upstairs that I need to take photos with," she added casually.

Trent paused briefly, shaking his head. He'd never met a girl who gave more mixed signals in his entire life. "Crazy chick," he mumbled to himself.

Elle slowed to a stop and turned around. "Did you say something?" she asked.

"Nope," he said with a popping sound.

He paused in front of her, looking down with intense eyes. Opening his mouth, he debated telling her exactly what he thought. Deciding against it, he snapped his jaw shut and instead took a deep breath and exhaled.

Elle could feel the warmth of his breath sweep across her face, making her body hot. She swallowed slowly and continued to hold his gaze. Then, all too soon, he turned away and barreled down the hall. He was walking so fast that she had a hard time keeping up with him. Silently cursing her choice of four-inch heels, Elle looked around and realized she had no idea where she was. Nothing looked familiar to her. Just as she was about to ask Trent where they were, he came to a stop in front of white metal doors. He grabbed the handle and flung it open, disappearing behind it, into the unknown room.

Where the heck does he think he's going? Elle thought in confusion. She briefly contemplated turning around and attempting to find her way back when the door opened again and Trent poked his head out.

He slowly looked her up and down before settling on her face. "Are *you* coming?"

"Do I even have a choice?" she asked, rolling her eyes.

"I just thought you'd like to see the room where all the *magic* happens," he said with a smile.

"Fine," she huffed before the door swung closed again. Elle was reeling with excitement at getting anything behind the scenes that was related to the Eagles. And she wasn't going to deny her desire to get a sneak peak at one Eagle in particular. She smiled at the thought and took one calming breath before pulling open the door.

As soon as she stepped in, she was greeted with the large Eagle emblem on the wall. Turning to the right, she scanned the room for a minute before she realized where they were. Wood lockers lined the walls and extended almost the entire length of the room on both sides. And above each locker was a plaque announcing each player's name.

"Pretty cool, huh?" Trent's rough voice broke the silence.

He was near the center of the room, sitting on a bench in front of what Elle assumed was his locker. Her heartbeat quickened as her eyes trailed over his body, taking in all of his features. His wide muscular frame, his hands which lay casually on his lap, his strong jaw line that led to his full lips, and his bottle green eyes that peeked out from behind his dark lashes. He was sexy and rugged and it was all topped off by a head of sandy blond hair.

A shudder racked through Elle's body as she looked him over. Tearing her eyes away, she rolled her shoulders and forced herself to focus on something else. The way her body was reacting to him—the way *she* was reacting to him—was not normal. And to pounce on him right now was not an option. Slowly taking a step forward, she continued until she stood directly in front of him and looked down. "So this is where the *magic* happens?" she asked in her most seductive voice.

His eyes met hers and she saw his chest expand as he held his breath. "If by 'magic,' you mean me getting naked? Then, yes." He stood slowly, brushing against her as he surpassed her by a few inches.

Elle almost moaned and had to bite down on her lips in an attempt to keep quiet. Just when she thought she was under control, she felt the tips of his rough fingers trail up the length of her arm, stopping when he reached her shoulder.

"Is something wrong?" he asked, his voice husky. It was clear that she was turned on by him, and Trent was just glad he wasn't the only one.

"Not at all," she lied quickly before stepping back. Desperate to change the subject, she circled around him and walked over to his locker. "So, you're the ever-infamous T.A.W., in the flesh." She ran her fingers across his nameplate on the locker.

"That's me, but you know you can call me Trent." He laughed loudly and the sound sent a chill down Elle's spine.

"Okay then, Trent." She swallowed and turned her back on him nervously. "Why don't you tell me a little about yourself?" She tried to keep her voice steady, but there was no hiding its slight waver.

Trent didn't say a word. Instead he silently walked towards the nervous girl who was finally showing the break in her tough exterior. He placed a hand on either side of her, trapping her against the locker. "What do you want to know?" he whispered in her ear.

His hot breath blew across her neck, making every little hair stand on end. Dropping his head lower, he placed his lips on her shoulder and slowly turned his head to the side, until they came in contact with the bare skin of her neck. Elle's breath caught and her knees went weak. She could feel the heat radiating from his body and could smell the clean cotton of his shirt. Her mouth started to salivate and before she could stop herself, she spun around and pressed herself against him.

"Anything," she panted.

Trent dropped his hands from the sides of the locker and wrapped them around her waist, pulling her off the ground and closer to him. He didn't ask permission; he knew he didn't have to. Without a moment's hesitation, he pressed his lips to hers. She tasted like peppermint and everything good and he wanted more. Sliding one of his hands up from her waist to her back, he gently massaged the muscles of her back and continued until he reached her shoulder. Her dark hair tangled around his wrists. Placing his fingers at the base of her neck, he held her to him.

Fire licked up Elle's spine, and she felt the heat of it pulse through her entire body. Something in the back of her mind told her that she could spend the rest of her life kissing the man wrapped in her arms and she'd be perfectly content. Because she wasn't sure if he felt the same way, she knew she couldn't give in easily. She wanted him to work for it, so she continued to kiss him hungrily and let her hands roam free—down his back, over his butt, and to the fronts of his thighs. His legs stiffened slightly under her touch, but she didn't stop until she reached a few inches above his knee. Elle had no idea if he was ticklish or not, but she was willing to take her chances. Sliding her thumb and forefinger apart, she slowly wrapped them around the front of his leg and squeezed hard. It only took a second and he dropped to the floor with a thud.

"Damn it! What was that for, Elle?"

Attempting to hold in her laugh, she looked down at him. "Just making sure you're not as indestructible as you are on the field." She smirked. Taking a step around him, she walked across the locker room and stopped when she reached the door. "Well, are you coming? You've got to walk me back before going to sit with the team," she said with a wink.

Still sitting on the floor, Trent dropped his head back and laughed. He hopped up and followed her out into the hallway. As soon as he caught up with her, he swung his hand in the air and slapped her butt—hard. "Come on, sweetheart, I don't have all day. I already missed kickoff." he said with a chuckle.

Elle's eyes instinctively narrowed at hearing that word. Normally, she would have spat back with a sassy comment, but this time something else happened. She smiled.

❧

Ethan watched Elle walk off the field, keeping her eyes locked on Trent, and laughed to himself. He was pretty positive his best friend was in for the ride of his life.

"I think she likes him." Kate's soft voice spoke beside him.

He turned to face her and reached down for her hand. "Yeah, I think he likes her too," he said, giving it a squeeze.

Just then, Sophie poked her head between the two of them. "Of course they like each other. I was fairly certain she did when she told us about meeting him on the side of the road. And when you told us about Trent's response to her, well, then I was definitely sure. They're meant to be together. I just had to figure out a way to get them both here," she said simply.

"I'm guessing that a casual dinner would have had the same effect." Kate laughed.

"That wouldn't have worked." Sophie shook her head. "They both needed to be in their element."

"How did you arrange this, anyway?" Ethan asked.

"All it took was a few phone calls and—"

"You told them what to do," Kate finished.

Sophie looked to her friend with innocent eyes. "Like I was saying, I made a few phone calls and just found out exactly where Elle would be and when. Graham was able to help with that. And Ethan, if it weren't for you, it wouldn't have worked. Good job keeping the magazine away from Trent." She winked.

Ethan smiled. "I don't think I had a choice. Something tells me that once you set your mind to something you don't give up."

"Because she doesn't." Logan walked up beside her and wrapped his arms around her waist. "The first time I met her, I wasn't quite sure what to think. I was almost intimidated by her."

Sophie laughed at Logan's ridiculous statement, but Ethan understood exactly how Logan could feel that way. She was tenacious and some people didn't know how to handle that.

"I've never heard the story of how you both met," Ethan said as he sat, pulling Kate down on his lap.

"They have a fun story," she whispered in his ear before placing a soft kiss on his cheek.

"So, who's going to tell it?" Ethan looked from Sophie to Logan.

"I'll start!" Sophie sat in the seat beside them and curled her feet under her. "It was the summer before ninth grade and I was out for a jog—which is something I never do, mind you; I'm more of a Pilates girl. But, for some reason when I woke up that morning I decided to go for a run." She paused for a moment, recalling the memory like it was yesterday.

Logan took advantage of her brief pause and jumped in. "I was playing soccer for a summer league and we were having a game that day. I remember being nervous because I was new to the team and barely had any time to practice."

"You shouldn't have been nervous," Sophie added. "You were the best player out there. And the cutest."

"Thanks, sweetheart, but I don't think my looks would have kept me on the team." He laughed. "So anyway, I was running down the field, waiting for an open shot when I saw her." This time he paused.

"I knew as soon as I saw him." Sophie's blue eyes were intense. "He was so cute and I just felt something different. It was like a spark went off."

"I could barely keep focused," Logan said, laughing again. "She stood on the sidelines and watched the entire game, screaming at the top of her lungs every time I got the ball or scored a point. I remember thinking 'Who is that girl? Do I know her?' When the game was over, I searched the field, but didn't find her. For a second, I thought that maybe I was going crazy and imagined the whole thing, especially after weeks with no sign of her.

"It wasn't until the first day of school that I saw her again. I was standing in front of my locker putting my books away and she walked right up to me and introduced herself. There wasn't a shy bone in her body. The rest is pretty much history. We've been together ever since."

"Wow," Ethan said in shock.

"I know, right? I told you it was a great story." Kate smiled and nuzzled into his chest.

"That's one of the best stories I've ever heard. I think the only one that could ever come close to that, would be if Elle and Tr—"

"Oh, come on, sweetheart. Don't get your panties in a twist," Trent said, effectively cutting Ethan off. He was following behind a fuming Elle who'd just barged into the room. "You know as well as I do that he had that coming," he continued.

"I don't care what you think he had coming. He was just asking for an autograph. You can't tell every guy that comes within a foot of me that you'll beat them down if they touch me!" She spun around and poked her finger at his chest. "And don't even start with the panties talk. You haven't earned the right, yet, to talk about my underwear."

"Yet? Does that mean I *will* be getting a chance to talk about them?" Trent's face lit up with a smile.

"Look, if you think that acting like a jerk in front of all those people made me want to rip off my knickers and toss them in your face, you have got another thing coming!"

His eyes went wide. "Wait a minute. You would *rip* them off?" he asked, clearly not paying attention to a word she was saying. "That's just hot. You can't say something like that and not expect me to—"

"To what, Trent? Overreact?" With clenched fists, she stood ramrod straight, anger rolling off her in waves.

"No," he said softly, ducking his head down so he could look her in the eyes. "Elle?" Taking a step forward, he wrapped his large hands around her fisted ones and gave them a squeeze. "What I was going to say is, you can't say something like that and not expect me to want to kiss you again, right here, right now, in front of everyone." He kept his eyes on hers and, ever so slowly, Elle's body relaxed. "I'm sorry about what I said to those guys," he continued. "I've never been good at that sort of thing. But I know I'm going to have to work on it."

By now, Elle had cooled off enough that she could speak with a clear head and level voice. "You're going to have to work hard, you know. I'm not easily won over," she challenged.

Trent's laugh ripped from his chest as he closed the little space between them and wrapped his arms around her waist, pulling her close to him. She allowed him to hug her for a minute and then playfully pushed him away, before saying her goodbye. Trent promised he'd see her after the game and left.

Muttering something under her breath, she walked over to the rest of the group and sat down. "So, what have I missed? What's the score?" she asked, picking up Logan's drink and taking a large gulp.

"Umm…" Logan trailed off, still staring at his sister in shock. He was certain he'd never seen her cool off so quickly or act that way toward a guy before.

Having not received her answer, Elle looked at her brother and was confused by the expression on his face. "What? What are you looking at me like that for? I just asked what the score was."

Sophie leaned forward and glanced at Elle casually, not surprised at all. "We just scored another touchdown. So that ties us up at fourteen-fourteen."

"Thanks, Soph."

"Yep," she replied with a satisfied smile.

Ethan looked at Kate and saw the same satisfied look on her face. "Meant to be," she whispered with a shrug, answering his silent question.

"Yes. It's meant to be," he repeated the words aloud and pulled Kate closer to his chest, resting his chin on the top of her head. Those three words, something that Ethan had never considered a possibility for himself, rang true to him for the first time ever.

❧

Halfway into the third quarter, Ethan's phone rang. He considered ignoring it, especially after he looked at the screen and saw that it was Henry. The last thing he wanted was to be called into work on his day off.

"Hey, Henry. What's going on?"

"Before you ask, I'm not calling to ask you to come in. I know you've had this day marked off for a while."

Ethan relaxed with a sigh. "Well, in that case, how can I help you?"

"I actually wanted you to relay a message to Trent for me. I tried his phone earlier this morning, but I couldn't reach him."

"Yeah, we went hiking this morning. Must have been out of range," he said, stifling a laugh.

"I see," Henry said. "I bet he's aching to get out on that field. His team doctor told him to give it a few more weeks and he should be ready."

"Surprisingly, I don't think he's complained at all today about not playing. Then again, he's been pretty distracted. At least, he seemed pretty content to me."

There was a moment of silence and then Henry cleared his throat. "I have no idea what you're talking about."

"Oh, you'll find out soon enough. Believe me, if this goes where I think it's going, Trent will be sharing the news with every guy that will listen."

"Well, then, I'm excited to hear about it. So, can you do me a favor and tell my son that his mom wants him to come by this weekend? She has a few things for him to sign."

"Sure, no problem, Dad. I'll let him know."

Ethan ended his call with another promise that he'd relay Henry's message and flipped his phone shut.

"Did you just call Dr. Williams 'Dad'?"

"Yeah, it started years ago. I let it slip once by accident and it's stuck ever since. Besides, he's like a father to me anyway."

"What did you just say?" Elle leaned forward in her chair and looked over at Ethan and Kate. Her eyes were huge and her face pale. "Did you just say that Dr. Henry Williams is your dad?" she asked the question, but never quite closed her mouth. It continued to hang open in amazement.

"No, he's not my dad," Ethan assured her.

Elle breathed a sigh of relief. "Good, I was going to say that would—"

"He's Trent's dad. Did he not tell you that?"

As soon as the words were out of his mouth, Elle's back went straight. Her once-shocked face turned to one of agony as she slowly blinked, processing the words she'd just heard. Both Sophie and Kate were holding back laughter as they watched what was transpiring in front of them.

"Come again? Who's his dad?" Elle asked calmly. Her voice held a slight waver and try as she might to disguise it, it didn't work.

"Henry Williams," he repeated slowly. "I work with him at the hospital. Why?"

"Ah … Umm … no reason in particular. I've just met him a few times, that's all. He's treated me and Kate before. He's really … nice," she mumbled.

"Oh, stop being so shy, Elle. We all know why you know Dr. Williams." Sophie let her voice trail off suggestively and was met with a don't-you-dare look from Elle. Deciding to keep quiet, she giggled softly and tucked herself back into Logan's side.

"What was that all about?" Ethan asked Kate quietly.

Very casually, Kate leaned in. "Ever hear the term 'MILF'?"

"Yes. Why?"

"Well, you see, Henry is Elle's 'DILF.' Dad I'd like to … ya know …" She nodded her head.

"Dad I'd like to what?" he asked with a smile, enjoying her inability to actually say the word.

Kate rolled her eyes and looked back at him. "Come on, you know what I'm talking about."

"Maybe I do." He shrugged. "I just want to hear you say it."

She blushed slightly in embarrassment, but then ever so slowly she leaned in, placing her lips against his ear and finished the sentence. Her warm breath blew over his cheek and made the hair on the back of his neck stand on end.

Taking a deep breath, Ethan tried to put his thoughts into coherent words. "Do you—"

"Want to get out of here?" Kate finished.

He closed his eyes and nodded with a laugh.

"I'd thought you'd never ask." She winked.

With a new sense of excitement, Ethan cleared his throat loudly. "Well, guys, I think Kate and I are going to take off. We've seen enough football for one day." He met the other three pairs of eyes that accepted his excuse, although they probably didn't believe it.

"How can you leave halfway through the game?" Elle asked. "It's like stopping in the middle of opening presents on Christmas. You just don't do it."

Ethan shook his head in disbelief. Elle and Trent were more alike than he ever imagined, and it was a comment like that which proved it. Sliding Kate off of his lap, Ethan grabbed hold of her hand and started for the door. They said their goodbyes and were in the car heading towards New Hope in no time. The start of the drive was silent, but the energy in the air surrounding them was palpable. On more than one occasion, Ethan had to unlock their intertwined fingers so he could wipe the palms of his hands on his jeans.

"Is someone feeling a little nervous?" Kate asked with a giggle.

"No, I wouldn't necessarily call it nerves," he partially lied.

If he was being honest with himself, he was nervous, but only slightly. And even then, it was the anxious kind of nervous. Kate was the one person who he felt completely calm and peaceful with; yet she could also make his heart react in ways he never thought possible. He wanted to be with her all the time. Wanted to be close to her, so he could hear her voice, touch her face, and look into her eyes at any moment. He knew that leaving her tonight would make his chest ache, and he was dreading that moment already.

"Do you have to work tomorrow?" she asked, breaking his train of thought.

He nodded. "I go in early and I'm working a long shift, so I'll be there all day."

"Oh." She dropped her head down, hoping the disappointment didn't show on her face. Instead, she focused on their hands resting on her lap.

"Why the sad face?"

"It's nothing." She shook her head quickly.

"Kate," he said. Over the past few weeks together, Ethan had become an expert at reading her little mannerisms. He could tell when she was nervous about something or having a hard time understanding something. It was in the subtle tilt in her head or the fake smile on her face. Usually, all he had to do was wait and eventually she'd say what was on her mind.

"I just hate when I don't get to see you," she said quickly. "I miss you, and I know we'll talk on the phone, but it's still not the same." She twisted the fabric of her coat between her fingers.

Ethan dropped her hand and cupped her cheek. "I miss you too. More than you know."

She smiled and placed a soft kiss on his palm before taking his hand back in hers. There was something in the connection that the two of them shared that always amazed Kate. All it took was a few comforting words from Ethan and she felt at peace. She'd never had that before—ever.

The rest of the drive continued with moments of comfortable silence and casual conversation. There was always something new to learn, some small fact that was left unknown. Childhood stories of tree houses, and riding horses, and trips to the beach that always ended with a stop at the candy store. It was clear that neither of them could get enough of the other and that their feelings were mutual.

Kate was in the middle of a detailed description of her father attempting to remove a hornets' nest that hung by their shed when they pulled up to her townhouse and got out of the car. As they walked toward her front door, she was laughing so hard she could barely get the words out while she fumbled with her keys.

"Watching him swing that stick around was the funniest thing I've ever seen. And from a distance, you couldn't even see the bees, so he just looked like a wild man." She tossed her head back and laughed freely, color staining her cheeks.

Ethan watched her in amusement. He always thought Kate was beautiful, but at that moment, seeing her carefree and laughing took his breath away. She was so vibrant and full of life.

"What?" she asked, upon noticing the way he was watching her.

He shrugged his shoulders innocently. "I just like watching you."

Taking a step forward, Kate placed her hand on the back of his neck and pulled his lips to hers. She kissed him softly at first, then gradually grew more eager. Pulling away, she kissed along his jaw until she reached his ear. "I like watching you too," she whispered.

Looking down into her eyes, Ethan saw that familiar glint and took it as his go-ahead. He pulled her body close to his and captured her lips once again. Kate wrapped her arms around his waist and fumbled with the doorknob behind him, attempting to get it open. A second later, it swung open and Ethan pulled Kate inside, kicking the door shut behind them.

☙

Later that evening, they sat on the couch, watching the yellow and orange flames dance in the fireplace. The only sounds were their breathing and the occasional pop and sizzle of moisture from the logs. Ethan looked down at his lap where Kate lay, her eyelids heavy with sleep. Light flickered across her face and shadows outlined her straight nose and full lips. Very gently, Ethan lifted his hand and placed it on her cheek, turning her toward him. Looking down into her eyes, a feeling of love overwhelmed him, filling his chest with warmth.

I love you, he thought, the words rushing through his mind as the realization hit him. He wasn't sure how she felt, and the last thing he wanted to do was scare her off, so he bit down on his tongue in an attempt to keep those three words from spilling out.

"Kate," he said slowly. "You are amazing. Actually, you're so much more than amazing." His words were simple, yet he hoped that she would understand the feelings behind them.

"You're amazing too, Ethan. I'm so glad I have you." She lifted her head up and placed her lips to his, before curling herself into his chest.

The two of them stayed wrapped in each other's arms until all that was left of the fire was golden embers. Ethan knew it was time for him to go since he had work early the next day, but he was reluctant to leave. Kate sighed, knowing without words what he was thinking.

"I guess you need to get going, huh?"

"Unfortunately, yes."

"Okay," she said, sounding defeated. "Let me run to the bathroom really quick and then I'll walk you out."

"Sounds good to me." He gently squeezed her body, holding her close and savoring her warmth.

"Be right back," she whispered and climbed off the couch.

Ethan watched her until she was out of sight and knew at that moment that he'd never tire of her. He smiled and let himself enjoy the feeling of contentment as it settled over him. A moment later, a phone beeped, signaling a text. Ethan turned his head to the side and saw it lying on the ground a foot away. Without thinking, he picked it up and flipped it open. His eyes focused on the screen and his heart, which was once fluttering in elation, stopped.

In simple black text, against the blue screen read the name, Scott. In the second it took for the name to register, a hundred questions flitted through his mind. The last text Kate had received from Scott had been at the restaurant almost a month ago and, as far as he was aware, she hadn't received any more. *But what if she had?* he thought. Surely she would tell him if they were talking to one another again. He couldn't stop the questions and couldn't help but think of the worst case scenario. So he tried not to.

Placing the phone on the coffee table, he stood up and headed for the door. The only thing he wanted was space and time to think and he couldn't do that in Kate's home. He was just about to the door when he heard Kate.

"Ethan?" He took a deep breath and turned around to face her as she walked toward him, a look of worry etched on her face. "Were you going to say goodbye?" Her eyebrows pulled together.

"Of course. Yes. I just…I'm sorry." His voice trailed off, never giving the reason for leaving in such a hurry.

"Is everything all right?" She took a step toward him.

He tried to form the words to ask the question that was burning inside of him, but he couldn't. Instead, he just reached forward and wrapped his arms tightly around her. Placing his chin on top of her head, he breathed in her scent. As happy as he pretended to be at the moment, he couldn't escape the awful feeling deep in his gut that told him something was wrong. He swallowed hard and once again pushed those thoughts from his mind.

"I really should get going. I'll call you later, all right?" he asked.

"Sure." Kate looked up at him and knew something was off.

"Goodnight. Sleep well." He leaned down and kissed her softly on the lips before walking out the door.

Chapter 20
Complications

"Crap. Oh, shoot. Dang it!" Kate's hands flailed around helplessly, trying to somehow magically stop the milk that she'd just spilled from dripping onto the floor.

"Here, use this," Elle said, tossing her a towel, which she unfortunately missed.

"Stupid ... idiot," she mumbled to herself before picking it up.

Elle's hands went to her hips and she glared at her friend. "Hey, hey. What's with the bashing?"

"I wasn't talking about you, Elle." She sighed. "I was referring to myself." She turned her attention back to the spilled milk and began to clean up the mess.

"Okay, what's wrong?"

Kate closed her eyes and tried to focus on anything but the reason why she was upset. It didn't matter how many times she ran through the events of last night, because the more she did, the more confused and frustrated she became. She wasn't planning on bugging Elle with something so stupid, but her friend's question changed her mind. After all, that's what friends are for, right?

"Last night, Ethan and I came back here to hang out."

"Sure, you guys 'hung out,'" Elle said with an eye roll. "If that's what you want to call it. And?"

Pressing her lips together and inhaling through her nose, Kate tried to put her thoughts in order. She was pretty sure that no matter how she explained it, her concerns would sound ridiculous. "So, when it was time for him to leave, I got up to use the bathroom, and when I came back, he was already at the door. He said he had to get home to bed since he was working early this morning."

"Um hmm." Elle nodded her head, letting her friend's words register.

"Look, I know this sounds stupid, but I just felt like something was wrong."

"Like what?"

"I don't know … something. He just looked like he had something on his mind. Ugh, I don't know. I'm probably being stupid and completely overreacting." She dropped her head onto the table and buried her face in her arms.

"Look." Elle placed her hand on Kate's back. "I'm sure everything's fine. He probably was just thinking about work, especially since he had to go in early."

"Maybe you're right. I'm just reading into things too much. I'm sure everything is fine." She sat up and nodded. *Everything is fine; nothing is wrong.* She repeated the words over and over a few times in her head, willing herself to believe them. The only problem was that no matter how much her mind believed it, her heart didn't.

"What are your plans for today?" Elle asked, trying to help change the subject. She hated seeing her friend worry, especially if there was nothing to worry about.

"Not too much. I have a few more pictures I have to take into the city, then I'm meeting Scott for coffee." As soon as the words were out of her mouth, she paused. She hadn't told Elle or Sophie about her rekindled friendship with Scott. Not that it mattered—he was just a friend. But then again, he was a friend they both hated.

"What?" Elle asked in shock. "Do you mean Scott—as in Scott Christiansen?"

"Yeah," Kate mumbled. "I guess I forgot to mention that we're kind of friends again?" Her statement came out sounding like a question, and she waited patiently for the onslaught she knew was coming.

"Friends!" Elle yelled. "Are you serious? You're actually trying to be friends with that jerk?"

"Come on, he's not a jerk," she defended him. Elle folded her arms and glared at Kate with raised eyebrows. "Okay, so maybe he can be a jerk sometimes. But he used to be our friend," Kate reminded her. "And he wants to be again." She shrugged, hoping the topic would be dropped.

"Friends? Do you honestly think you can just be friends with him?"

"Yes, I do," she said truthfully.

"What makes you think it will be different this time?"

Because I love someone else. The thought caught Kate off guard. She knew she was falling in love with Ethan, but she hadn't actually said it yet. "Because, Elle, I don't love Scott anymore. I want to be with Ethan, and that's it." She smiled as she said the words that she knew were true.

Elle studied her friend's face and could see the honesty there. "I want you to be happy, Kate. You're my best friend and I love you. And it's because I love you that I'm going to tell you to be careful. I know Scott says he wants to be friends, but he's said that once before and it didn't end well. Plus, I would think about Ethan."

"What about Ethan?" Kate asked in confusion.

"Well, have you told him about being friends with Scott again?"

"No," she replied, still confused.

"Don't you think you should? I mean, clearly, I'm not an expert on relationships. But I'm pretty sure that most guys would feel a little threatened by an ex trying to weasel his way back into the life of a girl they're dating. Especially if I found out she was meeting him for coffee."

"But Ethan has nothing to worry about. I don't love Scott anymore. He's just a friend."

"A friend who you *were* in love with who also happened to break your heart."

Up until this point, Kate hadn't thought of the way Ethan would see it. She didn't think it was a big deal, but maybe to him it would be. And now, after hearing Elle's words, she feared that maybe she was right. Maybe Ethan would be worried. Maybe he would doubt the way she felt about him. Kate immediately felt sick as she thought of Ethan doubting her love for him in any way.

"I'll tell him, then," she said frantically. "I don't think I could handle losing him over something so stupid." Tears welled up in her eyes just thinking about it.

"Hey, don't be worried. Everything is going to be fine." Elle pulled her friend into a hug and rubbed her back in reassurance.

It was times like this when Kate was grateful for her friends. Friends who would still be there to comfort her when she needed them, even though they weren't happy with the choices she made and would tell her that flat out.

"So, how was hanging out with Trent last night? You guys went out, right?" Kate teased, desperate for a change in conversation.

"What? No! I mean, kind of. In a way."

Kate stood back and watched her friend stumble over her words. Elle was *never* flustered. "Elle," she said, lifting her eyebrows. "Do you have something you want to tell me?"

"No." Spinning around quickly, she scurried out of the kitchen.

"Hey! Not so fast, missy." Kate followed after her and found her sitting on the couch watching ESPN. "You know I'm not letting you off that easily." She stood in front of the TV with her hands on her hips. "I saw the way you guys looked at each other. And don't think I didn't hear what he said about kissing you *again*."

Elle closed her eyes tight and dropped her head back on the couch, letting out a sigh of frustration. This conversation was what she'd been trying to avoid. Last night had ended up entirely different than she thought and just thinking about it made her angry.

"What is the matter with me?" she finally yelled. "I mean, he is such an ass. But I can't help but like him. I'm pretty sure he likes me too, especially after that kiss." She pressed her fingers to her lips, remembering the way they felt on his. Just when she started to smile, she remembered how things had ended last night and she immediately forced all hopeful thoughts of him aside. "But you know, I'm not holding my breath or anything. He's probably one of those guys who has a different girl every day of the week, and I refuse to be another notch in his belt. No biggie." She shrugged. "He's just another jock, anyway, right?"

Kate looked at the sad eyes of her friend and knew she didn't believe her own words. Placing her hand on her knee, she gave it a reassuring squeeze. She knew she didn't have to say a word for Elle to know she understood. The two friends sat in silence for a moment, both pretending to watch the TV and both knowing what the other one was thinking.

"I have to get going," Kate said, grabbing her keys and phone off the table. "I only have two hours before I have to meet Scott." At the mere mention of his name, Elle rolled her eyes. Choosing to ignore it, Kate continued talking. "Will you be around later? I think we need a girls' night. Just the three of us and, of course, Maverick, Goose, and the Iceman. Half-naked. Playing volleyball."

"Mmm, you sure know the way to a girl's heart." Elle placed her hand over her chest and sat back dramatically.

"Does that mean you're on?"

"Sure. I'll call Soph." She flipped open her phone and was already talking to her as Kate walked out the door.

Over the next two hours, Kate's mind was disconnected from her body. Her body ran errands, picked up dry cleaning, and made the drive into the city, but her mind was stuck on Ethan, like it had been all night. Every time she started to feel anxious, she would repeat the phrase from earlier. *Everything is fine; nothing is wrong,* she would tell herself. And, just like earlier, she would feel comforted—at least for a few minutes.

The few times she tried calling him, it went straight to voicemail. She knew he was working all day and eventually accepted that she would have to wait until tomorrow to talk with him.

Before she knew it, the time had passed and she was walking to the coffee shop where Scott had asked to meet. She was only a block away when her phone beeped, signaling a text.

Hurry up, have a surprise for u.

She quickly replied that she was around the corner and tucked her phone away. As soon as she opened the door of the coffee shop, she both saw and heard her surprise.

"Katie!"

There standing a few feet away was Brian, one of Scott's friends who she'd grown to love and missed dearly. She smiled and ran to him, throwing her arms around his neck. He gripped her around the waist and swung her in a circle.

"Man, you *do* look good," he said, placing her on her feet and taking a step back to admire her. "Scott wasn't lying." He smiled.

Scott coughed and shot Brian a look. "I was hanging out with this guy here earlier," he said, nudging Brian in the shoulder, "and I accidentally let it slip that I was having coffee with you. He insisted on coming to see you, so I hope you don't mind."

"Are you kidding?" she asked. "Why would I mind?" She smiled at Brian. "It's been so long since I've seen you, or all the guys for that matter. What's new?"

"Funny thing you should ask that," Brian said with a hint of something underlying his voice, earning yet another glare from Scott.

"What's going on?" Kate asked, feeling out of the loop. The two boys kept giving each other secretive, silent glances, and it was driving her crazy.

"I think I better let Scott explain it. I have to get going, anyway." Brian stepped forward and gave her another hug.

"Okay, I guess I'll see you later?" she asked, hopeful.

"Of course you will, now that you're back in the group." He winked. The words didn't register in Kate's mind until he was at the door. "I'll see you tonight," he added over his shoulder, and then the door shut behind him.

Staring after him in complete confusion, Kate turned to Scott. "What was all that about? And why am I seeing him tonight?"

"I guess he was kind of hoping that you would come to McLaren's tonight. I've been meaning to tell you that Christine and Mike finally got engaged. The group of us is getting together as kind of an engagement party."

"Oh." She didn't know what else to say. The thought of seeing everyone again made her excited, but she also felt a little wary. McLaren's was *their* place, the place where the group of them used to hang out when both she and Scott were together.

"You have to come," he pleaded. "Everyone is dying to see you. Plus, it would be really nice to have you there again." He reached forward and took her hand, holding it in his.

Kate stared at their intertwined hands before what she was doing registered. As soon as it did, she yanked her hand back and shoved it in her pocket.

"Scott," she said, dropping her head.

He took a step toward her and lifted her chin up, forcing her eyes to meet his. "Katie, can we talk?" His eyes bore into hers, familiar and loving. "Please," he said before leading them to a corner booth and taking a seat.

Kate took a deep breath and held it before sitting down across from him.

"These past few weeks have been great. Wonderful, even," he started.

"They have been. Scott, I'm really glad that we can be friends again."

He visibly cringed. "Friends," he repeated the word.

"Yes, friends. That's what you said you wanted, right?"

"It was. But now, I don't know."

"You don't want to be friends anymore?" she asked in confusion.

"No, I do." The words rushed out of his mouth. "I just can't help it. I mean, I never thought that it would happen again. And then…" He trailed off again, looking away in frustration.

Kate's nerves were beginning to unravel as she tried to understand what he was attempting to say. "Okay, Scott, enough with the cryptic talk. What are you talking about? If you don't want to be friends with me anymore, then fine, just say it. And if you don't want me at McLaren's tonight, then just tell me. Stop beating around the bush and just spit it—"

"I love you," he said, cutting her off.

She sat back quickly, pressing her spine flat against the seat, not able to breathe. The three words hit like giant rocks thrown at her stomach, pushing her back and rendering her speechless.

The two of them sat in silence for a few moments as the words hung in the air. Kate knew that she should say something, but she didn't know what to think, let alone say.

"Are you going to say something? Kate, please. Just talk to me."

"What do you want me to say?" she whispered as her stomach twisted in knots. "What about your girlfriend? I thought you were happy with her."

"Samantha's a really nice person, but she's not *you*. No one will ever be you, Katie. So please, just tell me that this is a good thing. Tell me that I'm not too late."

"Too late? Scott, it's been months. Do you just expect me to jump up and throw my arms around you and act like nothing happened? I can't do that. I won't do that. I thought that being friends again was a good thing, but now..." She trailed off, shaking her head.

"I don't expect you to jump up and be excited. That's not what I'm asking." He sat forward and looked at her closely. "What I'm asking is that you think about what I said. I want you to know that I love you; that I've loved you for as long as I've known you. Ever since that day you sprained your ankle and I carried you home. We have a history together, and I know you better than anyone. Yes, I've screwed up in the past. I've been a complete idiot. But that doesn't change the way I feel about you now. I want to do this. I want to be with you."

Kate sat listening to the exact words that months ago she'd ached to hear. Except now when she heard them, all she felt was confused and frustrated. Her head was spinning so fast that she had to close her eyes to keep from falling over. Knowing that she had to get out of there, she swung her legs off of the vinyl chair and stood up quickly.

"Where are you going?" Scott stood to his feet.

"I need...umm...I need to get out of here and think."

"What's there to think about? You either love me or you don't."

His words stung, and she felt like she'd been slapped. Spinning around with clenched fists and anger-filled eyes, hundreds of thoughts rushed though her mind. Hateful words hung on the tip of her tongue, waiting to be projected at him, but instead she clamped her mouth shut tight. "I can't believe you said that," she managed through her teeth.

"What? It's the truth, Katie. Either you love me and want to be with me, or you don't."

"You don't get it, do you?" She shook her head in disbelief. "You know what? I'm leaving. I can't do this right now."

Turning around, she ran out of the coffee shop and could sense Scott behind her. He hated leaving things on bad terms as much as she did, but right now she needed to get away and think.

She was almost to the corner when she heard Scott calling out her name. Keeping up her fast pace, she hoped to get to her car before he caught up. Just as she rounded the corner, her foot caught a raised edge of pavement. Her body lurched forward, and she fell to the sidewalk. Instinctively stretching out her arms to break the fall, she felt the searing pain shoot up her left wrist as soon as she hit. She whimpered and rolled onto her back, clutching her wrist to her chest.

"Kate! Are you okay?" Scott's voice was panicked as he ran toward her.

"No, dang it. I think I might have sprained it," she said, still lying in the ground.

"Well, if you weren't running away from me, maybe you wouldn't have fallen."

"I wasn't running. I told you I needed some time to think." Scott took a step forward and grabbed hold of her forearm in an attempt to help her stand. Shaking his hand free, she glared up at him. "I've got it," she snapped, and pulled herself to her feet.

"Here, let me look at it," he said, holding out his hand.

Ignoring him, she kept her head down. "What are you, a doctor now or something?" she asked coldly.

"No, but I was a life guard in high school, remember? I have a little bit of training."

"Life guard? Scott, that hardly constitutes being a professional." She rolled her eyes and continued examining her wrist.

"I'm serious. Let me look at it."

"You know what? I think I'll go the hospital and have a real doctor look at it." Her heart fluttered at the thought of seeing Ethan and she smiled to herself.

"Okay, let me go get the car and I'll take you." He reached in his pocket and pulled out his keys.

"Please. I can take myself to the hospital." She turned to walk away.

"Well, you shouldn't. And you know your mom and dad will be pissed if they find out I let you drive yourself."

"Then let's not tell them," she called over her shoulder.

"I can't promise anything. You know how word travels back home. Gossip spreads like wild fire amongst friends." There was a playful undertone to his voice, but she was still angry at him so she continued to walk, ignoring his comment. "Aww, come on. Stop being so stubborn and let me just take you. I promise I won't talk about what I said earlier. I'll be perfectly nice. I'll even tell you about Brian's new girlfriend."

Kate groaned. He had her with that one. She was always a sucker when it came to Brian. He was almost like a little brother to her. "Fine," she huffed as she spun around to face him.

He smiled wide. "Good. Wait here and I'll go get the car."

He took off down the street. Figuring he'd be a few minutes, Kate took a seat on the curb, pulling her jacket up around her neck to shield herself from the cold wind.

She sat there, frozen, staring down at the bits of gravel at her feet. Her insides, however, were anything but still. To say she was freaking out would have been an understatement. Her mind was split in a million different pieces, each focusing on something else. She was angry at Scott for springing something like that on her. And she was even more frustrated with herself for putting herself in that situation. For a half second, she'd even questioned her feelings, and the thought made her sick. She knew that Ethan was who she wanted to be with, yet there was a small part of her heart that couldn't let go of Scott. He was such a part of her past—like a habit she couldn't break.

"Katie, get in!" Scott yelled, waking her from her trance.

Slowly standing up, she made her way into his car. It had been over six months since she'd sat in that very spot and realized immediately that it was a bad idea for him to drive her. It was like crawling into a time capsule. There were simply too many memories bottled up within the four doors and the steel frame.

Sitting in silence, Kate listened as Scott went into full detail of Brian and his new girlfriend. He explained how they met, and how long they'd been dating, but Kate didn't hear a word he said. She stared out the window, lost in memories, both happy and sad. It wasn't until the car came to a stop and she was nudged that she realized they were at the hospital. He pulled into the Emergency Bay and put the car in park.

Inside the building, Ethan stood leaning against a wall, lost in thought. "Doctor Montgomery, please report to the ER."

The voice piped throughout the hospital halls woke him from his trance. He groaned internally, feeling his frustration growing. He'd been called over the intercom all day long and it was starting to bother him.

He knew it was his own fault for keeping his phone turned off, but he didn't know what else to do. Although he felt bad about his obvious avoidance of Kate, he knew that after leaving her house last night he needed some time to think things through. It didn't take him long to realize that he was stuck in an impossible situation. He was in love with a girl and had no idea if she felt the same way. Not only did he not know if she felt the same way, but there was a good chance that she was spending time with her old boyfriend, a jerk who'd broken her heart more than once and left her shattered.

Ethan's hands clenched tight at the mere thought of Scott talking to her or making her laugh. It made him sick. He wasn't sure if his assumptions were true, but he intended to find out. He knew he should have asked her last night after seeing the text, but something inside him was too afraid of what the answer would be.

After staying up all night thinking about the situation and spending all morning going over the conversation he would have with her, Ethan was certain that she needed to know how he felt. She deserved to know, even if she didn't feel the same way for him. And if she told him her feelings weren't reciprocated, then he'd step down. He wouldn't push her; he wouldn't try to convince her that Scott was wrong for her. Doing that would only hurt her and he refused to cause her any pain.

With a resigned sigh, Ethan pushed way from the wall and walked over to the elevator. His stomach churned, from both hunger and nausea. He hadn't been able to eat all day and finally understood what people meant by the term 'love sick.'

As soon as the doors opened, he regretted not taking the stairs. Both Cindy and Lisa stood side-by-side, heads pressed together in conversation. He still couldn't understand why they were friends.

"Hello, Dr. Montgomery," they sing-songed.

"Cindy, Lisa." He nodded in acknowledgment and stepped into the elevator.

Keeping his eyes facing forward, he hoped they would see that he was in no mood to carry on another agonizing conversation.

"So, Ethan," Cindy started as she turned her body to face him.

"Yes?" he deadpanned.

"I'm assuming that your parents will be here for the annual benefit? You know they're hoping to raise enough money to help with the remodel."

"Yes, I was aware of that."

"So, your parents will be here?" she asked, annoyed that she had to repeat her question.

Ethan exhaled slowly before responding. "Yes, I believe they will be."

"Good." She smiled in excitement. "I've been anxious to see them again, and I was hoping to touch base with Sabrina. I'm sure she'd want to help in the planning."

He rolled his eyes at Cindy's enthusiasm. Up until this moment, he hadn't thought about his parents coming to town for the benefit or the fact that Cindy would be there. Unfortunately, the pharmaceutical company she worked for was a sponsor every year, which meant she would be in attendance. Thankful when the elevator doors opened, Ethan stepped out without another word and saw Henry waiting for him.

"Still haven't fixed your phone, I see," he said, taking a step toward Ethan. "Here, until you get everything situated." Handing over a pager, he offered a friendly smile.

"So, are you the reason I was paged here?" Ethan asked.

"Yes. I wanted to give you that," he pointed to the pager, "and I wanted to ask if you and Kate wanted to come over for lunch this Sunday." He studied his colleague's face carefully.

"I would love to come over for lunch, but I'm not sure if Kate will be there," Ethan said honestly. Surprisingly, Henry didn't say a word. Instead he stood in silence and waited for the explanation. Taking a deep breath, Ethan told him everything, right down to the fears and doubts he was having. It wasn't until he told Henry of his decision to back down if he felt that Kate wanted to be with Scott that his mentor spoke up.

"Ethan, I'm not so sure that's the best thing to do. If you care about her like you say you do, then you need to fight for her. Tell her you love her; show her that she has options. Don't step down because you think that's the right thing to do."

"I won't make it harder on her. I don't even consider it a choice." There was finality in his voice and even Henry could hear it. He'd already made his decision.

"Well, let's hope it doesn't come to that then. I'm sure once you tell Kate of your feelings, everything will work out."

Just as Ethan opened his mouth to voice his doubts, the head nurse, Kristen, walked past.

"Hey, Dreamy and Divine, we've got a trauma coming in!" she yelled over her shoulder while pulling her hair back. The two men laughed at their given nicknames and followed her outside.

❧

"Sorry I've been so quiet," Kate mumbled from the passenger seat.

Scott smiled kindly. "It's okay. I can tell you have a lot on your mind."

"Yeah," she paused. "Well, thanks for the ride." She grabbed the handle and started to open the door when he stopped her.

"Wait! I'm coming with you. Let me go park, and I'll meet you inside."

"No! No, you're not!" she yelled at him, suddenly frantic at the thought of having to explain Scott to Ethan in front of him. The whole situation was bound to be awkward, and she wanted to avoid it like the plague.

"Katie, I'm not just going to let you go in by yourself. Plus, how are you going to get back to your car?"

"I can handle going to the hospital by myself. I've done it before. And if I need a ride to get my car, I'll call Sophie. I think she's in the city today."

"I guess that's all right." He was silent for a moment, then he looked at her hopefully. "Will you come tonight?"

"I don't think that's such a good idea."

"Why?" he questioned. She looked at him with raised eyebrows. He knew why. She didn't have to tell him. "I promise I'll be good. I'll just be your friend, nothing more."

"Friend?" She scoffed, but he ignored her gesture.

"Everyone is planning on seeing you there. Christine and Mike would be disappointed if you don't come."

As he spoke, an ambulance pulled up, causing people to scramble about. Kate didn't pay them any attention; she was too lost in the pulse of the swirling red lights and the decision she was about to make.

"Please. I promise I'll behave," he added, knowing that her silence meant she was thinking about it.

"Fine. I'll go. But I'm not staying long. I've got plans with Soph and Elle."

"Great! I promise, it'll be fun and you won't regret it." His smile was infectious and she couldn't help but grin back at him. Before she had time to react, Scott had his arms around her, crushing her in his excitement. Not wanting to be that close to him, Kate started to pull back, but not before she saw Ethan. He was standing next to the ambulance, watching her with confused eyes.

Kate gasped and flinched away from Scott, effectively cutting off her view of Ethan. Ignoring the sharp pain that shot up her wrist, she wrenched open the door and jumped out, slamming it shut behind her. She rushed around the side of the ambulance towards Ethan. In her haste, she tripped and almost fell onto him.

"Are you okay?" The sound of Ethan's voice calmed her frantic heart.

"Yeah, I'm fine," she sighed, relieved to be near him. "I'm glad you're here."

"Really? Why?" His face looked pained as he looked at Kate's worried face.

Before she could respond, Scott ran up, out of breath. "Katie, are you okay? I saw you trip and I swear one of these days you'll—"

"I'm fine," she said quickly, cutting him off. "Why don't you go home? I'll be fine."

Scott searched her face to make sure she was truly okay, then eventually looked over at the man standing beside her. It took a minute for it to register that it was Ethan and the look on his face was not welcoming. "Sure, I'll just get going then." Scott nodded. "I'll see you later tonight, okay?"

Kate nodded and Ethan's body stiffened as he processed the words he just heard. The flicker of hope he'd felt a moment ago slowly faded as he realized his fears might be right.

The two stood in silence and watched Scott climb back into his car, waving to Kate as he pulled away.

"Kate," Ethan finally said. "Are you all right?"

"Yes, well ... no, not really. I fell and hurt my wrist. I think it's just a sprain."

"You did? Here, let me see."

Holding out her arm, he gingerly took it in his hand. He felt the bones in her wrist and turned it over a few times, moving it slowly back and forth, asking brief questions as he did. He kept his voice professional, but Kate could tell there was something wrong. The emotions on his face were something she'd never seen before and uncertainty settled heavily in the pit of her stomach.

"So, you were with Scott today?" Ethan asked, breaking the silence.

Kate took a deep breath and prepared herself for the conversation that had been running through her head since the morning.

"I met him for coffee," she said casually.

"Oh" was the only thing he could manage.

"I'm actually kind of his friend again."

"Friend?" he said skeptically, fighting the urge he had to tell her she was crazy. He'd only seen Scott with her for a few minutes and it was clear that he looked at her as more than a friend.

"Yes, friend," she confirmed with a nod.

"And how does Scott feel about you being friends?"

"Well, he … I mean, he said he … Scott will always be …" She fumbled with her words, trying to find the right way to explain the situation; but to Ethan, her fumbling meant only one thing. She'd already made her decision and she wanted to be with Scott.

Before he had time to think about what he was doing, before he could remember how important it was for him to tell her that he loved her, he broke. "I can't do this," he said, cutting her off before she said the words that would kill him.

Kate looked around nervously and realized he must be talking about his work. Clearly having a conversation about their relationship should not be done outside of the hospital. She almost laughed at herself for not thinking it through better. *Nice one, Kate. You really want to confess your love for him in the two minutes he has before running back to work?* she thought.

Ethan watched emotions dance across her face. Knowing that he had to spare her any guilt or pain that she might feel at his expense, he forced himself to continue. Instead of lying and telling her that he didn't care about her, that he didn't love her, he settled for something else—something that would turn things on him and make it all his decision.

"I think we need to take a break from each other," he finally said. "I need a break … from you."

"What?" Kate repeated the words over in her head, not understanding them fully until he looked up at her. Once he did—once his eyes focused on hers—she knew what he was saying. He was done.

"Oh." Her words came out in a whisper, barely audible. "I see."

The voice inside Ethan's head was screaming, begging to let him speak the truth. But he bit down on his tongue and continued. "I just think it's best if we both take some time to figure things out."

Kate nodded and dropped her gaze to the ground, allowing the words to sink in. She wanted to yell at him and tell him that he'd promised he'd never hurt her, but she couldn't. All she could do was stand there; and the longer she stood, the deeper his words cut, leaving ragged edges as they ripped through her. She was faintly aware of Ethan saying something more, but she didn't hear him. All she could hear was the blood rushing through her veins, pumping fluid to a heart that felt as if it would stop beating at any moment.

"I have to get inside," Ethan said quietly. "Henry will be wondering where I am. You take care of yourself, Kate." He exhaled as he said her name for the last time, and felt his heart leave his body with it. For no matter what happened, it would always belong to her.

It was another minute before Kate could look up, and when she did, she realized she was alone.

❧

She spent the entire afternoon curled up on her bed, trying to physically hide from the pain. The tears had stopped falling after the third hour, and her face was tight and dry from the salt. She must have run over the scenario a hundred times in her head. Each time she said something different, changed the words she'd used, but in the end, it didn't matter. Every time, the scene ended the same: her standing alone, watching glass doors open and close with no Ethan in sight.

Attempting to find some solace, she tried telling herself that she was crazy— crazy for falling in love with someone after only three weeks. But it didn't work. She even tried telling herself that what she felt wasn't love. That there was no possible way she loved him as much as she thought she did. That didn't work either. She loved Ethan; there was no doubt about it. She felt it the first time she saw him and still felt it now. It was with this realization that she climbed out of bed. No matter what Ethan felt for her, it wouldn't change the way she felt for him, and Scott needed to know that. Having made a decision, she felt a little better and forced herself to get up and shower.

The sound of the water running must have alerted her friends of her presence, because as soon as she pulled back the curtain, there was pounding at her door.

"Kate! Come on, open up!" Elle yelled. "We know about your wrist. Ethan called us."

As soon as she heard his name, her heart stopped. Grabbing the door, she flung it open. Her friends took one look at her puffy red face and gasped.

"Where's the jerk?" Elle spat, anger in her voice.

"Very tactful, Elle," Sophie said with a roll of her eyes before looking back to Kate. "Where's the bastard?"

"That's more like it." Elle wrapped her arm around her blond friend and dragged her into the room.

"You guys, he's not a jerk." Kate sighed. "I love him."

"What!" They both yelled.

"Are you serious? Kate, he broke your heart three times and you're going to let him have another shot?" Sophie yelled, her fists balled up at her sides.

Kate looked at her friends, confused. "What are you talking about?"

"Scott." They said it in unison.

"Oh. I thought you were talking about … Ethan." She swallowed thickly after saying his name.

"Wait, what about Ethan? What happened?"

Kate closed her eyes, willing herself to keep it together long enough to tell them, and started from the beginning. She shocked even herself when she told them about Scott's tentative marriage proposal the last time they'd gotten back together. They were livid that she hadn't told them, but kept their comments to a minimum so she could continue with her story. She told them all about the emails that started a few weeks prior and about the honest excitement she felt at actually being friends with Scott again—just friends and nothing more. When she told them what happened at the coffee shop earlier that morning, both of their mouths hung open in shock.

"Are you going to give him another chance?" Sophie asked, eyes wide.

"There's no reason to. I'm going to tell him that tonight. I don't love him anymore. I love Ethan." As soon as she said his name, tears pooled in her eyes.

Falling back on her bed, she buried her face in the pillow and let the tears that she thought were dried up spill freely.

Both Sophie and Elle looked at each other in puzzlement. They couldn't understand her reaction. "Kate, what's wrong? I thought it was a good thing that you love Ethan." Elle sat down beside her and rubbed her back soothingly.

"He doesn't want me," she said through her sobs. "He said he needs a break."

"Did he give you a reason?"

She couldn't speak anymore, so she simply shook her head.

"He didn't? That doesn't make sense. Why would he call here if he didn't care about you?" Sophie bit on her lip in confusion.

Up until that point, Kate had almost forgotten about what they'd said earlier. Ethan had called, and now she desperately wanted to know what he'd said, even if hearing it would hurt. "What did he say?" she finally asked, bracing herself for their reply.

"He called and said that you came into the hospital with a hurt wrist, but didn't see a doctor. At least he said he didn't see a chart for you. What happened?"

"I left," she said, tears running down her cheeks. "I couldn't stay there. I couldn't see him again."

"And how's your wrist? Do you need us to take you somewhere to have it looked at?" Elle asked in concern.

"It's okay. It's still a little sore, but the swelling is already better."

After they were sure Kate was truly fine, the two friends lay down beside her, one on either side and wrapped her in their arms. They did what all best friends do and assured her that things would be okay. Even if they hadn't figured out how just yet, they would be. They stayed at her side until the sun began to set, casting dark shadows across the room.

"You guys, I have to get up and get ready." Kate's voice was scratchy from all the crying.

"You're still going?" Elle asked, sitting up.

"Yes. I have to. I care about Scott. It's not right to let him think that things can be different between us. Besides, it will be good to see everyone again. I need a distraction."

"Well, let's get to work then. I can't have you leaving the house looking like that. Your face looks like you had some kind of allergic reaction." Sophie waved her hand in her friend's face.

"Gee, you always know how to make me feel better, Soph." She hit her hand playfully and smiled for the first time since the morning.

"Come on. Let's get you ready." Sophie hopped off the bed and stood next to Elle. The two friends reached out their hands and pulled Kate to her feet.

"Everything is going to work out. I just know it," Elle whispered in her ear before giving her a tight squeeze.

Back at the hospital, Ethan was as miserable as Kate. Though he tried to hide it, he couldn't fool Henry. "Ethan, I really think you should leave for the rest of the day. I know you said you could work a double, but I don't think you're in any shape to do that." Concern was etched in his face as he looked at the young man who was like a second son to him.

"No, I think I'll stay. Thanks. This place needs all the help it can get." He was being harsh and he knew it. Ever since Kate had left, he hadn't been able to think straight. She hadn't stayed at the hospital to have her wrist looked at, and when he'd called her house, Elle said she hadn't seen her. All the events of the day were piling up and slowly eating away at him. He'd already snapped at three nurses for screwing up on something they couldn't possibly have known, and he knew it was only a matter of time before he lost it on a patient.

"I mean it, Ethan. Finish up with the head laceration in room four and leave. I can't have you here, not like this. And frankly, I don't want you here."

"I can't go." He hung his head. "If I leave here, then my mind will be free to wander. I know what I'll think about, and I can't. When I think about her being with him," he swallowed slowly, "it makes me sick."

"So, go to her and tell her that. Tell her that you were wrong. Tell her that she has options; tell her *you* are an option."

"Not any more I'm not. I took myself out of the equation," Ethan said.

"Did you tell her?"

"What?"

Henry raised his eyebrows knowingly. "Did you tell her that you love her?"

"No."

"She deserves to know that, Ethan. And you know that. If you say nothing else, then fine, that's your choice. But at least tell her that."

Ethan remained silent, but knew Henry was right. The advice he gave was the same as the thoughts Ethan had earlier that morning. He'd told himself that Kate deserved to know how he felt, but somewhere along the way, he'd forgotten to tell her. He hadn't followed through when he had the chance.

"Go. Tell her." Henry smiled. "And if she still tells you that she doesn't want you, then you can come back here and continue being miserable."

Ethan laughed. "Thanks for the confidence." Rubbing his hands over his tired face, he thought about what he should do.

"Stop thinking and just go."

Giving one last smile, Ethan ran for the door. He had no clue what would happen, but he had to find out.

❧

"Please be here, please be here," he whispered under his breath as he shifted his weight from one foot to the other. Taking a deep breath, he started knocking.

"I hear you, I hear you. Now stop with the pounding!" Elle yelled from behind the door. "Now what in the world do you—" She stopped mid-sentence as soon as she saw Ethan. Crossing her arms in front of herself, she glared at him with accusing eyes.

The two stood in a silent stand-off, waiting to see who would be the first to speak.

"I need to talk to Kate. Is she home?"

"Yeah, I bet you need to talk to her," she said with a sarcastic smirk. "Look, Ethan, I know you're an old friend and everything, but that doesn't mean I still won't kick your butt. And if I were you, I would run and hide because Sophie is here and if you think *I* can be mean, you haven't seen anything yet."

His brows knit together in confusion. He'd assumed they would be slightly angry for telling Kate they needed space, but he figured that since it left her free to be with Scott, like she wanted, they would take it a little easier. "Look, Elle, I know that Kate has made her choice, but—"

"No," she said, cutting him off. "You made your choice. You told her *you* were done." She pushed her finger into his chest hard, making her point known.

"I only told her that because I knew she wanted to be with Scott. I mean, come on, you know Kate. She'd beat herself up for months over this if she thought she hurt me. And I can't stomach her being upset."

"What are you talking about?" Elle's face looked even more confused than the man standing in front of her.

"I'm talking about Kate and her choice to be with Scott."

Elle's jaw dropped as she studied his face. "Get in here." Grabbing his hand, she pulled him into the townhouse.

"Sophie!" she yelled. "Get in here now!"

"Uhh, Elle, didn't you just say I should run and hide from Sophie?"

She waved her hand dismissively. "Don't worry, that was before."

"Before? I'm confused. Will you please explain what's going on? Is Kate here? Can I see her? I really need to talk to her."

"You don't get to talk to her, *or* see her for that matter!" Sophie's venom-filled voice stung, and Ethan slowly turned around to find her standing in the hallway with her hands placed firmly on her hips. "I told you that if you hurt her, I would beat you down. It's so nice of you to turn yourself in for me. That way I don't have to drive around and hunt for you." She started to walk toward him, and for a split second, Ethan actually thought she was going to attack him.

"Hang on, Soph. I think there's been a miscommunication." Elle stepped forward and placed her arms on her friend's shoulder.

"I don't care about miscommunications. All I care about is my best friend who spent the entire afternoon crying her eyes out because this guy broke her heart."

Ethan buried his face in his hands. *Crap, I made her cry. I made her cry after I promised her I would never hurt her.* Guilt and pain washed over him. But even in his remorse, none of it made sense to him. If Kate had cried because of what he'd said, then there was a possibility that everything he thought could be wrong. "Sophie, Elle," he said, keeping his voice low. "Please tell me what you're talking about."

"I'm talking about Kate coming home after you broke her heart and told her you needed a break from her."

Ethan was already shaking his head. "I only did that because I knew she wanted to be with Scott," he repeated for the second time since arriving.

"What?" she yelled, her voice so high that it hurt his ears.

"That's what I meant by miscommunication." Elle took a step aside and plopped down on the couch. "So, are you saying that you want to be with Kate?"

He exhaled, for what felt like the first time since he'd arrived. "Yes. More than you can possibly imagine."

"Then what was all that talk about needing a break from her?" Sophie hadn't relaxed from her defensive stance, but her shoulders dropped slightly, signaling the fight was over.

"He was trying to spare her feelings. He thought that she wanted to be with Scott, and since we all know how Kate is—more concerned about other people's feelings than her own—smart aleck here figured he would make it seem like it was his decision to end things. That way, Kate wouldn't feel like she was hurting him." She took a breath before looking over at Ethan. "Right?"

He nodded and Sophie's eyes lit up. "Then you need to tell her how you feel," she said with a smile.

"That's why I'm here." He motioned to the room around him.

"Yes, and she's not here. She's with Scott. But not in the way you think."

"What do you mean 'not in the way I think'?" he asked.

"I think you and Kate need to have a long conversation. Go find her. Drag her out of that restaurant by her hair if you have to. Just go get her and talk; make her listen to you." Sophie walked to the counter and wrote something down on a piece of paper. "Here's the address. They always sit in the back corner booth." She smiled. "Go get her."

***

Kate walked into McLaren's and took in the familiar atmosphere. It had been a while since she'd been there, but it was still the same. It had the same laid-back, casual feel—the kind of place where you could sit with friends, eat good food, and laugh over drinks.

Before she even made it to the bar, she heard Scott calling her name. She didn't have to look to know where he was. He would be at the same table they'd always sat at. Making her way back to the corner booth, she saw all of her old friends smiling back at her. It was like walking back in time.

"Katie, you came!" Brian jumped up from the table and ran over to her, scooping her up in a hug.

"All right, all right, enough tossing me around." she groaned, feeling out of breath.

Brian laughed as he set her to her feet. "I'm just glad you're here." He wrapped his arm around her shoulder and led her to the table.

Surprisingly, Kate felt more comfortable than she thought she would. It was like she'd never left. They spent most of the dinner sharing stories. She heard the exact details of Mike's proposal to Christine, and Brian gave the run down on his girlfriend. It wasn't until they asked about the guy she was dating that she clammed up. Hoping that no one would notice her aversion to the question, Kate quickly offered to buy the next round of drinks from the bar.

Thankfully, the bartender was busy with a few other orders and it gave Kate the chance to gather her thoughts before going back to the table. Just a few hours ago if someone had asked about her dating life, she would have said she was with someone. Now everything was different. It was still so new that she'd barely had time to process it. Without warning, she felt the familiar tears prick her eyes. Not wanting to lose control in the middle of the restaurant, Kate closed her eyes tight and took a deep breath. Just as she started to collect herself, she felt an arm wrap around her waist.

"What a surprise seeing you here."

The unfamiliar voice made her skin crawl, and she whipped around to see who was touching her. As soon as she saw him, her stomach heaved and a feeling of panic swept over her. She recognized his yellowed eyes and sharply angled face immediately and memories of her night at Rain came with clarity. It was the man who'd grabbed her by the wrist on the night she'd seen Ethan.

"Where's your boyfriend, sweetheart? I'd hate to think that he left you here all alone." He leaned in as he spoke. The smell of the liquor on his breath blew past her nose.

"Her boyfriend is right here, so I advise you get your hands off of her. That is, if you want to keep them."

Looking over her shoulder, she was happy to see Scott behind her, towering over both her and the drunken man beside her. Instead of flinching away or backing down, the man simply smiled, looking from Scott to Kate.

"Looks like you get around. Last time I saw you, I could have sworn you had a different boyfriend." He smiled at Scott, provoking a response.

Fire burned behind Scott's eyes and he took a step closer. Kate knew him well enough to know what would happen next. "Scott," she warned. "Let's just go. I'm fine." She wrapped her hands around his arms and attempted to pull him away from the bar. Thankfully, he followed.

"Who was that creep?" He scowled watching the man leave.

"He's just some jerk that can't take a hint."

"What did he mean about 'last time'? What different boyfriend?"

"I saw him at Rain a month ago and I was with—" She paused. "Ethan. I was with Ethan then." She bit on her lip and swallowed back the emotions that were threatening to take over.

"What do you mean *was?*"

"Well, we're not … together anymore." It came out in a whisper. She could barely think the words, let alone say them without cringing.

"You aren't? Katie, does this mean that you're giving me another chance?" She didn't have a chance to respond before he'd pulled her into a hug "I knew you would. I knew you just needed time to—"

"Wait, Scott." She placed her hands flat on his chest and pushed him back, feeling a slight sting in her wrist. "That's not what I'm saying."

"I don't understand. What *are* you saying?"

She let out an exhausted sigh. Although she'd been planning to tell him tonight, now that the time was actually here, she was dreading it. "Can we go somewhere and talk?

"Sure." He nodded. "Let me go tell the guys. I'll meet you out front."

Pushing open the doors, the cold wind whipped across her face, clearing Kate's mind and giving her a sense of courage. Walking to the end of the street, she stood under the light and waited.

A moment later, Scott strolled to her side. "All right, I'm all ears," he said with a smile.

Kate took a deep breath and thought the words slowly before she said them. "I've been thinking about what you said earlier this morning; I've been thinking a lot about it."

"So have I. And Katie, I hope that you realize I never meant to hurt you. Or make this more difficult for you. I just want you to know you have options."

She laughed at his comment. "Options? I'm pretty sure that only applies if there is more than *one* thing to choose from."

"That's right. Ethan." He nodded. "You two broke up, huh?" There was no hiding the excitement in his voice even if he tried.

Shaking her head at him, she held back tears. "You know you could try to be a little bit more understanding. I haven't been handling all of this very well."

"I'm sorry." He paused, looking down at her with kind eyes. "Did you break up with him today?"

It was clear that he was under the impression that she'd broken up with Ethan to be with him. "No," she clarified. "*He* broke up with *me*."

"He did? So, I guess now we can—"

"Here's the thing, Scott." She cut him off. "I realized something during all of this. I realized that even if Ethan didn't want to be with me, it didn't change the way I felt about him or you. I guess what I'm trying to say is that I don't lo—"

Before she spoke another word, Scott pressed his lips to hers. He pulled her close, wrapping his hand around the back of her head, holding her there. Kate kept her lips closed tight and placed her hands on his chest in an attempt to push him away.

Across the street, Ethan was just climbing out of his car when he spotted Kate in the arms of Scott. His heart squeezed in his chest and his stomach dropped. Everything that Sophie and Elle had told him left his mind in an instant. Without thinking, he got back in his car and shoved the keys into the ignition, revving the engine. The tires spun and screeched as he peeled out of the parking spot and blew through the stop sign at the corner.

At the awful sound of tires screeching, Scott pulled back. Kate turned her head just in time to see Ethan's car speed down the street. "No!" she yelled, realizing what he must have seen.

"What's the matter?" Scott stepped close to her again and wrapped his arms around her waist.

She instantly recoiled and shoved him away. "You can't just kiss me. Were you not listening to a word I just said?"

"I was, but look, I love you, and that's not going to change. I need you to—"

"No!" She cut him off angrily. "*You* don't need me to do anything. *I* need you to leave me alone right now." Turning away from him so she wouldn't say something she regretted, she started walking down the street. She didn't hear him behind her and was thankful that this time he didn't follow.

Once she was alone, she paused and leaned up against the cold stone wall of the closest building. Her heart was pounding loudly and her head was beginning to ache. *How did this happen?* she wondered, swiping at the tears that she just noticed had begun to fall. Everything was such a mess. With a defeated sigh, she pushed away from the wall and headed down the street in the direction of her car.

She made it to the corner and was just about to cross the street when she heard footfalls behind her. Knowing that Scott must have decided to follow her, she began to turn around to confront him when a hand reached out in front of her and covered her mouth. Trying to pull away, she felt a second arm wrap around her waist, pinning her arms down to her side. She kicked her legs as she attempted to free herself, but it was no use. The lights from overhead wrapped everything in a blanket of gray haze. She couldn't see the face of her attacker, but she could feel him. She could feel his breath brush over her neck, could hear the sound of air rasping as it was pulled into his lungs. Fear crept up her spine and nausea swept over her.

"Looks like you're all alone now. No boyfriends here to save you this time."

Though she'd only heard his voice twice before, she recognized it at once—the voice that matched a hollow set of eyes that she'd seen just moments ago back at the bar. Her entire body froze as panic set in. She looked around for an escape, someone to help her. It wasn't until the man began to pull her into the dark that she heard a sound she wasn't sure she'd ever hear again.

Chapter 21
Fix You

Ethan weaved in and out of traffic as he raced back to the restaurant. It had only taken eight blocks for him to realize that he was running away from the one person he wanted, and he wasn't going to let her go without a fight. He would tell her exactly how he felt and then let her make a decision. Buildings flew past in a blur of stone and brick, and after a few blocks, he pulled over at the first spot he found. Climbing out of his car, he slammed the door shut behind him and set a quick pace in the direction of the restaurant. Keeping his head down against the wind, his mind replayed the words he wanted to say to her.

The awning of the restaurant was less than two blocks away when Ethan lifted his head. And when he did, it was as if time stood still. Everything slowed like lava flowing over dark rocks. Kate stood at the end of the street under the glow of an overhead lamppost and she wasn't alone. There was a man who stood behind her, closer than he should have been. Before Ethan could blink, the stranger's arms wrapped around her. The man held her close and said something into her ear. Kate's face went white with raw fear. Without a moment's hesitation, Ethan started to run.

"Kate!" he yelled out. The attacker didn't flinch. Ethan cursed, thinking he was still too far away to be heard. When Kate turned her head to him, her eyes wild with fear, and he knew that she, at least, had heard him.

He was half a block away when the man pulled her out of the light from the lamppost and into the darkness of the alley. The muscles in Ethan's legs burned as he pushed himself faster, harder, desperate to get to her. When he reached the corner, he dug his cell phone out of his pocket and dialed 911. He heard a woman's voice on the other end ramble, but didn't pay her any attention. His turned the corner and placed his cell on the ground, keeping the phone line open, knowing that the police would respond.

Kate was only a few feet away, and Ethan's adrenaline coursed rapidly through his veins.

Rage boiled within him and he closed the space between himself and the man that held Kate in three long strides. With both hands, he gripped the attacker's shirt. As soon as the man realized he was no longer alone, he shoved Kate away, sending her body colliding into the brick wall behind her. He tried to pull away, but Ethan held him tight and yanked his body around. When the attacker was finally facing him, it only took a second to recognize that he was the creep from the club. Ethan felt a flicker of regret for not doing something more extreme a month ago when he'd first grabbed Kate. He wouldn't make that mistake twice. Pulling his arm back, he put all of his weight behind him and punched the man square in the face. The man's head flew back and he crashed into the nearby Dumpster. The loud clang of metal rang in the alley, echoing off the brick walls.

Ethan ignored the pain that pulsed in his hand—in fact, he welcomed it and wanted more. He wanted the guy to stand up and fight back, but he didn't. He lay still on the ground, the rise and fall of his chest the only sign that he was alive. Taking a deep breath, Ethan spun around to Kate who was sitting on the ground with her back against the wall. Her eyes were wide as she looked from Ethan to the man who lay unconscious a few feet away.

"Kate," he panted. She remained silent until he repeated himself a second time. "Kate, are you all right?" This time she blinked, and he heard her take a deep breath. He crouched down and sat by her side, placing his hands on her shoulders. "He didn't hurt you, did he?"

She shook her head and looked up at Ethan. "No. No, he didn't. I'm fine; just a little freaked out."

"That's okay. You're allowed to be shaken up after something like that." He breathed a sigh of relief and pulled her into his arms.

Kate let herself relax for what felt like the first time in hours. Her shoulders rolled forward and she rested her head on his shoulder. Try as she might, she couldn't hold back the tears as they streamed down her checks. Pulling her tighter, Ethan kissed her on the head and whispered words of comfort.

Just as Ethan expected, the police arrived a few minutes later. By then, the man on the ground had started to groan, holding his hands to his face. Wanting to keep Kate as far away as possible, Ethan led her out of the alley. They were immediately greeted by two officers and explained the situation. Kate told them exactly what happened, and Ethan confirmed it with what he saw. After assuring them that she was fine, Kate was allowed to leave with the promise that she'd go into the station the following day if needed. Ethan was told that unless the attacker decided to press charges, which was highly unlikely considering the situation, he would be free to go as well.

Curious onlookers had begun to gather outside of the restaurant, and they took it as their cue to leave. Wrapping a comforting arm around Kate, Ethan led her to his car and helped her in. As soon as she sat back, she hissed through her teeth and arched her back.

"What's wrong?" he asked, worry etched in his face.

"It's just my back." She sat forward. "I must have scratched it on the wall."

"Will you be okay until I get you back to your house?"

Kate nodded. "You'll stay with me, right?" Her eyes searched his face, and she wondered how long he'd stick around. Clearly if he wanted space from her, hanging out at her house for the evening was not an option.

"Of course I will." He lifted his hand to her face and brushed his thumb along her cheek.

Ethan held her hand the entire way home, stealing glances at her constantly. He knew there were words that needed to be spoken. Things needed to be discussed, but now just didn't seem like the right time. Right now, all he wanted was to be close to her, to feel her safe in his arms and not let her go. When they pulled up to her townhouse, Ethan grabbed his medical bag out of the trunk before walking around to help Kate out of the car. He knew she didn't need the help physically, but there was no way he was letting go of her now that he had her.

As they approached the door, Kate sighed. "Prepare yourself for Self-defense Elle," she mumbled.

"Self-defense Elle?"

"Yeah, once she finds out what happened tonight, she's going to flip." Kate laughed. "She means well; she just worries about me. A year ago, she got both Soph and me self-defense classes for our birthdays. Did I ever tell you that?"

Ethan shook his head and laughed. "Well, you could always tell her that you gave him a good kick in the balls. You can trust me not to say anything." He winked.

Smiling, Kate placed her hand flat on his chest. "I think I'll stick with the truth. Although I'm not sure she'll believe that I have my own personal superhero."

"I don't know if I'd go with superhero," he said, rolling his eyes.

"Thank you," she whispered. "For being there."

Ethan swallowed the guilt he felt. "If I hadn't driven off before...I could have been there and none of it—"

"That's not important." She shook her head. "Nothing happened. He didn't hurt me. What *is* important is that you were there then and that you're here now."

He placed his fingers under her chin to ensure that she wouldn't look away. "And I'm not going anywhere. I'm staying right here." At that moment, he felt the need to tell her everything. He wanted to tell her the reason behind his actions earlier that day and he wanted to tell her that he loved her. He wanted her to know it all. "Look, Kate, about what happened earlier today at the hospital. When I said that I needed—"

"Let's not talk about that right now," she cut him off. "I just want to enjoy being with you for however long you'll—"

"I'm *not* leaving," Ethan said a second time. "I'm here for as long as you want me."

"That may be a long time, you know." The corners of her mouth pulled up into a hint of a smile.

Returning her smile with one of his own, he leaned in to pull her into a hug when he remembered her back. "Let's get you inside so I can take a look at your back," he said, eyeing the door.

They walked inside, and Kate led them through to the kitchen where she flicked the under-counter lights on. "Looks like we're safe from Elle." She held up a sheet of paper. "She's spending the night over at Sophie's."

"Good, then we won't have to explain anything tonight." Ethan stepped toward her and brushed his hand over her arm. "How's your wrist feeling? I wish you would have stayed and had it looked at," he said, feeling guilty that his words had sent her home before she was cared for.

"It's actually okay. Not as bad as I thought." He looked at her closely to make sure she was telling the truth. "I promise," she said, knowing that he needed that assurance.

"All right." He nodded. "Why don't you go lay on the couch?"

She walked out of the kitchen and paused by the doorway until he was beside her.

Ethan set his bag on the coffee table and removed the few things he knew he'd need. As he set out the gauze and tape, Kate watched him with loving eyes. It would be the second time he'd taken care of her, and the feelings it stirred were ones she'd never before experienced. There was something in his touch that made her feel so loved, so protected and safe. It was almost overwhelming.

"All right," Ethan said, standing up. "You'll need to take your shirt off so I can take a look."

With a silent nod, Kate lifted her hands and began to fumble with her buttons. She knew it was ridiculous to be nervous, especially since he'd seen her with her top off before, but she couldn't help it. She was on the second button when Ethan stepped forward and placed his hands over hers, stilling her movements. His eyes met hers, and he gently placed her hands at her side before taking over where she'd left off, carefully working the buttons open. When he finished with the last one, he gingerly slid the fabric over her shoulders, making sure not to rub her back in the process.

With both hands, Kate gathered her hair to the side and turned around to show him her back. Very carefully, she slipped one of her bra straps off her shoulder and followed with the other. Not wanting her to twist around and risk hurting her back, Ethan reached forward and undid the clasp. She slipped her bra down both arms and climbed onto the couch, lying down on her stomach.

Wanting to get a better look, Ethan dropped to his knees. It didn't look as bad as he'd thought and for that he was grateful. "It's just a few superficial lacerations; nothing too serious. Let me go wash my hands and I'll get it cleaned up. I'll be right back."

He grabbed a few washcloths and some ibuprofen from the hall closet and a bottle of water from the kitchen. When he walked back into the living room, Kate was lying still with her eyes closed. Her lips were parted slightly as she breathed in and out in a steady rhythm. She was beautiful, and he took a moment longer than normal to just enjoy the sight of her.

Eventually he walked over to the couch and cleared his throat to announce his presence. "I want you to take this for the pain," he said, holding out the bottle of water and tiny pills. "I'd feel better if it was something stronger, but that would require a trip to the hospital, and—"

"Shots," she said, cutting him off. He nodded and she opened her eyes to meet his. "No. I'd like to stay here. These will be fine." Tilting her head back slightly, she popped the pills in her mouth and drank deeply from the bottle of water. When she was finished, she buried her head into the pillow and sighed loudly.

"Just try and relax," he said calmly. "This will probably sting a bit."

He set to work cleaning the area with sterile saline, making sure it was completely clean before dabbing it with the washcloth. She only winced once, and for that Ethan was thankful. It was already hard enough knowing that she was in pain, and the thought of hurting her further was too much. After making sure everything was clean and dry, he continued with the dressings.

"That should do it. I'll want to take a better look at it tomorrow at the hospital and that's not up for negotiation."

He expected her to put up a fight and when she didn't, he sat back and looked down at her face. Her breathing was steady and deep and the features of her face were calm. She'd fallen asleep. Watching her with a smile, Ethan knew at that moment that everything was going to work out. They would be together, and all of the confusion between them would be in the past. Feeling as if a weight had been lifted from his shoulders, Ethan stood and started cleaning up when there was a knock at the door. Not wanting to wake Kate, he quickly hurried over to the door and opened it. As soon as he did, he wished he hadn't, because standing on the other side was Scott.

"What are you doing here?" Scott asked.

"I think I should be asking you the same question."

"Look, I don't think I need to explain myself to you. I'm here to see Katie." He placed his hand on the door and began to push it open.

In one quick swing, Ethan shot his hand out and blocked his entrance. He glared down at Scott's hand which was still on the door and briefly contemplated ripping it off. Noticing the expression on Ethan's face, Scott took a step back. Following his lead, Ethan stepped out into the hall and pulled the door partially closed behind him. "Kate's not really up to having company right now," he said through a tight jaw.

"I'm not company. I'm her ... friend," he said, swallowing back the word.

"It doesn't matter what you are. I'm still not letting you in. And what are you doing here anyway? Isn't it kind of late to be stopping by?"

"I think I should be asking you the same question." Scott gave him a condescending smile.

"I'm here because Kate asked me to be. *She* wants me here with her."

"Look." He held his arms out. "I heard some stuff happened a few blocks away from the restaurant where we were tonight, and I just wanted to make sure she's okay."

"She is now. Good thing *I* was there."

"What's that supposed to mean?"

At that moment all the anger and frustration Ethan felt for Scott bubbled to the surface. "It means that you left her alone. You walked away from her."

Inside the townhouse, Kate woke to the sound of arguing. It only took a second for her to recognize Scott's voice. She quickly grabbed her shirt and was buttoning it as she walked to the door. Just as she was about to walk out, she heard Scott shout. Her whole body tensed and she froze behind the door, listening.

"She walked away from me!" Scott yelled, his face contorted in anger. "And besides, she's a big girl; she can—"

"I'm not just talking about tonight," Ethan said, cutting him off. "You walked away from her six months ago. You left her broken and now you think you can just waltz back into her life and say you want her again? I'm sorry, but it's not going to happen. This time, she has me, and I *will* fight for her."

"Yeah, well, if memory serves me right you left her too, earlier today in fact. So, shut the hell up. You think you're better than me?"

For the second time that night, Ethan clenched his fist tight and pulled back. He didn't hesitate as he let go and decked Scott in the face. "Don't you *ever* compare yourself to me, especially when it comes to Kate," he seethed. Scott clenched his fists ready to strike back but Ethan continued talking. "You had your chance and you blew it. It's my turn now. I am in this for the long haul, and believe me, I'm not going to let you stand in my way. She is *everything* to me. I love her."

On the other side of the door, Kate gasped. She stood in shocked silence, trying to process what she'd just heard. Perhaps her shock should have rendered her immobile, but it didn't. She found herself grabbing hold of the handle and pulling the door open. Still dazed, she walked out into the hallway and stood at Ethan's side, not taking her eyes off of him.

As soon as he noticed her beside him, he looked down at her. Her eyes were wide with shock and her mouth hung open slightly.

"What did you just say?" she whispered.

"I said I love you."

She smiled as the realization of his words registered in her mind. "I love you too," she said simply, knowing without a shadow of a doubt that it was true.

Scott tensed as he heard her words and ran his hands over his face. The girl he loved stood silent while staring into the eyes of another. As he shifted his feet, Kate finally noticed Scott.

"Hi," Kate said, biting her lip nervously.

"Hey."

An awkward silence hung in the air as all three of them waited for one of the others to speak.

"Could you give us a second?" Kate finally asked. Ethan immediately looked at Scott with hard eyes but nodded.

Once alone, Scott looked down at Kate with a half smile. "I take it this means you guys are back together?" he asked, tilting his head to the side.

There was no hiding the happiness from her face as she smiled. "I guess so, yeah."

"And there's no way you'll think about giving me another shot?"

"Scott."

"I mean, come on, Katie. You honestly love this guy? You hardly know him. You've been together, what, like a month?" He shook his head. "You're just confused."

"No, I'm not," she snapped. "You don't know what you're talking about. I do love him. I want to be with him, and I'm not confused." He harrumphed and it only angered her further. "You know, I can't even believe I doubted myself for one second. I don't love you anymore, Scott—plain and simple. And I'm not—"

"But I love you. Doesn't that mean anything to you?"

"Are you kidding me right now?" She pushed the palms of her hands into her eyes. "You *know* me, Scott. You know that it means something to me. My friends are everything to me—a fact of which you are completely aware and have used against me on more than one occasion."

His arms crossed in front of himself. "What are you talking about?"

"What about dinner tonight?" she asked.

"What about it?"

"I told you I needed space, but you wanted me to go. So, what did you do? You told me that Brian would be there and that *he* wanted to see me. You know I can't say no to him, but you did it anyway because *you* wanted me there."

"I only did that because I love you, and I was hoping that maybe things could be like they used to be."

The pain and honesty in his eyes was clear, and the one spot in her heart that would always care for him ached. "I don't want to fight with you, Scott. I'm done." She dropped her head. "I will always care about you, and you will always have a place in my heart. Maybe some day, years from now, we'll be able to be friends again, but not now." She lifted her eyes and looked into the face of her oldest friend, a face that she knew so well. The face she'd once loved.

With tears in his eyes, he took a step closer. "I'll always love you, Katie," he whispered as he brushed his hand against her face.

"I know."

Before she could take a breath, he had turned away and was out of sight. Kate stood for a moment and waited for the signs of heartache to come, but they didn't. For the first time in forever, she was able to say goodbye to Scott and know that it was the right thing. Her heart, which had been missing pieces for so long, felt whole and fixed. With a calming sigh, Kate walked back into the living room, but didn't see the one person she wanted anywhere.

"Ethan?" She called out to him as she walked down the hallway.

"I'm in here. Hope you don't mind. I wanted to give you guys some privacy, and I could hear everything you were saying when I was in the living room."

She walked into her bedroom and saw him standing by the large window. The curtains were pulled back and the light from the moon was pouring in, casting a silver glow over everything. She couldn't see his face very clearly, but the light outlined his figure. His hair was messier than normal and his scrubs were wrinkled. At that moment, she realized that today had been just as hard on him as it had been on her.

"Sorry you had to hear all that," she said softly.

"Don't apologize." He walked toward her with open arms and she rushed to him, burying her face in his chest. She could feel the love he felt for her radiating off of him like heat, enveloping her and pulling her close to him. It was so easy to feel, and she wondered then how she'd ever doubted it.

Leaning back, he gazed down at her and traced his fingers over her face. The way he looked at her, studying her like she was the most precious thing he'd ever seen, took her breath away.

"Beautiful," he whispered. Lowering his head, he brushed his lips back and forth gently against hers before pressing them softly to her. Their mouths moved in perfect rhythm, recognizing each other's motions as if they'd always been one. Pulling back, Kate kissed his chin, his jaw, his cheekbone, feeling the rough stubble against her lips. His hands moved to the front of her shirt and began unbuttoning it for the second time tonight, but then froze. "Are you okay with this?" he whispered in her ear, sending a chill down her spine.

He looked down at her and Kate could see love and concern in his eyes. After everything that happened today, she could have said no, but she didn't. All she wanted was to feel his love for her. To feel safe in his arms and to show him how much she loved him.

"I'm more than okay." She looked up into his blue eyes and felt her heart fill with happiness.

Silently nodding, he ran his hands over her bare shoulders as he slid the shirt down her arms. His eyes grazed over her, drinking her in, before he slowly leaned down and kissed the soft skin of her neck. Sliding his tongue and lips along the line of her collarbone, he traced an invisible path to the curve of her shoulder.

Kate's head fell to the side and she closed her eyes, enjoying the touch of his lips on her skin. Everywhere he kissed left a trail of warmth. Little sparks of electricity pricked up her arms and worked their way through her entire body, setting fires along her skin. She could hear herself panting loudly but couldn't control it, and didn't want to. When his name passed from her lips, he lifted his eyes to hers. Even in the darkened room, she could see the depth of color and the way they changed from blue to gray as he looked at her.

Running her fingers up the base of his neck, she fingered the soft hair at his nape before pulling him down and covering his mouth with hers again. Once she was certain he wasn't going anywhere, she dropped her hands from his hair and slid them between their bodies until she found the hem at the bottom of his shirt. She gave him one last peck and pulled away, only to lift his shirt over his head and feel the bare skin of his chest under her hands. He was perfect. The lines of his wide shoulders, neck, torso, all of him...

Skin pressed against skin as they embraced and stepped backwards toward her bed, their lips never separating. He laid her down gently and held himself above her, looking deep into her eyes. In that one simple look, Kate felt safe. She felt at home and it was unlike anything she'd ever felt before. She wanted all of him—his mind, his heart, his soul, and his body. His soft yet desperate touches told her he felt the same way.

His hand brushed over her face, tucking her hair behind her ear as he peered down at her. Placing her hand over his, Kate held it to her cheek before turning to kiss his palm. Their fingers intertwined and slowly began a descent down her body, working the last few articles of clothing away.

Their touches were both gentle and desperate as they made love, each showing the other how they felt in a way words couldn't describe. Every touch of his fingers, every kiss of his lips was memorized and stored away in Kate's heart. And later, when they lay wrapped up in each other, the darkness of the room their only blanket, Ethan knew that he was with the person he'd spend forever with.

"I love you, Ethan," she said, as if reading his thoughts.

He tilted his head down and kissed her forehead. "I love you too."

Glancing up under dark lashes, Kate's brown eyes met his blue, and she knew then and there that she was looking into the face of her future.

Chapter 22
Clean

The sound of rain hitting against the glass window brought Ethan out of his deep sleep. He opened his eyes slowly and looked around. It only took a moment for his mind to register where he was and only a second longer for him to realize why he felt so happy, so complete. He looked down in his arms and saw Kate. She was fast asleep, a peaceful look on her face. He took in every feature as if he was seeing her for the first time. Every curve, every angle, every detail imprinted itself into his mind. He had no doubts that waking up with her next to his side was something he wanted every morning. Seeing her face and feeling her touch would be the perfect way to start his day.

Kate shifted and buried her head further into the pillow and Ethan could hear her faint mumbles. He smiled and wondered if she was dreaming of him. Heaven knows he dreamed about her every chance he got. Since the first time he'd met her, she'd been starring in them. Every morning he woke up with the picture of her in his mind, her smile captured like a photo for him to remember throughout the day. And now she was actually there in his arms. For the first time in his life, he didn't need a dream. He was living one.

Closing his eyes, he let himself enjoy the feeling of elation that filled his chest. He drifted back to sleep listening to the sound of Kate's deep breaths, keeping time with the pouring rain. Sometime later, he woke to the touch of Kate's lips against his.

"Wake up, sleepy head," she whispered against his mouth between kisses.

"Hmm," he moaned with eyes closed. "I could get used to this."

"Good. Because last night was the best night's sleep I think I've ever had. I'm pretty sure sleeping alone from now on will *not* be an option for me." Ethan finally opened his eyes and looked down at her. She was propped up on her elbows, her chestnut hair falling over her bare shoulders and sticking out in random pieces. Her face was crinkled with sleep, and she had never looked so beautiful.

"Sounds good to me." He laughed and wrapped his arms around her waist, rolling them onto his back.

Kate smirked down at him. "Yes, I could definitely get used to this."

"Oh, so that's all you want me here for? You just want someone to keep you warm and help 'scratch an itch' whenever it's needed?"

She eyed him playfully. "I'll admit. The warmth of your body is nice. But I don't need you here to 'scratch my itch,' Ethan. I've been just fine for the past six months."

"Oh, really?" he laughed.

She tried to hide her smile, but it was impossible. "Yes, really. Apparently you don't know me as well as you think you do."

"Well, believe me, I'm more than excited to learn all the little ins and outs of Katherine Thomas." He placed his hand under her chin and made her look at him.

"Really?" Her playful smile faded, and she almost looked insecure.

"Yes, really." He reassured her. "I want to know everything."

"Everything?" She raised her eyebrows in question.

"Yes."

"I don't know. There's a lot you don't know…" She trailed off, using her playful voice again.

It only left Ethan wanting more. If there was one thing in the world he wanted more of, it was Kate. "In that case, please enlighten me."

"Okay. So…" Her nose scrunched up, and she pressed her lips together in concentration. It was a look that always made Ethan smile. It was like he could see the wheels spinning in her head as she worked things out.

"I don't squeeze the toothpaste from the bottom of the tube; I do it from the middle." Her eyes met his in complete seriousness. "And," she continued, "I have to have the toilet paper hanging the right way. It has to roll from the top, not the bottom. I like fruit candy and chocolate, but not together. They have to be eaten separately; none of those chocolate covered fruit gummy things."

Her face scrunched a bit, but he held back his laugh and continued listening. "I despise mint flavored toothpaste, which pretty much leaves me with very few options in the cinnamon category. But strangely when it comes to candy, I only like mint and not cinnamon."

She continued to prattle with random facts that he was sure she felt were nothing but ridiculous habits and preferences. Ethan, on the other hand, listened intently, soaking in every last detail and routine she recited. She paused after a moment and looked at him.

"What?" she asked.

He shook his head in disbelief. "Amazing. You're simply amazing."

"Yeah," she said with a sarcastic laugh. "I've been known to mystify and surprise." She dropped her eyes down and focused on the trim of the sheet, twirling it between her fingers nervously.

"It's true, you know. You do amaze me. And you did leave a few things out. Like the fact that you have such a giving heart you can't help but draw people near you. Your smile brightens a room as soon as you enter it. You're the best friend anyone could ask for. You fidget when you're nervous about something or when you're concentrating. You're smart, funny, caring, understanding, thoughtful, beautiful, and sexy as hell. The fact that you have all of these adorable habits only makes me love you more."

There was a moment of silence as they both looked at each other. It was a wonderful feeling, knowing that they both felt the same way.

"As much as I'd love to lay in bed all day with you, we should probably get up." Kate sat up. "I think I'm going to hop in the shower." As disappointed as Ethan was, he understood. But before he had a chance to tell her he agreed, she spoke up again. "Care to join me?"

"Join you?" he swallowed, processing the words

The look on his face was all Kate needed. "I'll take that as a yes. Why don't I go get started and you can join me whenever you're ready." She smiled down at him and gathered the sheet up around her chest, making sure to keep herself covered. Very carefully, she kicked one of her legs around and climbed off of Ethan. He watched her as she made her way over to her bathroom, never taking his eyes off of her swaying frame. She paused as soon as she reached the door and looked back at him over her shoulder.

"Don't keep me waiting too long. I don't want to run out of hot water." She dropped the sheet and let it fall to the ground, sweeping over her silky smooth skin as it pooled around her ankles. Giving him one last sexy smirk, she disappeared behind the door.

Ethan lay on the bed, frozen, staring at the spot where she had just been. His breathing was heavy and he had to remind himself to calm down. Closing his eyes, he dropped his head back onto the pillow and heard the water turn on. He listened for a few seconds and heard the shower curtain sliding along the rod, signaling she'd stepped in. Without a second thought, he leaped out of the bed and ran towards the bathroom. Pausing in the doorway, he peered inside the room and could faintly see her silhouette through the light shower curtain. The curve of her hip and way her back arched was beautiful. When the room began to fill with steam, he stepped inside the bathroom and shut the door behind him with a click.

Thirty minutes later, they lay in bed, legs tangled together and their skin still damp from the shower. It wasn't until Kate's stomach growled with hunger that either of them stirred.

"Hungry?" Ethan asked, lifting his head.

"How'd you guess? I didn't really eat much yesterday. It was a crazy, stressful, amazing day."

He laughed. "That's quite a mix of adjectives."

"Well, it was quite a day. I'm just glad it ended with you."

He placed his hand on her cheek and looked into her eyes smiling. "I'm planning on ending every day and starting every day with you." He kissed her and felt her smile against his lips. "Let's go get you some breakfast. I can't have you passing out on me from lack of nutrition. Plus, I need you to have plenty of energy."

She smirked. "Yeah, I bet you do."

"I can't help it if I can't get enough of you." He shrugged.

"I know exactly what you mean." She nodded with a smile. "Come on. I'll make you breakfast." She hopped out of bed, walked over to her dresser and started pulling on a pair of little shorts and a tank top.

Ethan begrudgingly followed suit, grabbing his scrub bottoms from the floor and pulling them up around his waist. He hadn't noticed Kate had stopped getting dressed and was watching him. "I knew there was a reason I loved you being a doctor," she purred. Confused, Ethan turned and saw her devouring his body with her eyes.

"Kate," he warned. "If you want me to *let* you go eat, you're going to have to stop looking at me like that." She tore her eyes away from his body and felt embarrassed. He chuckled. "I love that you get flustered even after everything that we've done."

"I can't help it," she mumbled, dropping her eyes.

Taking a step forward, Ethan grabbed her hand in his. "Come on, beautiful. Teach me how to make those famous pancakes I've heard so much about."

❧

Six pancakes and an hour later, they sat on the couch in Kate's living room, watching *The Price is Right*.

"Come on! You honestly think a bottle of Centrum is $1.99? What year is this? 1970?" she yelled.

Ethan's eyes hadn't left Kate since the show started. He'd never seen her get so worked up over something and found her reactions more entertaining than the show itself. Not to mention, she was better than all of contestants who had played so far.

"I knew it. She should have switched the Centrum with the Metamucil." Huffing, she sat back, annoyed. He could barely contain his laughter. "What?" she asked, turning to look at him.

"I never knew you were such an expert on geriatric products," he laughed.

"Hey! I spent every Saturday morning watching this show with my dad, followed by the amazing Bob Ross and his happy little trees."

She joined his laughter and when her giggles died down, she rested her head on his lap. They spent the rest of the show in that position, with Ethan running his fingers through her hair, both of them relaxed and happy. The show was just coming to an end when there was a knock at the door. By the confused look on Kate's face, it was clear she wasn't expecting any visitors. With furrowed brows, she climbed off the couch and walked to the door with Ethan on her heels. She opened the door to reveal a nervous-looking Trent.

"Trent? What are you doing here?" Ethan asked, stepping around Kate.

"I'm here to beg you to come home because I miss you too much." He rolled his eyes. "What do you think I'm doing here? I'm here to see Elle."

"Really?" Kate poked her head out from behind Ethan, but stayed close, wrapping her arms around his waist and pressing her body against his.

Trent looked from Ethan to Kate and back again, studying his friend's expression, when suddenly a huge grin spread across his face. He'd known Ethan long enough to know his just-got-laid look.

"Someone had a great night," Trent said, raising his eyebrows up and down.

Ethan didn't have to look at Kate to know that she was probably embarrassed beyond belief. "Trent," he warned, just as Kate placed her hand on Ethan's chest and looked at Trent with a smirk.

"If you must know, we did have a great night. In fact, it was the best night *and* morning that I've ever had." She was met with two sets of wide eyes but continued talking. "And Elle isn't here. She stayed over at Sophie and Logan's last night. But I'll let her know you came by, and I'm sure she'll call you."

Trent shifted his weight from one foot to the other. "See that's the thing. I'm not sure if she will. I mean, we talked before and I … I think that I …" He let out a huff of air and looked at Ethan. "Can I talk to you for a minute?"

Kate gave Ethan's arm a squeeze. "I'll just go in the other room."

"All right," Ethan said, crossing his arms. "Hit me. What's going on?"

"See, that's the problem. I have no clue. For the first time in my life, I'm clueless." Trent was met with doubtful eyes. "All right, let me rephrase that. For the first time in my life, I'm clueless when it comes to a *girl*. I mean, I know chicks—it's my thing; it's what I do."

Ethan nodded. If there was one thing Trent was good at, it was girls. He knew them almost better than football.

"But for some reason, I keep getting these mixed signals from her," he continued. "One minute I think she's interested, and the next …" His voice trailed off as he rubbed his hands over his face in frustration.

Never in his life had Ethan seen his friend so confused over a girl, and he had to admit, it was fun to watch. "Have you told her you like her?" he asked.

"You know that I—"

"Look," Ethan cut him off. "I know it's not a typical 'Trent move' to admit that you actually like a girl but … wait, you do really like her, right?"

"Like her? Man, I've had more visits from Rosy Palm and her five friends in the past two days than I've had in a month." He laughed. "But it's not just that. She gets under my skin, and not in the normal, annoying chick way."

"Trent, you have to make a move and you have to make your intentions clear. If there is one thing I've learned in the two past days, it's to say what you feel."

He nodded. "Okay. I can do that. Right?" He looked to his friend for silent confirmation. "I mean, I've never done it before, but there is a first time for everything, right?"

The two stood in silence for a minute, both of them thinking. After a brief pause, Trent turned around to leave, but stopped at the top of the steps.

"You guys have plans for Friday night?"

"Not that I'm aware of. I work Saturday morning, but I'm pretty sure I'm free."

"Good. Keep that night open. We're going out."

The wide smile on his face signaled he had something planned, but Ethan didn't question it. He simply gave him a nod before shutting the door. Kate was lying on the floor on her stomach when he walked back into the living room.

"Let me guess. Problems with Elle?" she asked, still facing the TV. "Is he questioning whether or not she's actually interested?"

"Yes. What made you guess that?"

"Because that's Elle; she's the queen of mixed signals. Then again, from what she said about him earlier, he seems to be the same way. She doesn't want to be just another girl to him, another notch in his belt."

"I think he feels the same way. You know, it's funny though. I've never seen him so worked up over a girl before. It's almost painful to watch. Almost." He smiled, remembering his friend's confused face.

"I know, I thought the same thing with Elle. You know what this means, right?" She propped her head up on her elbow and faced Ethan.

"They're perfect for each other," he responded.

She nodded. "Completely."

He sat down on the floor next to her and glanced down at her back. Realizing that he hadn't re-bandaged it after the shower, he pulled the bottom of her shirt up so he could take a better look. "I need to get this covered." He grazed his fingers along the small of her back, raising goose bumps over her skin.

"Are you sure you want to cover me up?"

"Not really, no," he said simply. "But I do want you healed. I don't want it to get infected and make it hard to move around."

"I'm pretty sure I don't have any problems *moving* around," she said smirking.

"No, I guess you don't." He slid his hand up her back and along her shoulder. "But still I need to be responsible and take care of you. We can swing by the police station on the way to the hospital and see if they need any more information about last night." He started to stand when he felt Kate's small hand on his wrist, stopping him.

"Why don't you be responsible by checking my range of motion?" A sly smile took her lips as she looked into his eyes.

Ethan went back and forth mentally, debating his options, but knew by the look on Kate's face that this was one argument she was going to win. "I think I can manage that, as long as you let me take you in later," he said.

"I'll do whatever you want, *Doctor.*" She smirked and looked up at him from under her dark lashes.

He swallowed thickly and stood up, pulling her to her feet. "I hope you have a good water heater, because as your doctor, I suggest cleaning your back again."

"That sounds good to me." She smiled. "After all, one can never be too clean, right?"

"Never."

Chapter 23
Four Seasons

ome on, Elle, you have to go. All of us are going. It'll be fun," Kate pleaded.

Her tall friend rolled her eyes for the tenth time and exhaled before turning over in bed and glaring.

"Kate, I told you. I'm not interested in going." She stood up, walked over to her closet and began searching for her favorite patent leather peep toes. "Especially if Trent's going to be there," she mumbled under her breath.

"Please. Are you seriously going to let him keep you from having a fun night out with the girls? Or are you just afraid to be around him? Maybe he's too much for you to handle." Kate turned around casually and walked toward the door. Knowing Elle as well as she did, she knew exactly how she'd react.

"Hold on," Elle said with narrowed eyes. "First off, let's get a few things straight." Pausing, she held her finger up in the air. "I'm not afraid to be around Trent Williams. If anything, *he* should be afraid to be around *me*. And since when have I ever not been able to handle guys like him?" she asked with raised eyebrows.

"Never."

"That's right." Elle nodded.

"So…"

"So, what?"

"So, are you going to come with us or not?"

"Yes, I am." She spun around and slipped into her shoes. "That fine man can send me all the mixed signals he wants. I'll send them right back. Two can play that game."

"You *do* realize that sending mixed signals is not the best way to win a guy over."

"Who said anything about winning a guy over?"

"Elle," she warned. "I happen to know for a fact that you like him. And I'm pretty positive that he likes you. So why don't you guys just stop this game and get on with it?"

"Because," she sighed, sitting down on the edge of her bed, "I tried making it clear to him and it didn't work."

"When?" Kate sat down beside her and waited for an explanation.

"A few days ago." She shook her head trying to forget the awkward memory. "I don't know. Maybe it's because I don't have much experience in this area." She was met with silence. "Fine, let me rephrase that. I've never actually had to *work* to get a guy."

"Tell me something I don't know." Kate laughed. "Have you ever stopped to think that maybe you and Trent are more alike than you think? I mean, you both seem to be professionals at giving off mixed signals."

"Believe me, the signal I got was not mixed." She was speaking more to herself than to Kate, but she knew she'd been heard. Not wanting to explain further, she squared off her shoulders and took a breath. "It's no big deal. I'm going with you guys tomorrow night, Trent or no Trent." Her tone was final and she hoped that the subject would be dropped. "So, do you have another hot date tonight with Dr. Hottie?" she asked, hoping to help the flow in subject change.

"No," Kate said. Her face fell. "He's working late since he has off tomorrow night."

"Guess it's just the two of us, then." Elle smiled. "I've got to run out now. But when I get back, let's order takeout." Grabbing her purse, she walked to the door and yelled over her shoulder, "And be prepared, because I want details!"

Kate laughed and didn't even bother yelling anything back. If she knew Elle—and she did—there was no way she'd be able to get out of spilling at least a few details about the past few days with Ethan.

As Elle walked out the door, she heard her friend's laughter ringing in the hall. It made her smile to know that she was so happy. The changes she'd seen in Kate over the past week had been significant. She was definitely happier than Elle had ever seen her. It seemed as though all of her past fears and worries, most of them stemming from Scott, were gone. She'd made her decision and so had Ethan.

Try as she might, there was no denying the bit of jealousy she felt. She was more than happy for her friend, but seeing her happiness only made her realize what she was lacking. After the football game a week ago, she could have sworn that Trent was interested, but now she knew she couldn't have been more wrong. She climbed into her car and let her mind wander back to the night that started all the confusion.

The first fifteen minutes had been great, but then a few guys approached her and asked for an autograph. She'd been approached by fans before; but something told her that with the release of the *Sports Illustrated* swimsuit issue, things were going to be different. Having some experience with it already, she knew she had to play the part—the part of the "friendly and sometimes flirtatious Elle."

She had been a little nervous about how Trent might react. After all, he'd almost ripped a guy's head off at the football game for holding her waist a little too tightly. Making sure to be extra careful with her wording, she had made sure to keep her distance. Things had gone great for about five minutes, and then it had been like someone flipped a switch. Trent had, all of a sudden, become buddy-buddy with the guys, telling them to step closer and get a good picture. She had felt like she was out with her publicist, not on a date with a guy that liked her.

Not knowing how to react, she had done the only thing she could do when in an uncomfortable situation. She stepped it up a notch—the flirting, the touching, and the carefree attitude, all of it. Even though she knew it was childish, she waited for the reaction she was hoping to get—the same reaction that she had received on the night of the football game. The one that, even though she had yelled at him and called him a stupid jerk, had made her feel special. It let her know that he cared. But it never came.

That night she had left the bar alone, confused and pissed. It was a serious blow to her self esteem, and for the past few days, she'd been questioning what she could've done differently. Not one to ever let her guard down when it came to men, she was angry at herself for giving him a chance and thinking that maybe he was different. *That's what you get for leaving your choice up to the fate of a coin toss,* she thought with a roll of her eyes.

She continued to scold herself for being stupid as she pulled into the dry cleaners. Grabbing her clothes, she folded them over her arm and climbed out of the car, making her way across the parking lot. Her heels clicked on the pavement and set a perfect beat to her natural strut. She was almost to the door when she noticed a good looking older man walking toward her. Keeping her head held high, she made sure to turn up the sway of her hips as she sauntered closer to him.

Without needing to check, Elle knew he was watching her. She could feel his eyes on her, looking over her body. When she reached the door, she took a quick peek over her shoulder and her suspicions were confirmed. The man's head was craned around, his jaw open and eyes bulging. Giving him a smirk and a quick wink, she earned a smile and sigh in return. With a quiet giggle, she flipped her hair over her shoulder and walked into the store, feeling a boost in confidence.

Yep, I still got it, she thought. *Friday night is going to be fun. Watch out, Trent.*

☙

"Elle, are you almost ready?" Kate yelled.

"Almost," she yelled back, giving herself another glance in her full length mirror.

She'd spent most of her afternoon making sure she had a perfect outfit that would bring Trent to his knees. And looking back at her reflection, she knew she'd found it. The sexy skirt and heels were perfect. *Trent, baby, eat your heart out,* she thought with a wicked smile. Grabbing her clutch, she walked out of her bedroom and headed down the hall. Before she even made it into the living room, she heard the familiar laugh and felt her heart flutter. She gave herself a little pep talk and took a deep breath before turning the corner.

When she walked into the room, Sophie was sitting on Logan's knee, fidgeting with the buttons on his blue oxford. Kate stood beside Ethan, wrapped in his arms as he ran his fingers over the hair that brushed her shoulder. All four of them had their eyes on Trent, who was in the middle of telling a story. His vibrant green eyes glowed in contrast to the black shirt that clung to his broad chest and muscular arms. With serious difficulty, Elle forced herself to peel her eyes off of him just before he noticed her presence. As soon as he did, his voice cut off in a muffled choke.

He whistled. "Damn, Elle, don't you look good enough to eat."

"Sorry, but you better get used to fasting." She smiled pleasantly even though her voice was laced with venom. Turning on her heel, she started for the front door. "Well, are we going or not?" she called over her shoulder.

The five friends looked at each other and quickly hopped to their feet. It was clear Elle was in a mood and none of them wanted to push her buttons. Except, of course, for Trent. As far as he was concerned, her fiery temper made her even more interesting. The group walked past Elle, who stood at the front door, but Trent paused when he reached her. Leaning in slowly, he placed his lips only an inch away from her ear. The warmth of his breath blew over her neck, sending chills through her entire body.

"Something tells me you'll regret your little comment," he whispered.

When her chest grew tight, she realized she wasn't breathing. Silently cursing him for having that effect on her, she attempted to regain her composure and rolled her shoulders back confidently. Unfortunately for her, none of it went unnoticed by Trent, and she watched as a huge, knowing smile spread across his face.

"Speechless?" He laughed and turned away, walking down the front steps.

"Ha," she harrumphed, following quickly at his heels. "You wish you had that effect on me."

He stopped abruptly and spun around. Taking her by surprise, she slammed into his chest—her nose stopping an inch away from his collarbone. "Actually, I do wish." He smirked. "And I'm pretty sure you do, too." He looked at her, but she refused to meet his eyes.

Stepping back, she placed her hands firmly on her hips before finally looking at his face.

"You know, despite what the fairytales say, wishes and dreams don't always come true. Cinderella and that little green guy didn't know what they were talking about."

"Jiminy Cricket."

Her face pulled together in confusion. "Who?"

"The little green guy. His name is Jiminy Cricket."

"Whatever." She rolled her eyes. "Let's go."

Ignoring the way her heart was hammering within her chest, she walked past him quickly and was almost to her car when Sophie stepped in front of her, effectively blocking her path.

"Hey, why don't you drive over with Trent? I'm leaving early with Logan, and Kate and Ethan have plans later. I'm sure he won't mind dropping you off." She turned and smiled up at Trent, who was grinning back at her with a smile just as wide. "Right?" she asked.

"Sure don't." He shook his head.

"Good, then it's settled. See you there!"

Before Elle could even open her mouth to protest, her friend hoped into Logan's car and sped off, with Ethan and Kate following close behind them.

"Come on. I promise I won't bite."

She let out a huff of annoyance, but followed him over to his SUV anyway. After settling in to the gray leather, Trent started the car and backed out.

"How have you been, Elle?"

"Fine," she deadpanned. "You?"

"Can't complain. I got cleared medically so I can play now."

"Really?" There was no hiding the enthusiastic tone of her voice, and it took her a second to remember she was supposed to be playing hard-to-get and not interested. "Really?" she asked again, this time sounding nonchalant.

"Yep. You'll have to come to my next game."

"You'd get me tickets?"

"Sure. I get tickets for chicks all the—" He immediately caught himself and was about to apologize when Elle started talking.

"That would be really great. I'd love to take…" She scrambled for a name and quickly remembered one of the guys she'd met at the bar the other night. "…Richard to a game. He's a big fan of football and you already know how much *I* enjoy it." She waited for his response, expecting to finally get the reaction she wanted.

"Like I said, there's no problem getting you tickets at all. But," he paused. "I hope you won't mind sitting next to Candy. She's a big fan of mine and insists on sitting in the best seats. You know, so she can get a better view of me."

She recoiled and had to bite on her tongue to keep from snapping at him. "I don't mind sitting next to *Candy*," she sneered at the name. "But if she's hot, you may want to watch out. From what I've picked up on, Richard is into numbers…" she trailed of suggestively. *After all, what accountant isn't?* she thought to herself.

She snickered, but kept her eyes forward. There wasn't a sound from Trent, but she could've sworn she noticed his body stiffen. Waves of tension rolled off them both and clashed together in a silent storm. The already confined space suddenly felt even smaller, and Elle had to force herself to breathe.

She sat silently, not making a move although her body was screaming at her to pounce on him, right here in the car while he was driving. Her mind was telling her to speak up and ask him what the hell his problem was. Either he liked her or he didn't. She was sick and tired of not knowing. She knew what she wanted—why didn't he? The entire drive into the city lasted an eternity, and by the time they pulled up to Rain, Elle felt as though she was losing her mind—so much so that it took her a minute for the shock of where they were to register.

"Rain?" She couldn't hide her surprised tone.

"Yeah, I know. It's a little popular, but don't worry, *I* can get you in," he said confidently.

She almost laughed in his face, but then realized he was being completely serious. He obviously had no clue that Elle was more than familiar with the bouncers at this particular club. Biting down on her tongue, she prayed to God that Sophie and Kate wouldn't ruin the moment for her. It was a Friday and that meant that Chad and Greg would be working the door. She also knew that they rarely let guys in the club before ten, especially if there were a bunch of girls waiting in line, which there was.

"Oh, really?" she asked excitedly. "That's so great, because I've been dying to get in this club for a while. I'm so glad you have connections." She batted her lashes for extra measure.

Her sweet demeanor did nothing but throw Trent for a loop. He sat in silence for a minute watching her. "Something tells me, Elle, that you would have no problem getting into a place like this, especially if you walk up looking like *that*." His eyes roamed over her body, following the entire length of her legs before returning to her face.

With a satisfied smile, she realized her plan to drive him crazy was going to be easier than she thought. Still smirking to herself, she climbed out of his SUV and started walking to the door, hoping to catch her friends before they made it to the doors. Luckily, fate was on her side, and they were just approaching.

"Ladies, why don't we stay here for a second? Trent's going to go see if he can get us in." She winked and looked over her shoulder at Trent, who had a wide grin on his face.

"Hey, what can I say? Sometimes having my career has its benefits. I'll be right back." He walked past them confidently in direction of the main entrance.

Elle watched him as he walked, admiring his backside.

"Elle, did you hear me?"

"Huh?" she mumbled, still lost in her daydreams.

"I said why are you making Trent go up there?" Kate asked. "You know Chad and Greg won't let him in. He's a guy and it's before ten."

"And I'm betting the guy quota is already filled. The male meat always shows up early so they're guaranteed to get in. Everybody knows that." Sophie tapped her foot, annoyed.

"First off, Blondie, don't tap your foot at me," Elle said, pointing her finger. "I should still be mad at you for making me ride in the car with him. And second, do you not think I know all of this? I want to see him sweat it a little. He's overly confident. Which, I will admit, can be a turn on. But still, he needs to learn that not all things in life come so easily."

Sophie looked at her friend with a knowing smirk. "Are you talking about him getting into the club or something *else?*"

Elle narrowed her eyes and ignored her suggestion even though she was right. If Trent wanted her, he was going to have to work for it. "Let's just watch and see what happens. I want to enjoy the moment."

Turning her attention to the happenings in front of them, the girls watched things unfold. Trent stood in front of Chad and Greg, who were indeed working, as the girls expected. He moved his hands around nervously, alternating between rubbing his jaw line and neck. Ultimately, both hands ended up shoved deep in his pockets as he walked towards them, a look of rejection on his face.

"Problem?" Elle asked innocently.

"The guys I know aren't working tonight and those pricks say they're not letting anyone in, no matter who they are, until after ten o'clock. Some *quota* they have to meet."

She smiled sweetly and looked up into his eyes. "Maybe I should go try. I mean, I'm not an NFL star athlete, but maybe I can sweet talk them." She didn't wait for him to object before walking away.

"Why, if it isn't our favorite bombshell!" Chad held his arms out and she gave him a quick hug.

"Hey, Elle," Greg said without taking his eyes off her breasts.

"Greg, honey, I do believe I've told you before that you need to make eye contact with the ladies. We like that sort of stuff. Makes us actually believe you are interested in what's up here." She snapped her fingers to get his attention before tapping her head.

"I'm sorry. I swear I've been working on it," he apologized. His eyes roamed over her body once again.

"All right, all right. Are you done ogling?" Elle asked. "Because you know, I'd really like to get inside."

"Sure. Are Sophie and Kate here with you tonight?"

"They're right behind me."

At that exact moment, both guys looked over her shoulder and nodded in acknowledgment. "That guy looks pissed," Greg said with a laugh.

"What guy?" Elle spun around. All it took was one look and it was clear to see that he was referring to Trent. His thick arms were crossed in front of him, and his face wore a scowl. His expression softened when he locked eyes with Elle, but only slightly.

"Who is he anyway? And why is he standing next to Soph and Kate?"

"He's my date. No, wait, not my date," she corrected. "He's a friend of Kate's boyfriend."

"Kate's got a boyfriend now?" Chad asked.

She nodded. "Yes, she does. Now can you get us all in or what?"

"Elle, babe, have we ever let you down?"

"I'll take that as a yes." She gave them each a quick wink and walked back over to the group.

"They said no, huh?" Trent asked, never taking his eyes off Chad and Greg.

"Nope. They said we could go in." She smiled. "Never underestimate the power of sexual favors, Trent."

Without saying a word, she grabbed hold of her two girlfriends' hands and left a gaping Trent in her wake.

"Oh, that was mean," Kate said through a laugh.

"Mean and perfect," Elle corrected.

Sophie tucked her blond hair behind her ear and looked over at her friend. "You really are going to make him work for it, huh?"

"You bet I am. So far all I'm getting is the 'It's ok if you're dating other guys because I have other chicks' attitude. This, in subtle text, says 'I'm a player and girls like you come around every day.'"

"All I'm saying is: don't be blind. It may be harder for him to show what he's feeling than you think. Don't be so hard on him that you miss it, all right? Let him show you in *his* way," Sophie said.

"Sure, Soph." She nodded. "Whatever you say."

Doubt overwhelmed her, but deep inside, there was a small flicker of hope that maybe her friend was on to something. Walking into the loud club, the pulsing music rang through her ears, swallowing her in a world where she could forget all about Trent…almost.

☙

One hour and countless drinks later, they all stood on the sticky dance floor. The girls stayed close by each other, a tactic they learned could block out any man who wasn't welcome to rub against them. Only this time, that wasn't an issue since both Ethan and Logan stood behind them, staking their claims. Trent kept his distance most of the night, something which was slowly wearing on Elle. She was stuck in an endless cycle of berating herself for liking him so much and hating him for ignoring her. He'd only talked to her once, and it was only to offer her another drink. Not enjoying herself anymore, Elle decided to take a breather when she felt someone beside her.

"Do you want to dance?"

She looked up into an unfamiliar set of eyes and was stung by the disappointment that they weren't the green eyes she'd hoped they would be. Normally, she would have politely turned him down since she wanted a break, but this time she hesitated. She took a quick glance across the room and noticed Trent talking to a short red-head. *I see. Talk to the girl with frizzy hair and ignore me,* she thought with a huff. "Sure. I'd love to dance with you," she blurted before fully thinking through her response. Grabbing his hand, she pulled him into the center of the dance floor, within perfect view of Trent.

Once in position, she wrapped her arms around the stranger's neck and pulled him close so she could peek over his shoulder. Sure enough, just as she hoped, Trent's eyes were locked on her and the guy who held her in his arms.

It only took him six swift strides and Trent was standing directly across from Elle, dancing with the red-head he was talking with a second ago. The short girl rambled on about her career, but Trent didn't pay her any attention. Instead he was watching Elle with fiery eyes. The two stayed locked in each other's gaze, refusing to be the first one to back down or look away.

Elle wasn't sure if the room had suddenly spiked in temperature, but the heat she felt under his stare was suffocating. Strangely, it made the hair on the back of her neck stand on end and the tips of her fingers tingle. Without being aware of her actions, she stopped dancing and stood still. It was then that she felt the hands of the guy she was dancing with slide down her waist and over her butt. Before she could remove his paws, she felt them being ripped away.

"What do you think you're doing?" Trent seethed. "Get off of her!"

Her first reaction was to smile, because finally he was showing some emotion, but instead she snapped, letting all of her thoughts and doubts rip through her as they spilled out of her mouth. "What, so I can't get touched, but you can?"

"I wasn't getting felt up, Elle."

"Maybe not by her, but I'm sure *Candy* has had her hands all over you."

"Candy? What the hell does she have to do with all of this?"

"Oh … nothing, except everything! She just perfectly represents all the women I'm sure you've had and tossed aside without a second thought."

"What? And you haven't done that? What about Richard?"

"Who?" she asked, confused and angry that he was turning it on her.

Trent clenched his large fists and folded his arms across his broad chest. "Richard, who I'd like to call Dick."

"You don't know what you're talking about. Richard and I aren't together," she admitted.

"Then why did you make it sound like you were?"

"Because *someone* just so happens to get 'tickets for chicks all the time,'" she quoted with her fingers. "And I refuse—refuse!—to be just another chick!"

"Damn it, Elle, you're the most confusing person I've ever met."

"Yeah, well, it takes one to know one."

She spun around quickly, leaving Trent standing in the middle of the dance floor and didn't look back. With a huff, she flopped down in a chair at their table and reached for another shot. Tossing it back, she let it burn all the way down.

"Are you okay?" Kate stood a few feet away, watching her beautiful friend stew in all her fury.

Elle shook her head. "Is it possible to have a fight like you're in a relationship, even though it doesn't even exist? I mean, I don't even know what's going on. I swear he likes me. I know it. I *feel* it." She dropped her head. "I'm just so confused."

"You're not confused. He likes you, and you like him. You want to know what I think the problem is?"

"What?"

"You've found your match," she said, gently laying her hand on Elle's shoulder.

Suddenly the blaring music stopped abruptly, leaving nothing but a high pitch ring, echoing in Elle's ears. It was only silent for a minute before the music started again, but it wasn't club music at all.

"What kind of song is this?" Elle asked, sitting up. "I swear, they play anything these days." Kate didn't get a chance to comment before the sound of someone singing along with the song piped through the speakers. "Oh, man. I feel bad for whoever that poor schmuck is singing to. I mean, come on, who sings to someone at a club like this one?"

"Apparently Trent does."

Elle's head snapped to the side and met Kate's face with wide, horrified eyes. "What?" she asked, hoping that it was all a joke. But the look on Kate's face was serious, minus, of course, the playful smirk that was fighting to emerge. Following Kate's line of sight, she froze when she spotted Trent. He stood in the middle of the dance floor, holding a microphone to his mouth, singing loudly and staring directly at her. "You have *got* to be kidding me," she whispered.

He kept his eyes locked with hers and grinned, flashing his perfect gleaming teeth as he continued to sing. Everyone in the club was standing still, watching him as he made his way toward her. He swayed to the rhythm of the song, changing the lyrics at random and adding her name in whenever he could.

She watched him and couldn't hold back a carefree laugh. All of the ridiculous thoughts she'd had a minute ago melted away as she watched him sing the corny song. It was exactly what she needed to hear and exactly what she needed to know. Her heart thumped loudly, and at that moment, she knew she would be his.

Keeping his eyes locked on hers, he walked over and sat down next to her. He tried to read her expression, but couldn't tell if what he saw was good or bad. Either he was going to get punched for being an idiot or kissed for being an idiot. Fortunately for him, he didn't mind which one she chose. Both were hot. Luckily, his second guess was right and she lunged forward, crashing her lips to his, and nearly pushing him off the seat in the process. He could hear the people in the club hollering and clapping, but all he could think about was how much he missed kissing Elle. *Please don't let this stop,* he silently pleaded as he wrapped his arms around her waist and held her close. He was so consumed with thoughts of her that he didn't notice her slowing their kiss and before he could pull her back in, he was slapped in the chest.

"What the hell was that?" Elle snapped.

"I believe it's called a slap, although I must say, I was kind of hoping you'd punch me. Seems like something you'd do. Slapping is so … girly."

"In case you've missed it, I *do* happen to be a girl."

"Believe me, sweetheart, there's no missing that." His eyes drifted down her body and paused briefly when he reached her legs.

"Stop trying to change the subject. What was all that singing for?"

"Isn't it pretty obvious?" he asked with raised brows. "I mean, I know I send out mixed signals but I—"

"So you admit it." She cut him off. "You send out mixed signals." Folding her arms in front of herself, she waited for him to speak.

"I don't think I ever actually denied that. Apparently, I tend to do it often; at least that's what Ethan tells me. And as far as the singing goes, I wouldn't do that for just anyone." He paused. "Hell, what I'm saying is I *wouldn't* do that for anyone … but you."

Elle looked at him with narrowed eyes and contemplated whether or not he was actually telling the truth. "So, you're saying that you like me," she finally said with a smirk.

"I'm pretty sure I've made that obvious."

"How much are we talking here? Is it the 'we'll go out for a few weeks and one day you'll get tired of me and decide the new cheerleader is looking good'? Or it is the 'I like you—"

"More than any other girl I've ever dated," he finished. "More than I like to admit to myself because I don't know what I'm doing."

They stayed silent for a minute, both of them realizing the importance of his revelation.

She swallowed slowly. "Well, are you going to take me somewhere like a proper gentlemen or are we going to hang out at the club all night?"

"I thought you said dreams don't come true?" he teased.

"Let's just say if you play your cards right, maybe I'll be your fairy god-mother." She winked and took his hand in hers as she stood up.

As soon as he was to his feet, he pulled her in and bent down to her ear. "I was hoping you'd say that." Without waiting for her response, he wrapped his arm around her waist and practically lifted her off the floor. Elle waved to her friends over his shoulder and Trent craned around to give Ethan the don't-come-home-unless-you-want-to-die look, before disappearing in the crowd.

The remaining two couples burst into laughter as soon as they were alone.

"What did we say?" Sophie asked through her giggles, looking at Kate.

She nodded. "They're perfect for each other."

Chapter 24
Firsts

"Come on. You have to at least tell me how old you were. I told you my story." Kate rolled her body toward Ethan and nuzzled his neck, hoping that her close proximity, combined with her begging, would be enough to make him cave.

"It was … awkward, and I was young and … inexperienced."

"How young?" She lifted her head and looked at his face. His eyes were closed and his lips were pressed together in a tight line. "Please," she added, hoping that would be enough.

"Sixteen."

"That's not too young. I was only a year younger, and believe me, what Kevin did could hardly even be considered a kiss. Was she your girlfriend?" she asked, wanting more information, but secretly dreading the answer. The last thing she wanted was to find out that she had a beautiful mystery girl to live up to.

"She wasn't my girlfriend *per se*. More like a good friend who took it upon herself to uh … *teach* me."

"Teach you?"

"She was older than I was, and after spending the summer together, we decided to, you know …" His voice trailed off as he looked at her face, hoping he wouldn't have to actually say the words.

Her eyebrows knitted together and a moment passed before she realized what it was that he was talking about. *Oh,* she thought. All this time she was talking about first kisses and maybe stealing a few bases, but clearly he was talking about the whole shebang. It also didn't escape Kate's notice that the mystery girlfriend was older.

"Define older."

"Only two years."

"Two," she repeated and ignored the jealous, insecure feelings the crept up on her. It only took a few seconds to realize that the age had nothing to do with it. She was simply jealous of the mystery girl who was Ethan's first at everything. Although she knew he'd dated other girls, she wanted him all to herself. She wanted his past, present, and future, no matter how impossible and ridiculous it seemed.

"So, the two of you …?" she suggested.

He nodded and waited for her response.

"Wow." She paused for a few minutes and for the first time wondered about all of his past relationships. In the time they'd been together, they hadn't discussed the subject in detail. Even though the thought of knowing made her stomach churn, she couldn't stop the curiosity. Before she could figure out a casual way of asking her questions, they poured from her mouth, uncensored and rushed. "Did you ever see her after that summer? I mean, did she ever meet your parents and stuff? Did it get that serious? Have you taken a lot of girls home? What about your last girlfriend? What was she like? How long were you with her? Did you love her?"

He gave her a lopsided smile and laughed. "Hearing you get jealous is quite interesting."

She huffed in defeat and dropped her head. She knew as well as the next girl that jealousy was not the most becoming feature, but she couldn't help it.

Ethan, seeing her struggle, immediately thought over her questions. "No. No. No. Only two. Crazy, overbearing and fake. A few months. And no."

"Wait, what?" she asked in confusion.

"Kate." He placed his hand on her cheek and waited for her to look into his eyes before he spoke. "I've had girlfriends in the past. All of them taught me something about myself and they each helped me realize the kind of woman I wanted to ultimately be with. I guess, in a way, they were preparing me … for you."

Stunned by his words and unable to move, she held her breath. The blue of his eyes were the most vibrant she'd ever seen them, and in that moment, she felt as if she could see into him. The love she felt for him spread from her chest through her entire body. Not wanting the moment to end, she smiled up at him and enjoyed it a little longer before breaking the silence. "Preparing you, huh?" She smirked. "I must say they did a good job."

"Oh yeah?" His carefree laugh echoed through the room as he wrapped his arms around her and pulled her close to him. They lay in silence for a few minutes, their bodies intertwined with one another.

"Kate?"

"Um hmm," she sighed, keeping her eyes closed.

"Henry invited us over to his house for lunch tomorrow. And I'd love it if you would come. I really want you to meet Lori. She's like a second mom to me, and well ... it will give you practice."

"Practice?" She lifted her head.

"For meeting my parents."

His tone was so matter of fact that she almost swallowed her tongue in shock. "When am I meeting them?"

"In a week."

"Ethan!" she yelped.

"What?"

"A week! When were you planning on telling me?"

"Right now," he smirked, enjoying the reaction that he was getting.

"Your parents." She paused. "Wow, I mean, I haven't even seen your apartment yet," she teased.

As soon as the words were out of her mouth, Ethan hopped out of bed and walked over to his clothes, which were still on the floor from last night.

"Where are you going?" She sat up, pulling the sheet around her.

"*We* are going to my place," he said, smiling.

Kate watched him pull on his pants and sighed quietly to herself. He really was the hottest thing she'd ever seen. "Are you sure you don't want to just stay here?" she purred, trying desperately to sound seductive.

Ethan looked over at her and immediately knew what she was thinking. "If you keep looking at me like that, we won't ever leave."

"Then let's not." She threw the covers back and began crawling across the bed, closer to him.

He clenched his hands into tight fists. "Kate," he warned. "I'm serious; I really do want you to see my place. After all, it would be a little awkward if you meet my parents and can't even say you've seen it. Plus, I have something I've wanted to show you."

He was right, like always. And if she were thinking clearly, she would have remembered that she did want to see his place. It was the only part of him that was still a secret to her, besides his parents.

"Fine, I'll go." She sighed. "But only because I'm dying to try out your bed."

"I love you too," he said, laughing. "And I *am* going to hold you to that."

"Believe me. I'm planning on it." Giving him a quick wink, she hopped out of bed and hurried into the bathroom to get ready.

An hour later, they pulled onto Ethan's street. For reasons unknown to him, he felt a little nervous. But that nervousness was easily overpowered by his excitement. It still surprised him to realize that he and Kate had been together for over a month and she still hadn't been to his home. There wasn't a reason other than the fact that Elle was gone so often on jobs that they were able to be alone at her place. But now that Kate was here, he couldn't wait to get her inside.

Quickly walking around the car, he opened the door for her and took her small hand in his as he led her toward his building. Together they walked hand in hand down the long hallway and came to a stop outside of his door.

"This is it." He smiled down at her before opening the door. "I hope it's not too much of a mess, Trent usually tries to—" He stopped mid-sentence as soon as he stepped over the threshold and looked at the living room.

The normally organized, spacious room was in shambles. All of the pillows from the couch were on the floor, some all the way across the room. Magazines from the coffee table were scattered everywhere haphazardly. The lamp at the end of the couch was tipped on its side, leaning up against the armrest; its shade was lying on the ground. One of the pictures on the wall was hanging sideways, on the verge of falling to the floor like the other one that normally hung beside it already had.

His first thoughts were that someone had broken in. Immediately shooting his arm out, he blocked Kate from walking further and tucked her behind him. If he had been robbed, there was a slight chance the person was still in his apartment. Reaching into his pocket, he pulled out his cell phone and handed it to Kate. With wide eyes, she took the phone and got ready to dial the cops if needed.

Ever so slowly, Ethan took a step forward, listening intently for any sound that was unusual. He didn't get more than four feet when he heard a rattling from the kitchen to his left. Taking a glance back at Kate, he took a step into the dining area that connected to the kitchen. This room was as much a mess as the living room. All of his mail was scattered on the ground as well as random pieces of half eaten fruit. The two looked at each other in confusion and before either of them could speak, they heard someone yell from another room.

"Hey, baby, get some more fruit! Do you have any grapes?"

Ethan's head shot up quickly because he recognized the voice at once and so did Kate. The rattling noise they'd heard just a moment ago started again, and this time there was the distinct sound of someone singing. With a shake of his head, Ethan walked directly into the kitchen and flicked on the overhead light. He could just barely make out the naked butt of his friend sticking out from behind the refrigerator door.

"Trent Williams. What the hell happened to our apartment?"

Trent jumped at the sound of his friend's voice and cursed out loud when he hit his head.

"Dude! E, you're lucky I have this helmet on or I'd be tossing you on your ass." Trent slammed the refrigerator door and turned to look at Ethan. He was standing completely nude in nothing but his football helmet, grasping a bunch of grapes that he quickly moved in front of himself when he saw Kate walk up.

Trying to stifle a giggle, she attempted to cover it up with a cough but failed miserably.

"Hey, Kate," Trent said casually, surprisingly unaffected by his current situation and still ignoring Ethan's previous question.

"Hi, Trent, it's good to uhh … *see* you." She smirked.

"Trent," Ethan interrupted. "Why is our apartment a wreck? And why is there half eaten fruit all over the—"

"Hey, baby!" Elle yelled from the other room. "Remind me to call Graham later. I want to make sure he doesn't have anything for me this weekend." Elle walked into the kitchen wearing one of Trent's oversized jerseys and nothing else. She smiled at both Ethan and Kate and easily grabbed some grapes from the bunch Trent was still holding in front of himself. Popping them in her mouth, she reached up on her toes and kissed Trent on the cheek before turning back to her friends. "Hey, guys," she said with a smile.

"Hi, Squish," Ethan said, trying to keep his voice calm since he now knew what had been happening. It didn't take a genius to put two and two together. The destroyed living room, the half eaten fruit on the floor next to the cleared off table, the—*Oh no, the table,* he thought. It was his mother's and he didn't even want to think about what had happened on it. He opened his mouth to yell when he felt Kate's hand on his back, rubbing soothing circles, instantly calming the anger that was building inside of him.

"How about you show me around?" Kate asked quietly.

Ethan gave one last warning look at Trent. "Don't even *think* about putting those grapes back after where they've been," he said, pointing his finger.

"Totally," Trent said with a nod.

Satisfied, Ethan looked down at Kate. She smiled back at him and gave him a quick wink before sliding her hand into his. "Well, this is the kitchen." He waved his hand around the room. "And you already saw the dining area." A shudder went through him again as he looked at his mother's table.

There was no hiding her laugh this time as she looked at the expression on Ethan's face. "I'm just glad they didn't go back to our place," she said, still laughing. "I'd hate to think about the damage they would have caused to my old coffee table. That thing can't hold Trent's weight."

Kate's laugh was infectious, and pretty soon Ethan was joining her, forgetting all about the messy state of his home. By the time they made it to his bedroom, their laughs had died down and the excited nervousness from earlier returned. Opening the door, he pulled her inside beside him.

"And here's my bedroom." He turned to look at her face and gauge her reaction. Her wide, dark brown eyes dashed around the room quickly, taking in everything. Letting go of his hand, she silently walked over to his bookcase. She stood for a few moments, trailing her fingers over the bindings as she read the titles. He noticed her face light up when she spotted titles that she herself owned, and after finishing with the books, she moved on to his music collection.

"You've got quite a collection," she mused.

He laughed. "It's kind of an addiction. My mother's a great piano player. I think she always secretly wished I'd studied music instead of medicine."

"A mother who doesn't want her son to be a doctor? Somehow I find that impossible."

"Don't get me wrong. She's very proud of me. I think she just wished I'd continued playing."

Kate held up her hand motioning for him to stop talking. "Hold on. So you actually play? You play the piano?"

"A little." He shrugged.

"You really are perfect, aren't you?" She meant to be playful, but there was no denying the truthfulness of her statement.

"Believe me, I'm far from perfect."

"You are to the person who loves you. You are to me." She smiled. "Unless, of course, there's some big secret flaw you aren't telling me about." Stepping forward, she wrapped her arms around his waist and looked up at him.

"The only secret I've ever kept from you was that I loved you. And I could only keep that from you for a day. I'll always be honest with you. Always." Dropping his head down, he kissed her; their tongues touched, and they both felt the spark of energy between them ignite. When he pulled away, he brushed his lips along her ear. "I have something I want to show you," he whispered.

"Okay," she said, eyeing him suspiciously.

"Close your eyes." She rolled her eyes playfully before shutting them tight. Ethan kept his arms around her waist and led her to the opposite side of the room, closer to his bed. Once they were in position, he turned her body so she faced her picture and stood behind her. "All right … open." He couldn't see her eyes open from where he stood, but her gasp signaled when she did.

"When did you …? I mean I never asked who it was, I just … when?" She turned around to face him, her eyes full of question.

"When I first saw you standing there in front of this picture, I had no clue that you were the person who took it. I had already seen it once earlier that night and had my eye on it. Then, after seeing you, after *speaking* with you, I felt this indescribable connection and I had no clue if I'd see you again. There was no doubt in my mind that I *needed* any tie to you that I could have, anything that would make me remember you. And this picture was the closest thing I could get. Seeing you the next night and then at the hospital and then the grocery store and practically every day since then has been amazing."

Kate's cheeks blushed pink, and tears pooled up in the corners of her dark eyes. She ducked her head down and placed it against his chest, directly over his heart. "I love you, Ethan," she whispered.

He held her in his arms for a few minutes and simply enjoyed having her there, in his room, in his arms. He felt happy and complete in a way he'd never thought possible.

"You know, I'm still freaking out about meeting your parents in a week," Kate finally said, breaking the silence. "You really should have prepared me a little better."

"Now where's the fun in that? You should have seen your face. That alone was worth waiting to tell you," he teased.

Kate flipped her head back and glared at him, her eyes squinting in an adorable way.

"I promise that the next time I have something to tell you I won't wait to spring it on you last minute. Better?"

"Better," she said, grinning.

"Does this mean that you'll come to lunch at Henry's tomorrow?"

"Of course."

He smiled and wrapped his arms around her waist, lifting her off the ground. Walking back slowly, he stopped when his legs hit the bed and sat down, pulling her with him. She settled her legs on either side of his waist and slid her fingers through his hair.

"The first time I saw you, I got lost in your eyes. I remember thinking that they were the most interesting shade of blue I'd ever seen. They almost looked gray. I had a hard time talking when you looked straight at me; I felt so stupid. But at the same time, I didn't want to look away either; I couldn't." Kate's eyes looked far away as she told her story, reliving it like it was yesterday. "When you answered your phone and walked away, I was sure I'd never see you again. And then I thought for sure someone was playing a mean trick on me when I saw you the next night, only to have you leave again. I figured I'd pressed my luck at that point and that it would be the last time I'd see you." She was silent for a moment and her smile slowly faded. Emotion flashed in her eyes and she dropped her head.

"Ethan, I'm sorry."

"Sorry? For what?"

"For everything that happened with Scott. I'm sorry that I didn't tell you about seeing him again. I should have told you. And I should have said something at the hospital when he was with me, but then you said you couldn't do it anymore." She paused to catch her bearings. Even remembering it brought her heartache. "I just couldn't help but think that you'd finally realized you were too good for me. But even then, I should have made you stay and talk to me. I should have told you right then that I loved you. I should have—"

"Kate," he cut her off. "You can't take all the blame. I should have said something too. I should have said something when I saw that he texted you the night of the football game."

"Wait, you saw that?"

"Yes. And I automatically assumed you were letting him back into your life and that was wrong of me. I should have asked you about it, but I didn't. And then I had a second chance outside of the hospital, and I still didn't do it." He shook his head. "I saw you with him and I thought for sure you were getting back together. I should have listened to my heart and fought for you."

"As I remember correctly, you did fight for me," she said, her eyes sparkling.

"I guess I did. I'm not normally a violent person, but when he started comparing the two of us, I lost it. I would never, could never, do to you what he did." He dropped his head in disgust. "I'd never ask for your hand that way. *When* I do it, I'll mean it."

Kate's eyes went wide and she paused. It took him a second to realize why she was so shocked, and when it did, he berated himself for dropping something like that so casually. Preparing to apologize, he opened his mouth to speak when Kate cut him off.

"I know you would never do that to me. And I ... I look forward to the day that you mean it." She stumbled over her words, her cheeks red.

The smile on his face signified the joy he felt. He didn't have to say a word. Instead he simply kissed her deeply and let her *feel* the love and happiness he had for her.

When their tongues touched, his heart beat quick and strong and she enveloped him, heart and mind. Leaning in closer, never taking her lips off his, Kate pushed him back and held her body over his.

"Ethan," she said between kisses.

"Yes."

"I know this isn't the best time to ask, but I'm kind of hungry. Do you think Trent left any food in the house?"

He laughed and pulled back, looking at her. "I'm sure I can find something. I go check and we'll eat in here."

"Sounds perfect."

Without another word, he bounded off the bed, threw open the door and headed for the kitchen. But before he made it down the hall, he heard Kate yelling from his room.

"Make sure you don't grab any grapes!"

"Kate, you look fabulous. Why are you so nervous anyway? It's not like you're meeting his actual parents or anything. That's next week." Sophie's hand flew up to her mouth, trying to stifle the giggle that was threatening to escape.

Ever since Kate had gone home yesterday and told her about the big 'parent meet,' she'd been laughing it up, constantly reminding her of the impending appointment.

"Soph, you could at least try to be more sympathetic. Do you remember what it was like the first time you met Logan's parents?"

"As a matter of fact, I do. I wasn't nervous at all. I knew they'd like me," she said, shrugging.

"Yeah, well, you had Elle as a friend to help soften the blow."

"True." She nodded. "But don't forget, you do know Henry. You told me that he was really nice to you."

"He is, but I mean…Sophie, I'm not you. I don't *glow* like you do." She flailed her arms out, motioning to her cheery friend.

Stepping forward, Sophie grabbed hold of Kate's hands and looked her in the eyes. "You *glow* to Ethan. And that's what matters. You are fabulous, Katherine Thomas, and they will know it as soon as they meet you."

Kate knew she wasn't only talking about meeting Henry and Lori. It was her way of calming her nerves; not only for today, but for the meeting she would have in a week. She smiled appreciatively. "I hope you're right."

"I'm always right." Sophie rolled her eyes sarcastically. "Now that you're nice and calm, what do you say we go torture Elle?" Her eyes gleamed.

"All right, but let's go easy on her. I'm pretty sure she's more nervous than I am."

Smiling, Sophie took off down the hall with Kate following at her heels. Just as the two of them were about to enter Elle's room, they heard her talking.

"Is Trent here already?" Kate whispered. "He and Ethan were supposed to come together."

"I don't think so. I didn't hear the door, did you?"

She shook her head at Sophie, took another step forward, and listened. She could faintly hear Elle speaking and she couldn't believe what she heard.

"It's so nice to see you again, Dr. Williams. This is a beautiful house you have. Mrs. Williams, this is a beautiful house. Oh, hi, Dr. Williams. It's good to see you again too. Trent talks about you guys all the time. Ugh, who am I kidding?" She groaned. "This is completely ridiculous. I can't believe I'm doing this."

Both Kate and Sophie peeked around the doorway and saw Elle standing in front of her mirror, nervously adjusting her outfit while she continued to mumble to herself. Kate contemplated leaving her to calm down on her own, but Sophie had other plans.

"Elle," she said in a sing-song voice. "Are you excited?

She spun around. "Seriously, Soph, do I look excited?" Her hands shot up towards her shiny face. "Would I be sweating like a freaking race horse if I wasn't nervous?"

"I'm sorry," her blond friend said with repentant eyes. "I guess you're a little more nervous than I thought."

"Nervous? Sophie, have you even stopped to think about the fact that Henry Williams, Dr. 'Do-Me' Williams, is his dad? His dad." She repeated for emphasis. "The very guy I've had fantasies about and the same guy who makes it almost impossible for me to even smell Band-Aids without getting excited. So, yes, Soph, I think you can say I'm a little more than nervous."

"Band-Aids? Really?" Sophie's face scrunched up, trying to understand the appeal.

"That's beside the point!" she snapped. "Right now, I just need help calming down. Because I'm this close to calling Trent and telling him I can't go."

Both friends' mouths dropped open. They'd seen Elle nervous before, but this was something different. She was terrified.

"Elle." Sophie stepped up and placed her hands on her friend's shoulders. "Sweetheart, everything is going to be great. You care about Trent, right?" Elle nodded quickly, twisting her fingers nervously. "Then that's all that matters. So what if you think his dad is hot?" Sophie shrugged.

"Who doesn't?" Kate added, and walked over to the two of them. "And believe me, I've had my fair share of fantasies that included Dr. Do-Me."

"Really?" Elle looked at her with hopeful eyes.

"Yes. And from what Ethan's told me, all the females who work in the hospital feel the same way. They even have a nickname for him – and Ethan, for that matter. They call them the two Ds, Dr. Dreamy and Dr. Divine. So just forget about it. You like Trent, he likes you, and you're meeting his parents. No big deal. You just so happen to know one of them. And if this helps, I hear his wife Lori is wonderful. They're perfect together."

At Kate's words, Elle took a deep breath and relaxed for the first time all day. "Thanks," she sighed.

"No problem. But I'll have you know, I expect you to do the same thing for me before I meet Ethan's parents next week. If his dad looks anything like his son, I'm going to have just as difficult a time." Both of her friends doubled over in laughter, and she couldn't help but join them. Their giggles were cut short when they heard someone calling from the front room.

"Kate?" Ethan's voice echoed down the hall and was soon followed by Trent's and Logan's.

"We're back here!" the three yelled in unison.

Logan stuck his head around the corner first, his brown eyes lighting up as soon as he saw Sophie. "Hey, sweetheart," he said, walking into the room. "Guess where we've just been invited?"

"To lunch at the Williams'?" she squeaked.

"Yep. Trent figured that since the four of them were going, we needed to tag along. Apparently his mom is a the-more-the-merrier type."

"She sure is. If she could, she'd adopt everyone," Trent said as he walked into the room, hearing the end of Logan's comment. "Hey, baby." He walked over to Elle and wrapped her up in his arms. "You ready to hit the road?"

"Ready as I'll ever be." She gave a weak smile.

Ethan wrapped his arms around Kate and pulled her in. Ever so gently, he kissed along her neck and worked his way closer to her ear.

"Ethan," she whispered.

"Yes?" he asked, knowing exactly what he was doing.

"If you keep doing that …" she trailed off, her voice breathy.

"If I keep doing it, what? Are you saying we won't be able to leave?"

"Maybe." She smirked.

"Oh, really?" he teased.

"Yes, really."

"All right, all right." He straightened his back and put a few inches between them. "I'll let you go this time. Besides, I think I could have some fun playing with you at the Williams' house."

"Playing?" she asked in confusion.

He nodded once. "Playing,"

Kate hadn't a clue what he was talking about, but the look on his face made it clear that he had plans.

Grabbing her hand, Ethan started for the door. "Let's get this show on the road. I don't want to be late."

❧

A short drive later, they were winding through the back roads of Pennsylvania.

"Trent, where do your parents live, exactly?" Elle asked and turned around to peer at her two friends with wide eyes.

Trent placed a hand on her knee. "My mom has always loved nature. So when they built this house, they made sure to surround themselves with it. Don't worry, baby. I won't let any bears get you," he said, laughing.

"Damn right you won't."

Kate laughed at her friend, but it came out sounding a little strained because of the nerves that were wreaking havoc on her insides. She knew it was ridiculous to be so nervous, but she couldn't help it.

"Don't be nervous. They'll love you, and so will my parents." Ethan said, pressing his lips to her forehead.

She felt her body relax instantly and dropped her head on his shoulder. Instead of focusing on her nerves, she studied the green foliage streaming by in a blur of green and brown. Just when she thought they couldn't go any further, they pulled off the road.

Standing on a slight hill, surrounded by tall maple trees of varying heights, stood a large, three-story, red brick, colonial home. Black shutters popped against the white framing around the house's many windows, which seemed to sparkle in the sunlight that filtered in from between the trees. A typical New England porch, complete with a swinging bench and rocking chairs, gave the house a welcoming feel, and Kate was suddenly anxious to see the inside.

"Wow," Sophie gasped. "This place is gorgeous."

The rest of the group nodded in agreement, not taking their eyes off the house as they pulled up. Ethan opened the door and held it open as the rest of them piled out. Taking Kate's hand in his, he smiled at her and led them toward the house.

Trent barged through the double front doors first and was yelling out for his parents before the rest of the group were even up the steps.

"Mom, Dad! We're here. Where are you guys?"

"I'm in the kitchen, honey." A woman's voice called out.

Trent spun around on the polished, dark, hardwood floors and motioned to the foyer. The butter yellow walls and white decorative molding made the entry bright and cheery. "This is it. Make yourselves comfortable." He wrapped his arm around Elle and walked off, leaving the rest of his friends standing there.

"I guess I should apologize for my son. Sometimes he forgets that not all people are as comfortable as he is in strange places."

Kate recognized the voice and turned around to see Henry standing in the doorway. Behind him, she could see the light colored walls continued into the sitting room where potted plants of vibrant green stood beside floor-to-ceiling windows. Taking a minute to admire Henry, Kate noted his casual jeans and collared shirt. It was different seeing him in something other than scrubs, and she couldn't help but smile when she imagined what Elle's reaction might be once she saw him.

"Well, Ethan, it seems as though Trent has neglected his duties." He laughed and walked toward them. "Hello, Kate, it's great to see you again."

"You too, Dr. Williams." She smiled.

"Please, call me Henry."

Kate nodded, and he turned his attention to Sophie and Logan. "You must be Sophie and Logan. Both Trent and Ethan have told me a little about you two, and I'm very interested in hearing more. Please, make yourselves comfortable while you're here. Lori and I wouldn't have it any other way."

Logan reached out and shook Henry's hand while he spoke. "Thank you so much for having us."

"Yeah," Sophie added. "Your house is beautiful."

"I'm afraid I can't take any credit in that department. Lori did everything."

"Then I'll have to pick her brain. I'm always itching to change our décor." Sophie's face was alive with excitement.

"I'm sure she would be more than willing to help. I believe she's in the kitchen, which is where I'd bet Trent ran off to." He laughed.

Not needing any more permission, Sophie grabbed Logan's hand and sped off around the corner, out of sight, and in the same direction that Trent had gone.

"Why don't you show Kate around, Ethan? I'm sure she'd like a tour."

Kate looked up at Ethan and nodded in interest.

"No problem," he said with a shrug.

Henry smiled at them both before turning around and disappearing back into the sitting room. As soon as he was out of sight, Ethan turned around and peered down at Kate with a mischievous smirk.

"What?" Kate asked.

Leaning down, he quickly pressed his lips to her cheek. "Tag, you're it," he whispered in her ear before slapping her butt and running for the stairs. What he'd said didn't register in her mind, and Kate stood motionless. "Didn't I tell you we'd play?" he asked with a raise of his eyebrow.

"Umm ... yes," she mumbled.

"Well, then, let's play." He smirked down at her and dashed up the rest of the stairs, disappearing out of sight.

All right, Ethan Montgomery, you want to play? Let's play, she thought. Taking one deep breath, she looked around and took off after him.

Chapter 25
Play Time

Kate ran up the stairs as fast as her legs could carry her. She thought that once on the landing she'd be able to see Ethan, but he was nowhere in sight. *All right, sneaky, where are you?* she thought. Taking a step into the hallway, she looked both ways, trying to decide which way to go. The house was larger than it looked from the outside, if that was at all possible. Numerous doors were open, letting light stream through into the hall. There was no possible way for her to know which room he'd gone into, so she began her search. Standing in the doorway of the first room, she stuck her head inside.

"Ethan, are you in here?" she whispered, looking around the wine colored room. It seemed to be the first of what she guessed were many guest bedrooms. Taking a step further into the room, she peeked over the opposite side of the bed to make sure Ethan wasn't hiding. Satisfied that he wasn't there, she walked back into the hallway and repeated the process in the next two rooms. By then, she was starting to feel slightly annoyed and didn't notice her voice was getting louder.

"Damn it, Ethan. I thought we were playing tag. This is starting to feel more like hide-and-go seek!" she yelled out into yet another 'Ethan-less' guest room, this one having a nautical theme. Just as she was about to walk out, her cell phone rang.

"Geez," she gasped, pulling her phone from her pocket. She smiled as soon as she saw who it was. Flipping the phone open, she began speaking immediately.

"You know, I'm getting a little annoyed with this game of yours. I thought we were playing tag. Doesn't that usually entail running up to someone, tapping them quickly and running away?" she asked.

"All right, so maybe I'm combining the two games. Just go with it and have some fun. Come find me, Katherine." His voice was teasing yet sexy, and it was the first time she recalled him ever calling her by her full name. It made her heart thump a little louder. Collecting herself, she walked out of the third room with new determination.

Making her way down the hallway, she peeked into each room she passed. When she reached the second to last door, she peered in and ended up staring in shock. It was quite possibly one of the prettiest bedrooms she'd ever seen.

The giant sleigh bed was the first thing to catch her eye. Its dark wood gleamed in contrast to the rich burgundy bedding and pillows which adorned it. The rest of the room was in similar tones: rich reds, creamy tans, and brilliant whites. It looked like something straight out of a Pottery Barn catalogue. It didn't take a genius to know that it was Henry and Lori's room and that Ethan surely wouldn't, in a million years, be there. As she was about to turn around and leave, she felt someone's arms wrap around her. She almost screamed in shock, but recognized Ethan's touch and calmed herself.

"I'd say you're getting hotter, sweetheart," he whispered in her ear, as he slowly trailed his fingers from her neck down her arm.

Goosebumps spread over her skin and her breath hitched. "I thought it was my turn. I'm supposed to find you, remember?"

"I know, I just couldn't resist sneaking up on you." He chuckled, and Kate could feel the vibrations of his chest against her back. Leaning forward slowly, he placed his lips to her neck and kissed her softly.

"So…" She swallowed thickly, trying to concentrate, something which was difficult with his lips touching her skin. "Is it my turn next?"

He shook his head side to side, brushing the length of her neck. "Nope, I get to hide again since, technically, you never found me."

"Hey, that's not fair." She spun around quickly in challenge, but noticed he was already gone. She clenched her fists in determination and walked out of the room. There was only one room she hadn't checked and it was at the end of the hall.

Twisting the brass knob, she pushed the solid wood door open and instantly knew whose room it was. All she had to see was the football paraphernalia and enormous plasma flat screen to know that it was Trent's. Where some parents might change their child's room into a sewing or workout room, it was clear that Lori had gone the other route. She'd only added improvements and even framed and hung one of Trent's jerseys above the bed.

Taking a step into the room, Kate silently closed the door behind her. "Ethan," she whispered as she tiptoed over to the huge bed. "Are you in here?" She listened for a sound, anything to let her know he was there and when no response came, she felt ridiculous. *What am I doing? Clearly I'm not cut out for this game.* She laughed at herself and rolled her eyes.

Then, when she was about to leave the room, she heard a sound. It was so faint she wondered if she'd even heard it at all. Closing her eyes, she held her breath and listened carefully. It was another moment before she heard it again, but this time she was sure she'd heard something. She turned her ear to the sound and realized it was coming from behind the door only a few feet away. Happy that she'd finally found him, she pressed herself against the wall and sidestepped her way closer. She carefully turned the knob as quietly as she could manage and with a quick inhale, she flung the door open wide.

"Ah hah! Found you!" she yelled into the dark closet.

Her excited smile quickly fell when she didn't see him anywhere. From where she stood, it was difficult to see far into the closet so she opted to step inside. The sunlight from the bedroom faintly illuminated the space so she could just barely make out the clothes that hung inside. Knowing she was at a disadvantage without light, she felt around on the walls for a switch. It was when she turned to her left and took a step forward that she heard him. The distinct breathing that was familiar to her.

"I can hear your breathing," she said quietly, "which means I found you. So you might as well come out and face me." There was a slight shifting behind the clothes, and it was another moment before he emerged, his hair wild and sticking out at random. "Looks like I won this round." She smiled in satisfaction. "So what's the prize for—"

"Not so fast, sweetheart." He cut her off. "I don't think you've technically won yet."

Crossing her arms in front of herself, she glared at him. "Excuse me?"

"I haven't officially been tagged. So that means—"

Before he could say another word, Kate pounced on him, offsetting his balance and causing him to stumble backwards. He reached blindly for something to help break his fall, and as his fist closed around the closet rod, Kate's lips crashed against his. The sound of wood splitting filled the air and both he and Kate froze, lips still locked together.

"Did you just break the closet?" she asked against his lips.

"I think *we* just broke it."

The two of them pulled apart and turned their heads to the side, cheeks pressed together. Sure enough, one end of the rod had been pulled away from the wall, a chunk of plaster stuck to the end. They looked at it in shocked silence, and then suddenly burst out in laughter. Through watery eyes, they both attempted to put it back in place, and ten minutes later, they were hanging up the few articles of clothing that had made it to the floor.

"I'll just tell Lori that I tripped and grabbed the bar to stop myself," Ethan said, still laughing.

"Do you honestly think that a small trip could result in the bar being torn from the wall? It wouldn't have happened if I hadn't attacked you." Kate hit her face with the palm of her hand.

"Don't be so hard on yourself. You're just competitive and wanted to make sure you won." He shrugged, hanging up the last shirt.

Kate rolled her eyes playfully and then took a step out of the closet. "Come on, let's go before I break anything else," she said over her shoulder as she headed for the door. Before she could get too far, Ethan grabbed her hand and yanked her back, pulling her in tight to his chest.

"Kiss me," he said, looking down at her.

"I'm not so sure that's a good idea." Her hands fiddled with the hem of her shirt and Ethan knew she was thinking about it.

"Why not?"

"Because I can't promise more damage won't ensue." She laughed.

"We're in Trent's room. He trashed my place, remember?"

"Well, in that case." Her eyes went from his lips to his eyes and back again, before she leaned in to kiss him. Once he felt her tongue with his, he deepened the kiss and picked her up. Taking a step forward, he sat her down on top of the entertainment center. There was a distinct creaking sound from under her, but she ignored it as they continued to kiss each other like teenagers. When they finally pulled apart, their breathing was heavy and Kate had to suppress a giggle. It always amazed her how she reacted around him, and it was something she knew would never change.

Ethan dropped his forehead to her shoulder, and when he caught sight of what she was sitting on, he erupted in laughter.

"What's so funny?" She pulled away and looked at his face.

"How would you like to help me get Trent back?" He cocked an eyebrow.

"What are you talking about?" she asked in confusion.

He nodded and cast his eyes down. Kate followed his gaze, and for the first time realized she was sitting on top of a DVD player.

"A DVD player?"

"It's his Xbox," Ethan clarified. "He has two of them, one at our place and one here. But *this* one," he pointed to the box Kate was sitting on, "has his best *Halo 3* score stored on it. He's never been able to top it. It's his baby, his pride and joy. It's the perfect payback."

"For what?"

Ethan wrapped his arms around her waist and lifted her down from the entertainment center. "Two things really. First, he had sex with Elle on my mother's table. And second, he used fruit. And that is clearly *our* thing." He motioned his hand back and forth between the two of them with an expression of complete seriousness.

Kate had to bite down on her cheeks to prevent the outburst of laughter. "So what do you want me to do? Tell him that we made out on top of it?"

Ethan looked at her mischievously. "Actually, I have a better plan."

❦

Five minutes later, both Kate and Ethan laughed together as they walked down the stairs, discussing the various reactions Trent might have when he discovered their surprise. When they walked into the kitchen, everyone was sitting around the table playing cards.

"What's so funny?" Trent asked, looking up from his hand toward them.

"The fact that Elle is kicking your butt," Sophie chimed in.

"Hey, Blondie, it's Uno. It's not a real card game. It takes practically no skill, even a dog—" Trent stopped speaking as soon as his eyes caught a glimpse of Elle, who was glaring. "I mean, any dog can tell that it's not just skill. It requires patience and cleverness."

"Good one, T," Ethan mumbled under his breath as he sat down and pulled Kate onto his lap.

"Did Ethan give you a nice tour of the house, Kate?"

Kate looked to the person who was speaking and realized it was Lori. She hadn't met her yet, but she looked just as Kate had suspected: tall, blond, and beautiful. Her clothing fit her lean frame perfectly and matched the style of her house—classic and comfortable. There was no surprise that both she and Henry were Trent's parents. He was a perfect mix of them both.

"He did, thank you." Kate nodded. "The rooms are beautiful. I love the way you've decorated them."

"She *loved* your room, Trent," Ethan interjected, smirking at his friend who was still engrossed in his game.

Kate nudged Ethan gently and looked at him with wide eyes before directing her attention back to Lori. "Do you need any help with lunch?" she asked, hoping for a distraction.

"I do need some help setting up the fruit tray." Lori smiled.

As if someone had announced the second coming, everyone around the table froze. It only took a second to recover, and when they did, all five of them wore smiles.

"Sure, I'd love to help." Kate fought off her embarrassment and hopped up from Ethan's lap. Both she and Lori talked as they set up the fruit tray. Lori filled her in on stories about Ethan and Trent in school. She gushed over how much she adored them both and how Ethan was like a second son to her. How his friendship with Trent was the best thing for him and how they balanced each other so well.

"I've known him for so long and I don't think I've ever seen him this happy before. I know that sounds silly. It's the type of thing that's said in a Hallmark movie, but it's true. There's something different about you, and I know he sees it. I'm sure his parents will too."

Kate tensed at her words. The thought of meeting them in a week was still fresh in her mind, and the more she thought about it, the more nervous she became.

Lori placed her hand on Kate's and gave it a gentle squeeze. "They will love you, trust me."

Kate smiled hesitantly. "Thank you."

"Thanks for what?" Ethan asked, walking up behind them and grabbing a piece of pineapple off the tray.

"Kate was just thanking me for having you all over. Now be a dear and go place this in the other room." She handed the tray to Ethan and turned to her son. "We're ready to eat, Trent. Go tell your father."

Eager to eat, Trent hopped up from his seat and ran out of the room while the rest of the group followed Lori into the dining room. Vibrant colored plates and cups were set against a crisp white tablecloth, and the spread of food was amazing.

Surprisingly, even though Trent was the last one in the room, he was the first one to sit. "Let's eat," he said, and picked up his plate.

They spent most of the afternoon sitting around the table, sharing stories and laughing. Elle was making a good impression on both Henry and Lori, and it seemed her previous attraction for Henry wasn't causing any problems. Trent did his fair share of bragging for her, telling them all of the new shoots she had planned and how successful her *Sports Illustrated* cover was.

Henry spent a lot of the time talking academics with Logan, and was genuinely interested in his field of study. Sophie, Lori, and Kate talked a little about photography, and Ethan jumped back and forth between all of their conversations, never once removing his hand from Kate's.

The sun was starting to set by the time they all got up from the table. Ethan and Kate helped clear and carry all the dishes into the kitchen, where Trent, Elle, Logan, and Sophie continued their Uno game from earlier.

"Hey, Mom, are we having dessert?" Trent asked without looking up from his hand.

"Do I ever cook you a meal without one?" she asked.

"Score." He nodded. "I'll take that as a yes." Placing his cards down, he stood up and reached for Elle with an outstretched hand. "Will you let us know when it's ready? I want to show Elle the shop."

"Shop?" Kate questioned.

"Trent likes to work on cars. He's restoring a 69' Camaro. I told my dad about it, and he insists I get all the details," Elle said.

"I bet." Kate laughed.

Trent cleared his throat loudly and wrapped his arm over her shoulder. "You kiddies have fun. I'm gonna go show my baby, my baby." He walked past them and paused when he reached the door. "Oh and Ethan, when I come back in, I'm taking you on, bro. *Halo 3.* My room. Be ready."

"Don't worry, Trent. I'll be ready." Ethan smirked and Kate bit back a laugh.

As soon as Trent disappeared around the corner, both Logan and Sophie turned to their friends. "You'll find out," Kate answered before they could even ask.

"Why do I have a feeling that I won't want to miss this moment?" Logan said with a grin.

The sly glint in Ethan's eye said everything. "Because, Logan, you won't."

The next fifteen minutes were spent sitting in front of the TV waiting for Trent and Elle to be done while Henry and Lori got dessert ready. Kate was thankful for the TV as a distraction, but it hadn't stopped Ethan from glancing at the clock every few minutes.

"What's his deal?" Sophie whispered, leaning toward Kate.

"He's waiting for Trent to *find* something."

"I'm sorry, what?"

Kate looked down at her hands and nervously twirled her ring in an attempt to delay her answer.

"What's he finding?" she asked again.

"Umm," she hesitated, looking up at her friend who had a new determined look on her face. "My underwear," she finally whispered.

"Pardon me—your what?"

"Soph, don't make me repeat it. I'm already having doubts as it is. I mean, we didn't actually do anything, but Trent won't know that. It's just for payback."

"I'm not following. Just explain it to me. What are you paying him back for?"

Taking one deep breath, Kate closed her eyes and started to talk. "Ethan is anxious for Trent to find my underwear that he left on top of his Xbox—which is where we made out earlier. Ethan is hoping that Trent will think we did more than just kiss, since he and Elle had sex on Ethan's mother's table. It's just a little payback. Plus, they took our fruit thing. And let's face it, that's our thing." Kate finished speaking and looked at her friend, hoping she wasn't horrified.

Sophie's jaw hung open as she stared. She stayed silent for a few moments, and then her shocked expression slowly melted away as a wide smile stretched across her face. "Katherine Elizabeth Thomas, I never knew you had it in you." She laughed. "This is going to be fabulous. I can't wait to see his face."

At that moment, Trent strolled back into the room. "Come on, Ethan. Let's go." He paused. "That is, unless you'd rather wait until Kate's not around to see you cry like a girl when I beat you."

"Oh, I'm pretty sure I'll be crying, but they'll be tears of joy. You can bet on that." Ethan stood from the couch and approached a confused-looking Trent.

"Whatever you say, bro. It's your reputation."

The four of them followed behind Trent and Ethan as they walked up the stairs to his room. As soon as they walked in, Ethan sat down on one of the leather chairs and positioned himself right in front of the TV.

"Do you want to start with *Halo 3*, or should we start with something a little easier for you? That way you can keep some of your dignity," Trent taunted.

"We can play whatever you want. But I'll have you know, I've been practicing. Kate thinks I'm really good."

From across the room, Sophie's laugh filled the air, and she sat down on the floor a few feet away, ready to watch.

Trent ignored her outburst and walked over to the entertainment center. Pulling out two controllers, he tossed them to Ethan. So far, he hadn't even noticed the red lace panties that lay directly on top of the Xbox. But soon enough as he began to turn around, he froze.

"What the …?" he mumbled to himself as he picked them up with two fingers.

"Oh, sorry," Ethan said loud and clear. "I must have left those here earlier." He stood up, walked over to a bewildered Trent and took Kate's underwear from him. "Here you go, honey. Sorry about that." He tossed them to her with a wink.

With deliberately slow movements, Trent looked back and forth between Ethan and Kate, trying to catch on to what just happened. Then suddenly his eyes grew wide as it dawned on him. He looked at the Xbox, then at Kate, before finally settling on Ethan.

"Wait, are you telling me you … you …?" His mouth hung open at a loss for words. "Dude," he finally said to Ethan, "you had her *box* on my Xbox!"

Ethan smirked at him and held up three fingers. "Three words, Trent: table, fruit, and payback."

Chapter 26
Impressions

So, tell me again how the company started." Kate sat back on her bed, rubbing her eyes with the palms of her hands, imagining that she could somehow force the information into her brain.

"Gunpowder. They were the largest suppliers of gunpowder during the mid-nineteenth century. After the war was over, they branched into dynamite and smokeless powder. They studied cellulose chemistry, you know, lacquers and other stuff." Sophie waved her hand around. "The company kept its emphasis in material science, and pretty soon it was dominating the entire field. They discovered neoprene, synthetic rubber, polyester superpolymer, nylon … The list goes on and on. The Montgomery family itself stepped back from running the company after Ethan was born, but his father still keeps a place on the board of directors. Oliver and his wife, Sabrina, are highly involved in numerous charities and run the Kids First organization that helps to fund children's hospitals nationwide."

Kate kept her eyes closed and mumbled off the list again, committing it to memory before groaning in frustration. "Ugh, Sophie, I still can't believe I didn't know this. I mean, what, was I living in a hole?"

"Kate, honey, *I* didn't even know this. And I know *everything*. The company name isn't Montgomery Industries, so how were we supposed to know?" Her friend nodded, but stayed silent. "Also, they stay out of the spotlight. Sure they go to fund raisers and charity events, but they aren't your typical high society family."

"I guess that's good, right? I mean, that they aren't the typical high society snooty type?" she asked, searching for the positive amongst the negative.

"Of course it is." Sophie sat down next to her on the bed and started playing with her hair. "But either way, they'll be nice. They raised Ethan, one of the nicest, sweetest, most amazing guys."

"I know, I know," Kate said, still in a daze. "I still can't believe Elle didn't tell me, or Logan. Didn't they know that I had no clue?"

"Logan said he thought you knew. So did Elle. They both figured it must have come up in your conversations. I mean, usually you talk about that type of stuff with the love of your life."

"Sophie," she sighed. "We did talk about it. He told me that his parents worked with an organization that helps fund children's hospitals. He even told me they were big on charity events, and he once said something once about how his family started a company way back, but I never once thought it was to this capacity. So yes, he did tell me. He wasn't trying to keep it from me."

She knew the tone of her voice sounded like she was still having doubts, but she wasn't—at least not anymore. At the time, however, she'd felt quite differently.

They were on their way home from Henry and Lori's a week ago. Trent was driving, still giving both Ethan and Kate the silent treatment. Apparently, he was a little put off by Ethan's choice of payback, even after being informed that nothing really happened on his Xbox.

Thankfully, Trent wasn't one to stay angry, and soon everyone was laughing and poking fun as they shared stories of their past. Kate made sure to listen closely to every story that involved Ethan, adding more reasons to love him. It was about halfway through Elle's story about a horse that Kate felt confused.

"Wait, a horse? You rode horses, Ethan?" she asked, turning toward him.

"Of course he rode horses. It was required of all 'prestigious academy boys.'" Trent answered in a mocking tone, earning a scowl from Ethan.

"If I recall correctly, Trent, you enjoyed it just as much as I did. And yes, Kate," he turned to face her, "I rode. But I haven't since my last visit home."

"Wait," she paused. "You have a horse?" She almost laughed at the thought.

Ethan shrugged his shoulders casually. "Sure, we have a few."

"Momma Sabrina loves horses," Trent said with a snort. "You should see her at the Derby, she goes nuts."

"The Derby?" Kate asked, not out of confusion but out of shock.

"The Kentucky Derby. In the past, we've had a few horses race." He smiled.

Shaking her head, Kate imagined ladies in large hats, sipping mint juleps and speaking with a southern drawl. She tried to imagine Ethan there, but couldn't picture it.

That moment was Kate's first sign that there was an invisible billboard hanging above Ethan that flashed the words "loaded" in florescent lights. Other signs came as more stories were told. Like the time that Ethan ran away when he was six and the nanny couldn't find him. Or the time that Elle snuck into Ethan's mom's closet and tried on all her clothes, ruining her three thousand dollar Versace gown, and blamed it all on Ethan.

"Squish was determined to fit into that thing." Logan said through tears, referring to Elle by her childhood chubby nickname. "She didn't even get it over her butt before the ripping started."

"Logan McLean!" Elle snapped.

Trent placed a comforting hand on her thigh. "Hey, Logan," he yelled over his shoulder. "I'll have you know there isn't a squishy part on my lady's body."

"Trent, that's my baby sister." His warning was said with a smile, but it was enough to end any further discussions that involved Elle.

Trent immediately changed the subject and started in on stories of vacations he'd taken with Ethan's family. It was when they discussed one specific trip—in Europe—that Kate interrupted.

"What exactly do your parents *do* again?"

"I thought I told you. Mostly they own an organization that helps fund children's hospitals."

"And when you say mostly … that means what exactly?"

"Well, Dad still sits on the board at GS. He couldn't quite step away completely. Had to keep his feet in the company somehow."

"GS—as in Global Science? What does that have to do with your family?"

Everyone in the car burst out in laughter, except for Kate and Sophie who looked at Ethan in confusion.

"Kate," Trent said, looking at her in the rearview mirror. "Ethan's dad is *the* Oliver Montgomery whose great-grandfather owned Montgomery Industries, now known to the world as Global Science."

"What?" she asked in shock. Her eyes flashed to Ethan and she expected him to laugh it off or at least correct Trent. Instead he shrugged his shoulders.

"Yeah, it's no big deal. I thought I told you about it."

"Well, you didn't." She snapped, feeling slightly annoyed that all of a sudden her Ethan seemed like a mystery to her. Like there was an entire world, an entire side of him, that she knew nothing about. She knew that he came from a comfortable background, but this was more than that; this was luxurious. Keeping her mouth shut, she was lost in her thoughts for the entire drive home. It wasn't until they were back at his home that they spoke about it.

"Kate, I'm sorry that I never told you, but I never thought it was a big deal."

"How can your family owning one of the largest companies in the country not be a big deal?"

"For starters, we don't own it anymore," he said, crossing his arms in front of his chest, taking a defensive stance.

"Well, excuse me for not knowing that."

"I didn't expect you to know it. I'm just stating a fact. Yes, my family *used* to own the company, but I still don't see what the problem is." His face softened, and she knew he didn't want to fight.

"The problem is you belong to a world that I can't even begin to understand. A world of nannies, trips to Europe, going to 'The Derby', and thousand dollar dresses."

Ethan took a step forward and placed a finger over her lips to stop her rambling. "Where I *belong* is with you. Where and how I grew up has no bearing on who I am. You *know* who I am Kate."

"But your parents, won't they want you with someone who—"

"They'll want me with someone," he said cutting her off again, "who makes me happy. They want me with someone who is kind, and funny, and understanding, and smart, and sexy…" He trailed off. His comment got her to smile, something that he'd been trying to do for that last hour.

"Sexy?" Kate doubted. "Something tells me that sexy is not a trait your parents would scour the earth to find for their son."

"Of course it is. They *do* love me." He laughed, pulling her close to him.

Kate laughed with him, but it was half forced. The worry and fear she felt was still present.

"Look, they will love you just like I do."

His comforting words had soothed her temporarily, but now, a week later, she was just as nervous and terrified as she had been then.

❧

"Soph, what if they don't like me? What if his *mom* doesn't like me?" She resumed pacing her bedroom, like she'd been doing all morning, wearing a pattern in the carpet. "You know, it's never a good thing if the mom doesn't like you."

"Stop worrying so much. They're going to love you. You just wait and see," she said confidently.

"I wish I could feel as sure as you seem. I'm just so nervous. These people could be my … I mean they could end up my … Well, we haven't actually talked about it, but I know they might end up—"

"As your in-laws." Sophie finished her sentence. Kate looked at her friend and nodded. Her heart raced at the very thought of the word. "Well, then," Sophie continued, "let's get you ready to meet your possible, potential future in-laws."

"I still wish I could meet them for the first time in a different setting."

Ethan tried to get his parents' schedule free before the benefit so they could all get to know one another without all the hoopla. But between all the meetings they had, there simply wasn't time. Instead, Kate was meeting them for the first time during the dinner amongst Pennsylvania's elite.

With a deep exhale, Kate willed herself to relax and think positively. "I couldn't do this without you. You know that, right?" she asked Sophie.

"Of course." She nodded.

"And you do realize I need to go over all of the information again, right?" She nodded again. "Of course."

"Good," she said in relief. "Start quizzing."

Sophie grabbed her notepad of Montgomery facts, along with her giant toiletries bag, and led the way into the bathroom, shouting off random questions along the way.

❧

One hour later, Kate stood in front of Elle's full-length mirror, wearing a fitted strapless black dress that came right below her knees. Her hair had been blow-dried and curled, and her face looked flawless. Every detail was perfect, but it still wasn't enough to calm her nerves. The fluttering butterflies she'd had earlier had turned into giant balls that were ricocheting inside her stomach, pounding harder with every minute that ticked by. Without even realizing it, Kate found herself talking quietly, practicing her greeting—just as Elle had done only a week before.

"Doesn't look so stupid now that you're in the same situation, huh?" Elle asked with a smirk, as she sat down on her bed and opened up the latest edition of *Vogue*.

Kate looked at her through the mirror's reflection. "No, not nearly as stupid," she agreed. "I wish I was as lucky as you. Henry and Lori are wonderful; they're so laid back."

"Ethan's parents are just as great. And you have the added benefit of not lusting after his dad. Although I will tell you, Oliver is one attractive older man." She smirked.

"Gee, great." Kate deadpanned. "How was that, by the way? I mean, has Trent caught on to anything?" She spun around to face her.

"Oh, he knows. He says he's used to it. It's really not an issue. I mean, Henry is attractive but…he's no Trent." The smile on Elle's face said it all. She was completely head over heels. Hot dad or not, she was in love with him. Her eyes were glazed over, and she was still for a moment before turning her attention back to her magazine.

With a deep breath, Kate smiled and went back to practicing her greetings again. After probably the eighth "It's a pleasure to meet you," there was a knock at the door.

"Have fun," Elle said, looking up with a smile. "You look beautiful. Go knock 'em dead."

With a quick thanks, Kate left the room and walked as fast as her heeled feet would carry her. When she reached the door, she could hear Ethan talking from the other side. She pulled the door open and gasped when she saw him. He was standing with one hand tucked in his pocket, the other one holding his phone to his ear. His black tux fit him perfectly, accentuating the width of his shoulders and the V shaped angles of his torso. Even with his crisp appearance, he still had that slightly rugged look. She looked him up and down, taking her time to enjoy the view and didn't hear a word he said. It wasn't until she heard her name that she snapped out of it.

"Kate is looking forward to it also." His smoky blue eyes locked with Kate's and he smiled. "All right, Dad, I will. Okay. Yes, that's fine. Okay, we'll see you soon."

Ethan snapped the phone shut, but didn't say a word. Instead, he took a small step back and dropped his eyes down Kate's body. The way he looked at her made her heart race, and she couldn't look away from him. He took his time as he slowly worked his gaze higher, eventually settling on her face.

"Beautiful," he said in a tone so sure, so honest, that she had no choice but to believe him.

"Thank you," she whispered, dropping her eyes.

He closed the distance between them in one step and wrapped his hand around the nape of her neck. Pulling her forward, he pressed his lips to hers, kissing her gently.

"Thank *you*," he said with a smirk. "So, are you ready for this?"

She took a calming breath. "Ready as I'll ever be."

❧

"Where are we going, exactly?" Kate asked, looking around at their surroundings. They had been in the car longer than she'd planned and was beginning to think they were lost.

"My parents decided that they wanted a place to stay when they come out to visit."

"And a hotel isn't okay?"

"My mom likes the feeling of having a house to come home to. She thinks it feels more personable, and it's easier to hold events without having to find a location that can accommodate everything."

"I thought a pharmaceutical company was throwing this thing?"

"They're sponsoring it, but after my parents decided to purchase a house, she convinced the person in charge to have it there. She loves entertaining; plus, after telling the hospital that they would get more contributions if it were held in a comfortable setting, they couldn't deny her. Not that anyone can ever deny my mother anyway."

"I see." Kate nodded. "So, they bought a home out here," she repeated.

"Yep."

Kate continued to nod and tried not to think about how nuts it all sounded to her. She was fairly certain that buying a home just so you could have somewhere to stay when you visited your son twice a year wasn't the typical thing to do. After all, her parents lived a few hours away and they never once thought about purchasing a place close by. Feelings of inadequacy started to creep up on her at the thought of how different their upbringings were. Just as quickly as the panic crept in, she pushed it aside and forced herself to focus on the then and there.

She kept her thoughts positive as they talked about random things. Just as she was about to ask him how much further they had to go, he turned off onto a side road. There was a large wrought iron gate blocking the entrance. There were trees as far as Kate could see, and no sign of a house. Ethan pulled up to the intercom and announced their arrival. The voice told him to pull forward and that the garage would be open for him. The huge gates slowly parted, and they crept forward. Kate couldn't escape the feeling that she was entering a compound, and in the back of her mind, a voice screamed for her to turn back now.

Ethan, sensing her nerves, placed a calming hand on her lap. He took her hand in his and squeezed it gently before giving her a reassuring smile.

The road twisted languorously around narrow trees and rows of tall hedges, cut and pruned to shape. Kate could only imagine how amazing it would look in full summer, when the trees were lush and green. When the surroundings began to thin, the road straightened and the house finally came into view. To say that is was larger than Henry's and Lori's would be an understatement. It was huge. Built of blue-gray stone, it stretched the entire length of the clearing and had more windows than Kate had ever seen on one house. Chimney stacks sprouted up from the slate roof and she was fairly certain she'd counted at least five.

"Geez," she said quietly.

"Yeah, I know. They go overboard sometimes."

"I'll say." She continued to watch in awe as they pulled up the winding driveway and into a separate, detached garage. Ethan turned off the car and got out while Kate sat still, motionless, trying to get her legs to function. Before she had time to move, the door was opened and she was being lifted out by her waist.

"Don't be nervous," he whispered into her ear as he nuzzled her neck. His warm breath brushed past her shoulder causing goose bumps to cover her skin.

"Hmph, that's a lot easier said than done, you know."

"It will be great, I promise. Look, we don't even have to stay very long. We'll make an appearance and say hello. I'll see if we can have brunch tomorrow morning with my parents to catch up, okay?"

Kate could tell he was trying to appease her, trying to make her feel as comfortable as possible, and she immediately felt awful. He hadn't seen his parents in a while, and there she was making him change his plans.

"No." She shook her head. "It will be fine. We'll stay as long as you want." She smiled up at him, trying to sound as genuine as possible.

"We'll play it by ear. But the minute you say you want to leave, we leave. All right?" She nodded and he kissed her forehead before running his hand down her arm and grasping her hand in his. Side by side, they walked out of the garage and across the wide driveway to a side door. He didn't bother knocking but just walked in, pulling Kate behind him.

The sounds of banging pots and crystal glasses tinkling together filled the air, like a culinary symphony. Delicious scents of rosemary and citrus wafted in from the next room and her mouth watered instantly. When they walked down the long hallway and into the kitchen, Kate's jaw dropped. It was gorgeous. Every state-of-the-art, top-of-the-line appliance you could imagine was tucked away amongst cherry cabinets and granite countertops. The giant island in the center had two side-by-side stovetops and every burner was occupied. Men and women dressed in white chef attire crowded the space, calling out orders and directions to the other workers standing by. It looked like a working kitchen at a restaurant and Kate was in heaven. She couldn't stop the smile that spread across her face as she took it all in.

Ethan gave her one look and laughed. "Smells good, doesn't it? Mother only gets the best to cater these things."

"It smells wonderful, but Ethan I . . . I can't get over the kitchen. It's amazing." She gaped.

"I'm sure my mom would love to hear that." Ethan motioned with his head toward something, and when Kate followed his gaze, she tensed.

Standing across the room was Ethan's mother. Kate didn't have to ask to know it was her. Her dark hair was the same shade as Ethan's, and even from this distance, she could see a slight resemblance. Her fair skin looked flawless, and it glowed against the dark green gown that draped her body perfectly. She was speaking with one of the chefs and just so happened to glance up at the doorway.

Once she spotted Ethan, she smiled. "Ethan," she crooned as she made her way toward them. "I was wondering when you would arrive. How was the drive? Did you find it easily?" She wrapped her arms around his shoulders and pulled him in for a tight hug, causing Kate and Ethan's hands to separate.

"It was fine, Mom; easier than I thought." He pulled back from her arms and looked down at Kate. "Mom, this is Kate, my girlfriend."

Sabrina kept her eyes locked with Ethan's for a little longer than normal and silent words passed between them. It only lasted a second and then she was looking at Kate. "Kate," she said with a half smile. "I'm glad you could accompany Ethan. I'm sure we'll find time to talk later. Please enjoy your evening." She gave him one last parting smile and turned her attention back to the preparations.

Kate stood speechless. She hadn't even had a chance to say hello and wondered if perhaps she was imagining the cold greeting she'd just received.

"Sorry about that. She gets short sometimes when she's stressed. Once the party starts, she'll calm down a bit." Kate nodded in understanding, but couldn't shake the feeling that her behavior had nothing to do with stress. Ethan intertwined his fingers with hers, lifted their clasped hands and placed a kiss on the back of her hand. "Let's go find my dad," he suggested.

"Sure."

Ethan led them through the kitchen and out into a dining room. The long table looked as though it could seat twenty people quite comfortably, but today no one would be sitting there as it was covered with desserts of all kinds: cakes, Danishes, cream filled pies, custards, fresh fruits dipped in chocolate—anything one could possibly imagine. Kate's mouth watered at the sight of it.

"He's probably hiding in the study, wherever that is," Ethan said, interrupting her dessert-filled haze. "If we find it, then I'm sure we'll find him."

"Your guess is as good as mine." She shrugged and turned away from the spread.

"I guess half the fun is the searching. This place has got to have all kinds of empty rooms. Maybe we can play another game of hide and seek." He raised his eyebrows.

"Not so fast, lover boy. You're lucky you got me to agree to that at Lori's house and look what happened. I ended up breaking her closet. There is no way I'm playing that here. I'll probably end up breaking an antique worth a hundred thousand dollars."

He laughed. "Fine, we'll play it your way." Together they walked out of the dining room to begin their search.

It took them longer to find his dad than they'd imagined it would, but then again, the house was even bigger than it looked from the outside. The high ceilings and formal décor made it feel almost like a hotel. No doubt it had enough rooms to be counted as one.

They walked into the study, and immediately Kate knew it should be called a library instead. It was huge, with a second story on one side and floor-to-ceiling built-in bookshelves lining every wall. She felt like she'd just walked into a fairy tale and blinked slowly to make sure it wouldn't all disappear. Ethan walked into the room farther and found his dad, just like he thought. He was sitting in a large leather chair next to a giant bay window. Hunkered down in his seat, he was engrossed in the pages of the book he held.

"Dad," Ethan said, alerting him to their presence.

His head snapped up. "Ethan." He smiled and placed his book down. His eyes dashed to the person beside his son, and his smile grew even wider. Standing quickly, he walked over to them, stretching his arms out as soon as he was in reaching distance. He pulled Ethan into a bone crushing hug and gripped his shoulders upon release. "It's so good to see you. And you must be Kate." When he turned to look at her, Kate saw that his eyes were almost the exact color as Ethan's, only a little darker. He had hair a shade lighter than his son's, and although she thought she'd seen a resemblance between Ethan and his mother, that was not the case here. Ethan was definitely his dad's son.

"Hi. It's so nice to meet you," Kate said, smiling.

"Have you received a tour of our home?"

Ethan laughed. "Dad, I don't even know my way around; how can I show her?"

"It's your home too. Just wander around. It's not that hard to figure out. Although, I must admit, it took me a little while to find all the bathrooms." He let out a loud laugh and slapped his son on the back. "I take it your mother is in the kitchen bossing everyone around?" It was a rhetorical question, and his dad didn't even wait for a response before he continued speaking. "Henry and Lori should be arriving soon, as well as all the other representatives from the hospital. I know Cindy is hoping to get a good turn-out. They put a lot into it this year."

Kate could feel Ethan's hand stiffen in hers at the mention of the girl named Cindy, and for some reason, it sounded familiar. She looked up at his face in question, but his eyes were still on his dad.

"I hope we get a good turn-out. The hospital could really use a new wing for pediatric cardiology."

"With the guest list that Cindy and your mother came up with, I'm sure there will be enough to break ground next spring," he said, laughing again. "Speaking of those two, I better go find them and see if they need help." He looked down at Kate and placed his hand on her shoulder. "Again, it's great to meet you. I'm sure we'll have plenty of time to talk later. Take care of my son, here. Don't let him get carried away with the silent auction." He leaned down and spoke softly in her ear, even though it was clear Ethan could hear every word. "He always outbids me, and this year I'm determined to beat him in something. I may enlist your help with that later. I'll come find you." He stood up and gave Kate a quick wink before he walked toward the door. "Go look around, you two, but make sure you're back by the time we start."

As soon as his dad was out of the room, Kate turned to face Ethan. "Cindy?" she asked, knowing he understood her question.

"She's a … colleague, but I used to date her."

"What!" she shrieked. "Are you telling me that the girl in charge of this thing, the girl who has been working side-by-side with your mother making a 'perfect,'" she sneered the word, "guest list is a girl you dated?"

"Yes."

"How serious were you?" He rubbed his hands over his face and Kate's stomach dropped.

"She was the girl I was dating when I first met you."

Kate thought back to the day at the hospital, that day that seemed so long ago, and clearly remembered the moment. The nurse, who she now knew as Lisa, had interrupted them for what seemed like the third time and announced that Ethan's girlfriend had called and wouldn't be able to make it for dinner.

Just the simple memory made her feel sick. She knew Ethan had been dating someone. It had been something that she'd lost sleep over for days until she finally saw him at the grocery store. At the time, she was so excited to find out that he was single that she hadn't even begun to think about how serious the relationship had been.

Thinking back to their conversation over a week ago, she tried to recall what Ethan had said about past girls he'd dated. He had said his last girlfriend was crazy, overbearing, and fake, that they only dated a few months, and that he didn't love her. For some reason, these facts meant little to Kate now—now that she was faced with the knowledge that this girl, this Cindy, was someone his mother obviously liked. A girl who already had a relationship with his family, something that she was just now beginning.

"Kate." Ethan placed his hand on her cheek and guided her head to look at him. "She is just a colleague. And honestly, I don't know what I ever saw in her. For work purposes, I have to put up with her."

His words made her feel a little better, but it still wasn't enough to erase the panic that was brewing beneath the surface. She knew that jealousy wasn't the most attractive quality, but right now she was raging with it. Just as she was about to ask him how long they dated, another more important question came to mind. A question that Kate wasn't sure she wanted the answer to.

"Does your mother like her?" He hesitated for a moment, and that alone answered the question. "Hmm, I see." She nodded.

"It's only because they had mutual friends," he explained. "Well, that and tennis. That's all it took." He rolled his eyes.

"Tennis?"

"One of my mother's many obsessions." He laughed to himself and pulled Kate into his chest. "I'm sure Mom will love you and it won't be because you play tennis."

"Well, thank goodness for that. If my tennis playing skills are any sign of the relationship I'll have with your mother, then I'm afraid I'd be a lost cause." They both laughed and Kate tried to relax a bit by telling herself that she had nothing to worry about.

"Come on, let's go take a tour of the house and get ourselves lost." Ethan started for the door and Kate followed a step behind him.

"As long as you promise me that we'll be back on time and not miss anything important. I don't want your mom disliking me even more."

"She doesn't dislike you." He stopped and turned around.

"Did you not hear her? Wait, let me rephrase that—did you not see the way she looked at me, or should I say *didn't* look at me?"

"My mom is hard on everyone she meets. There is this unspoken fear she has that every person we let *in* has ulterior motives."

Kate stayed silent and let his words stew in her mind as they began their walk through the house. Every room was more amazing than the next, and after ten minutes, she was fairly certain they hadn't seen them all. Deciding to take a break from touring, they returned to the main level where the festivities were being held.

As they walked into the main room, Kate stared in awe. It was breathtaking. Two large fireplaces stood on either end and were emitting a soft glow, giving the room a comfortable feel. What normally served as a living room had been transformed. All the couches had been removed and replaced with round tables, each one adorned in colors of vibrant green and white, accented in silver. All the guests were filing in and a few had taken places at various tables. Kate looked at each woman carefully, wondering if perhaps she was Cindy. She didn't have time to ask Ethan before he noticed someone across the room who waved him over.

"I'll be right back. Would you like something to drink?" he asked.

"Yes, please. I'll have whatever you're having, unless what you're having is water, and then I'll take a glass of wine." He chuckled softly in her ear and was gone before she said another word.

She watched him as he walked away and wondered how she'd ever gotten so lucky. Smiling to herself, she took another look around the room and paused when she noticed a few pictures on the mantle of one of the fireplaces. Taking a closer look, she noticed Ethan right off. In one of the pictures, he must have been around fourteen years old. He was on the back of a black horse that was draped in flowers and he held a ribbon in his hand. She chuckled to herself because she wasn't at all surprised that he was an accomplished rider. The rest of the pictures followed a similar theme. They were either all of Ethan or of Ethan with his parents. There were a few from various places around the world and one from his graduation from medical school. He looked genuinely happy in all of them, and it was clear he loved his family.

Just as Kate was about to turn away, the last photo in the lineup caught her eye. It was a more recent photo and when she took a step closer to get a better look, her heart sank. There, looking back at her, was Ethan with his arms wrapped around the waist of someone else. The girl was a few inches shorter than him and had light blond hair and blue eyes. It took Kate all of two seconds to figure out who the mystery girl was.

"I just love that picture. It's one of my favorites. I'm so happy Sabrina decided to put it up."

Kate didn't have to turn around to know who the sickeningly sweet voice belonged to. Instead, she kept her eyes forward and waited for the voice to speak again, silently begging for her to disappear. Unfortunately, she wasn't so lucky.

"You're Kate, right? I heard Ethan say something about him coming with a friend tonight and your name was mentioned. So, I'm just assuming."

Kate's eyes narrowed in defense and she spun around to face her head on. "Yes, I'm Kate. I'm Ethan's girlfriend." She emphasized. "And you must be Cindy, his colleague." She crossed her arms and watched as Cindy's face puckered. For a split second, she felt like she had the upper hand; that was until she saw Ethan's mom walking toward them.

"Cindy," she called out. "I was wondering where you disappeared to. Ethan was just talking to the Governor and it seems as though he has an eye on number twelve in our auction." She wrapped her arm around Cindy's shoulder and laughed. "You might want to step in and tell him about Ethan's habit of outbidding everyone. Then maybe he'll stand a chance of leaving here tonight with something."

"That son of yours is quite something," Cindy replied.

They faced each other for a moment and had a quiet conversation, never once looking in Kate's direction. *She hates me,* she thought as a flood of rejection washed over her.

Standing in shocked silence, she watched them for a moment before turning around. She tried to focus on anything other than the couple behind her. Even the painting above the fireplace couldn't hold her attention.

"It's beautiful, isn't it? It's one of my favorite pieces." Kate chanced a look over at Sabrina who was now standing beside her. She was alone, and Kate realized that now was her shot.

"It is. I took a class that studied Impressionist painting when I was in London; Monet is amazing."

"That's right, you studied art and photography." Her tone wasn't questioning, rather it was stating. "But surely you can't expect to be able to make a living for yourself by taking Polaroids."

Kate ignored the stab and swallowed down the emotions she felt surfacing. "That's what I'm doing now actually. I've sold a few pieces in a gallery, and my schedule is full shooting weddings and other events."

"Ahh, that's right. Ethan told me he purchased one of your pieces. It was rather pricey, if I recall. I'll have to see it sometime."

"Umm … sure. I'm sure he'd love to show you," she stammered. "He's very supportive of my work."

"Of course he is, my dear. You're probably very talented. Although I'm sure he wouldn't tell you honestly if he felt otherwise. But he has been exposed to the arts his entire life, so I can only hope he knows good work when he sees it."

Kate was baffled, mystified really. She couldn't understand if Sabrina's comments were complimenting or insulting.

"Ethan's been exposed to a lot more in his life than art. He's been places and seen things I'm sure you've only dreamed of. I'm not sure of your intentions, but if you think that working your way into his life will grant you all of those things, then you're mistaken. I hope the crush you have is short-lived because I'd hate to see you get hurt, sweetheart."

A wave of anger and sickness rolled over Kate. Not only was his mother calling her a gold digger, but she was questioning what she felt for Ethan, what they shared. On most occasions, she prided herself on being able to speak her mind—to defend herself—but at the moment, the sickness and rejection she felt far overpowered the anger. It was obvious that Sabrina had decided that Kate was not good enough for her son.

She felt the tears well up in her eyes and she blinked them back, forcing them not to fall and show yet another weakness that could be added to her list of faults. "Excuse me," she whispered, dropping her eyes as she ran out of the room, refusing to look up in fear that Ethan would see her. She hurried down the hallway, willing herself not to break down until she found a room to hide in. Yanking on the handle of the first door she came to, it flung open. But before she could take a step inside the room, she slammed into someone.

"Oh, man, I'm sorry. I didn't see—"

"It's okay." The sound of her voice cut through Kate. If there was one person she didn't want to see her cry, it was Cindy.

"Cindy." She nodded in acknowledgment.

"Are you all right?" she asked in an overly fake tone.

Taking a calming breath, Kate lifted her head. "I'm fine."

"Sabrina can be hard to win over. I wish I could say it took me a while, but it didn't. You see, I fit. I *belong* here and a girl like you," she looked her up and down, pausing briefly at her shoes. "In last season's Prada heels," she smirked, "can't possibly fit. Sabrina knows that, and it's only a matter of time before Ethan does."

Kate kept her jaw locked tight and ignored the stabbing pain that Cindy's truthful words caused as they ripped through her chest. Giving one last smirk as she watched her reaction, Cindy stepped out of the room, letting the door close with a click behind her.

Finally alone, Kate let the pain take over. She let the words Sabrina had said soak into her mind and the facts work their way through her body until they rendered her weak. She'd always had a fear that she wasn't good enough for Ethan, and for the first time, she felt it. Falling to the ground, she pressed her face in her hands, letting the tears fall freely as she blocked out the world around her, the world in which Ethan belonged and she didn't.

Chapter 27
Confrontations

Ethan watched in horror as Kate fled the room. The expression on her face was one he couldn't quite place. She looked … confused, upset, angry, hurt? He wasn't sure, but he knew he'd seen it before. He closed his eyes in concentration, then, like a bolt of lightning, it came to him; he knew where he'd seen that expression before.

His memory flashed to the two of them standing outside of the hospital. He'd just lied and told her that he needed a break, that he couldn't do it anymore. He remembered having to look down at the ground so he wouldn't have to watch her face any longer as she realized what he was telling her. Days later, after all the confusion was cleared, Kate had told him that she felt he'd finally realized that she wasn't good enough for him, a thought that was completely ridiculous.

Now, standing in his parents' house, his blood began to boil as he realized something must have been said to her in order to draw that same reaction, that same pained expression. His stomach churned and he felt like he was going to be sick. The very idea of Kate being upset on behalf of something his mother said was nauseating.

"Excuse me, Governor, I need to take care of something." Ethan tried to keep his tone light, but knew that it sounded strained. He walked swiftly across the room to where his mother stood, talking to another guest and interrupted her. "May I talk with you, Mother?"

"Just a minute, dear, Mrs. Dawson was just telling me about—"

"Now," he seethed through clenched jaw.

Without waiting for her to excuse herself, he wrapped his arm around her waist and led her to the exact spot she and Kate had been standing just moments ago.

"Ethan, do you really think it's a good idea to interrupt Mrs. Dawson? You know how she—"

"What did you say to her?" he asked, cutting her off.

"Excuse me?"

"To Kate, Mom. What did you say to Kate? I saw you over here talking to her, and I also saw the look on her face before she ran out of here."

"I didn't say anything that wasn't true."

"What did you say?" he repeated again, beginning to feel even more frustrated. He turned toward the mantel and was just about to rest against it when a picture caught his eye. "What the…?" He glared at the picture of Cindy and him, and felt the bile rise to the back of his throat. "You didn't." He shook his head in disgust.

"Ethan, she's a very sweet girl, I'm sure. But she is not meant for you. Cindy is—"

"Manipulative, overbearing, in some cases, psychotic… my list could go on."

"Sweetheart," she started in an almost warning tone, but Ethan didn't stay around to hear the rest. He grabbed the frame off the mantel and turned on his heel. He knew his mom would follow, so there was no reason to wait for her. Sure enough, he could hear the click of her heels as she walked behind him down the hallway. As soon as he made it to the study, he spun around to face her and was surprised to see his dad had joined her.

"What's going on?" he asked, looking at his son's furious expression.

"Why don't you ask Mom. She still hasn't told me what she said, but I have a feeling I know what it was."

His dad turned and looked at her with questioning eyes. "Sabrina?"

She let out a soft sigh and took a few steps closer. "Ethan. I only want what's best for you."

"And what do you think is best for me?" He ran his hands over his face in an attempt to calm himself.

"Someone who understands what it means to be a Montgomery. Someone who is strong and more than capable of standing on her own. Someone who is interested in you for who *you* are, not our family name."

Ethan had to hold back his laugh. His mother had no clue what type of person Kate was. She was all of those things and more. Just as he opened his mouth to tell her that she couldn't have been more wrong, he realized that she still hadn't answered his question. "You still haven't told me what you said to her and I'd like to know—word for word."

Sabrina held her head high, and Ethan braced himself for what she was about to say. "Well, we talked a little bit about her profession. And I expressed my concerns for her ability to support herself by taking Polaroids."

"Polaroids?" he repeated in disgust. "Kate is one of the most talented people I've ever met. I know good art when I see it, Mother, and believe me when I say her picture was worth every penny I spent."

"A picture that you bought *after* you met her. I'm sure she found some way to coerce you into—"

"Coerce me?" he spat, cutting her off.

"You know how people are. You've dated girls in the past who were only in the relationship for the money."

"How would you know? I've only ever brought a few girls home. Have you ever stopped to wonder why that is? I didn't bring them because I didn't want *this* to happen."

"You brought Cindy, and I think she is—"

"I think you've made your feelings about Cindy quite clear." He held up the framed picture, making his point before throwing it in the trashcan. "And I'll have you know I only brought her home to meet you because she demanded it. You didn't get a chance to ever meet the real Cindy. Someday I'll have to introduce you to her, because she's not the person you think she is."

"She's not a . . . gold digger, I know that."

"And you think Kate is?" She remained silent and then he knew. Ethan knew that's what she had said to her. He felt his heart ache at the thought of Kate being accused of something so ridiculous. "Please tell me that I'm wrong," he said, his voice was so low it was almost inaudible. "Please tell me that you did not call her that."

Her eyes dropped to the floor slightly before looking back up at him. "Not in those words, no."

"Sabrina," Oliver gasped.

"Sweetheart, I'm just trying to look out for him."

"Is this something you've perceived after talking to her?" Oliver asked. "Have you talked to her? Actually talked to her? Because I have. Granted, it was only for a moment, but I didn't pick up on anything other than her genuine kindness and affection for our son."

Ethan's mother looked at her husband for a moment before answering. "He's only known her for a month; she doesn't belong—"

"She *belongs* with me, and I belong with her," Ethan said. "I may have only known her for a month and a half, but it has been the best month and a half of my life. Kate is loving, and smart, and funny, and understanding, and the best friend anyone could ask for. She's not pretentious in any way. In fact, she didn't even know I was a 'Montgomery' until last weekend. She was scared and nervous to come here today and meet you both. She was worried that she wouldn't fit in. And you know what? Maybe she doesn't, and I'm glad. She's better than all of this."

He looked around the room. "I know you think everyone has ulterior motives, and I understand why. You experienced it firsthand, and that must have been painful for you. But that was a long time ago. This judging, this thinking that everyone is only after one thing, has got to stop. Because I love her—I love her and I am going to marry her someday." He spun around on his heel and headed over to the doorway, but stopped before leaving. "I'm going to go find her and try to convince her that you aren't as awful as I'm sure she thinks you are. If you want me to stay, then I advise you think of what you are going to say to set things straight. I love you, Mother, but I go where she is." He looked at his mom and tried to smile, to let her know that he wanted a life where both she and Kate were involved.

"I'm sorry, Ethan," he heard her say as he walked out of the room.

It took all the strength Ethan had to walk out of the study, to stand up to his mother, a woman who he loved dearly and meant the world to him. She was always so protective, and he knew it was because she had his best interests at heart; but this time, she had gone too far. He never wanted to choose between Kate and his mother, and was hoping he wouldn't have to. He was leaving it up to her.

℮⁀

I don't belong here . . . I don't fit. Kate repeated the words over and over in her head until they didn't make sense any more. Tears continued to fall down her face, but she made no effort to wipe them. From experience, she knew they wouldn't stop until they were dried up, until she had nothing left.

She lay curled up on the floor and stared out the window, trying to find patterns in the white clouds that drifted across the gray sky. The daze-like trance was beginning to set in and she welcomed it—welcomed the numbing ability it brought. She didn't want to feel undeserving and not good enough, so instead she focused on the feeling of nothing and tried to let her thoughts fade away.

Eventually, the floor began to feel hard and her arm started to tingle. She regretfully sat up, and for the first time, looked around the room in which she was sitting. It looked like a guest room that was decorated to look more like a master suite. It fit perfectly with the rest of the rooms she'd seen today. All of them were exquisite and fancy and extraordinary. All of them had tasteful furniture that must have cost a fortune, and all of them were perfect and beautiful. While she sat, taking in all of her surroundings and every little detail, it hit her.

Ethan had grown up in this. He grew up in a place that was fancy and perfect and pretentious and felt like a hotel; yet he was nothing like this. He was perfect and beautiful, yes. But he wasn't overpriced pillows and thousand dollar paintings. He was simple and honest and good, and that was the man she belonged with.

I belong with him, she thought. She closed her eyes and repeated the new phrase over in her head, willing herself to know its truth. She said it until she *felt* it, until she knew there was nothing that could make her think otherwise. It was then that she realized that Sabrina might think she knew her, but she really had no idea.

Kate wiped the wetness from her eyes and forced the tears to stop. Taking a deep breath, she slid her feet underneath her and stood up. Rolling her shoulders back, she walked over to the mirror that hung on the wall and looked at her face. It was red and splotchy, and it looked like she'd been crying, but she didn't care. She ran her fingers through her hair and was just about to leave when there was a knock at the door. Before she could answer, the door opened and there stood Sabrina.

"Kate," she said quietly. "I'd like to talk to you if that's all right."

Kate was taken aback by the gentle tone of her voice, but realized it might have been her way of softening her up for another round of verbal insults. Drawing on all the strength she had, she took a deep breath and looked Sabrina straight in the eye.

"No. I need you to be quiet. It's my turn to talk."

Behind the door, standing out in the hallway listening, was Ethan. He'd seen his mother walk into the room and had a feeling he should follow her. As soon as he'd heard his mom say Kate's name, he'd frozen. The protective side in him wanted to barge into the room and pull Kate away. He wanted to tell her that he was so sorry for all the things that had happened and tell her that she didn't have to talk to anyone. The only thing that stopped him was Kate's response. Now he stood in silence waiting for his mother to say something. Very few people ever spoke to her that way, and he wasn't sure how she would take it. When he didn't hear anything, he assumed she must have decided to listen to Kate and stayed quiet.

"I'm going to talk and I want you to listen. After all, I think I have been more than fair by listening to your opinion of me up until this point." Kate balled her fists and gathered more courage. "I don't know what you've heard about me or what Ethan has told you, but you are seriously mistaken by thinking that I am some kind of gold digger. I could care less about your money. I didn't even know that Ethan was a Montgomery. I mean, I knew his last name was Montgomery, but I never imagined it was *the* Montgomery. So, for you to assume that I'm trying to work my way into his life to get all the things that come with his privileged title is completely ridiculous.

"As for my choice in career, I am doing just fine for myself. I have my work in numerous galleries and my calendar is booked almost six months in advance. For someone who shoots *Polaroids,* I'd say that's pretty good. I don't need Ethan's money; what I need is Ethan. So, I don't care what you or Cindy or anyone else says to me. I don't care if I fit in here, because I know where I belong; I know where I fit. And that's with your son." Kate looked at Sabrina after she was finished with her rant and breathed for what felt like the first time since she'd walked into the room.

"Well, I must say I was not expecting that. You, my dear, are nothing like I thought you were. I seem to be mistaken about a few things."

"Look, if you're here to insult me further, I think I'll leave. I've heard more than enough slandering comments today. I don't need to hear any more." Kate turned away and headed for the door.

"Wait," Sabrina called out. "I seem to have a … problem projecting my concerns when it comes to the welfare of my son. And I owe you an apology."

"I'm listening," Kate said softly.

"What do you know about me, Kate? Did Ethan ever tell you my maiden name was Whitmore?"

"No, he never mentioned it." She made a mental note to take the matter up with Ethan later.

"So, you've heard of my family?" Sabrina continued.

"I know I've read the name somewhere. It's associated with wealth, much like the Montgomery name."

"That's correct. So, you see, I've grown up in this."

"And that explains your actions toward me in what way?" Kate snapped, earning a sigh from Sabrina. "Sorry. I'll let you explain," she whispered.

"My parents were wonderful people. They tried to keep me sheltered my whole life but it was harder as I grew older. We can't keep a tight hold on our children, even if we want to." She was quiet for a moment as she thought of her son. "As I was saying," she continued, "they couldn't control all of my actions, no matter how badly my father wanted to. When I was nineteen, I moved out of the house so I could live on my own, and that's when I met Charles."

Ethan, who was still outside of the room, listened intently. He'd never heard the entire account of what had happened between Charles and his mother, only bits and pieces.

"We met at the library at the University where I was studying," his mother continued. "He was a gentleman and helped me reach a book that was too high for me. After a few minutes of talking, he asked if he would see me again there tomorrow. We met every day, in the same spot, and talked for hours about … everything." Her voice was wistful.

"I remember feeling so excited about finally finding someone who knew the real me. Someone who didn't care who I was, but loved *me*. He told me I meant the world to him; that he'd waited for so long for someone like me. We didn't date for very long before he asked for my hand. Of course I said yes, and we both agreed on a quick engagement, much to my parents' disapproval. They insisted there was no way that I really knew him; that it was impossible to really be in love. I refused to listen to them. Even after my father said he had a reliable source with proof of Charles' intentions.

"I told my parents that they could either accept him in my life or I was gone. Neither of them wanted to lose me, so we continued with the wedding plans. Charles, for the most part, completely understood. He took little part in the wedding plans and wasn't around very often, but I simply thought that was normal. After all, what groom enjoys picking out flowers and concerning themselves with seating arrangements?" she said in an almost laugh.

"A week before the big day, a few of Charles' friends arrived in town. He spent a lot of time with them, and I was thankful that he had something to keep him busy, since I was so tied down with last minute wedding things. One night after a nice dinner at my parents' estate, Charles and his friends were in the parlor having drinks. I knew they probably wanted some male bonding time and decided to give him some space.

"After an hour or so, I went to check on them. I could hear the laughter pouring from the room and knew they must have been having a fun time. I was just about to enter the parlor when I heard my name. I froze, merely out of curiosity, and waited to hear what they were talking about. Pressing my ear to the door, I heard the conversation that turned my life upside down." Sabrina paused for a moment and her throat tightened. She didn't like remembering the moment, let alone talking about it. Swallowing down the knot that had formed, she continued.

"'I can't believe how lucky I got,' Charles said. 'Who knew landing a rich one could be so easy? The fact that she's got a pretty face makes it even easier.'

"They laughed amongst themselves for a minute, and I stood in horror, not believing my ears. I contemplated running away, either that or barging into the room to confront him; but I couldn't move. I stood there, listening as they talked about me.

"'You're lucky she doesn't seem to care about you being gone a lot,' one of his friends laughed. 'You can go out, get your fill with the ladies, and still come home to her. Then you can give her a good screw to thank her for keeping the bed warm while you spend her money.'

"I could hear Charles laugh along, and I just knew. I knew that what his friend had said was true. The conversation continued on much like that until, finally, the door opened. Charles took one look at my face and he knew that I had heard everything. I slapped him hard, then turned around and left him there. I never looked back and never saw him again. I told my parents about what I'd heard, and my father made sure he'd never bother me again. I found out months later that Charles had been sleeping with other women while we were together. Apparently, he found out about the new 'Whitmore' girl on campus and set out to find me. He had it all planned from the beginning."

Silence hung in the space between them, and Kate sat down on the nearby bed.

"I learned the hard way not to trust people's intentions," Sabrina said, finally breaking the silence. "Ethan is my only child, and I feared for the day that something like this would happen to him. Then he told me about you. About how amazing you were and how much he enjoyed being with you. It all sounded too good to be true. It was like I was listening to myself talk about Charles. And then I mentioned you to Cindy earlier today, and she seemed to think that your intentions weren't as they should be."

"I don't know Cindy very well. But from what I've gathered, she is not the best person to trust in terms of character judgment," Kate said.

"Ethan did mention that she isn't quite what she appears to be, which I must admit is quite a shock. I usually consider myself a good judge of character, but this time I must be wrong. She's always seemed pleasant, but I'll be the first to admit perceptions can be wrong. As I have obviously demonstrated today." She smiled apologetically. "Ethan loves you, and from what you've said, you love him. All I've ever wanted for my son is love and happiness, and he seems to have found that in you."

"I want you to know that I can't promise that I'll fit in here," Kate said. "All of this is new to me. I don't play tennis, I don't know the 'who's who' of society, and I certainly don't know the difference between last season's Prada collection and this year's. But I can promise you that I love your son. I love him for who he is, and I'm not going anywhere."

"That's all that matters. You'll get used to everything else with time. And if anyone asks, last season's Prada collection was much better than this year. Much classier, if you ask me."

Both ladies laughed and there was immediate release of tension. They knew that things had changed for the better, if only slightly. Either way, it was enough for now.

Ethan took the moment to enter the room and finally see Kate's face. "Are you all right?" he asked, needing to hear her say it to his face.

"I'm fine. Better than I was." Kate looked at his mother briefly and then at him before smiling.

"Well, I've got a party to get back to," Sabrina said, keeping her voice light. "Why don't you two take your time and join us when you're ready? I'm sure Lori and Henry will love to see you." She looked at Kate and smiled kindly, offering another silent apology, then turned to her son. Placing her hand on his cheek, she gave him a quick nod before leaving the room.

When they were finally alone, Ethan crossed the room quickly and pulled Kate into his arms. Without giving her a chance to speak, he kissed her deeply. And when they separated, he looked at her with love in his eyes. "Are you sure you're okay?" he asked again, still not satisfied with her previous answer. "I saw you leave and you looked so sad. Then I talked to my mother, and when she told me what she said, I..." Taking a deep breath, he forced himself to stop rambling. "Kate, I am so sorry. I never should have left your side tonight."

"No." She shook her head. "You can't be sorry for something you didn't expect to happen. You can't always protect me, I'm—"

"I can try," he said, cutting her off.

"Yes, you can." She smirked. "But I still need to learn to stand up for myself."

"And stand up, you did."

"You heard me?" She looked at him in shock.

He looked away innocently. "I *may* have been listening to some of the conversation."

"Did you know that whole story about your mother?"

"No. At least, not all of it. I knew she'd been hurt and that it had something to do with a guy and her parents' money, but I never imagined it was that."

"It does explain a lot of her actions. I mean, she—"

"Kate, she still shouldn't have said those things to you."

"I know that. But she was just being the protective mother. I know that if our only son came home with a girl that I didn't know, I'd question her motives. We can't always trust—"

"Our son?" he repeated with wide eyes. He had to admit that hearing it come from her mouth offered more comfort than he ever imagined.

"Umm...er...well..." Kate's face turned the color of a tomato, and Ethan instantly placed his hand on her cheek, feeling the warmth against his palm. She wouldn't look up at him, so he bent down slightly.

"Hey," he said, trying to catch her eye. "Look at me."

She closed her eyes briefly before opening them again and staring right at him. "What? So, I've thought about it." She shrugged and shifted her weight from one foot to the other nervously. "Is there something wrong with that?" Her tone was challenging, but there was no masking the panic that was there as well.

"There's nothing wrong with it, except for the fact that you said *only* son." Kate dropped her head and sighed his name so quietly he could hardly hear it.

He worried for a second that perhaps he said too much, but immediately knew that he hadn't. He knew how Kate felt and knew that she wanted the same things he did. He also knew that talking about having kids together was a completely overwhelming conversation, so he attempted to change the subject.

"What do you say we go see if Henry and Lori are here yet?" he suggested, taking her hand in his.

She smiled at him, her dark brown eyes the color of melted chocolate. "Sounds like a great idea."

Together, they walked out of the room and made their way back to the party. It didn't take long for Lori to spot them, and both she and Henry were standing next to them in a matter of minutes.

"I was wondering if we would see you two. Sabrina said you two lovebirds were off hiding somewhere," Lori said, smiling. "These events can get a little stuffy if you ask me."

Kate laughed and rose up on her toes to give Ethan a peck. Just as their lips touched, Ethan's dad came up beside them.

"Mind if I steal your girlfriend for a bit?" he asked with a playful glint in his eye.

"Trying to recruit another spy?" Ethan laughed. "Dad, every year you try, and every year I still outbid you."

"I know, I know, but I didn't have Kate all those other years. Something tells me she's a lucky one."

They all laughed at his dad who immediately wrapped his arm around Kate's waist and led her out of the room.

"No, Dad, I'm the lucky one," Ethan said mostly to himself.

Kate, hearing him, looked back over her shoulder and smiled. Her mouth parted and he watched her lips as she mouthed back to him. "Me too."

Chapter 28
Paging Dr. Hunter

*W*hat I want to do—well, no, let me rephrase that—what I *have* to do, is outbid Ethan on at least one item. I don't know what I do wrong. Every year I think I'm the highest, and then I always lose." He tossed his arms up in the air in frustration.

Oliver and Kate had been walking side-by-side for the past few minutes, strolling past tables that held either pictures of items or actual items that were up for auction.

"Why don't you just bid obscenely high and call it good?" she asked, feeling slightly stupid for asking the question.

"Well, for starters, Sabrina would not approve of me buying a trip to Fiji for half a million dollars. The other reason is that Ethan and I always play fair. We made a promise not to go overboard and try to actually keep the bidding realistic. There *are* other people here and we have to give them their shot." He gave her a smile that looked so much like Ethan's that she couldn't help but giggle.

"Okay, so you play fair," she confirmed. "How does it all work?"

"It's pretty simple actually. Each item has a description and a base price for what the item is worth. People write a bid on small sheets of paper and deposit them into the box on the table. At the end of the auction, the bids are calculated and the highest bidder wins the item, for whatever price he or she offered."

She nodded. "That is pretty simple. So, what do you need my help for?"

Oliver turned and smiled mischievously. "I need you to tell me what he bids."

"Mr. Montgomery, I—"

"Please call me Oli," he said, cutting her off.

"Okay, Oli. Look, you should probably know that when it comes to keeping things from your son, I'm lousy. He's going to know something is going on."

He folded his arms across his chest and thought over her statement. "All right. So, what about a distraction?"

"Distraction?" she asked hesitantly. "Like what?"

"I don't know, but I'm sure you can think of something. We still have some time. The bids are collected at the end of the evening and then the winners will be announced. I trust you can figure something out."

Something about the childlike glint in his eyes made Kate want to help him, but she knew that it probably wouldn't work. Stealth was not her strong suit. Before she could tell him, a pair of warm arms wrapped around her waist. Ethan dropped his head down and grazed his lips along her neck.

"Miss me?" he whispered into her ear.

"Ethan, glad you could join us. I was just explaining the silent auction to Kate." Oliver gave her a quick wink.

Rubbing the small of her back, Ethan turned to his dad. "And by 'explaining,' do you mean persuading her to help you beat me this year?"

"Why would I do that?" his dad asked, smiling innocently.

"Because you're competitive."

"That's true, I am competitive. But at least now you know where you get it from."

Kate looked up at Ethan. "You're competitive?"

He didn't get a chance to say a word before his dad started laughing. "Have you played any games with my son?"

"We've played a few, but he wasn't too bad." She shrugged.

"Well, then, you weren't playing the right game. Sit down and play a game of Monopoly against him and you'll see what I mean. Why, he couldn't even play Chutes and Ladders properly when he was a kid. This one time—"

"Dad," Ethan said, cutting him off. "I was six years old! And stop trying to change the subject. Were you, or were you not, trying to get my girlfriend to help you cheat?"

Oliver rubbed the back of his neck and thought carefully. He didn't want to actually lie to his son.

A laugh rumbled in Ethan's chest and Kate turned to look at him. "Did my dad ask you to help him?" he asked.

Chancing a peek over to his dad, who was smiling, Kate didn't say a word. She knew that if she spoke up she'd say something that would give her away.

As it turned out, that was all the proof Ethan needed. He laughed again and shook his head at his dad. "What do you say we take our walk?"

"Walk?" Kate asked in confusion.

"We walk around and take a look at the items, decide what we want to bid on, and then place our bids."

"I'm ready when you are, son." Oliver had a look of determination on his face as he spun around, leading the way.

Kate glanced around the room as they started walking and spotted Sabrina standing across the room talking with Cindy. She felt her stomach churn as she thought about the discussion they might be having. Although she knew that Sabrina was going to reconsider her opinion of Cindy, it didn't completely do away with the unease she felt. The last thing she wanted was any kind of competition with Ethan's ex. In an attempt to distract herself from thinking the worst, she focused her thoughts back on the subject at hand. And that was Ethan and his dad.

"You know you should let him win at least one thing this year. Make him feel a little better about himself," she whispered quietly to Ethan.

"I already planned on it."

"You did?"

"Yeah, and beating him last year put a slight dent in my pocket."

"Dent?" she questioned. "How big of a dent?" He opened his mouth to answer and she quickly held up her hand. "No, never mind. I don't want to know." She knew that money wasn't an issue for him, but didn't want to think about it in terms of actual numbers. Things just felt easier that way.

Kate meandered away from Ethan and his father as they started debating about whether or not a sailboat would be a practical item to bid on. She walked around the large living room and focused on the items that covered the tables. They ranged anywhere from box seats for the Pennsylvania Ballet, to a five-carat yellow sapphire Tiffany pendant. Kate was never much of a jewelry collector, but there was no denying that the pendant was beautiful.

"I see you decided to come out of hiding."

The voice grated on her nerves. Clenching her fists, she squared off her shoulders and turned around to face Cindy. "I wasn't hiding," she said confidently.

With narrowed eyes, Cindy watched her expression with a false smile and took a step forward. She peered at the table and brushed her fingers over the glistening pendant. "I see you've already set your sights on what you want. Using the Montgomery money to buy yourself a little present?" she said in an accusing tone. "You know, Sabrina was eyeing it earlier. She asked my opinion on it, and of course, I told her I loved it. I wouldn't be surprised if I received it as a thank you for all my efforts for the evening."

Kate kept her face composed even though she wanted to gape. She had a hard time believing that Sabrina would actually spend that kind of money on a gift for someone, let alone Cindy. "Well, that would be very nice of her. She is definitely a very giving person." Kate smiled sweetly. Her extra-kind response threw Cindy for a loop and she hesitated. "Of course," Kate continued, "being a giving person and a good judge of character are two very different things. She seemed to be confused and under the impression that you're a good person. But don't worry, I made sure she was informed of her inaccuracy."

Again Cindy was left speechless, but it only lasted a moment. "That's right, sweet, innocent Kate. You keep on believing that you have any type of influence over Sabrina. You may think she likes you, but all it takes is one afternoon with me and she'll be singing a different tune. I'm quite good at twisting words." Her eyes dashed from Kate's face to something behind her. Then she quickly reached forward and patted Kate's cheek. "I'll be seeing you at the next family get together, and I'll make sure I wear the pendant. After all, I wouldn't want Sabrina to be offended."

Kate's hand itched with the desire to slap the girl in front of her. She was never a violent person, but something about Cindy brought it out in her. Before another word could be spoken, Cindy spun around and was gone.

Kate narrowed her eyes. "I'll make sure she gets hers later," she mumbled under her breath.

"Who?" Ethan asked from behind her.

"Cindy," she answered, and turned around to face him. "She's a piece of work. What did you ever see in her anyway?"

"She's good at hiding the real her. Even my mother had a hard time seeing it."

"Well, if that isn't the understatement of the year." Kate rolled her eyes.

"Don't worry. Mom believes us both. And she likes you, I can tell."

She shook her head a little and held her tongue. She didn't want to mention the pendant. After all, Cindy could have whatever she wanted. Kate had Ethan. She smiled at the thought. "So, are you and your dad finished making your bids?"

"I think so. I had to fight him on the boat. I mean, honestly, he has no experience with sailing."

"Do you?"

"Of course. I spent an entire summer on a sailboat when I was in high school."

"You did?" she said in awe, imagining a tanned Ethan standing on the bow of a boat with the wind blowing in his hair. "Do you think that maybe someday we can go sailing together?" She took a step closer, placing her hand flat against his chest.

He looked down at her hand, then her lips, then her eyes. "Is that something you'd like?" he asked in a deep voice.

"Mmm hmm." She nodded, sliding her hand up his chest and over his shoulder, following a line up to the nape of his neck.

"Kate," Ethan said breathlessly.

"Yes?"

"You're making it difficult for me to think straight."

She dropped her hand and giggled softly. "Sorry," she apologized. "When we get back to your place, I'd like to see some pictures from your sailing days."

"I'd be more than willing to show you." He winked.

"Good."

Ethan clasped her delicate hand in his and led them across the room to where his parents stood talking to Lori and Henry.

"Kate," Sabrina called out as they stepped closer. "Have you seen anything that interests you?"

"Everything being auctioned is great; it's almost overwhelming."

"I know. Every year it tends to get more and more extravagant. But it's all for a good cause." She looked over at Henry, who nodded. "Make sure you keep us posted on the hospital's progress," she continued. "We'll be heading back to San Francisco in a few weeks. Which reminds me, Ethan, if you want access to your piano, I can give you a key to the house."

At her words, Kate perked up. "I'd like to hear you play," she said, grinning.

"I'm sure you have time before the winners are announced," Sabrina assured.

Ethan laughed and wrapped his arm around Kate. "Make sure you keep an eye on Dad. I don't want any peeking going on while I'm gone," he yelled over his shoulder to his mom as they walked out of the room.

"I really like them." Kate smiled. "Especially your dad."

"They like you too. I know it was a rough start with my mom, but she's the type of woman to admit when she's wrong about something, and she was. I actually think that's the first time a woman stood up to her like that." He shook his head. "It was amazing. Now my dad … well, he loved you right from the start. I have a feeling that he's going to steal you away at all of our family get-togethers."

"I like him too. Then again, I think I have a soft spot for Montgomery men." She winked.

Ethan laughed and came to a stop in front of two glass French doors. He dropped his arm from around her and pushed down on the handles before stepping into the room. Kate followed behind him and paused in the doorway to take in the room around her.

It was gorgeous, with clean lines, rich colors, and dark woods. Everything about it felt warm and inviting. Two large bay windows along the back wall gave a great view of the immaculately landscaped backyard. On the far wall to her right was the largest sound system she'd ever seen. Shelf after shelf of records and CDs lined the walls beside it. Everything about the room said "music." Standing in the middle of the room as the focal point was a grand piano. She watched Ethan as he walked over to it and sat down on the bench. His fingers trailed over the keys softly, not eliciting any sound.

"Play something for me," Kate said, breaking the silence.

"It's been a while. How about 'Heart and Soul'?" He asked while pushing down on the ivory keys, playing the first few recognizable chords.

Kate took the few steps to the piano and sat down beside him. For a moment, she almost considered playing the upper hand, but paused when she noticed the melody changing. Ever so slowly, another song began to unfold. It was one she'd heard before, but she couldn't place the composer.

Sitting beside him, completely at ease, Kate watched his fingers dance across the ivory. When the last note hung in the air around them, she looked up at his face.

"That was beautiful," she whispered, hoping not to disrupt the music that was still resonating in her head.

"Thank you," he smiled. "I always forget how much I miss it until I sit down and play. I need to consider turning Trent's room into a music room."

"Something tells me that Trent wouldn't like having to share his space with a baby grand." She laughed as she imagined Trent's reaction.

"Yeah, well, I'll just kick him out," he said with a shrug, "I'm sure Elle wouldn't mind having him as a roommate, although I'll have to warn her. He can be a bit messy sometimes."

"Great," Kate deadpanned. "How did you know I always wanted a roommate who probably doesn't even wash his own clothes? And I just love the idea of my grocery bill tripling."

"Your grocery bill won't triple. Honestly, I don't eat that much, although I'm sure that will change after a week of your amazing cooking. And don't worry about me; I know how to wash my own clothes."

"Wait, what?" she asked, confused, not grasping what he was talking about.

Ethan laughed while shaking his head. "If I kick Trent out, it's because I want *you* in."

"What?" she repeated again.

"Kate," he said, tucking a piece of hair behind her ear. "If, and *when*, Trent moves out of my place, I fully expect *you* to move in with me. I want nothing more than to have the guarantee that I'll wake up next to you every morning."

Her mind thrilled at the thought. "When that day comes, I'll be more than ready," she said with a smile that mimicked his.

Cradling her face in his hand, he brushed her cheek with his thumb. "I love you," he said softly, before leaning in and kissing her.

They pulled their bodies closer and deepened the kiss, both of them never wanting to part. His hands ran up and down her back and bare arms, setting little fires along her skin. Kate's body felt alive with energy, like it always did when Ethan kissed her. It didn't matter how brief or how soft the kiss was, she always felt it. He pulled back for a moment and brushed his nose along the line of her jaw, tickling her cheek with his hair. She jumped slightly at the sensation and hit the piano with her hand, filling the air with a cacophony of notes. The once intense moment changed instantly and they both sat back laughing freely.

"Why is it that we can't seem to keep our hands off of each other while we're in other people's homes?" she asked through her giggles.

"Sweetheart, it's not just in other people's homes. I can't keep my hands off you, period. And believe me, I'm not at all complaining." He leaned forward and gave her another quick kiss before grasping her hand. "We'd better get back to the party. Something tells me they'll be announcing the highest bidders soon."

When she nodded her head, Ethan wrapped his arm around her waist and stood up from the bench, setting her on her feet. Making sure her dress was smooth, she ran her hands over the fabric and fiddled with her hair. Ethan stood at the door, waiting for her with his hand outstretched. She went to him, and immediately found her place by his side.

As they made their way into the great room, they noticed the announcing of the top bidders was about to start. Ethan gave his dad a smile and veered the two of them in his direction.

"I thought for sure you'd miss the announcement. I was fully prepared to accept anything on your behalf," his dad said, laughing.

Ethan reached out to pat his back. "Yeah, I bet you were, Dad."

All other conversation was cut short as an older lady with silver hair and an indigo wrap stood at the front of the room, holding a sheet of paper. The room fell into a quiet hush as she began speaking, noting that she'd been asked to fill in for Cindy who had to leave early for the evening. Kate couldn't help but feel both relieved and disappointed. Relived that she wouldn't have to watch her smug face as Sabrina gave her the gift and disappointed that she wouldn't be able to rub Ethan in her face any more. She knew the latter was a bit childish and ruthless, but she was forced to work with what she had.

Standing in silence, she ignored the woman speaking and thought about what she'd actually say to Cindy if given the chance. The sound of Ethan laughing at his dad brought her out of her thoughts. "What did I miss?" she asked, keeping her voice low.

Instead of answering her, Ethan kept his eyes on his dad with a look of disbelief. "I can't believe you bid on it. We both agreed that—"

"No, *you* agreed."

"Dad, you don't even know how to sail." Father and son smiled at each other, neither one standing down.

"Whenever I'm in town, you can teach me. And when I'm not here, you can take it out. I'm sure Kate would enjoy it." Oliver looked at her and winked.

"I'm sure she would. And I'm sure we'll take you up on that offer."

His dad grinned at the both of them and turned his attention back to the lady at the front of the room.

"So, he got the boat?" Kate asked.

"He sure as hell did." Ethan laughed and shook his head. "A ninety-eight foot, 2007 Ketch. That must have cost him a pretty penny."

There was no stifling her curiosity. "How many pennies?"

"Last one I saw was a few years old, and it ran a little under a million."

Kate almost choked on her spit, but swallowed slowly in an attempt to play it off as no big deal. "You didn't bid on anything that expensive, did you?" She held her breath, horrified of his answer.

"No, not … *quite.*" Kate opened her mouth in protest, but he held up his hand. "I'm not telling you, so don't ask."

She shut her jaw with an audible snap, and instead tried to focus on the lady who was speaking. She announced that the Governor got the box seats to the Ballet and an old lady, decked out in more jewelry and fur than Kate had ever seen on one person, won a pair of emerald earrings.

"Damn," Ethan mumbled.

"What's wrong?"

"Oh, it's nothing. I just … it's nothing," he said, forcing a smile.

Kate narrowed her eyes at him in disbelief, but before she could question him, the lady spoke up again.

"The two week stay at the villa in Tuscany goes to number fourteen, Ethan Montgomery."

Whipping her head to the side, Kate gaped at him with wide eyes. "Tuscany. You bid on a trip to Tuscany?"

He shrugged his shoulders and smirked. "Sure, I've always wanted to go. I've been to Rome but never Tuscany. Plus, the villa is gorgeous; it's right on a vineyard. You're going to love it."

"*I'm* going to love it?"

"You can't possibly expect me to go without you."

She stared at him in shock. "Ethan, you don't have to—"

"I know I don't have to. I want to. Besides I'm your boyfriend, and if I want to buy you nice jewelry or a trip to Europe, I'm allowed."

Nice jewelry? she thought. Then it hit her. "Ethan," she said calmly. "You bid on those earrings, didn't you?" She tried to sound upset, but he didn't look apologetic in the least.

"Yes, I did."

"They were huge! I'm not even sure I could pull something like that off. I mean they'd look out of place on—"

"All girls look fabulous in jewels." The soft yet commanding voice of Sabrina spoke up behind them. Kate turned around and noticed that she was directly behind her and probably heard their entire exchange.

"Well…sure, I mean…I—"

"And," she continued as if Kate hadn't said a word, "if you marry into this family, you'd better like them." She cocked her perfect eyebrow and gave her a knowing smile before leaning in and whispering, "Because we tend to have a lot."

"Mom, let's not scare her off," Ethan teased before pulling Kate to his side.

"I'm not scaring her. In fact, I came over here because I want to help ease her into it."

Confused by her comment, Kate pulled away from Ethan to ask what she meant; but as soon as she looked at her, she knew. Sabrina's hands were outstretched and hanging from her fingertips was the sparkling yellow pendant hanging on a small chain.

Kate's jaw dropped. Words jumbled in her mind and she couldn't bring herself to think clearly. Sabrina's laughter rang through the air as she took a step forward and motioned for her to turn around. Still rooted in place, Ethan had to assist in guiding Kate's motions and turned her to face him. When the cold stone hit her chest, her hand automatically covered it. Spinning around, she forced herself to speak.

"I thought…I mean, Cindy said that you—"

Sabrina shook her head. "I think we both know that Cindy says a lot of things that aren't true."

"But she's—"

"Cindy may be able to play tennis, Kate, but that's not what makes a Montgomery."

They stood silent for a moment, looking at each other, both of them knowing that there was more meaning behind her simple statement than was said. In her own way, Sabrina was welcoming Kate into the family and telling her that she was good enough—better in fact—than Cindy was or ever would be.

Rolling the cold, smooth stone between her fingers, Kate smiled. "Thank you, Sabrina."

She smiled in return, then looked at her son. "I wanted to give you a warning. Your father just got the First Base Line Box Seats for the Phillies home opener."

"Great." Ethan's head dropped down, defeated.

"What does that mean?" Kate asked.

"It means, my dear, sweet Kate," Oliver walked up beside her and planted a kiss in her cheek, "that I won!"

℘

Two weeks later, Kate lay in bed watching clouds scudding across the sky outside of her window. She contemplated spending another day in bed, under the illusion that if she did nothing then Sunday would arrive sooner.

Sunday would be the first entire day in a week and a half that she'd have with Ethan. He'd been working such crazy shifts at the hospital that she'd hardly had a chance to see him. On more than one occasion she contemplated telling him that it was time for him to convert Trent's bedroom into a music room. She was ready.

Rolling her eyes at herself, she turned over with a huff, pulling the covers over her head in the process. But being under the blankets didn't help in dispelling the voices in her head that told her to take some initiative and do something. Giving in, she sat up quickly, allowing the thick morning haze to clear from her mind and she started planning. She had an idea of what she wanted to do, but knew there was no way she could pull it off by herself. Rolling over, she grabbed her phone and called in reinforcements.

℘

"Kate, if you want to get full shock value, you have to wear it," Sophie yelled from behind the bathroom door.

Kate looked at her reflection in the mirror and knew that she was right. After all, she was going for shock value. She smiled to herself as she picked up the little lace garter skirt and stepped into it. After attaching the clasps to the tops of her thigh highs, she slipped into her sexy black dress and stood back, giving herself one last look over. Sophie had spent half of the morning shopping on her behalf and the rest of the afternoon making phone calls to arrange everything.

"Okay, guys. I think I'm good," she said, running her hands over her dress nervously.

"Get out here and show us then," Elle demanded. "You know we have to approve."

Taking a deep breath, Kate swung the door open and earned smiles of approval from both her friends.

"If I weren't a chick, I'd be all over you," Elle said, wiggling her eyebrows.

Kate laughed. "Trent's rubbing off on you."

Her face lit up and she grinned triumphantly. "Good. I'm perfectly okay with that."

Still smiling, Elle walked to the bed and returned with a pair of red heels. "These are my favorite. They're good luck. And besides, you can't wear an outfit like that," she motioned to her friends outfit, "and not wear red heels."

"Thanks." Kate grabbed the heels and slipped them on.

"Don't forget this," Sophie said, scampering over and securing Kate's necklace in place. "Perfect." She smirked, looking her friend over. "And don't forget, go to the front desk and ask for them to page Dr. Hunter. If they give you any trouble, ask to speak with Kristen. She'll know what to do."

"Got it." She walked over to her bed and grabbed her long cream coat. She gave her two friends one last smile before turning to leave. "Wish me luck," she yelled over her shoulder.

"Luck!" they both yelled back. The sound of their laughter echoed down the hallway as Kate walked outside and shut the door.

❧

Almost an hour later, Kate stepped out of her car, pulling her already tightly wrapped coat even tighter to keep out the cold. She hurried into the hospital, anxious to get into the warm building, and walked up to the front desk. The platinum blond girl behind the counter was huddled down low in her chair, biting on her nails absentmindedly and completely engrossed in the book she held. The lazy smirk across her face made it clear that she was enjoying what she read, and Kate felt bad for interrupting her.

"Can I help you?" she asked without looking up.

"Umm … sure, I'm … umm, I need you to page Dr. Hunter for me, please?" She tried desperately to hide the nervousness in her voice, but it was useless.

The blonde lifted her head and smirked. "Was that a question or an answer?"

"Answer."

"And you are…?"

"Kate."

The girl behind the counter eyed her knowingly. "You're Kate. Dr. Montgomery's Kate." She wasn't asking. It was clear that she already knew the answer, but Kate nodded anyway. "I've been waiting for you." She smiled. "I'm Jess. And if it's not too forward of me, I'd like to say, damn girl, you are lucky. They don't make many guys like Dr. Montgomery. Trust me."

Kate's couldn't help but laugh. "Yeah, he is pretty amazing."

"Mmm hmm." She nodded before hopping up from her chair. "Come on, I'll take you to Kristen. She and Dr. Hunter have been waiting for you."

"Thanks," Kate said, feeling herself relax a bit more.

As they walked down the hall, Jess's eyes dashed down to Kate's shoes. "I like the heels. Red is a *very* good choice. Happens to be my favorite color," she added casually.

"Thanks. It *is* a great color," she agreed.

They walked down a few halls and through a couple sets of doors, before stopping at another counter, this one looking more like a nurse's station than an information desk. One of the girls with dark brown hair looked up as they came into view.

"Is this her?" she asked, looking at Jess.

She smirked back. "Yep."

Kate looked back and forth between them and realized that the dark-haired girl must be Kristen, and wondered what it was exactly that Sophie had told her, or the both of them for that matter. Jess turned and gave a quick wink before walking back the way they'd just come.

"Let's go find Dr. Hunter. I think we found the perfect place. You're lucky an entire wing is under construction," Kristen said, standing beside her.

Nodding, Kate swallowed back her unease. Honestly, the only reason she was even attempting the entire thing was because she knew she wouldn't get caught. Or at least hoped she wouldn't. She opened her mouth to ask Kristen a question when a male nurse walked up.

The two of them bantered back and forth, each comment more sarcastic and witty than the first. When the guy finally left them alone, Kate couldn't help but wonder if they were involved, but kept her mouth shut.

"He's my surfer boyfriend; at least that's what I like to call him," Kristen said, answering her unspoken question.

"He cute." Kate smiled.

"Cute and young—eight years younger, to be exact. He's not really my boyfriend, but the boy can bake some brownies." She laughed.

"Well, a guy that can bake is always a good thing."

"Exactly. And when I say they're good, I mean they're gooood. He makes 'em from scratch." She continued to tell all the other concoctions the young nurse could make and only stopped when she noticed a woman in a white lab coat walk out of an exam room.

"Dr. Hunter!" she yelled, probably louder than necessary.

The woman with a short strawberry blond bob lifted her head and smiled as she walked over to them. "I take it that you're Kate?" she asked.

"That's me."

"It's nice to finally meet you. Ethan can't stop talking about you, so you can imagine how excited I was when Sophie called me." Her eyes danced in anticipation.

She was genuine in her excitement and Kate felt an immediate kinship to her. It was a miracle that Kate remembered her name from a few months ago, but she was thankful that she did. Almost two months ago, when she and Ethan had first started dating, Dr. Hunter had interrupted their early morning smoothie date. She'd needed a favor and asked if Ethan would cover her shift. Of course, he'd told her it wouldn't be a problem, but that she owed him big time. Kate counted this as the payment.

"I want to thank you for doing this, Dr. Hunter. I know that you owe Ethan, but this goes above and beyond."

"Please, call me Debbie," she smiled, "And I don't mind. In fact, I'm thinking that after setting this up, Ethan's going to owe *me*."

Kate laughed. "So," she started. "Where are you guys—"

"Ugh," Kristen moaned, cutting her off. "Bitch alert, twelve o'clock."

The distinct clicking of heels echoed down the hall, and in the pit of her stomach Kate had a feeling she knew who it was. Her stomach folded in on itself, but she rolled her shoulders back. She'd had two weeks to think about this, and there was no way she was backing down. Plastering on her fakest smile, Kate spun around.

"Cindy," Kristen sneered. "Isn't there a plastic surgeon somewhere looking for you?"

"Or I'm sure I can find you an intern who needs to practice his Botox injections," Debbie offered kindly.

"Ladies, that's so nice of you. But I think I'll stick with what I have. After all, those of us with natural beauty shouldn't rub it in your faces any more than necessary; that's just rude."

A silent standoff was taking place between the three girls, and Kate couldn't resist jumping in.

"Cindy, it's so good to see you again," she smiled, keeping her voice as sweet as possible. "I was hoping I'd get a chance to see you today."

Cindy narrowed her eyes slightly, but kept the fake grin on her face. "Oh really? That's so sweet. It really is a pleasant surprise to see you here. And you know it saves me the trouble of calling Sabrina and asking how she's doing. I'm sure you've talked to her recently."

"I can't say that I have. She likes to give Ethan and me our space, but we'll see each other before they leave town."

"That's right, they're leaving soon. I'll have to call her and see if she's up for a little tennis match. I'm sure she'd like the opportunity to see me before she leaves. Maybe even give me a small token of her appreciation."

The fake smile on Kate's face turned genuine as she listened to Cindy speak. "Token?" she asked, playing dumb.

"Yes, you know, the pendant."

"Oh, you mean this?" She brought her hands up to the collar of her coat and pulled it open, exposing the yellow sapphire pendant that hung around her neck. Cindy's eyes went wide. "You see, Cindy," she said walking toward her, feeling her confidence grow with each step. "You may be able to play tennis with Sabrina, but that doesn't make you a Montgomery."

"And you know what does?" she snapped.

"Of course I do, because you see … someday soon *I'm* going to be one." Kate reached out and patted her cheek gently. Cindy's jaw clenched tight, but she didn't say a word. Instead she spun around and stormed down the hallway, clunking loudly in her pair of last season's Jimmy Choo's.

Feeling a new sense of relief, Kate turned around to face Debbie and Kristen, who both wore smiles.

"Ohh, I love you," Debbie said, shaking her head with a laugh.

"That was perfect." Kristen nodded.

"Let's just say, I've had plenty of time to think about what I've wanted to say to her." She took a deep breath and felt a new sense of relief. "So, ladies, what's the plan?"

Both girls smiled at each other before turning back to her.

"Ethan should be back from lunch soon, so let's hurry. We'll fill you in as we walk," Debbie said, stepping to Kate's side. With a quick nod, the three set off for the abandoned section of the hospital.

❧

Downstairs, Ethan sat at the lunch table, absentmindedly folding and unfolding a napkin. His thoughts were on Kate and how much he missed her. Being on call and working double shifts translated into zero down time. He spoke with her on the phone whenever he had the chance, but it wasn't the same. Lately he'd come to realize just how important the sound of her voice or the touch of her hand was to him. It had an almost calming effect, and he was growing antsy waiting. Somewhere between thinking about kissing Kate and lying next to her, his pager went off, waking him from his daydream. Disappointed that he wouldn't be able to catch some sleep after eating, he stood up and slowly headed for the elevator.

"Hey Dreamy," Kristen called out as soon as he stepped off the elevator.

"Did you page me?" he asked while rubbing his hands over his scruffy face.

"Yeah, Dr. Hunter asked me to. She wants your opinion on a patient."

"Okay, sure." He nodded, still halfway in a haze. He turned around and was just about to walk away when Kristen called out.

"Oh, she's in second floor radiology."

"Wait, what?" he asked in confusion.

"Don't ask me. You doctors are always doing your own thing. But she did say something about the temp wing being too crowded. So, I don't know." She shrugged her shoulders and quickly walked away from Ethan, mumbling under her breath.

Ethan stood still and watched her retreating form. He simply didn't have the energy to think, let alone argue, about why he was being sent to the section of the hospital that was under construction. So he stepped back into the elevator and pushed the button for the second floor.

He walked through the halls on the second floor until he came to the roped off section. There were sheets of plastic hanging from the ceiling to keep the dust caused by construction from spreading too far. Pushing back the sheet, he stepped into the dark hallway that was lit with only the emergency escape lights and the large window at the end.

"Dr. Hunter?" he called out.

Her head poked out from one of the exam rooms. "Hey! You got my message," she said, smiling.

He nodded. "Why are you over here? I thought that everything had been moved temporarily."

"Oh, it has been. I just had a special patient. She requested some privacy, and I couldn't say no to her."

His face pulled together in confusion, and Debbie started to laugh. "Perhaps you could come take a look. I'd really like your opinion." She stepped aside and motioned with her hand for Ethan to enter.

"Sure." He shrugged, taking a step forward. As soon as he walked into the room, he paused. Standing at the far end of the room in a long cream coat and red heels was Kate.

His heart thumped, and he felt himself smile. "Kate, what are you doing here? Are you all right?"

"I'm fine." She smiled. "I called in a favor." She shrugged casually, looking at Dr. Hunter.

Ethan looked back over his shoulder and noticed Dr. Hunter grinning mischievously. "I'll see you guys later." She giggled before walking out the door.

The door shut with a click, and Ethan looked back at Kate. She was stunning and his hands twitched with the desire to touch her. He started to take a step, but she motioned for him to stop and brought her hands to the front of her jacket. Ever so slowly, she began to unbutton it, never taking her eyes off of him. She slid her fingers down the hem of her coat and pulled the sides back. He didn't want to take his eyes off of her face, but he couldn't resist; he had to look down at what she was wearing.

Dropping his eyes, he looked at her and felt his breath catch. He took in every last detail of the black dress—the way it dipped in at her waist and hugged the curve of her hips. His eyes continued their descent all the way down her legs, ending on her red shoes.

"I figured Sunday was too long to wait, and if I remember correctly, you once told me that you liked a girl in a short skirt and a long jacket," she breathed.

The sound of her voice calmed him instantly. Reaching back, he turned the lock on the door, the bolt sliding into place with finality. Desperate to be close to her, he crossed the room in three long strides and wrapped his arms around her waist. He pulled her body to his and brushed his lips against hers, immediately feeling at home.

Chapter 29
Full Circle

Sophie, you have got to be kidding me!" Kate yelled over the dressing room door.

"Just come out and let me see it," Sophie pleaded.

"No freakin' way am I coming out there."

"Katherine Elizabeth Thomas. This is *my* wedding, and the bride always gets what she wants."

There was a defiant tone to her voice which made it clear that she meant business. The way Kate saw it, she had two options. She could either (A) refuse and put her jeans back on or (B) realize that if she didn't do as Sophie asked, she would be forcefully removed from the dressing room and shoved *back* into the dress she was currently wearing.

"Fine, but if you and Elle laugh, I'm leaving."

"She's not here. She's getting a taller pair of heels from the sales lady. I promise not to laugh. Now, come out before I knock down the door and make you."

Kate huffed in defeat and opened the door in one quick motion. Stepping out into the room, she heard her friend giggle quietly.

"Okay, so maybe orange isn't your best color," she said, her giggle turning to a full-blown belly laugh.

Glaring with narrowed eyes, Kate faced her friend. "I said no laughing. And seriously, what did you think it would look like?" She stepped up onto the platform in front of the three-sided mirror and flinched at her reflection. It looked like she was wearing a life jacket disguised as a dress. The bright orange color clashed with the pale tone of her skin, giving it a light bluish hue. *Great. Just what I wanted—skin the color of skim milk,* she thought with a roll of her eyes.

"Yeah." Sophie walked up behind her. "Orange is definitely not your color. Why don't you go try on the wine-colored one?"

"Whatever you want," Kate teased. "After all, it's *your* day."

"You bet it is, and don't think I'm not putting you in four-inch heels either. Speaking of which, where is Elle with the shoes?" She spun around quickly and scurried out of the room before Kate said another word.

Laughing quietly to herself, she walked back into the large dressing room and peeled off the offensive orange dress. Ever since Sophie had gotten engaged six months ago, she seemed to have been running on an even higher level of energy, if that were at all possible. Apparently planning a wedding in eight months was close to impossible to accomplish. But she'd insisted on a late fall wedding since the color palette was ideal, and waiting for the following fall was not even an option. She had waited long enough for Logan to propose, and once he had, she was determined to be Mrs. Logan McLean before the new year.

Stepping into the wine-colored dress, she had it up around her waist when her cell phone rang. She hurried over to her purse, tripping over her jeans and nearly ripping the dress in the process.

"Hello?" she said breathlessly, not even pausing to check the caller ID.

"Hey, how's the—wait, are you okay? You sound out of breath?"

"I'm fine; I just tripped. You know, the casualties of running in a tight, fitted dress."

"I take that you didn't hurt your—wait, tight?" Ethan's voice dropped slightly to a gritty undertone.

"Yes. It's deep red and *very* snug. Clings to all my curves just the way you like it," Kate said, lowering her voice and playing right along with him.

"Am I going to get a chance to see you in it before the wedding?"

"I'm not sure. Sophie has the final say. This may not even be the dress she wants."

"Do me a favor. If she vetoes it, buy it anyway. It sounds amazing, and I want to see you in it."

Kate smiled and felt her heart flutter. His words still had a way of affecting her, and she knew it was something she'd never get used to. And for that, she was thankful.

"When do you think you'll be done with Sophie and her torture?" he asked, breaking Kate away from her thoughts.

"Not sure; it all depends. Once she gets around shoes, time ceases to exist, and all else is put on hold."

"Make sure she's not too long. I have plans for us tonight," he reminded her.

"Plans which you're still not going to tell me about, are you?"

"Nope," he said, popping the 'p.'

"Fine, I'll remind her that I have to be done by six o'clock."

"Sounds great. I'll see you at home."

Kate said her goodbye and hung up, smiling ear to ear. Every time Ethan referred to his apartment as 'their home,' she grinned. One would think that after four months, she'd be accustomed to it, but she wasn't. With a content sigh, Kate sat on the chair in the corner of the dressing room and stared back at her reflection, letting her mind drift back to the day *his* apartment became *theirs*.

❧

It was the beginning of summer, and she and Ethan had spent the entire day together outside, enjoying the warmer weather. He'd insisted that she show him the path she used to run along the river. The same path where she'd had her fall months before, which resulted in a trip to the hospital and ultimately his exam table.

"I couldn't believe you were there, you know, at the hospital. I'd been thinking about you all day and was hoping that by some miracle I'd see you again. I planned on going to Rain every weekend, on the off chance that you'd be there," he said, wrapping his arm around her shoulders.

"Yeah, well, I was completely mortified and ecstatic that you were the doctor treating me. I was so nervous, I remember almost panicking at the thought of even taking my shirt off."

"It's a good thing I'm a professional."

"A professional that almost kissed me," she reminded him, looking up at his face.

He turned his head away from her and looked out over the water. "I don't know what you're talking about," he said innocently.

"Ha-ha," she deadpanned. "You know as well as I do that we almost kissed." She hit him playfully, but Ethan continued to ignore her statement. "Can't say

I'm not happy we didn't kiss. First kisses are always awful and uncomfortable," she said casually. "The last thing I needed was for it happen while I was cut and bleeding in a hospital surrounded by the smell of antiseptic."

"Hang on." He placed both his hands on Kate's shoulders and turned her to face him. "Our first kiss was anything but awful and uncomfortable. If I remember correctly, it was pretty damn hot, and you enjoyed it quite a bit."

Kate's carefully composed face gave way and she smiled up at him. "Yeah, I have to agree with you there. It was pretty hot."

"Hot enough that you want to re-enact it sometime?" He smirked.

She nodded and started playing with the buttons of his shirt. "I think I'd like to re-enact it somewhere a little more *private*."

"Sounds good to me; let's go home." He took her hand in his and started walking in the direction of his car.

The drive to his apartment didn't take much time, but Kate couldn't stop twisting her fingers and fiddling with the fabric of her shirt.

"Someone's a little fidgety." Ethan laughed.

"I can't help it. I just … you know … I'm anxious," she said, shrugging.

Ethan responded with a mumble.

"What did you say?" Kate turned to face him.

He swallowed thickly and leaned forward, turning up the volume on the radio. "Oh, nothing."

Kate watched him for another minute and noticed there was a sudden change in the atmosphere. She couldn't quite place it, but she was sure something was off. Continuing to watch him, she noticed his back become straighter and his body tense even more the closer they got to his apartment. "Ethan, are you all right? You seem tense about something," she asked, feeling slightly nervous as they got out of the car.

"I'm fine—no, I'm more than fine. I'm great." He reassured her.

His words did little to comfort her, and her mind began to backtrack over the conversation they'd just had. She wondered if perhaps she'd said something that would have upset him but came up with nothing.

Just as she was about to tell him that she knew something was wrong, he spoke up. "Well, here we are. *Home* sweet *home*." His voice wavered.

"Ethan, seriously what is going on? And don't tell me it's nothing because I can tell that you're acting strange."

"Kate, I'm fine. I just … look let's just go inside, okay?" He gave her a reassuring smile and turned the knob, pushing the door open. As soon as they walked inside, he turned left and headed into the kitchen.

She followed behind him in silence, keeping her panicked thoughts to herself and slammed into him when he stopped suddenly. "Omph," she mumbled, her face pressed between the shoulder blades of his back. "Sorry." She took a step back as Ethan turned around to face her.

"You don't have to apologize. It's my fault for stopping so abruptly. I just got a little ahead of myself." He spoke so quickly that she could barely make out what he was saying. "I'm just a little nervous about how you'll react to the whole thing, and I don't know. Maybe I—"

"Stop! Now *I'm* freaking out a little. What are you talking about?"

"This." Ethan stepped to the side and turned around motioning to the kitchen before them.

It took Kate a minute to register what he was talking about but then she saw it. Her towels, her blender, her KitchenAid mixer, her platters displayed behind the glass cabinet doors, her cookbooks filling the bookshelf in the corner, her lotion next to the sink. All of it was hers, and all of it was there in Ethan's house.

She walked across the room and opened the first cabinet she came to. There, sitting on the first shelf, stacked neatly, were her dishes and cups. It didn't take her long to put two and two together, and once she did, her vision started to get cloudy. Tears stung her eyes and slipped down her cheek, leaving a trail of silver.

Stepping up behind her, Ethan wrapped his arms around her waist. "Like I said, I was a little nervous about how you'd react."

Kate was speechless, stunned, excited, nervous, and happy—utterly and completely happy. She was amazed at the emotions that seeing one stack of dishes brought on, but she couldn't help it. Quickly spinning around while still wrapped in Ethan's embrace, she flung her arms around his neck, pulling herself as close as she could get.

"Does this mean what I think it means?" she asked, looking into his smoky blue eyes.

"What do you *think* it means?"

"I think it means that you finally have a music room and that I get to wake up next to you every morning in *our* apartment." Without saying a word, he nodded. Excitement bubbled up inside Kate's chest, and she reached up on her toes, pressing her lips to his. "When can we move the rest of my stuff?"

"It's already done," he said with a smirk.

Kate pulled back and looked at him in disbelief. "What? All of it?"

"Why do you think I needed you out of the place all day? I swear, I owe the gang big time for helping. I couldn't have done it without them."

"I'd say we both owe them. How about having them over for dinner?" She was bouncing on the tips of her toes feeling a little like Sophie and not caring in the least.

"Sounds good to me. I'll go call them."

"Uh, uh, uh. Not so fast, mister. You can call them *later*." She grabbed his shirt before he could walk away from her.

"What?"

"I want another kiss in *our* apartment." Apparently Ethan had no problems complying with her request and walked toward her swiftly, scooping her up in his arms.

The two of them spent the rest of the evening making every room in the house theirs, and when it was finally time for them to go to sleep that night, Kate lay in bed staring back at her reflection in the window. She was enveloped in Ethan's arms and could see his hair in disarray sticking up behind her. She listened to his soft, deep breathing, and a feeling of comfort rushed over her. It was at that moment that she knew she was home.

☙

"Elle McLean! I mean it, I'm not kidding. It's my wedding day, and I'm going to have you in those shoes if I want to."

"Calm down, Soph, you know I'm just teasing you. Besides, since when do I question your fashion sense?"

The voices of Kate's friends fighting brought her out of her memories, and she quickly finished zippering the back of the dress before stepping out of the changing room. "Hey, no fighting," she called out as they came around the corner. As soon as they saw their friend, they both froze. "What?" Kate asked touching her face self consciously.

"That's it!" Sophie gaped. "I *knew* that color would be perfect. I'm not sure about the length yet, and I think I want a different waistline, but I am *certain* about the color. And it will look flawless against your skin too, Elle," she commented while running her hands up and down the length of the dress. "Maybe I should go longer, or shorter. What about tea length?"

Both Elle and Kate looked at each other and smiled. Sophie was always the optimist. "Soph, whatever you choose will be perfect. Either way, I'm buying this dress."

"Oh, planning something special for Bones?" Elle teased, using Ethan's childhood nickname.

"Maybe." Kate smirked. "He called just a minute ago, and I told him what I was wearing. Apparently he wants to see me in it.'

"Well, he's going to flip. It really is a beautiful dress. And the color is just … it's perfect." Sophie sighed.

"It is, babe, it's perfect." Kate patted her shoulder. "Hey, when do you think we'll be done here? I need to be home by six o'clock." She turned around and walked back into the changing room and slipped out of the dress.

"Making plans on my day of wedding shopping? How dare you." The future bride laughed, her voice echoing off the mirrors. "Of course we'll be done by six. In fact, I think we're done here. Why don't we go grab some lunch, and we can discuss whether to do a peep toe, sling back, or stiletto."

Elle applied her lipstick in the mirror and watched as Kate walked out of the room behind her with the dress slung over her arm. "All right girls." She smiled. "I'm ready. Let's go."

❧

"Bake at four hundred degrees for thirty minutes until hot and bubbly." Ethan stood hunched over the counter, reading out of the new cookbook he'd purchased earlier that day. Originally, he planned on giving it to Kate as a gift and taking her out to dinner, but the more he thought about it, the more certain he was that he wanted to cook for her.

There was no comparison between the two when it came to cooking, but Ethan wasn't that bad. He'd only cooked a few things for her since they'd moved in together, and that consisted of boxed macaroni and cheese and pre-made pizza. Of course, Kate was always more than grateful for his efforts and ate with the enthusiasm of a starving child. Although he'd wanted to cook a more lavish meal for her, he'd never had the chance. Ever since she'd moved in, she'd become a cooking maniac. She said it was something to do with his stove. Whether or not it was all an excuse to cook for him, he'd never know. After all, he wasn't going to complain.

But tonight was different. Tonight Ethan wanted to pamper her, to show her just how much he appreciated her and how important she was to him. He had the entire weekend planned out and his only hope was that it would end the way he planned. He smiled to himself and covered the dish with foil before sliding it into the oven and setting the timer. Walking into the dining room, he checked the table and made sure everything was in place before heading into the bathroom to get cleaned up.

Twenty minutes later he heard the front door open and knew that Kate was home. He finished tossing the salad and added the last few cucumber slices before going to greet her at the door.

"Hi." She smiled as soon as she saw him. Ethan walked toward her, taking the bag out of her hands and wrapping his arms around her.

"Hello, beautiful. Did you have fun?" He looked at the bag he held. "I see you purchased the dress."

"Umm hmm." She nuzzled into his chest. "You smell nice."

"It's just the food you smell. I decided to try my hand at cooking."

"You cooked?" she asked in disbelief.

"I can cook. I just never have the chance. Plus, it would never be as good as what you make, so why even try?"

She looked up at him and grinned. "You're just trying to butter me up."

"So, maybe I am. It is working?" He flashed a smile.

"Most definitely." She reached up on her toes and he leaned down, meeting her halfway. Her soft smooth lips brushed against his, and Ethan knew that if he didn't stop, dinner would *not* be happening. There were a few things that made him lose touch with reality and kissing Kate was one of them. Regretfully pulling away, he gave her one last kiss before stepping back. "If we're going to eat this meal warm, then I have to stop. Because seeing you—and kissing you and tasting you—gives me *more* than enough reasons to forget about dinner," he admitted. "Why don't you go get changed into that dress and meet me back here?"

"Sounds good, as long as you promise we'll pick this up later."

"Believe me, it will be picked up later. I have plans for you." He looked her up and down slowly.

"Plans?"

"Yes, plans. Plans that might not work out, if you don't go slip into the dress."

"Okay, okay, I'm going." She giggled. "But it's only because I'm curious, and of course, because I can't wait to see your face when you see me in *this*." She grabbed the bag from him and shook it in the air.

She left the room and when she returned she looked just as phenomenal as Ethan thought she would. The form fitted dress was almost enough to make him forget about dinner—almost. He did, after all, have plans.

They took their time eating and talking. Some would think that after their time together they would know almost everything there was to know about each other, but there was always something. Something about Kate's day or week that she'd forgotten to tell him or a small childhood memory that hadn't yet been shared. Those were some of the things Ethan loved hearing about the most, especially if they involved her parents.

He'd met Annie and Doug over the Fourth of July weekend, and they were just as he'd imagined they would be. They were fun, down to earth, supportive and completely loving and accepting of their daughter. They balanced each other perfectly, and Ethan could easily see how Kate fit into their lives.

"You should have seen my dad's face. I thought he'd blow a gasket. He'd warned me not to go up there, but honestly, it didn't feel dangerous." She shrugged. "That was until it came to climbing down. That's a whole other story."

"If I'd known you liked climbing so much, I'd have taken you. I think some of my old gear is at my parents' house."

"You have rock climbing gear?"

"Yep, somewhere I do."

"Why am I not surprised? I should know by now that there is nothing you can't do. Like cook a delicious meal." She waved her hand over the table in front of them. "It really was amazing. Thank you."

"You're welcome. I'm glad you liked it. And you know you're wrong. There are a lot of things I don't know how to do."

She arched an eyebrow. "Like what exactly?"

"Photography. I'll never be as good as you. Of course, if you *teach* me..."

"Uh-uh, I don't think so." She shook her head. "I get to have one thing."

"Fine." He laughed. "So, are you ready for dessert?"

"I get dessert?" she asked.

"You do." He nodded. "But it's not here. We have to take a ride."

"All right." She smiled.

"Go grab your shoes, and I'll meet you at the door."

He stood at the door waiting for her, and a few minutes later, she came around the corner smiling and ready to go.

⁖

"You're still not going to tell me where we're going, are you?" she asked for the fifth time.

"Nope," Ethan responded just as he had the five previous times.

Kate sat back with a sigh and enjoyed the warm air as it circled around her, leaving behind the smells of summer. Through the light from the dash, Ethan could see her lazy smile and watched her hair dance around her face and cling to her neck. He continued to steal glances at her as they neared their destination. Once there, he asked her to close her eyes. He knew she'd figure it all out once inside, but until that point, he wanted it to be a surprise.

As he pulled into a back alley, he slowly drove forward until he found the door. Slipping the car into park, he killed the engine and walked around to her side.

"Can I open my eyes yet?" she asked, her face all scrunched up like it was a required expression while closing her eyes.

With a quick look around, he realized she wouldn't be able to tell where they were and agreed.

"Ethan, where are we?" she asked.

"You'll see. Come on." Grabbing her hand, he led them to the door and dug in his pocket for the keys.

Kate's face was full of questions, but she remained quiet as he unlocked the door. The room they entered was dark. Ethan guided them expertly past the stacks of boxes and tables. After making their way down a long hallway, they came to a stop in front of double swinging doors.

"Ready for your surprise?" he asked.

"Mmm hmm." She nodded.

Ethan grinned at her in excitement and pushed the door open. As soon as they entered, he heard her gasp followed by a laugh.

"How in the heck did you arrange all this?"

"I'm a doctor and good at saving lives," he said casually, shrugging his shoulders.

"How does your being a doctor have anything to do with this?"

"It's kind of a long story, so I'll give you the abridged version. A month ago, I had a patient come to the ER in cardiac arrest. I saved his life, found out he owns this store, and I called in a favor."

"I'd say. Isn't this grocery store normally open twenty-four hours?"

"Like I said, I called in a favor." The look on Kate's face was priceless and Ethan couldn't help but laugh. "Come on, let's go to our spot." By the glow of the emergency lights, they made their way down the aisles, and when they came within view of the produce section, Kate burst into laughter.

"I can't believe you did this."

"Believe it, because I did." He led them further and paused when his set up came into view.

On the floor lay thick blankets and soft fluffy pillows. Off to one side, there was a large tray that was piled high with fresh fruit. Without saying a word, Ethan slipped off his shoes, walked over to the blanket and sat down. He kept his eyes on Kate and waited for her to follow.

She stayed rooted in place, twisting the fabric of her dress nervously. "Are you sure about this? I mean, there aren't security cameras or anything?"

"Nope, no security cameras. We're completely alone. And if I wasn't sure about it, I wouldn't have done all of this." He motioned to the spread in front of him.

Swallowing thickly, she hesitated but only for a moment and ignored the butterflies. All she had to do was look at Ethan and she forgot everything else. She was always lost in him. "You thought of everything, didn't you?" She lowered herself to the floor pulling her feet up beneath her. "Well," she reached forward grabbing a deep red strawberry from the tray, "let's have some dessert."

❧

Kate woke the next morning to sunlight pouring in through the windows. Without opening her eyes, she searched the sheets blindly for Ethan but felt nothing. It wasn't normal for her to wake up not wrapped in his arms. Her eyes fluttered open, and she sat up looking around the room.

Where is he? she thought, straining her ears in an attempt to hear if he was in the shower or kitchen. Not hearing a thing, she gave up with a huff and fell back into bed. As she lay there, she allowed her mind to wander back on the events of last night.

Ethan cooking dinner for her was a surprise, but the grocery store was beyond what she imagined. She laughed quietly to herself. Never in a million years did she think he'd actually arrange something like that. In the very store where they'd bumped in to each other all those months ago. Closing her eyes, she relived the moments from last night and drifted back to sleep thinking of strawberry juice on red stained lips.

"Kate, wake up, love." Ethan's voice woke her from her sleep, and she immediately smiled.

Turning her head toward the wonderful sound, she pried her lids back. Ethan's steel blue eyes looked back at her, and his perfect lips were stretched in a smile. "Hi," she said, her voice still raspy from sleeping too long. "Where were you earlier? I hate waking up without you."

"I had some errands to run. Then I stopped by the store to pick up some things for lunch."

"Lunch?" She pushed up on her elbows and looked at the clock on the nightstand. Sure enough, it was already noon. "I missed breakfast." She flopped back down on her stomach. "I wanted to make you pancakes as a thank you for last night."

"Actually, I'd love some pancakes. I got up late and only had a cup of coffee, so I'm starving." He ran his hands over his chiseled jaw, still scruffy from not shaving.

"Really?" she asked into the pillow, her voice sounding muffled.

"Yep."

"What about the stuff you bought for lunch?"

"We'll have it later," he assured her.

Lifting her head, she peered at him through her messy hair. "Okay, let me go get the pancakes started then." She gave him a quick kiss on the lips and hurried out of bed.

They spent the rest of the afternoon lounging around, primarily in the music room. Kate sat by the window in the large comfy chair and read, while Ethan played the piano. Taking a break from the magical world in which she was engrossed, she turned her attention to the pianist. She watched his fingers dance across the ivory and smiled at the expression on his face. With brows knitted together, he concentrated on the music in front of him until the final notes rang through the air. After a moment of silence, he took his hands away from the ivory and turned to face Kate.

"Let's go for a hike."

"A hike, really?" she asked skeptically.

"All right, not so much hiking; more like walking."

The look of excitement on his face made it impossible to deny him. "Okay," Kate said. "But let's go before it's too dark."

An hour later they were walking in a park near New Hope and Kate had a feeling Ethan didn't know where he was heading. "Are we lost?" she asked.

"No, of course not."

She looked around the path they were on, not spotting a sign anywhere. "And you know this because…?"

"Because I've been lost here before, a few times really. I've pretty much memorized the area."

"You were lost here? When?" Kate thought back, attempting to recall a 'lost in the woods' story that he might have told her.

"The first time, I was with Trent. We went hiking before a football game. In fact, it was the game where he hooked up with Elle, remember? Sophie needed me to keep him busy and I'd wanted to go hiking for a while, so we went."

"And you got lost," Kate stated.

"Yes, but only for a few hours. And the second time, it wasn't even half that long."

She couldn't understand why he was so excited about getting lost, especially when something could have happened to him. "Why would you keep coming back if you get lost?" Her disbelief and slight anger was a distraction, and she didn't notice the root sticking up out of the dirt. Before she could catch herself, her foot caught and she stumbled forward, instinctively putting her arms out to break her fall. Only one hand hit the ground before she felt Ethan's arms around her waist.

"Careful." He pulled her body into his. "Let me see."

"It's just a scratch." She brushed her hand over her capris, ignoring the sting it brought and looked up at him. "You still haven't told me why in the world you go wandering in the woods, getting lost."

"I'll show you," he said quietly while wrapping his arm around her.

They walked for another few minutes, and strangely enough, the surrounding area started looking familiar to Kate. She couldn't quite place it, but it felt like she was reliving a dream.

"Notice anything familiar?" Ethan asked.

"I'm not sure. I—"

Just as she was about to tell him that she thought she might have been there before, they came around a bend in the path and she saw it—her tree. The same tree she'd stumbled across so long ago, the same tree in the picture which now hung in the bedroom that she and Ethan shared.

"How did you? I mean…what…how?" she mumbled incoherently. Her feet were stuck to the ground as she stared in shock at the large tree that stood off the path. It was just as perfect as she'd remembered, just as perfect as the moment that she'd captured it. The dark bark twisted and swirled around the trunk, and its full branches were bursting with vibrant green leaves. She was so entranced with seeing it again that she didn't even notice the blanket spread out beneath it.

"Ever since that day in the gallery when you said you had no clue where it was, I was curious. I wanted to find it, to sit under it and know that you'd been there too. Of course, after we got together, I had other reasons for wanting to find it. I wanted to come here with you." Ethan rubbed her arm affectionately.

"I can't believe you found it," Kate gasped, once she was composed enough to speak. Running over to the tree, she walked underneath the canopy of its branches while memories came flooding back to her. "You know, when I found this tree, I was so sad. So broken and hurt. I remember wondering if I'd ever be happy again. I sat here and wondered how old it was. I imagined that it had been around for a while and that I wasn't the first person to sit in its shade. I wondered if other couples had been here, had sat in this very place. Now being here…," she trailed off. "This time, everything is different. Is it weird to say I feel like I've come full circle?" She turned around and saw Ethan leaning against the trunk of the tree with his arms folded. The sun poured through the branches lighting up his face and making his hair look lighter than normal. Her breath caught as she watched him, completely enamored.

"I wondered the same thing when I found it. And I'm glad that *this* time, you're here under different circumstances, although you are hurt a little." He pointed to her hand. Pushing off the tree, he walked over to a picnic basket and pulled out a little first aid kit. "Occupational habit." He smirked, holding up the small box.

She rolled her eyes playfully and sat down next to him. Very carefully, he lifted her hand and wiped the dirt away. She watched his face as he studied her palm before applying an ointment and covering it with a Band-Aid. Even after he was finished, he held her hand, looking at it closely as if it held something important.

"I'm sorry I wasn't fast enough earlier," he spoke, still keeping his head down.

"Are you kidding? It was my fault. And look at the bright side. It could have been worse. You could be giving me stitches."

Her comment loosened him up a bit and he started laughing. "No more stitches for you. You have enough scars," he said, looking up at her.

"I can't promise I won't ever get hurt again. But if I do, at least I have you to fix me."

The smile on his face faded slightly and he reached forward, taking her other hand in his. They sat face-to-face across from each other, and that familiar, unidentifiable energy that they always felt pulsed around them.

"You may not be able to promise, but I can." He paused. "I can't promise you that you won't get hurt physically, of course. But I can promise you, Kate, that you will never feel broken again. You will never have to come to this tree and wonder if you'll ever be happy. You will never feel lost or alone, because I'll be here."

Kate sat silent, listening to his words and looking into his beautiful blue eyes. He stared back at her as if he could see right into her soul. Her chest felt tight, and she took a deep breath, reveling in the joy that rushed over her. Try as she might, she couldn't stop the tears that pooled in her eyes as she continued to listen to him speak.

"I knew the first time that I saw you. The first time I looked into your beautiful eyes, I knew there was something. I didn't even know you, but when I walked away … I *missed* you. And we'd barely even talked." He laughed, shaking his head. "Call it cosmic forces, magic, fate, whatever you want, but I *know* I'm supposed to be with you. I know that being with you has been the best part of my life. You make my life better. And I can't imagine a day without you in it. I've found my one—my other half that knows me better than anyone. The one person I can't live without. I want to have children with you. I want to watch them grow up to be just as loving and smart and funny and generous as their mother. You are my life, my missing piece, and my best friend. Please, Katherine Elizabeth Thomas, please say that you'll have me as your husband."

Tears, which once brimmed in her eyes, now ran down her cheeks in trails of silver. She didn't even bother wiping them away as she lunged forward, and crashed her lips to Ethan's. Wrapping her arms around him, she held herself as close as possible—as if squeezing him that tight could somehow bind them together permanently. She pulled away from his lips only so she could speak.

"Yes," she said, before kissing his cheek. "Yes." She kissed again, moving to his chin. "Yes." His eyelids. "Yes." His forehead. "Yes. " His jaw. She continued to kiss every inch of his face, and with every kiss came the word yes.

Ethan laughed at her enthusiasm, but never once tore his body or lips from hers. Together they sat under their tree, wrapped in each other's arms, and watched the sun set as another day ended.

Turning her head, Kate smiled up at Ethan and she knew, without a doubt, that although this day was ending, their life together was just beginning.

Epilogue

11:30 A.M.

"Come on! He was safe! Open your eyes, ump!" Trent yelled at the TV before running his hands over his face in frustration.

"What'd you lose?" Ethan asked, knowing that he was fond of betting on sports.

Trent's eyes didn't leave the screen. "Huh?" he asked under his breath.

"The game, how much did you lose?" Ethan repeated.

"I didn't."

"Then why are you all messed up over it?"

"Because I lost." He shrugged.

"I thought you said you didn't lose any money." By this point, Logan was leaning over as well, engrossed in the conversation.

"I didn't lose *money*," Trent said simply.

"Then what did you lose?"

"Nurse Betty," he sighed, hanging his head.

Both Ethan and Logan looked at each other on the verge of laughter and still had no clue what he was talking about. "Nurse Betty?"

"Trent, please tell me you're not thinking about cheating on my sister, because I will beat you," Logan said.

"Dude, I *am* talking about your sister." It took a second for what he said to register in Ethan's mind, and once it did he couldn't help but laugh.

Logan, on the other hand, was still a little lost. "What does my sister have to do with Nurse Betty?"

Trent sat back in the bar stool and grabbed the beer off the counter. He crossed his ankles and took one long pull from the bottle before speaking. "That same thing she has to do with Kristen the teacher, Rosanna the foreign exchange student, Michelle the cheerleader, and Linda the librarian. And now, thanks to that play by Wilson, it's going to be another week before I get to meet Nurse Betty."

Recognition spread over Logan's face. His eyes went wide and his lips pressed together.

"Are you telling me you make bets on games, and if you win, she has to dress up for you?" Ethan asked, honestly curious.

"Nope." He grinned like a kid. "If *she* wins she dresses up for me."

Ethan's eyes went as wide as Logan's, but didn't look nearly as angry.

"Trent, can you please not talk about my sister's sexual preferences."

"I'm not talking about preferences. I'm just saying she likes to role play. If I was talking about sexual preferences, I'd tell you about this one move she likes. It's when I—"

"Okay, let me rephrase that then. Can you please refrain from anything that may have to do with my baby sister in a sexual way?"

"I'll try." Trent grinned back. "But I can't promise anything."

Logan accepted his friend's 'almost promise' and went back to watching the game while Ethan looked around the room for a distraction. He knew he had a few hours until he needed to get dressed, and when he started thinking about it, he only grew more impatient. Being away from Kate made him anxious, and he hadn't seen her since yesterday morning. The only thing stopping him from going to see her that very moment were the Sassy Sophie and the Sharp Tongue Amazon Elle, who he knew would be guarding her door. With a sigh, he looked around the room. "Hey, anyone interested in a game of pool?" he asked, eyeing the table.

"Always," Trent responded, pushing back from the bar and heading over to the pool table. "Care to make it a little interesting?"

Ethan smirked. "As long as you don't want me in a bar wench outfit, I think I'm up for anything."

"Hmm, bar wench. I'll have to remember that one," his big friend said in a daze.

"Come on, Williams, let's play," Logan commanded, walking past with a roll of his eyes.

With a laugh and a shake of his head, Ethan was relieved to have two friends that might be able to keep his mind off of his beautiful bride that was on the opposite side of the building, even if the task would be impossible. He was always thinking of her.

11:33 A.M.

"Left together, right together, left together, right together," Kate mumbled as she held onto the bottom of her robe, pulling it up over her knees. She watched her feet practice for what must have been the hundredth time in the last eight months.

Ever since that amazing day when Ethan proposed, she'd been in a wedding whirlwind of flowers and lace. Not knowing exactly what she wanted, she was quickly schooled by Sophie, her mom, Ethan's mom, and even Lori on Wedding Planning 101—a job which they were more than happy to fulfill. Thankfully, her mother and Sabrina hit it off immediately. Apparently, planning a wedding was the best way for two people to become best friends because that's what happened. Their personalities balanced each other perfectly, and together they planned a wedding that anyone would be envious of.

"Kate, sweetheart, you do realize that you can't walk down the aisle like that, right? It would look a little funny," Sophie said while she arranged the pins in her friend's hair.

"Yes, despite what you think, I *do* know that walking down the aisle, staring at my feet with my dress pulled up over my head, is not normal. Ouch, be careful." She winced as a piece of hair was yanked from her scalp.

"I don't know," Elle interrupted. "I doubt Bones would mind seeing you walking like that."

Kate glanced at Sophie with a smirk, and the three of them doubled over in laughter, Kate's sounding a bit hysterical, no doubt a side effect of the nerves. Leave it to her bold friend to try and lighten the mood with a sexual comment. Once the giggles died down, the flutter of butterflies returned. "Time check?" Kate asked.

Sophie glanced at the clock. "A little over an hour and a half to go; we should get you in your dress in the next half hour so I can take your hair down."

"Already?" the bride squeaked. "Don't you think you guys should get in your dresses first, and then I'll get in mine?" Any nervous feelings she'd had over the past eight months suddenly tripled, and she felt her stomach go sour.

"No, it won't take us any time at all." Sophie waved. "Besides, you're the bride. We have to make sure *you're* perfect first."

She nodded quickly and felt the gurgling and churning begin. A cold sweat started to bead up on her forehead, and both her friends watched with wide eyes.

"Sweetheart, are you okay?" Elle asked, placing her hand on Kate's shoulder.

Before she could respond, she felt the bile rise in the back of her throat. Clamping her hand over her mouth, she took off for the bathroom, praying that she'd make it to the toilet in time.

11:51 A.M.

"Red stripe, left pocket," Ethan called before making his move and watching the ball sink right in as he wanted.

"Damn it," Trent groaned, throwing the pool stick on the table in defeat. "I hate playing with doctors. Your hands are too steady."

"Oh please, you always use that excuse because your dad and I are the only ones who can beat you."

"Hold on," he said, holding up his finger. "First off, you make it sound like you kick my ass all the time, which you know isn't true, and secondly, don't try saying that your steady hands don't come into play."

"If my doctor hands come into play, then how did I beat you when we were younger?" Ethan smirked, knowing he had him.

"Hell if I know. All I can remember is I could always beat you. Then that summer when we got back from camp, you picked up your game."

There was no hiding the triumphant grin that spread over Ethan's face. Trent was always asking him what happened that summer and would teasingly chalk it up as puberty or some other crazy excuse. What he never stopped to consider was that one of their camp leaders was very skilled at the game of pool, skilled enough that she was training to compete on a national level. They'd spent a lot of their nights playing, and she'd taught Ethan everything she knew.

"Remember that summer at Camp Winacoke?" he asked.

"Yeah, what about it?"

"Remember one of the counselors was great at pool?

It took Trent a few seconds but clarity started setting in. "Blonde, killer rack, the one who beat any guy she took on at the table?"

"Sure, sure, I guess she was attractive." He nodded.

"Dude, she wasn't just attractive—she was hot. Granted, she had nothing on Elle, but still, she was hot. What about her, anyway?"

"We were friends and she taught me how to play," Ethan admitted.

"She *taught* you?" he asked, completely blown away. "How did you manage that? She wouldn't give any guys the time of day, let alone take a minute to give personal lessons. We all swore she dug chicks."

"We were friends. She hated that you always beat me and decided to make sure it didn't happen again. Between her classes and my steady hands," he held up said hands, "I became unstoppable."

"Don't go that far. You're not unstoppable. I can still take you."

Logan tossed his pool stick from one hand to the other. "You guys are wasting your breath arguing. We all know I can take you *both* down."

"All right, let's go another round. You break."

The three friends spent the next twenty minutes playing pool, and between Logan and Ethan, they were in fact unstoppable.

"How did you learn to play so damn well? Don't tell me a hot chick taught you," Trent asked Logan after losing another round.

"Do you really want to know?"

Trent nodded and grabbed another beer off the bar.

"My sister."

Trent froze, bottle to his lips and spun on his heel to face his friend. He swallowed loudly and paused before speaking. "Elle can play?"

"Oh, she can play. Better than any of us, in fact." Logan looked at Ethan with a smile.

"He's right. I played her when we were kids and it wasn't pretty. I can only imagine how she plays now."

Trent didn't answer, but a wide grin spread across his face. "I think I just fell even more in love with your sister."

Logan laughed and patted him on the back. "Speaking of my sister, when are you going to ask her?"

They all knew that it was only a matter of time before he and Elle got married. They were perfect for each other, and they knew it just as much as their friends did.

"I already have the ring," he said, shocking the hell out of his buddies.

"Really?" Logan and Ethan both said in unison.

"Of course I do." He grinned.

12:00 P.M.

"Take a deep breath," Elle commanded. Kate did as she was told and lifted her head up.

She'd spent the last twenty minutes kneeling in front of the toilet, letting her nerves get the best of her. Yes, it was ridiculous, but she couldn't help it.

"Now exhale," Sophie said, rubbing her friend's back. "Everything is going to be great. You know that, right? I *know* it will."

Her reassuring words helped a little. After all, Kate knew everything would be okay. She loved Ethan more than anything in the world. He was the one, *her* one, of that she was sure. Her reaction to her nerves was something she didn't have any control over.

"Soph is right, babe. Everything about today will be perfect, and when it's over, you're going to be tied to Ethan, forever. You'll finally be his wife."

Hearing his name and the word 'wife' in the same sentence brought a smile to Kate's face. She hadn't seen Ethan since yesterday morning, and it was starting to wear on her. Being near him always calmed her, and she wanted nothing more than to see him, if only for a minute.

"Can one of you go get Ethan?" she asked hopefully.

"Absolutely not! The groom can *not* see the bride before she walks down the aisle!" Sophie yelled in protest, squashing her friend's hope in an instant.

Kate had a feeling that was going to be the response she received, but she had to try. With a huff of defeat, she stood up to brush her teeth. "It's just that I always feel better when he's near me," she said, slathering on enough toothpaste to clean a horse's mouth. "He makes me forget about all this wedding hoopla." She shoved the toothbrush in her mouth and started brushing, erasing any trace of her moment of weakness.

Sophie looked back at her friend's reflection in the mirror with sad eyes. After a minute of quiet contemplation, she glanced at Elle, who nodded her head. "Tell you what," Sophie said, standing behind Kate. "How about we get you into your dress now, and then one of us will go get Eth—"

"Thank you, Soph!" she yelped, spraying the mirror with toothpaste.

"Wait, wait. Let me finish." She held up her hands. "We'll get Ethan so you can *talk* to him. Talk, through the door. No seeing each other. Understand?" Her face was dead serious, and Kate knew she meant business.

In her desperation to see Ethan, she more than willingly complied. "No seeing each other, I promise."

With a pleased nod of her head, Sophie turned her attention to Elle. "You grab the dress; I'll get the accessories. And you," she said, turning back to Kate. "Get all of that vomit taste out of your mouth and get out of the bathroom. Enough nerves for you."

Kate nodded, again agreeing to her command, and watched as they left the bathroom. The two of them hurried around the bridal suite, gathering what they needed, and Kate looked on with a smile. Gratitude for her two best friends filled her heart. Two people who meant the world to her and who had been by her side through everything. She knew that without them her life would be completely different. It would be less full and definitely less fun.

After a minute, Sophie paused and noticed her friend's smile. "Are you ready to become Mrs. Montgomery?"

Excitement bubbled up inside her. "Ready as I'll ever be." She walked to the center of the room where Elle now stood with her dress.

"Be careful with that rock of yours. You don't want to snag the material," Elle said, motioning to Kate's ring as she helped slip the dress over her hips. "I still can't believe you didn't go for the four-carat Tiffany," she mumbled.

"For the last time, Elle, I can't wear a four-carat diamond."

After Ethan proposed, he pulled out three rings. He'd said after seeing her reaction to the emerald earrings he almost purchased at the auction, he wanted to play it safe and give her the option to choose. Staring at the three boxes in front of her, Kate had asked him to pick his first choice, the one he thought she'd like. He hesitated for only a moment, then pushed the black box forward.

As it turned out, he was right; the ring was perfect. It wasn't the smallest one and it definitely wasn't the biggest, but it was the one meant for her. The one-carat solitaire with a thin, delicate band woven gently around her finger.

"Tell me again why the four-carat diamond was so bad?" Elle asked, still not completely convinced.

"It just wasn't me. Plus, it was way too big. It looked ridiculous on my finger. You would agree with me if you'd seen it," Kate assured her.

"Heaven knows I'm not turning down a big rock."

"Considering Trent is a firm believer in 'bigger is always better,' something tells me the ring he gives you will be plenty big."

12:00 P.M.

"So, you have a ring?" Ethan asked in shock.

"Yep, got it a few weeks ago," Trent said with a casual shrug.

Logan leaned forward across the pool table. "Then what are you waiting for?"

"The right moment. It's been so crazy with all the wedding stuff, that we haven't had time to ourselves. But I'm thinking once things settle down, I'll take her away for the weekend."

There was a glint in his eye, and Ethan held back a laugh. He was used to Trent being happy, but his expression was almost blissful and ... romantic? That was something entirely new.

"Do it. I can't wait to see the look on my mom's face when we tell her she has a wedding this year." Logan laughed to himself and set up for another round of pool.

Just as they were getting ready to break, the door swung open and in walked Ethan's dad, Doug, and Henry.

"Where have you guys been?"

"Getting pictures taken. I think your mother has found her second calling in life and it has to do with planning weddings. It's a good thing you were a boy or you'd probably be going crazy right about now. Is it really necessary to have five hundred pictures of the groom's parents and the bride's parents?" Oliver gave a long sigh of relief and sat down on the couch next to Doug, who looked just as exhausted.

"He's being serious. You should see them. Annie is just as bad," Doug said, shaking his head.

Ethan looked to Henry and half expected him to be just as shocked as Ethan's dad and Doug, but he wasn't. "Lori has always been this way," Henry said, as if reading his mind. "She may not plan weddings, but you've been to our parties." He laughed.

The groom and the two groomsmen joined the dads in front of the TV. After all, there was nothing like a good old basketball game to waste some time and help them relax.

12:20 P.M.

Elle and Sophie stood at Kate's side, smoothing away imaginary wrinkles on her gown when the door opened.

"Oh my! You didn't tell us you were getting dressed already. You know we wanted to be here for this!" Kate's mother squawked as she ran towards her with arms flittering about.

"Surely you want the photographer here so you can capture this moment," Sabrina added, walking in after her, one arm linked with Lori's.

"Pictures are one of the most important aspects of any large event, weddings especially. But, of course, you already know that." Lori winked and escorted the photographer into the room.

"I'm sorry, Mom. I decided to get dressed early so I have time to talk to Ethan before I walk down the aisle." The three mothers gasped in unison, but Kate cut them off before they could talk. "Soph already warned me. It will be just talking. I won't let him see me. I promise."

"Well, in that case, we'd better hurry and get you ready." Sabrina stepped forward and motioned for her soon-to-be daughter-in-law to spin around. Her two best friends stepped aside for the time being and let both Annie and Sabrina pour over her while Lori directed the photographer.

When Kate was finished with the dress, Sophie and Elle sat her in front of the mirror and took over, pulling all the bobby pins out of her hair. Soft curls fell gently down her back, and the sides were pinned up loosely, showing off her grandmother's antique sapphire earrings.

Sophie insisted Kate follow all the bridal traditions and that included the 'something old, something new' rule. The earrings were the 'something old.' Her 'something new' was the lingerie she wore under her dress, which was, of course, a gift from her two best friends. Her 'something blue' was the delicate sapphire and diamond bracelet that was a gift from Lori and Henry. Apparently marrying Ethan didn't make just Sabrina and Oliver her in-laws, but the Williamses as well. The only thing she didn't have to finish out the tradition was the 'something borrowed,' which Sophie assured her not to worry about.

Just as the last pieces of hair were pinned into place, Sabrina walked up behind the bride. She smiled down at Kate's reflection and handed her a dark blue velvet box. Curiously running her fingers over the smooth surface, she almost asked what it was when her mother cut in.

"Oh, for heaven's sake, just open it," she said eagerly.

Both Elle and Sophie stood off to the side, looking on with eager expressions. It was then that Kate realized she must be the only one left out of knowing what was in the box. Shaking her head, she smiled and opened the lid.

As soon as she saw the radiant contents, her hand went to her throat and she gasped. There, lying perfectly nestled in the navy velvet, was the most beautiful diamond necklace she'd ever seen. There must have been hundreds of diamonds, some pear shaped and others brilliant, but all of them brilliantly sparkling. It was impossible to speak, so she continued to sit and gape with wide eyes. "Kate, I'd like for you to wear this as your 'something borrowed,'" Sabrina finally said, breaking her out of the diamond induced haze.

"I … I'd …" Kate stammered.

"I think what she trying to say is 'she'd be honored to,'" Elle finished, while leaning forward and closing her friend's open mouth.

Without saying a word, Sabrina slipped the necklace from the box and hooked it around Kate's neck while she looked back at her reflection in awe. The necklace was intricate in its detail but still looked delicate. It paired perfectly with the simple style of her strapless gown.

"It's beautiful," Kate said with a sigh, running her fingers over it.

"Then it's perfect for you."

"Thank you, Sabrina." She stood up and gave her a hug. "And thank you, Mom, for Grandma's earrings."

Her mother smiled back lovingly. "She would have liked for you to have them." Standing back, Annie gazed at her daughter, now completely ready. "Your father is going to have a heart attack when he sees you. You're the most beautiful bride I've ever seen." Her eyes welled up with tears as she wrapped her arms around Kate. "I'm so proud of you, sweetheart. Ethan is a wonderful man, and I know he makes you happy," she whispered into her ear before pulling away.

They both looked at each other for a minute, silently communicating in the way mothers and daughters sometimes do, before she took a step back.

"All right, let's get this show started," Sophie said, rubbing her hands together excitedly. "I'll go get Ethan and tell him to come to the door, and we'll be waiting for you downstairs."

Kate nodded and gave everyone one last smile as they left the room.

12:45 P.M.

About a half hour later, Trent cleared his throat and stood up from the couch, motioning for Ethan to follow him. Both he and Logan turned away from the game and walked to the bar where he was standing.

"Since Logan and I are your best men, we wanted to get you something," Trent said, looking at Logan with a smile. "Something that had sentimental value and would make you smile every time you saw it. We thought this over long and hard, and eventually chose something." He reached into his back pocket and pulled out a small envelope.

"You guys didn't have to get me anything," Ethan protested.

"We know, but we wanted to." Both he and Logan looked at him sincerely and gave a warm smile before handing over the envelope. Flipping it over, Ethan slid his finger under the seal and read the slip of paper inside.

A gift of health just for you.
Your one-year membership in our Harvest Club brings our
orchard fresh fruit right to your home every month!
Every piece of fruit is picked at its peak of flavor and delivered
to your door in our exclusive Watercolor Art Boxes.
Make this year a healthy year.

As soon as he finished reading, he began to laugh, shortly joined by his two friends. Ethan was fairly certain that now it was official. He had the two best friends any guy could ask for. It was a minute before any of them was calm enough to speak.

"Kate is going to love this," Ethan said, holding up the paper. "Thank you."

"Speaking of the bride, how do you think she's holding up?" Trent asked.

"Hopefully she's all right. Hey, what do you think my chances are of seeing her before we start?"

Logan looked at Ethan with raised eyebrows. "Are you kidding? Soph would eat you alive if you tried to see her. You know how she is about all this."

Ethan groaned. "I know. I just really want to see her."

"Dude, all you have to do is flash Soph the JB and you're in."

"Excuse me? The JB?"

"Yeah, what?" Logan asked, joining in his friend's confusion.

"The JB, you know…Junk Bulge. It's the one thing that can break through their defenses. Women are weak when faced with the JB," he said with confidence.

Biting back his laugh, Ethan was truly intrigued. "And you know this because?"

"Because it works. I even got out of a speeding ticket once. Just a little shift and roll and you're good." He circled his hips around in a move reminiscent of Elvis.

Ethan chuckled. "As much as I believe you, I'm not sure I can do that to Sophie."

"Whatever, I'm just telling you it works. Remember it when you want something from Kate. If she's anything like Elle, she'll—"

"Trent," Logan warned for at least the third time today.

At that moment, the door opened and in walked Elle, followed closely by Sophie. Both were dressed in their champagne-colored bridesmaids' dresses and looked stunning.

"You can talk to her," Sophie said, walking directly to Ethan. "Talk, that's it."

"And if we find out that you saw her, we will pull every last one of your perfect white teeth out of your mouth with our bare hands," Elle threatened with a friendly smile and wink.

Their words sunk in and Ethan smiled. "I love you guys, thanks." He kissed them both on the cheek and headed out the door.

"We mean it! No looking, just talking!" He heard them yell, but he was already halfway down the hall, his heart pounding in anticipation of just hearing her voice.

12:48 P.M.

Now that Kate was finally alone, she took a moment to simply breathe, to take in her surroundings and to feel the excitement of the day. She'd been so busy and nervous the past few days and weeks that she hadn't even had a chance to just enjoy the moment.

Walking over to the large window, she looked outside and her mind automatically thought of Ethan. She thought about the first time she saw him, the first time she touched him. She remembered their first kiss and the way her heart raced. The same way it still did whenever she got close to him. She thought about the day he asked her to be his and all the days after. She thought about the nights that they stayed up talking just because they couldn't get enough of each other, and those nights where they did anything *but* talk. She thought about the days they spent out on the boat with his parents. And she remembered the first time they talked about babies and how many they wanted to have.

She thought about all of these things, but mostly she just thought about the way Ethan loved her and she loved him. Her mind was still filled with images, flashes of them together and moments in time, when there was a knock at the door.

"Kate?" She heard Ethan's comforting voice and her heart skipped.

Gathering her dress around her, she hurried over to the door and pressed her hands flat against the wood. "Hi," she said into the crack.

"What did you say to make them cave?"

"Nothing really. I may have pouted just a little." Kate laughed. "Did they threaten you? Because I wouldn't put it past them."

"You could call it a threat."

"Did they make you promise like they made me?" she asked.

"Nope."

She could hear the smile in his voice and knew he was thinking of ways to break the rules and see her. She knew it was silly because she was going to see him in fifteen minutes, but it didn't stop her aching desire to throw open the door and see him.

"Are you doing okay?" he asked.

"Better now," she admitted. "Not seeing you drives me crazy. Plus, I'm a little nervous about walking down the aisle."

"You know we don't have to do this. We could just leave right now and get married at City Hall, or even Vegas."

"And have to face the wrath of four wedding planners? I don't think so." Kate paused. "I'll be fine once I see you. I'm always better when I'm with you, Ethan."

"I'm better with you too. *You* make me better."

Blinking back tears, Kate forced herself to hold it together and not mess up her make-up. "I love you," she said quietly, not sure if he could hear.

"I love you too. Now, are you going to marry me, or what? The sooner we say 'I do,' the sooner we leave for Tuscany and start our honeymoon."

She smiled and pressed her forehead against the door. "Yes, I'm ready. Believe me, I'm ready."

"Okay. I'll see you down there. And remember, it's just you and me."

Taking a deep breath, she waited in silence and heard him push away from the door. Once alone, she walked back to the vanity and took a seat, staring back at her reflection. The sound of the door opening drew her eyes away, and she turned to see Elle and Sophie standing in the doorway, grinning.

"It's time to get married," they said in unison.

12:58 P.M.

Ethan made his way downstairs and found Trent and Logan waiting by the side door. They looked at their friend's expression and smiled.

"I'd say someone is excited," Logan said. "I don't think I've ever seen you like this."

"What can I say? I'm ready. She's the one."

They both nodded in understanding and grasped the door handle.

"All right then, let's get you hitched." Trent pulled the door open in one quick swoop, and the three of them took their places on the platform under a canopy of flowers. The flowers were everywhere, splashes of white and cream draped around the room.

Ethan took a deep breath and looked out over the sea of faces, some recognizable and some not. His eyes landed on the large double doors in the back of the room, and he couldn't look away. He knew that just beyond them, Kate was waiting, waiting to be his wife. The music started to play, and happiness filled his chest. He knew that this was the moment he'd waited forever for.

1:00 P.M.

"Left together, right together, left together, right together." Kate's dad spoke in a low voice as he practiced his steps.

"If it helps, I'm not sure I'll get it right either." She spoke up behind him.

As soon as he heard her voice, Doug spun around and smiled when he saw his daughter. "You look beautiful, Katherine. Prettiest bride I've ever seen."

"Thanks, Dad." She fiddled with her flowers.

"Hope I get these steps right." He chuckled.

"I tell you what. I don't care how I get there, as long as you're with me."

"Well, that I can promise." He wrapped his arm around her waist and placed a kiss on her forehead.

The sound of Sophie's voice gathered everyone's attention as she placed everyone in line. Before Kate could register what was happening, the music started and her father linked his arm with hers.

1:02 P.M.

Ethan stood, watching the double doors closely. As they slowly opened, the soft murmur in the crowd died down and everyone turned to face the back of the room.

Sophie came through the doorway first, followed by Elle. The two of them looked beautiful, and they each smiled at Ethan when he met their eyes. He'd always imagined what it would be like to have sisters and now he knew. He loved them both like family, and the bond they each shared with Kate was an unbreakable one.

As soon as they were at the end of the aisle, the music changed and once again Ethan's eyes were drawn to the back of the room. It was then that he saw her. His breath caught and he froze. She was stunning, more beautiful than he could have ever imagined. Her white strapless gown was simple and clung to her body perfectly before flowing gently to the ground. He took in the moment—the image before him—and committed it to memory, positive that he would never forget it.

She was a quarter of the way down the aisle before she lifted her eyes to his. When their eyes locked, she smiled, and at that moment Ethan knew that everything he'd ever done in his life had led him to Kate. She was his beginning and his ending. The one he'd be with forever. This knowledge didn't make him nervous or afraid; it only made him feel at peace. Because when he was with Kate, he was home.

1:02 P.M.

The large double doors opened and the fragrance of a thousand flowers wafted towards Kate and her father. The entire room was filled with flowers in various shades of white, accented by champagne-colored ribbons. They lined the aisle and hung from the backs of every pew. They even hung over the altar, forming a canopy of white petals. It was one of the most beautiful things Kate had ever seen.

She could have stood there all day and taken in every last detail, but her father starting walking. Thankfully, her body acted on its own accord and followed his motions. She noticed all the people standing on the sides as she started down the aisle, but she didn't focus on them. There was only one person she wanted to see and that was Ethan. As soon as she saw him, her heart sped up. He was looking at her, his smoky blue eyes gleaming as he smiled. She grinned back at him, keeping her eyes locked with his, and forgot about everything else. All that mattered was the two of them; everything else faded into a blur of white.

When they reached the end of the aisle, Doug handed over his daughter, and Ethan took his place, taking her hand in his. She took a step toward him, and immediately felt the comfort of his touch. Ethan ran his thumbs over the tops of her hands and gave her a quick wink before the priest began their vows.

She listened to the words that were spoken and repeated every promise over in her head, trying to commit every single moment to memory forever. Ethan gazed back at her, looking deep into her eyes, and she knew he was doing the same thing.

When it was time for Kate to say her part, she paused, getting control of her emotions so her voice would be loud and sure. "I do," she said clearly before the tears began to run down her cheeks.

Ethan lifted his hand and lightly brushed them away, his fingers lingering at her cheek. "I do," he promised.

The priest closed with pronouncing them husband and wife, and Kate didn't waste a second before throwing her arms around Ethan. He pulled her close, holding her by the waist, and pressed his lips against hers. She let herself get lost in the moment and reveled in his touch, his lips, and his warmth.

Eventually they separated, but Ethan didn't let her go. Instead he dropped his lips to the side of her ear and whispered, "My wife."

The word sent chills down Kate's spine and filled her entire body with joy. She knew that she was finally his, and he was hers.

Burying her face into his chest, she felt his chin rest on the top of her head. They stood like that for a minute, lost on their own world. It wasn't until the crowd's cheering grew louder that they became aware that they weren't, in fact, alone. Very gently, Ethan slid his arm from around her waist and clasped his hand in hers, giving her a reassuring squeeze.

Then, together they took their first steps down the aisle as husband and wife. Kate smiled as she looked up into the eyes of her best friend, her lover, her confidant, her companion, her forever, and her happily ever after.

ACKNOWLEDGMENTS

HUGE thanks to:

My amazing family, for all their love, support and patience. To my super editor Meredith, for knowing my characters as well as I do, and for all of her hard work. To all of the friends that I've made throughout the writing process, whose support and laughs have kept me sane. To Elizabeth, for giving me this opportunity. And to the ones who have inspired me, and have taken part in making me a believer of true love.

ABOUT THE AUTHOR

Elizabeth makes her home in Delaware with her husband and spends the day with her two loves, her children and her writing. With a strong adoration for the East Coast as her foundation, she penned her first novel, *Stitches and Scars*, a delicious romantic comedy.

In her spare time, she enjoys taxiing her kids to every activity under the sun, baking enough to make Betty Crocker proud and finding inspiration for her writing in even the most mundane of circumstances.